"*The Merciless King of Moore High* combines terrifying monsters, palace intrigue, and authentic high school romance and angst with Lily Sparks's uncanny ability to make the fantastical believable, and to populate it with characters that are not only smart, sexy, and fun, but utterly compelling, in the moment and for a long time after."

—Jon McGoran, author of *Spliced*

"High school rivalry with end-of-the-world stakes gripped me from the first page. The unflinching Kay Kim, gritty world building, and slow-burn romance kept me reading into the night. Lily Sparks's *The Merciless King of Moore High* is a gruesomely twisted take on the zombie apocalypse filled with gory dragons, medieval pageantry, and dangerously shifting alliances. My heart was pounding by the end!"

—Katharine J. Adams, author of *Tonight, I Burn*

"A gripping thrill ride with monsters and deception lurking behind every page. Fast-paced and full of surprises, Sparks skillfully balances a world of fragile power and fraying loyalties with heartfelt emotion and the fierce will to survive."

—Linda Kao, author of *A Crooked Mark*

"I couldn't put down this action-packed post-apocalyptic adventure. Set in a world where all the adults have turned into dragons, this story is a gritty mix of *Mad Max* and King Arthur's court. High school rivalries and teen drama added plot twists that kept me guessing. I'm excited to see where the series will go next!"

—Tessa Barbosa, author of *The Moonlight Blade*

"*The Merciless King of Moore High* merges the cutthroat fantasy politics of *The Cruel Prince* with the post-apocalyptic high school setting of Netflix's *Daybreak*. Sparks lays out twist after twist like a winning hand of cards, turning the story on its head every time you think you've figured it out. Breathlessly tense, unpredictable, and a heck of a lot of fun."

—Claire Winn, author of *City of Shattered Light* and
City of Vicious Night

"Post-apocalyptic survival meets high school clique drama in this inventive and twisty young adult novel. *The Merciless King of Moore High* is going to revitalize dystopian literature!"

—Rachel Menard, multi-award-winning author of
Game of Strength and Storm and *Clash of Fate and Fury*

THE MERCILESS KING
OF MOORE HIGH

LILY SPARKS

flux
®
Mendota Heights, Minnesota

First Edition
First Printing, 2024

Book design by Kate Liestman
Cover design by Cynthia Della-Rovere
Cover illustration by Jensine Eckwell

Flux, an imprint of North Star Editions, Inc.

Library of Congress Cataloging-in-Publication Data (pending)
978-1-63583-096-5

Flux
North Star Editions, Inc.
2297 Waters Drive
Mendota Heights, MN 55120
www.fluxnow.com

Printed in Canada

For my sister, Cinnamon, who is honest to a fault.

MOORE HIGH

1st/Basement Floor

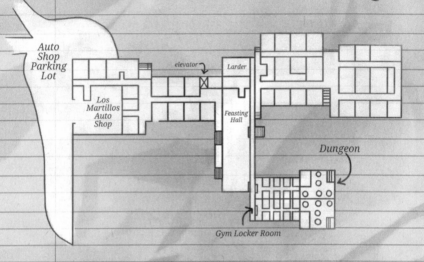

Auto Shop Parking Lot

elevator

Larder

Los Martillos Auto Shop

Feasting Hall

Dungeon

Gym Locker Room

Ground/2nd Floor

Motorheads

Dragon-Killing Lessons

Yard

Flower Aquarium

old vending machines

King's Room

Pool (Trial by Combat Arena)

Throne Room

Party Gym

Stairs to Choir Room

Cage

Hall of Faith & Martyrs

Skull Entrance

Lawn

3rd Floor

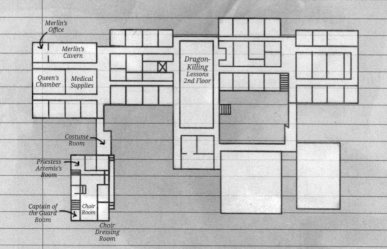

Merlin's Office

Merlin's Cavern

Queen's Chamber

Medical Supplies

Dragon-Killing Lessons 2nd Floor

Costume Room

Priestess Artemis's Room

Captain of the Guard Room

Choir Room

Choir Dressing Room

THE EXILE

KAY

Once upon a time, I could go outside and not think about dying. But now that being in the open means I could die at any moment, the warm spring sunlight feels sinister as I wait for the sound. The only way to know what direction they're coming from is the splintering of tree trunks. And they are always coming.

I stand in the waist-high grass of an abandoned backyard in my small hometown of Brockton, bloody wrists zip-tied in front of me, holding back a sob so I can listen.

Maybe a minute passes before it comes: branches crashing several blocks down.

I turn on my heel and hurl myself in the other direction.

I sprint through a suite of outdoor furniture overgrown with vines, barely dodging the dark brown pool beside it, clumsily scramble over a rotted white picket fence with my bound hands, and fall into the grass. Behind me, a tree lands in the pool so hard dirty water flecks my scalp.

Ahead is an old colonial house. I kick in the last shards of glass at the edge of its front picture window and hurl myself inside, catching myself on my forearms. The shriek of collapsing branches draws closer and closer as I curl up against the interior wall of the long-abandoned living room, clutch my locket like it can protect me.

Will it come into the house?

As secretary of the Student Council at Jefferson High, I take down the reports of the football team when they return from scavenging, especially when something goes wrong. *There were screams in the kitchen, and Jermaine stood by the cupboard, his arm half-gone, tendons hanging out of his sleeve like fat snails pulled from their shells*, says Tyler. *No, he walked in from the backyard*, Ameen says. *I saw the trail of red dots across the yellow leaves up the back steps.* The accounts are all like this, associations of vivid images, memories shattered by shock and fear. The football team cannot talk about these things publicly, by Law. I'm lucky to know so much, but I still know hardly anything. I saw the locket on its chain, back and forth, back and forth, in time with my rising heartbeat, debating.

Can it come in, or not?

Glass shatters in the next room and skitters across the floor. The wall across from me shudders, and a grid of framed family photographs goes crooked all at once. The frames rattle softly at first, then sharper, faster, clacking louder and louder until each smiling face falls down and smashes across the floor.

I jump up, hurrying away from the buckling wall as falling branches scrape its exterior, and almost slam into three girls coming down the stairs. Their faces are painted like red skulls.

They're all in threadbare cheerleader outfits.

"Wh—"

One of them looks from my bound hands to my face, then clamps a hand over my mouth, eyes cutting to the other two. Their expressions are unreadable behind the face paint. But some agreement is reached because suddenly they're dragging me backward up the flight of carpeted steps.

We're on the landing when a massive oak tree plummets into the living room. The wall crumples like cardboard; branches send heavy furniture screaming across the floor. A cloud of leaves and plaster dust rushes up toward us. We all turn and sprint.

Up the last set of steps. Down the narrow hall. Through a pink door and across a floor littered with toy ponies and broken glass and clots of mud. Straight for the open window, where a lace curtain billows in front of the sky.

The girl holding me, her face a blur of paint and sweat, puts a finger over her lips. I nod; she pulls her hand away. She points down, and I look out the window: an open-top Jeep idles two stories below.

We can get away!

But how do we get down?

The cheerleader with micro braids sits on the window frame, back to the blue sky. The cheerleader with the shaggy hair kneels before her. They exchange a look, and Micro Braids dives backward out the window. Shaggy braces her legs, anchoring her inside the room. Now the third one, Topknot, climbs over both of them and *out the window*.

"Lower!" I hear Topknot hiss, and Shaggy stands, dropping Micro Braids down farther until she's dangling Micro Braids out the window by her ankles. Then she *lets go*.

Two white high-tops float in midair, framed by blue sky and drifting lace curtains.

I dart my head over the sill, speechless, to see Micro Braids balancing on Topknot's upraised palms in a handstand. Micro Braids carefully lowers one and then the other sneaker onto Topknot's shoulders and rises to face me. She reaches out and mouths:

Jump.

The wall below us bulges as the creature inside barrels toward the Jeep.

And I remember the one thing all the casualty reports agreed on: once a Grown sees you, it won't stop until it kills you.

Like we're cockroaches, Tyler said.

"*Now!*"

I step onto the window ledge, touch my locket for luck, then throw myself into the open air.

Micro Braids's arms close around me, rough but sure. She passes me down to Topknot, who drops me hard into the back seat as a crack races up the exterior wall. The shutters rattle, and a gutter pipe pops and clanks down onto the Jeep's hood as the Grown rams the wall again.

Shaggy leaps overhead into Micro Braids's arms, and the three girls expertly collapse into the car around me. Then the engine roars, all of them screaming joyfully as we shoot forward:

"THAT'S RIGHT BITCH THAT'S RIGHT LET'S GO!"

We fly between houses, ignoring the lane lines and cutting corners across lawns until we're out on the deserted West Rocks Road, speeding toward the other side of my hometown. Micro Braids makes a dizzying series of turns, winding and cutting back, speeding up on the long hauls, then slowing before turning a corner. Topknot kneels in the passenger seat, facing backward, scanning the sky behind us for the sudden burst of escaping birds that means another one is near.

My head falls back. I'm dizzy from the speed and dazzled by the golden morning sun through the bright green leaves above me, dense as rainforest after nearly a year of most of us gone. The once-manicured lawns have churned out a new Eden. Behind green veils of overgrown grass, the dark-eyed houses look haunted, their front doors open like screaming mouths. I draw my knees up to my chin and try to breathe normally again.

"What's your name?" Micro Braids asks from behind the wheel.

It takes a few tries to get it out. "Kay."

"Where the hell did you come from, Kay?"

"Jefferson High."

A look flashes from cheerleader to cheerleader, eyes wide in their red-painted faces.

"Did something happen to your car?" Shaggy asks gently.

"I don't have a car."

"What, you just went for a walk? Jefferson is five miles away!"

Five miles. *Five miles.* Not even the Scavenging Team has gone out five miles. I will never see anyone I know again. The clique I sleep with, circled up on the gym floor at Jefferson, the same five girls I've shared a lunch table with since seventh grade, they're awake by now. They're expecting me back from the birthday room.

What will they think? That I turned? That I *walked out*?

I clutch the small locket that hangs level with my heart, nausea sweeping through me, but I know I won't puke. There's not enough in me to throw up.

"Kay? Kay!" Topknot snaps in my face. "How did you get here?!" And then, coldly, "Why are your hands tied?"

". . . Because I was dropped off," I choke out, hand still fisted around my locket.

Shaggy squeezes my shoulder. "Oh, honey . . ."

"Why?" Topknot glares over the headrest. "What did you do, Kay?"

"Leave her alone, Stokes!"

"What? Moore's never kicked anyone out. Why would Jefferson kick out some scrawny twelve-year-old bald girl—"

"I'm *eighteen*," I snap. That makes me one of the oldest people in town now. And I'm not *bald*. I get my head buzzed on the #2 setting once a week.

Topknot holds my stare. "I want to know why she got kicked out."

I look away, cheeks burning. I didn't do anything. I just found something out.

"We're almost at the fence," Micro Braids says coolly. "She coming in or what?"

"We bring her in," Shaggy says, hand still on my shoulder. "It's Tribute Day, so we can let King Max decide."

King Max?

A shadow falls over the car. We're pulling up to a fence that must be thirty feet high, a hasty construction of rough-edged particle board, slapdash plaster, and what look like giant broken bones with their jagged edges facing out. Lining the top of the fence are *bushels* of barbed wire.

How the hell did they stay outside long enough to build this?

Micro Braids taps the horn, and a panel just large enough to drive through rises, leveraged by considerable unseen force behind the wall. As we drive through, I twist around in the Jeep to clock a shirtless guy, very tanned, in a lawn chair under a beach umbrella. He directs two younger guys, who haul up the panel on massive rope pulleys with all their might.

"Any luck, ladies?" he yells to the Jeep, and Topknot reaches down into the passenger seat footwell and fishes up a Charms Blow Pop from a mini backpack. The sight of candy makes me sit up at attention. She throws; he catches it one-handed. Then he gets up and helps the other two lower the fence and latch it back into place.

We repeat this twice: drive down a neighborhood until we reach a similar fence, wait for a panel to rise before crawling through, and idle while the trio secures it behind us.

The last fence is the tallest but has no barbed wire. A figure silhouetted against the sun straddles the top instead.

"Who's with y'all?" he calls down.

"Not sure," Micro Braids calls back. "Some Jefferson girl."

"Okay, hold up," he says. He pulls out a pocket mirror and flashes it a few times. There's a pause, then he waves to unseen figures below him and the panel starts to rise. The Jeep climbs up the sloping drive toward Moore High School, Jefferson's larger and "rougher" crosstown rival.

Only the coolest kids at Jefferson had been invited to Moore High parties. But all of us heard about them afterward: keggers and game-night ragers like our more academics-focused magnet school would never dream of.

Since the nightmare day the Growns . . . happened, I'd assumed anyone not barricaded in Jefferson had been killed. Or starved during the endless Connecticut winter. The idea that any of the other three high schools in our town might have survived had never occurred to me. Because we barely made it through winter, and we had Nirali.

But Moore's front lawn looks like an outdoor music festival.

The grass is strewn with blankets and people lounging and laughing; the gleaming white front courtyard is covered with circles of beach chairs and smoking hibachi grills. Everyone is dressed in as little as they can get away with, even though it's barely June: bright bathing suits and strange headdresses and some kind of . . . chain mail?

Wait. What?

I'm still twisting in my seat to investigate as Micro Braids parks at the shaded edge of the front lot. The cheerleaders help me out, and as we walk toward the school, the impression of concertgoers quickly fades.

Everyone in front of Moore is heavily muscled and armed. Sharpened machetes and flea market katanas are slung from leather belts; short hunting swords or handles of box cutters jut from pockets and Ugg boots. One guy, his head thrown back in laughter, has a *sledgehammer* balanced on his shoulder.

There are no weapons allowed at Jefferson. It's in the top three of the First Ten. Law Three: *No student shall at any time brandish an instrument like a weapon; nor design, sell, or possess a weapon of any kind.*

Then something else pulls my attention: a dog! They have dogs? I haven't seen one since Before, and this one is beautiful. She's the size of a Saint Bernard but with a narrow face like a husky's, her pale blue eyes ringed with dark fur. But then she bristles, baring her teeth, because a jerk with plugs in his gauged ears is shoving something in her face. She backs away, tries to duck her head, but another guy has a choke collar cinched so she can't escape.

Because they're trying to get her to eat a lit cigarette.

Absolutely not.

I break away from the cheerleaders, rush over, and knock the butt to the ground with my zip-tied fists.

"Who's in charge here?" I demand, scanning the blank faces around us, still shaking with adrenaline. "I need to report something to whoever's in charge!"

A knot of people beside the guys breaks off talking to stare.

Topknot, just behind me, curses under her breath.

Shaggy puts her hand on my shoulder. "Come on, let's go, Kay."

"Who's in charge of the rules out here?" I ask her, scanning for the Moore equivalent of a Scavenging Team member. I lock eyes with a grim-faced dude shucking the skin off a dead squirrel in one piece, like he's pulling off a glove. ". . . Isn't anyone in charge?"

"Bitch!" the guy with plugs bawls. *"I'm in charge of your scrawny ass now!"*

Laughter booms around us, and people amble over to see what's so funny. My own confused expression slides across several pairs of mirrored sunglasses as onlookers circle closer. But if I back down now, this will just get worse.

The guy with plugs is in my face, eyes all black pupil with a narrow band of gray around the edge, patches of acne bubbling up under reddish stubble: "You want in Moore? When's the last time you showered, bitch? Rolling up smelling like ass! You want in, bitch? Huh?"

"Not if you're in charge, shit breath!"

The crowd brays with surprise, and Topknot pulls me back by my shoulder.

"Good one. Now shut up and let's go—"

"He tried to *burn a dog*!" I cry. To my relief, there are immediate sounds of disapproval, and with a surge of confidence I turn on the guy again. "Why don't you go try that with someone who isn't on a leash?"

I should have just gone. The guy grabs my bundled wrists with one massive hand as his other arm flies back and glints in the sun, and some crevice of my brain fires off:

Law Two: *No dispute shall be settled by physical violence, but by an impartial third party granted authority by Student Council.*

The glint is a blade. As it swings back down, an animal cry tears from me. But before it lands, someone catches his arm and twists it, hard. In another moment, my attacker is on his back, the silver straight razor spinning across the white concrete. His shrieks get the biggest laugh from the crowd so far, as a shirtless stranger pins his head against the ground.

"My arm!" my attacker yells. "Slayer broke my arm!"

"No, I didn't, Jimmy." The stranger's tone is cold and full of authority as he snaps up the razor. He whistles, and the massive dog leaps over Jimmy to his side. The stranger gently slips the choke chain off her neck, then coils it around his hand as he stands. He's easily the tallest guy in the crowd, his athletic frame built out by slabs of bronzed muscle. He stares at the guy who held the leash, his face still as the profile on a coin.

"You put this on my dog again," the stranger says, raising a fist wrapped with chain, "and I'll show you just how small it goes."

He pitches the choke chain at the guy, hard enough the guy falls backward catching it, and then he turns his full face to me.

I have no words.

The left side of his face is hardly more than skull. His nose is clipped past the cartilage; jagged lines emboss the flesh all the way around the eye socket and down to his lips. Or to where his lips *should* be; they're mostly missing. Half his mouth has been sheared off in one stroke, freezing it into a permanent leer. His left cheek is gouged so deeply the back teeth show through in places. Just imagining the pain is unbearable.

Our eyes have barely met before we both look away. A practiced jerk of his head sends long dark hair over the damage as he ducks down to comfort his dog, rubbing her neck. I think I hear him say "Thank you," but it's too low for me to be sure. When he straightens again, he hooks a finger through my bloody zip tie, pulling me toward him so abruptly I almost stumble. Then the silver switchblade cuts through it with one stroke, and my hands are free.

"Leila," he asks Micro Braids, "where'd she come from?"

"Jefferson," I answer, trying not to stare or flinch. "Are you in charge?"

"No." He stays focused on the dog. "I'm with King Max." There's a weight to the word *with* that I don't understand. "Tribute's at noon," he calls over my head, to the ring of Moore onlookers who were hoping for a fight. Then he nods to the cheerleaders to follow him, and I fall back beside Shaggy as we move into the shadow of Moore High, rubbing my tingling wrists.

"Who is this guy?" I ask her.

"Brick. He's the Captain of the Guard," Shaggy whispers back. "He's really nice. Swear on the Skull."

"He just broke that kid's arm," I point out.

"It's *maybe* sprained." Topknot rolls her eyes. "Jimmy is a pussy. I'll swear *that* on the Skull."

She points up to something bolted over the doors of Moore: a huge, elegant loop of bone, with jagged teeth all around its edge. Like the *Tyrannosaurus rex* skull at the New York Natural History Museum, except larger. Why would Moore have a . . . wait.

Wait.

Is that . . . a Grown skull?!

Did they kill it?

Growns can die?

My eyes blur, staring up at it, my head suddenly light. I don't realize I've stopped walking until Leila comes back for me and pulls me forward, and I stumble under the grinning skull of the dead monster mounted over the doors to Moore High.

THE KING

KAY

The halls of Moore feel alive. They breathe with flowing air, sunlight pouring in from the massive windows.

We have windows like this at Jefferson, but the work of those first few days was to board them up. Our top priority as Student Council is keeping them that way. Everything that happens in Jefferson happens in a dark miasma of body odor and damp that clings to us like a second skin.

But at Moore, the air tastes like blue sky, and the only smell I notice is the light coconut of Brick's sunscreen when I walk close to him. There's mud tracked on the floor, and dried grass has settled under the lockers, but I don't see a single roach.

At Jefferson, our steps crunch with them.

Passing the open doors of the classrooms, I glimpse muscular teens dozing in hammocks, circled in lawn chairs talking intensely, or laughing as they kick hacky sacks back and forth. They have cook fires going, which alarms me. (Law Four at Jefferson: *No use of open flames will be permitted except by those trained to handle them.*)

Some of them hang out of their open doors as we pass: "Bring back anything this time, Stokes?"

"Not much!" Topknot jerks her thumb toward me.

"What's your name?" I whisper to Shaggy.

"Amy." She smiles. "That's Leila, and her name"—she points to Topknot—"is Tiffany, but everyone calls her by her last name, Stokes."

We pass through double doors and under a cement flight of stairs, into a hall looking into an atrium walled in by plate glass. Inside the atrium are six dazzling cherry trees, white-pink petals shivering down like snow past the glass. It's the most beautiful thing I've seen in a long time.

"Pretty, huh?" Amy beams. "I like to think of it as the Flower Aquarium."

Against the walls facing the trees, dozens of girls and several gentle-looking guys are circled on blankets, chatting or crafting or styling each other's hair. All of them look up as Brick passes.

"*Slayerrr!*"

"Hey, Slayer, why don't you come to 225 for dinner tonight?"

"And 103 for dessert!"

"Who's that? A new girl! She better not be your girlfriend!"

A hot flush races to the tips of his ears and darkens the back of his neck, but Brick just keeps walking. He leads us around a corner and through a set of double doors into a narrower hall, which must be their music wing. It's almost identical to the layout of our own at Jefferson: there are entrances to the auditorium on one side and the orchestra, chorus, and band rooms on the other. Jefferson's auditorium is in constant use, seats crammed with students and their lawyers preparing to have cases heard, the stage crowded with desks where judges hear complaints and accusations before handing down judgments.

But no sound comes from Moore's auditorium doors. It's *eerily* quiet for such valuable real estate. The gym and the auditorium are the only two areas large enough to assemble the whole school at once. We hold cases in the auditorium, and we all sleep on the gym floor at Jefferson: order in one, safety in the other, the two most important things in the two most important rooms. But the only thing that issues from Moore's closed auditorium doors is the faint smell of some kind of woodsy perfume.

I expect them to lead me inside, but we turn instead to the first door on the other side of the hall, flanked by two more buff guys. One is holding a golf club with a sharpened clubhead, the other a pair of nunchucks that he flips idly. Both stand up straighter as Brick approaches.

"S'up, Brick. She clean?" Nunchucks asks.

Brick says, over my head, "Stokes, can you pat her down real quick?"

Stokes sighs, annoyed, then awkwardly pats around my waist and hips. "All good."

"Your name?" Brick asks me, looking at the ground.

"Kay. And you're Brick?" I try to look him in the eyes, but he won't let me. "Or Slayer?"

"My name is Randall Brick. Friends call me Brick. Idiots call me Slayer." And he steps past me through the door. I'm about to follow him, but Leila stops me.

"He has to announce you first."

"The King's, like, not always available," Amy says. "But I'm sure he'll make some time to see someone new."

I nod, like this is a perfectly normal statement. It is not, and though nothing is normal now, Moore's new normal might be more than I can take. Jefferson's new normal at least doesn't involve kings, or squirrel blood, or *switchblades*.

"That guy out front, he was . . ." I can't finish.

"Gonna cut your face up, yeah," Stokes says, hands on her hips. "Jimmy was high as hell! That's why I told you to leave it, but you popped off."

I remember his dilated eyes and grab my locket, sawing it back and forth on its chain. For once it doesn't comfort me.

"You *didn't* get cut, though." Amy shoots Stokes a look. "But maybe, like . . ."

"Maybe don't pop off at people you don't know," Stokes finishes.

"Just try being polite, okay?" Leila widens her eyes in warning. "*Especially* with the King."

The door opens, and Brick says solemnly, "You are granted an audience with His Majesty, the King of Moore High."

"Good luck!" Leila pats my frozen shoulder.

"We live in room 212 if you want to hang later!" Amy adds.

I nod and follow Brick into what I guess is the throne room, looking what I hope is polite.

It must have been the band room, because it's just like Jefferson's, with a floor descending in tiers down to the platform where the conductor would stand. But where musical instruments should hang on the walls are now weapons, the kind of flashy stuff they roll out at swap meets: two crossbows, hunting knives, ninja stars, several samurai swords. On the conductor's platform is a guy with his back to the door, wearing paint-spattered Dickies.

I was expecting a muscleman like Brick, but King Max is narrow and tall, with hair bleached yellow at the ends and black at the roots. He's painting gold scales on a red dragon that covers the chalkboard. He carefully finishes a row before turning around, pressing the wooden tip of his paintbrush into his full bottom lip, and scanning me with sharp black eyes.

He is definitely unimpressed.

"Um, hello, Your Majesty—" I start. He cuts me off.

"You need to bow first." He says it nicely enough, like a friend telling you his mom makes everyone take their shoes off at the front door. But it's still a command. I blink at him for a moment, then bob up and down awkwardly.

"Almost." He smiles, tight-lipped. "We'll get there."

I reflexively pull a face, and his smile drops. Leila's warning rings through me.

"Excuse me. We don't have a, uh, king at Jefferson."

"Well, you're a ways out from Jefferson now. Who sent you?"

"No one sent me. I was . . ."

Where do I begin?

Do I tell him I was bound hand and foot and thrown into the back of a van by a mystery assailant? That our own Scavenging Team captain drove me into our town, staring straight ahead, refusing to flinch no matter how much I screamed? I begged Tyler to at least cut the ties on my feet so I could run. And he did, before throwing me into the tall wet grass and speeding off. I chased the red taillights until they zeroed out into the black sea of night that lay between me and dawn.

Law One at Jefferson: *Forcing someone outside is murder*.

"I was dragged out and dumped close to where the cheerleaders found me."

"They were raiding on West Rocks and Elm," Brick adds, standing guard beside the door.

King Max leans against the chalkboard and daubs at his palette, eyes downcast. His olive skin is flawlessly tan, his expression almost bored as he considers.

"Tell the cheerleaders to put her back where they found her," he says at last, and turns back to his painting.

"Wait, *what*?" Panic jolts through me. "Why?"

"Because I don't buy it." King Max shrugs. "Someone at Jefferson sent you out here with a sob story so we'd take you in."

"You think I'm a *spy*?"

"Makes more sense than them dragging you out. Who'd be scared of you?" He turns to face me again, but he's still focused on his palette. "You're what, ninety pounds?"

"We've been below rations for two months," I confess. "We're not spying. We're starving."

King Max tilts his head back again, waiting for me to give him more.

"And believe me, if Jefferson *was* going to spy on you, I would be the *last person* they'd send." Everyone who knows me knows my little tic, knows why I can't lie to save my life. "But no one at Jefferson is even *thinking* about Moore. We're too busy trying to survive!"

"So, let's try this again." He stops mucking around in his paint and stares me down, face cold. "Who are you, and why the hell did they try to kill you?"

"My name is Kay Kim. I'm the secretary of the Student Council." I raise my chin. "I work with the president and vice president and eight student representatives to draft policy for the whole school—"

A silent laugh reveals a magazine-ad smile. "Just what people need most," King Max says, "when they're starving to death."

"That's why our president went out to look for help."

Gearing up President Kyle for a drive outside Brockton had been momentous work. It felt like we were launching an astronaut into space, outfitting his gray Volvo. We'd boarded up the windows with plywood, extended the side mirrors, and put a Jefferson Senators sticker on the bumper. Then we loaded it with precious food, gallons of water, and his lifeline: the ham radio, so he could call each day at sunrise and sunset.

When Kyle crossed the front quad to the Volvo that morning, everyone in Jefferson watched from the cracks between the boards. Kyle paused at the Volvo and, instead of scrambling into the car, turned to us. He smiled, then waved, and a cheer echoed through the length of Jefferson.

But the bravest and most beautiful thing was Nirali—Kyle's girlfriend, and our school's doctor—racing across the parking lot, her long black hair streaming behind her. Risking her life for a last kiss goodbye.

Kyle took off his varsity jacket and slung it around her narrow shoulders, and we all went hoarse cheering until a weeping Nirali hurried back inside.

"That was in April," I explain. "Kyle had been updating senior members of our Student Council over the radio every day since. Then I found out contact with Kyle had been broken, but they were still passing off important statements as his." I swallow hard. "That's why I was dragged out. So I wouldn't tell anyone else."

King Max raises his eyebrows. "Sounds like someone's figured out how to be king at Jefferson after all."

He rattles his brush in a coffee can of water, then swipes it on the side of his Dickies. "So you're, like . . . a political fugitive? No—a whistleblower? Except you didn't get a chance to blow the whistle . . . There's an old word for what you are asking for. It's *right* on the tip of my tongue—"

"Asylum." Brick's deep voice rings out behind me.

"Asylum!" King Max points to me with the paintbrush. "You're an exile who *seeks asylum*!"

"Sure." Whatever it takes. "I plead for asylum, Your Majesty."

He grins, glad I'm getting into the spirit of things. "Nice, nice. Okay, cool. You can hang around here through the next Expansion. If I can find someone willing to babysit you."

"I will," Brick says.

I dart a look over my shoulder and catch the blur of hair falling over Brick's face before King Max says, "That works for me. Hey, it's almost time for Tributes, yeah?"

"Right." Brick opens the door and calls for the guards. They come running. King Max turns to the teacher's desk in the corner of the room and opens a deep file drawer. He pulls out an ankle-length swimmer's coat with fake red shearling inside a satiny red nylon shell. It has a giant Moore mascot appliquéd on its back: a helmeted Spartan. Then, carefully, he lifts out a hammered steel circle with four spikes and holds it in front of him. The circle is crudely fashioned, but the way he considers it tells me it's his crown.

He looks up over my head to Brick and says, "The next time we do Tributes, let's have someone put this on for me. One of the hotter girls. Jessica maybe."

I roll my eyes before I can stop myself. Luckily, he's too caught up with reverently crowning himself to notice. I feel a brush against my elbow: Brick is kneeling just behind me. I sheepishly lower myself to one knee.

"When I leave your presence, you kneel," King Max explains. "All right. Let's do this."

He lifts his chin as he stands over us, enjoying himself.

"I, King Max, welcome you to Castle Moore, Exile Kay!" he says, putting on a bit of a voice. "While you are under my protection here, I am your liege lord, and you my bound subject."

A guy wearing Dickies, Converse sneakers, and a steel circle on his head is my "liege lord." Sure. If it keeps me from going outside again, I'll learn to curtsy.

"We only have two rules for those who live at Moore: you must obey your King, and you must face the dragons. You may only join Moore when you've proved you can do both of these things."

Dragons? I look up from the scuffed vinyl flooring to the beast he's painted, with its skull-splitting smile and multitude of rolling eyes. "Dragons" is not what we call them, but sure.

"Well, actually, I already faced a 'dragon' today, so—"

"No," King Max cuts me off. "You ran from it. We don't run from dragons at Moore. We slay them. You can help with that, or you can move on."

"That's . . . that's not even possible—"

"How do you think I became King? I killed the dragon whose skull is hanging out front." My expression must satisfy him because he nods proudly. "And since we are expanding at the next full moon, you'll have a chance to earn your place here in four days."

No way. There's *no way* they could expect me to kill one of those things. *Four days from now?!* But King Max's face is hard.

"You'll figure it out. If you want to stick around," he says. Then he turns to Brick and resumes his lazy stoner affect. "Now let's go get my shit."

+ + +

Aside from the fact that King Max wears a swimmer's coat and steel crown, the royal entourage acts like any group of high school guys, the guards playfully swatting at each other with their weapons and letting me trail behind them like a half-deflated balloon. Only the dog checks in on me, looking over her shoulder with confused eyes, unsure if I'm with the pack.

I keep seeing Kyle in my peripheral vision, but it's always Brick. They're roughly the same height, about six foot four, with the same straight brown hair and naturally pale, pinkish complexion. But Kyle wasn't as built, tan, or intense. Kyle wore button-up shirts and kept his hair neatly styled and smiled at everyone. Brick wears only cutoff sweatpants and, behind his long tangled hair, an expression like a brandished fist.

Once we get within earshot of the first classroom door, the guards move ahead and enter first, calling, "His Majesty, King Max!"

Everyone inside kneels, head down, like they're about to propose and pretty depressed about it. They don't look up until King Max says, "Hey!"

Then the twenty-odd occupants of the room crowd around him. The former classroom is made unrecognizable by racks of bunks kludged together from scavenged beds and unvarnished two-by-fours. A window frame has gone black from a cook fire in an old barbecue grill, and hanging on the walls are dozens of makeshift weapons and shields, at least two of which were once metal garbage can lids. MOTORHEADS is painted in giant block letters across three walls.

The center of the floor resembles a hasty yard sale: a pyramid of canned goods, a bunch of different-sized batteries, a mirror, trash bags stuffed with clothes, a bucket of loose detergent. King Max selects one small can of mandarin orange slices and all the batteries, which he praises them for finding. The batteries go in a duffel bag carried by Nunchucks.

King Max asks about a helmet, and one of the guys brings forward a bundled-up hoodie and unwraps a roughly hammered golden bowl with two sweeping points, a rough draft of an ancient Greek helmet.

"I need time to finish it in the Auto Shop," the guy says, "but you know what they're like before an Expansion."

"They'll give you the time. I'll make sure. We're crowning the Duke that night, so the helmet has to be ready." Then King Max switches into his stage-actor-royal-man voice to say goodbye as they kneel again, and it's on to the next haul.

Most of the rooms are coed, but there's a few smaller ones that are all girls or all guys. Some groups are ten, some are five, and most are closer to twenty, like a class from Before. But all have weapons, fire, and a name. And no one is hungry.

We're on the first floor, approaching the loudest room so far, when Brick turns to me. "You should go see the cheerleaders," he says, not a suggestion.

"Why? Did I do something wrong?"

". . . We're about to go see Los Martillos in the Auto Shop, where Jimmy lives." Brick seems unused to explaining himself. "When I tell his room and the King about what happened, I don't want him going off on you to impress his friends."

"Fair enough." I nod, as though he's waiting for my agreement.

"We'll pick you back up when we get to the cheerleaders," he says.

I keep nodding. And then, unable to resist, I sink to my knees and pet the big dog, riffling the fur on her chest so I don't block her vision, cooing, "Such a lovely girl, aren't you? Aren't you a lovely girl?"

"His name is Frank," Brick says flatly. "And he doesn't like strangers."

But Frank is already nuzzling his heavy head into my hands as I scratch behind his ears, a pleased whine escaping him.

"Guess I'm already a friend." I smile up at Brick, and the corner of his mouth that can move jerks a little in response. Then King Max calls from around the corner, and Brick moves on, Frank chasing after his master.

But I don't just hurry my silly little self up to the cheerleaders just yet. I may have no choice about living through an apocalypse, but I will not go quietly into the Dark Ages. I want to see how this boys' club deals with Jimmy. I want to see what I've gotten myself into.

Once Brick turns the corner, I scan the long, echoing hall: At one end, a girl is shaking a hair spray bottle in preparation for spritzing it through a Bic lighter. At the other, a guy is crouched, sucking a crude joint as he sharpens a pile of ninja stars.

No one here is going to ask me for a hall pass.

I duck through the fire doors straight ahead of me and move cautiously along the exterior of the building.

There's a garage-style door open thirty feet ahead, looking out on a tree-lined parking lot filled with vehicles in various states of repair. Hugging the rough brick wall, I edge toward the clattering metal and raucous voices inside.

It doesn't sound like anyone in this room is bowing.

Luckily, a giant mirror in a gilt frame is propped right at the edge of the garage door. It's taller than me, a statement piece from a girly boutique, and angled to catch the daylight and bounce it inside. In its highly polished circle, I can see inside the Auto Shop.

The mirror faces the shop's back wall, which has floor-to-ceiling shelves of car parts. They make a gleaming silver halo around a guy in a black coverall, arms folded across his chest, leaned back against the shop teacher's desk and staring out into the center of the room. He wears an expression of total disdain as King Max talks, which is immediately endearing. So is the fact that he's the most gorgeous person I've ever seen in real life. He has a James Dean quality, like he's the lead man without even trying. His skin is copper and his hair dark, but his eyes are pale blue and glow in the shop's milky, diffused light. And when Brick starts talking, those eyes burn.

"—opened a straight razor on an unarmed girl half his size!" is all I catch.

"Whatever." I recognize my attacker's voice instantly. Jimmy. "You know how Slayer gets if someone raises a hand to a bitch, Leo. Fact is, she started it."

Leo. The beautiful guy's name is Leo.

Leo shoots Jimmy a look of cold rage but keeps his voice neutral. "Los Martillos will talk this over tonight."

"What's to talk about?" King Max says casually. "Kick him out."

"We very well might. But with all *due respect*"—and the way

Leo says this suggests very little is due—"I wanted to use this time to discuss an Auto Shop tribute. People should be turning over the auto supplies they raid. I caught some kid keeping beer cans in a bucket of coolant. That's not just dumb, someone could get killed."

"Yeah, I've thought about it," King Max says. "And it's a no. Tributes are a royal thing, and the Auto Shop isn't royalty."

"Yeah, but . . . neither are you," Leo says, and as shocked laughter bursts free around the room, I feel a surge of relief that someone is willing to call "King" Max out. But the swift silence afterward tells me he's made a terrible mistake.

"Count them off," King Max says.

Leo's half smile disappears as Nunchucks strides into the mirror and hovers menacingly beside him.

"One, two, three, one, two, three . . ." Brick's voice bellows and his towering head flashes across the mirror as he counts off the members of Los Martillos. There's over fifty of them.

"It is my royal decree that Jimmy and all the threes are out of this room from this moment on," King Max says with authority. "You hear that, threes and Jimmy? You're not with Leo. You can work here, but you don't sleep here. Until you find new rooms, you can sleep outside."

There's a hiss of protest, but it burns out quickly in the tight silence.

"Twos . . . you get to clean out the latrines today! The shitters are getting deep."

More grumbles and whispered swears.

"All the ones . . ." A smile creeps into King Max's voice. "You get to stay here. *If* you punch Leo, right now. Below the shoulders and above the belt." An uneasy murmur rises. "Make a line, ones."

My empty stomach twists as Leo stands straighter, face grim. But he doesn't protest.

"Line up!" King Max repeats, and the unease in the room deepens. It says something—how unwilling they are to punch Leo to save themselves. But it says something, too, that none of them will protest out loud.

"It's okay," Leo tells them quietly. "Let's get it over with."

My own breath is rising, my hands balling into fists. I want to stop this, but there's no way.

"And make it count, ones. No throwing fake punches," King Max tells the room. "Here, I'll show you what I mean."

Max strides into the mirror and punches the beautiful guy so hard he doubles over. I clap a hand over my mouth to keep from crying out.

"Line up. *Now*," Brick growls, and I can't take any more. I turn and flee back inside.

THE WIZARD

KAY

"Yeah, Los Martillos have been acting up a lot," Leila proclaims from her bunk in room 212. "They're the biggest room besides the theater department, and they think just because they know about cars, they should be in charge. It's nice to have people who know about cars, but we're *all* learning now. I fixed our radiator a week ago, and Leo said he couldn't have done it better himself."

"That's the Auto Shop guy with the bright eyes, right?" I ask, and Amy and Stokes exchange a glance.

"Someone's crushing out."

"Girl sees Leo, girl wants Leo—that's how it's been since third grade—"

"When will you hoes realize that that man is *my fiancé*?!" Leila cries indignantly. "Or he should be. Stop laughing!" She laughs. "I'm serious. I've liked that boy since kindergarten, okay—" And I can't help laughing along with them.

The cheerleaders' room is definitely my favorite, mostly because of their twenty-gallon storage bin stuffed with every kind of snack food. Amy pulled it out from a corner and gave me a whole Kit Kat bar when I first came in, my first chocolate in nine months. It tastes like falling in love.

"You can have another one," Amy says, watching me lick the inside of the wrapper. "One of our first raids was the 7-Eleven. Now we're sick of candy. All we want is meat."

"Andrea is cleaning a doe right now," Stokes says, arranging stuff in the center of the floor for Tribute. Room 212, they've explained, is home to six cheerleaders. The other three only raid during Expansions and make up for it by doing most of the chores.

"What's the difference between raiding and expanding?"

"Well, you remember all the fences we drove through today," Leila says. "Expansion is when we go kill a dragon so we can put up more fences."

"Dragons don't go near one of their own when it's dead. Like, it repels them, until it's fully decomposed," Amy adds. "Which buys us time to put up more fencing."

"'*Expanding*' the safe area outside Moore." Leila makes air quotes.

"Expansion is when the whole school goes out, all together, to kill a dragon," Amy says. "Raiding is going out past the fences to grab some stuff and race back. And we're good at that."

"We're *the best* at that," Stokes corrects her. "People even pay us to help them train for Expansions. Question!" She holds up a car battery. "How would you guys feel if I just, like, slid this under my bed? Just this once?"

"Put it on the blanket, Tiffany," Leila says sternly. "You trade an unoffered car battery and Merlin will be on our ass in five minutes, and I am *not* heading into an Expansion with Merlin pissed at us."

"Merlin? Really. *Merlin?*" I laugh. "I'm sorry, but what is up with all this Ren-faire crap?"

Silence.

A long, mortifying silence. I might as well have just farted out of my mouth.

Finally, Amy leans forward, her voice gentle but firm. "It's not 'Ren-faire crap.' King Max was really into *Echellion* Before. He says he couldn't have killed the first dragon without it."

And suddenly everything makes a lot more sense. My little brother, Arthur, was crazy about *Echellion*, an epic sandbox game like *Elden Ring*, set in the medieval world. Players started off as lowly squires and, over the course of many missions, climbed to knight, then lord, then duke, and finally king.

"Like, I didn't play *Echellion* Before." Stokes plunks down the car battery. "But all the 'Ren-faire crap' makes everything seem . . . way less sad. I like being a Knight."

"Everyone who raids regularly can call themselves a Knight," Leila explains.

"And they're naming a Duke next Expansion. And the Duke gets one of the three royal crossbows!" Stokes looks around the room. "Duke Stokes? I mean, come on!"

"Wouldn't it be *Duchess* Stokes?" Leila says.

"*Duchess?*" Stokes screws up her nose.

There's a knock at the door, and for what feels like the fiftieth time today, I have to take a knee to this bully: Max, back on his stoner vibe, smiling and high-fiving the cheerleaders like he didn't just punch a guy who couldn't fight back.

When Stokes asks what he'd call a lady duke, he considers it seriously and says, "Technically the lady equivalent of a duke is a duchess, but I don't know, that sounds weird. High Lady?"

"Don't you think Duke Stokes sounds better?"

"Duke Stokes! Hell yeah. Hey, if you get it, it's your title. You tell me how to style it."

Because he's so chill, right. I'm positively seething when I realize Brick is staring at me. Why? Did he glimpse me in the Auto Shop mirror somehow? If he *did* see me, what will that mean? A lecture?

A punch to the gut?

He's still peering at me through his dark hair. To avoid eye contact, I look down at his chest, but that's no good, either—since he has the body of an underwear model, he probably thinks I'm checking him out. So I meet his gaze, defiant.

He instantly looks away.

And then Max wheels around and says, "Brick, why don't you show Kay to the Cage?"

Brick's thick neck flushes. Then he nods and walks out of the room so fast I have to practically run after him, trotting alongside Frank.

We catch up with him on the stairs and follow him in silence, through the now-emptied hallway beside the cherry trees, back into the music wing.

Brick lights a stake of seasoned wood from a pile beside a trash can fire, which someone's set out ahead of sundown. He hands it to me without a second thought, then stalks to a set of double doors beside the throne room and unlocks a combination dial that secures a heavy chain around the handles. Once open, he gestures for me to walk through the doors and into the dark. I'm terrified for a moment that he means to lock me up, but he follows after me, chain swinging from his hands. He threads it through the handles on our side of the doors and locks us both in.

Where has he trapped us together?

My heart thrashes, and I spin around to look for any kind of exit, or a window I can break. The torchlight ripples with a sound like wind and dances up a tall metal grate that locks into the floor: the instrument cage. But the shelves where the instrument cases should be are now stocked with priceless treasure: unworn shoes, solar chargers, water filters, protein powder, boxes of condoms, and cases of toilet paper.

"My room is up this way," Brick says, taking the torch back. He sleeps beside the King's treasure. Max must trust him a lot, which makes me sort of hate him. But I follow him through a dark doorway, and the torch's flame folds itself smaller as we climb up an airless staircase to an even narrower door.

He throws it open, and I recoil.

This room is so tiny I don't think it's technically a room. Was it a *closet*? There is one bed, a long narrow cot covered in plaid fleece blankets, and the teacher's desk is pulled into the middle of the floor. On the wall hang a crossbow and two shields, one new and one cracked almost in half. And papered over the concrete are big, detailed blueprints: for wheels and towers and other *Echellion*-type things.

Frank happily jumps up on the tiny cot, and just as I'm about to demand where Brick thinks *I'll* be sleeping, he lunges onto the desk. The torch flames leap upward and draw my attention to a fire ladder leading up to a skylight.

"I'll be staying on the roof while you're here," Brick says. "If you want to change before dinner, there's clean clothes in the desk. I'll knock before I come down." He puts the torch in an old flag holder bolted to the wall.

"You're going to sleep *outside*?" I frown. "Is that safe?"

"It's safe everywhere at Moore." Brick shrugs. "That's why King Max is King." And even though the torch is behind him and I can't see his face, I can tell he's staring again.

"We'll be meeting the King at Merlin's Cavern for dinner," he says. "Merlin wants to get a look at you."

Merlin again. I bite the inside of my cheek. "He does?"

"She," Brick says, and turns to the ladder. But then he stops and turns back again. "I scared you before. Out front, with Jimmy."

". . . Yeah."

"Well." He pauses. "Please don't be scared of me." Then he climbs up the ladder, the skylight window closing noiselessly behind him.

"So where are *you* sleeping, Frank?" I ask the massive dog. Frank lays his giant head on the pillow in answer.

+ + +

Moore at night is even more beautiful than by day. Moonlight fills the halls with a dreamy lavender tone, every doorway glows orange as we walk by, and giddy laughter like a late night sleepover floats from each room.

I look ridiculous, swimming in Brick's sweatpants and flannel. But it's wonderful to be out of the cocoon of layered hoodies and thermals and fear pheromones I'd been swaddled in the past six months. When I scuttled out of them, they kept my shape like a plaster casting. They should probably be burned.

Brick leads me to a large set of stairs with banisters in the middle that runs up all three stories of the school, the sort of staircase that would be mobbed first period Before. Now there are hundreds of bouquets of drying herbs knotted up and down its rails, the scent somewhere between a soap store and what I imagine an apothecary would smell like.

"So do you have a royal title?" I ask him.

"No." Brick laughs.

"Why not?"

He pauses so long I think he's purposefully ignoring me. Then he says, "Because I don't want to be in charge of anyone."

"Just me?" I mumble, but he catches it.

"Only until you find a room."

I'm not sure what that means, but we've reached the third story and are going through double doors to what must have been their science wing. Brick stops in front of a door with a star painted on it and turns to me.

"You should ask King Max how he killed the dragon," he says.

"Don't like being in charge, you say?"

Brick doesn't smile. "Just some advice. Take it or leave it," he says, and waves me in ahead of him.

"Merlin's Cavern" was clearly the biology lab Before. Rows of black-topped lab tables recede into the dark, and on the closest one, a maze of beakers, cylinders, and distillation tubes is bubbling away on three Bunsen burners. Some mysterious substance fades from blue to green to pink as it travels through the web of glass.

I can't smell whatever it is, but maybe the scent is drowned by the half-dozen incense sticks tucked into the bookshelves lining the walls. Hundreds of books have been gathered on the freshly built shelves, mostly biology and chemistry, but art and history, too, all carefully color-indexed with dot stickers, alongside jars and jars of carefully labeled seeds: rosemary, feverfew, allheal. The stacks climb from the floor to the ceiling, which is painted navy blue and covered with a diagram of planetary movement sketched out in chalk lines fine as lace.

I'm gawking at it all when a wheelchair rolls down the central aisle from the back of the room.

"You must be Kay." A girl with an oval face framed by short, neat cornrows glides toward me. Her broad shoulders strain against her hoodie as she expertly maneuvers the chair. Frank's whole body wags with excitement. At her glance, he sits at attention. She pulls a treat from her hoodie pocket, he freezes as she balances it on his nose, and, when she snaps, he gobbles it up. She beams, revealing a massive smile with the tiniest gap between her front teeth, then scans me with laser-focused eyes.

"Thank you for looking out for our boy today," she says, rubbing Frank's massive head. "I don't know if I'd smack the first person I saw walking into a new school, but I respect the balls."

She moves past me to a table covered with a spotless white cloth. There, she pulls the lids off three catering trays.

Oh, God.

Grilled meat glistening with oil, a bowl of mashed potatoes dotted with melted butter, a heap of hot rolls—everything else in the room goes out of focus. The sound that comes out of me startles Frank.

"Please, get started," I hear her say as I seize the food. The meat is like chicken but tougher—squirrel? I jam a roll into my mouth, remembering to sit only after the first couple swallows. When I look up, Merlin and Brick have taken their places at the table, Merlin across from me, Brick in the chair beside me. They look like they're either trying not to laugh or trying not to cry.

"Sorry." I grab a snowy napkin by my plate with an oily hand. "This is such a nice dinner, I don't mean to—"

"Just eat," Brick says. "Please."

Oh, I have no intention of stopping. Merlin lifts the lid of a cooler under the table; there's soda and water and beer. I take a water bottle, nodding gratefully.

"That's quite a test tube setup," I say to Merlin, after I've emptied the water in two swallows. "What are you making?"

"An important magical potion," she says. I laugh, but she frowns. "I'm not kidding. I'm a wizard. That's what I do: magic."

"There's no such thing," I say before I can stop myself.

She smiles, but it doesn't reach her eyes. "You can sit here, in a time when dragons roam the earth, and say there's no such thing as magic?"

I may not have faced a Grown, but I know they are not made of magic.

They are made of death.

"What do you think caused the dragons, at Jefferson?" Merlin asks, eyes locked with mine. "Why did every adult in this town die and rise again as monsters to kill their own children?"

My chewing slows, and I swallow hard. When I reach for my water, my hand twitches.

"Will it happen again?" she asks, so evenly. Like we're discussing the weather. "Will we join them, too, when we hit a certain age?"

I look over at Brick, to see if he's as shocked as I am. He is watching me intently.

"Did this happen to just Brockton," Merlin continues, "or is the whole world swarming with dragons? Really: What does Jefferson say?"

We don't say any of this at Jefferson, ever. Which is not to say we don't think it. We do. I have. All the time. That's why I'm wringing my napkin under the table right now, so hard my hands burn. Imagining the whole world covered with them, no help ever coming, no escape.

"Aren't you, like, afraid of sending me into a panic?" I manage at last. "Saying all this stuff?"

Merlin tilts her head. "Isn't it worse, to think it and not say it?"

Not according to the Rule. There are laws at Jefferson, which can be debated. But the Rule is written over all of them, at the very top of Jefferson's Constitution, because without the Rule, no law is possible. It can be a very hard rule to enforce, and the penalty for breaking it is cruel. But I quote now what Nirali always says when defending the Rule in council:

"Words have power."

"That"—Merlin points at me—"that is a *fundamental property* of magic. So there *is* magic at Jefferson!" I tense. She smiles wider. "But you're using it wrong."

"No, we're just trying to prevent a mass panic while we find real solutions." I sit up straighter. "We have an exploratory committee looking into what caused the Growns, or dragons." I'm speaking a little formally now, like I'm addressing Student Council, but still shredding the napkin under the table. "There were some serious waves of panic the first few days. Everyone was sure it was zombies, then it was definitely an alien invasion, then a theory about demons went around. So, we formed a committee of our best math and science kids. Their theory is that Brockton was hit by some kind of virus that's triggered by aging. So, we do the birthday rooms."

"Birthday rooms?" Merlin's eyebrows rise. "What are birthday rooms?"

I've never had to explain them to an outsider. We never really explained them to ourselves. The rooms developed quickly at Jefferson; no one was debating policy that first night. We were out of our depth, beyond logic or rationality, operating under horror-movie zombie rules. We isolated anyone who'd been hurt by a forming Grown to see if . . . to see what happened. The rules are different now, but the idea is the same.

"There's these two rooms in the back of the school with a couple vending machines in them. They have a sort of thick metal security grating you can roll down and lock to separate the machines from the hall—like the Cage." I nod to Brick. "On your birthday, you go in there for twenty-four hours to make sure that, uh, nothing happens. You're excused from your chores for the day. You still get rations.

Sometimes other people have the same birthday, and then it's, like, a social thing."

I give them a quick smile. I don't tell them about the guards on the other side of the grating, with the gasoline and the matches. Maybe they would understand. Or maybe they would think we were becoming monsters after all.

"Damn," Merlin says. "That's grim."

"Hold on." Brick clears his throat. "If Jefferson believes the dragons are caused by a disease, and all of you already have it, then you walk around thinking anyone, at any time, could turn into a dragon?"

"We prepare for the worst. We hope for the best. What else can we do?"

"At Moore," Merlin says calmly, "we believe magic has returned. And we must master this magic if we are to conquer the dragons and save the world."

Conquer them?

A loud knock at the door saves me from responding. Brick stands as Max strides in, so I do as well; Merlin puts her hands over her heart and inclines her head. One of the guards passes on to the back of the room, hoisting a duffel bag that clinks when Max slaps its side.

"'Tis a fair battery haul this day!" Max announces in a stage-actor voice.

"Nice!" Merlin smiles. "Your Excalibur turn up yet?"

"Only way to get Excalibur is to behead all the water nymphs at the lake."

"Only took us forty tries!" Merlin laughs. It's an *Echellion* reference; I remember Artie trying to beat that level. They don't believe in actual water nymphs . . . I hope.

Max looks over at me and does a double take at my bone-scattered plate.

"We let her start early," Merlin says.

I start to apologize, but Max puts a hand up. "Hey. You need it!"

He laughs, and everyone else seems to relax. Max lowers himself into the seat at the head of the table. He takes the crown off, rolls his neck.

"This thing is seriously heavy," Max says, and sets it down beside his plate with a *clank*.

"Deep." Merlin laughs.

"No, not like, I'm not even trying to be symbolic. I mean it's, like, literally four pounds."

"Gotta work those traps." Brick tsk-tsks.

"Shut up, Hulk!" Max hides his huge magazine-ad smile behind one hand as Brick flexes an arm. Merlin licks the tip of her finger and presses it to Brick's bicep, making a sizzling sound that gets swallowed in the guys' laughter. Their playfulness hits me hard. I miss hanging out with my friends, I realize, like we did Before. Even though we're together all the time now, we don't joke around anymore.

"So, Exile Kay!" Max grabs a squirrel drumstick. "How you liking Moore so far?"

"It's amazing," I admit. "And I can't stop thinking about what you said. That you killed the Gr—the dragon, excuse me, whose skull is out front?"

From Max's face, I can tell this question has made his night.

"I was actually expelled from Moore at the time," Max starts, staring off into the distance like an actor going into a flashback. "I'd been at home all week while my parents got ready to ship me off to military school. No joke! That day, I was in my room, playing *Echellion* in sandbox mode, when I heard the sound. That moan, you know?"

That moan the adults made right before their eyes went blank, before they sank down on all fours.

"So I go to my window, and I see my old man clutching the driver's-side door of his truck. Then suddenly, he's on the ground. I thought, *Oh shit, he's had a heart attack or something.* But then his head . . . went back." Max does a less-severe gesture of the neck-snapping motion I saw dozens of times. "And then it was like he was *dragged backward*, he moved so fast. But he was crawling. He crawled, backward, out into the street and collided with our neighbor, who was also on the ground crawling, so fast, all of them . . . like crabs or something, the way they moved, right before they started coming together. I'll never forget it. The way their spines lifted right out, pulling the ribs up with them through the skin, *pop pop pop* . . ."

I try to push back my own memories of the thing that came crashing through the wall of the teachers' lounge that day. The thrashing line of twisting bodies, blood-soaked clothes hanging in rags. The wet *pop* of the tendons pulling from their joints as the skeletons unraveled from their deep red muscles and the bones began to scrape together.

Max says, "I have lucid dreams. You know what a lucid dream is?"

"When you can control what you do in the dream," I answer. "I've had them, too." I dreamed I ate a box of donuts once, perfectly aware I was asleep, the imaginary glaze dissolving sweetly on my tongue.

"Yeah, well. When it started, I thought . . . this must be a lucid *nightmare*. And then I thought, *How can I play it?* Like it was a game."

My stomach twists.

"I went to my garage and grabbed all three of my dad's crossbows—"

"Coach was big into deer hunting," Brick says quickly.

"He took Brick and the King out hunting with him every season, so that's why there are three of them," Merlin explains further. She raises an eyebrow at Max. "Most people don't just *have crossbows*."

"Yeah, well, he did, and I do. So, I got all my dad's hunting shit in my Jeep, including his chain saw because why not, and I drove straight to the school. I think I played 'Scaring the Hoes' the whole way there."

Merlin and Brick laugh.

"It still hadn't fully hit me it was real, you know?" Max says, eyes wide. "So I get to the Moore parking lot, and sure enough, there's a *big one*, and I recognize most of the people it was made of. It was still forming, right."

I remember the paw of the Grown raking the wall outside the teachers' lounge, its claws resolving from dead, dangling hands, a wedding ring popping off a knuckle and bouncing brightly down the hall with a sound like a jingle bell: *tink, tink, tink!*

"A lot of those teachers I didn't like, sure. But it was still sad. To see anyone you know as part of *them*, it just . . . hurts. Even if you hate the person, it hurts. Even thinking it was a nightmare, I started getting, like, furious, right?"

I nod.

"So I drove straight at it, shooting bolts at its face, faces, whatever you'd call the front end. It reared back, and I drove after it. And then I see Brick's truck pulling in, he'd cut first period—"

"*Senioritis,*" Brick adds dryly, and Merlin laughs.

"Yeah, so, Brick's standing there with his mouth hanging open—this was when he had a whole mouth—"

Merlin whoops with laughter. I look to Brick; he's laughing harder than either of them.

"—and I throw him a crossbow and tell him, you know, *let's get this thing*, and we just go for it."

Max's face glows; his gestures take up the width of the table. "We get a couple of its eyes—that was crucial. It was stumbling around all blind, so we herded it into the power lines down by the edge of the parking lot. It got all tangled up, and that was that, man."

"Yeah, especially for our electricity," Brick says.

"So then Brick went over with the chain saw," Merlin prompts Max, "to take its head off . . ."

"To make sure," Brick adds, arms crossing over his broad chest.

"It got in one last swipe on its way out." Max looks at Brick, eyes soft. Like how Artie used to look at me sometimes. A knot rises in my throat. "And then Brick was all *BZZZZZ!!!*" Max mimes bringing down a chain saw.

"So that's why they call you Slayer?" I ask Brick.

The table goes silent. Merlin leans her chin on a tight fist. Max's smile drops.

"If King Max hadn't come with the crossbows, I'd be dead right now." Brick meets my eyes briefly. Then he gestures toward Merlin, as if to redirect my gaze. "And Merlin figured out if you have one dead dragon lying around, the others stay away. That's how we learned to expand."

"The elevator stopped working when the power went out. I could get my chair up and down the stairs, but it was a real pain in the ass. Fire marshal really shat the bed on that one." Merlin's fist, under her chin, is looser now, and when Max bursts out in laughter at this remark, it relaxes, and she sits back. "So I mostly hung out here and watched a real-life horror movie."

She waves at the tall windows behind her, the real stars starting to come out beyond the painted ones. Before Moore built its fences, from this vantage point, she probably could have seen for miles.

"And I noticed some things," she adds with a modest shrug.

Max leans forward and grips both of their shoulders.

"And now we have a plan. Kill the dragons, build the fences, take back Brockton!" He smiles, staring me down, demanding my reaction.

"That's an incredible story," I admit, and Max looks smug.

"So what's Jefferson's plan?" Merlin asks. I almost laugh.

"To stay alive," I tell them, "until Kyle brings back some help." Though I don't know if I've ever let myself fully picture what that help would be. Scientists and politicians in some bunker, maybe, or an army unit, sweeping up survivors. Some kind of adults who know what to do. Who haven't turned into Growns . . . yet.

"But then you found out Kyle might not be coming back." Max shoots a glance to Merlin.

"Is that right? When did you figure that out, Kay?" Merlin frowns.

Yesterday. Was it really only yesterday?

I was running around the school with my dog-eared legal pad yesterday afternoon, my crank flashlight's beam sending roaches scuttling for the seam between the wall and the lockers. The light announced me as a member of Student Council on official business before I even approached the department heads.

I asked each of them the same question: if you could walk into a Costco right now and fill a cart for your department, what would you most need?

"Filters," the chairwoman of the Department of Water said. "Brita filters. Coffee filters. Panty hose over a tennis racket."

The head cook was frantically busy, but my best friend since first grade, Reese, worked the cafeteria serving line. Reese helped me with a list of things the kitchen needed besides food: dish soap, sponges, charcoal briquettes.

It wasn't until I met the head of the Department of Power that things got grim.

"We might not have a Department of Power in another two weeks," Tassos said. He was leaning back in an ergonomic chair in the basement, deep rings embossed under his large eyes. "The main's on her last legs." He meant the large main generator squatting in the shadows behind him. "She was meant to cover blackouts of maybe thirty hours, once a year. Currently, I'm grinding sixty hours out of her every month. And she's struggling. She took the last forty-eight hours off, and it took my crew five resets to get her back on this morning. Missed breakfast."

"I'm so sorry, Tassos." I cringed. The cafeteria dispensed food twice a day; if you came late, you went hungry. "Is it a question of more fuel, or . . ."

He shook his head slowly and gave me a sad smile.

"So more portable generators, then." My voice came out thin. "Maybe they have solar ones at Costco?"

"Every form of power Costco has we will need, eventually. Deep cycle batteries, solar chargers, whatever," Tassos said quietly. "Or a lot of people better learn to see in the dark."

I was used to being hungry and tired, but the weariness that settled over me after speaking with Tassos went deeper than that. I dragged myself to the top of the school, to the last and smallest department: the AV room. This was where our radio was. Simon and Nirali were the only ones allowed to sit in when Kyle called in at sunrise and sunset. But the threads of orange light that broke through the particle board on the west staircase still shone straight, not slanted. I figured I had a little time to check in.

"Kay!" Nirali, who was our senior representative and doctor, smiled as I entered.

She was at a desk topped with a Sharpie grid and scattered with chess pieces. She still wore Kyle's green-and-gold varsity jacket, as she always did when not in the hospital. It swallowed her, the sleeves going right up to the last knuckles of her delicate brown fingers. Even in the harsh LED light of the camping lantern, her fine features and large eyes were strikingly beautiful.

"Happy birthday to our favorite secretary and my favorite candy striper!" Nirali went on. I'd spent more than a few all-nighters at the hospital, helping patch up the Scavenging Team. "That's tonight, right?"

"Yup." I swallowed hard. "My turn in the birthday room! That's why I'm here. Figured since I'll have the next twenty-four hours to myself, I could work on a proposal for council—"

"Do secretaries make proposals?" Simon asked Nirali.

Simon, the vice president of Student Council, did not look at me. He only squinted through his owlish glasses at the chessboard, his long, pinched face overhung by unruly brown hair. Before, he had made an affectation of wearing a too-tight camel sport coat with leather patches peeling off the elbows. Now it hung loosely over layers of hoodies and thermals. Winter had made a lot more room inside our clothes.

Nirali gave him a disapproving look. "Tell us about your proposal, Kay. Don't mind Simon."

Nirali, my personal hero, was waiting to hear my big idea.

"Well, I've just been thinking a lot about the Costco across the highway," I started nervously. "All the nonperishable foods that would be in there. Canned food and flour and sugar, along with everything our departments need." I brandished the legal pad. "And trucks, you know, to drive it all back in. We could send out five people and get months of food back if we—"

"Absolutely not."

There was a clapping sound of something being hastily shut, and Tyler shot into view. He had been crouched behind the booth where the radio was mounted, working on the portable Generac. The captain of the Scavenging Team and former football team center, he yelled now like he was calling a desperate last play across the field, vein bulging at the center of his forehead: "You want to send the Scavenging Team out *ten miles*?"

"Well. I mean, one long trip to a securable building like Costco could actually mean *fewer* casualties than several—"

"You don't know what you're talking about." Tyler moved forward quick enough that Nirali stepped out from behind the desk and got between us. She was taller than him, but he was much broader and, because the Scavenging Team always ate ahead of the regular students, still relatively muscular. "If you think any of us are going to agree to this shit—"

"It's just an idea," Nirali said soothingly. "The council hasn't discussed it yet—"

"The council hasn't seen daylight since October. I was out last week. With Jermaine." Tyler's voice broke.

Simon heaved himself from behind the chess table and put an arm awkwardly around Tyler's shoulder, steering him toward the door.

"Look, don't worry about her." Simon's voice dropped lower. "Kay's job is just taking minutes. Someone wants a promotion, that's all. Don't stress. We'll talk soon."

The door closed behind Tyler, but tension still hung in the air when Simon returned to the chess table, his glasses white circles in the LED light.

"Kay, why are you still here?" he said, still not looking at me.

I flushed. "I was going to ask what Communications needs. I'm guessing a new generator, if the Generac isn't fixed—"

"Yeah, it just fully broke down yesterday." Simon lifted a chess piece and held it above the board, considering.

"Oh . . ." I said. Then, "So how did you get that transmission from Kyle? About the elections?"

Nirali had made a motion to call elections a few days ago—and unleashed chaos among the Student Council. We hadn't had an election since Before, and no one knew what that would mean. As the person taking minutes, I'd marked a lot of my entries *shouting/ indecipherable*. So when Simon gave Kyle's decree at today's meeting, that we should hold off on elections until Kyle returned, we all breathed a sigh of relief.

"When the Generac craps out, we switch to the main generator." Simon was scanning the chessboard, distracted. "Keep up, Kay." Simon snapped his piece down and grinned at Nirali. "Someone forgot about her bishop."

"Someone forgot about my queen." Nirali swept the piece across the board, and he swore. "Check!"

"But the main generator wasn't running yesterday," I pushed. "It wasn't on until this morning."

Nirali dropped Simon's knight with a clatter.

Simon turned to me at last, his wide red mouth crimped by a sneer. "So Kyle must have told me at sunrise."

"But Tassos said they didn't get the main generator back on until *after breakfast*, so it wouldn't have been on at sunrise, either. It wouldn't have been on until we were already at the council meeting—"

"Simon is confused," Nirali cut in smoothly. "He must have talked to Kyle last night, when I was at the hospital, and then the Generac broke down right after. Right, Simon?"

"Sure." Simon's jacket shoulders twitched with a shrug. "Hard to keep track of the time when it's always dark. Speaking of which, it's just about sunset. Kyle will be calling in, so all underclassmen should be out of the room."

Nirali gave me a little wave. I was dismissed, but I was still buzzing with questions as I nervously wound my flashlight and drifted down the empty stairs.

I ate dinner with my clique, and they surprised me with lavish presents: pencils and erasers and a new legal pad. Then we split a pink packet of Domino sugar Reese had been hiding in the kitchens for the last three months. While they rolled out their sleeping bags, I tucked mine under my arm, gave them each one last hug, and headed down the empty, echoing halls to the basement.

The grate was rolled up, leaving the dim, unplugged, and long-emptied Fruitopia machines exposed. No guards were waiting, but something told me I wasn't alone.

"Hello?" I called into the breathing dark.

A metallic roar came from behind the fire doors. They snapped open, and a panicked cry escaped me before I realized it wasn't a Grown filling the empty doorway.

It was the back of a van.

Whoever had been hiding in the dark shoved me then, ran me forward until the lip of the van bit my shins and I sprawled into its interior. Tyler, waiting inside, spidered forward and zip-tied my hands and my ankles. His unseen assistant slammed the doors closed, cutting out the last shreds of light from my fallen crank flashlight.

"What are you doing?! What is this?!"

Tyler didn't answer. He hopped lightly over the console and into the driver's seat, and the engine rumbled below me.

"WHO ORDERED THIS?!" I screamed at him, bruises swelling my shins, sharp plastic digging into my wrists.

But he never answered.

+ + +

"So this Simon guy, the vice president," Merlin says when I finish, "is covering up that Jefferson's president is dead, so he can stay in power."

"Wait, hold on, I'm not saying Kyle is dead!" I shake my head. "Simon lied about speaking to Kyle when our generator was down, and I'm sure he played a part in kicking me out. But that doesn't mean anything's happened to Kyle! It just means Simon was desperate to shut down elections. Because he knows he would be voted out."

"What about the girlfriend?" Max taps his bottom lip with one long finger. "She lied, too. She covered for Simon."

"No, not necessarily. She misses a lot of the radio calls because she's our doctor—she works day and night in the hospital. That's why she proposed the elections in the first place—"

"Or she's given up on Kyle coming back and doesn't want to be left holding the bag," Max says, more to Merlin than me.

"No! No one has given up on Kyle. None of us will ever give up on Kyle!" I cry.

They are casually breaking the highest rule in Jefferson. Even exiled at Moore, I feel compelled to shout them down. A look of concern passes around the table, so I take a breath and compose myself before I explain: "She just wants to get out of doing council meetings. Because the hospital needs her more."

"I'm sorry, what?" Merlin leans back in her chair. "What do you mean she's a doctor? She has to be eighteen, nineteen at the most. So what, she started medical school at *age ten*?"

Max laughs. "Hey, Jefferson is the school with all the smart kids, right?" His tone drips with sarcasm: "'Tomorrow's leaders today' or whatever."

"'Leaders of Tomorrow,'" I say quickly. "And no, she didn't go to medical school, but she was accepted to Yale, where her dad was a surgeon, and she was going to do pre-med. And she did MediCamp for three summers."

"Three whole summers, huh?" Merlin widens her eyes. "Sorry, but that is *not* a doctor."

"Do you need a doctor," Brick says, his deep voice always a little startling, "if the problem is you're starving?" He slips some gristle to Frank under the table, and a thick tail swats at my ankles.

"Fair point." I look at the trays of leftover food on the table. "I know it's a big ask, but if there was any way Moore could possibly—"

"Hell no!" Max laughs, a charming laugh, even more beautiful than his smile. It makes me hate him completely. "I won't risk Moore lives crossing town."

"You'd rather *all of Jefferson* die?" I say before I can stop myself.

Brick tenses in the chair next to me. Merlin shoots a look to the King. But Max is not disturbed. He takes a leisurely swig of his beer.

"It's nice," Max says, "that you'd stick your neck out for the school that tried to kill you. But you just got here. We're not even sure if you're staying yet. Speaking of which: Can you drive stick?"

I nod, and my face immediately goes hot, the corner of my mouth jerking wildly. I didn't even *say* yes, but it's too late.

"What's so funny?" Merlin stares at me.

"No, I just . . . I'm sorry!" The grin stretches across my face, going wider and wider the more awkward the moment becomes. I start laughing, nervously. No one joins in. I clutch at my locket. "I'm really out of it. Sorry, I can't drive stick shift. I don't know why I nodded."

"Yeah, you're loopy. Go to bed." Max nods to Brick. "Take her to the Cage and sort out her car stuff before Expansion, okay? I have to talk to Merlin."

"Oooh, let me guess," Merlin says as Brick stands, hovering over my chair. "More sightings of the Blue Knight?"

"I wish they'd stop calling him that. Knights have to be *knighted*. I'd make an edict about it except it's not worth my time." Max sounds annoyed. "But all three guards on the first fence to the north swear they saw blue light on that block last night . . ."

Their voices drop, eyes locking on each other. Dismissed, I rise, my stomach going sour as I follow Brick and Frank into the hall.

"Why are you so red?" Brick asks once we're in the stairway.

"Me? Red? I'm red right now?" My voice comes out too high. "Huh, weird."

There's a pause. Then he asks, "Can you drive at all?"

"No," I admit. Immediately my face relaxes and starts to cool.

"You'll need lessons, then."

He says nothing else the rest of the walk to his room. He goes straight up to the roof, and I sink down onto the cot, next to Frank.

Brick took the torch with him, so I only have a rectangle of silver moonlight slanting across the concrete wall. It falls on one of the blueprints, and I get up to investigate. The precise, straight lines on the blueprint are all made with Bic pen and describe the measurements of what appears to be a water wheel. The kind of thing you'd see on a cover of a big book of nursery rhymes.

What have I gotten myself into? Fighting "dragons." Bowing to a King. Dinners with a wizard. Maybe this is all some dream.

Then, most dreamlike of all, I hear the opening notes of my favorite song.

I have to be imagining it. But the Coldest Lakes song keeps coming, every note hitting exactly where I need it to, unlocking memories of bus rides to Model UN debates at Sharpe Academy, and walking around Mill's Pond with Reese, and curling up on the couch with Artie while he played video games. Am I *hallucinating*? But the music gets louder underneath the skylight.

I climb up on the desk and realize it's coming from the roof.

Brick is a Coldest Lakes fan?

I would've thought *he'd* be into . . . heavy metal? The sounds of spear fishing? But no. He's falling asleep to Coldest Lakes' last album, *Kite Weather*, just like I used to. I stand on the desk listening until my chin nods. Then I creep back to the bed. I throw one arm around Frank and close one hand around my locket and fall completely asleep for the first time since Before.

+ + +

I open my eyes to a glowing stripe of sunlight curved across an overturned bowl, a folded note peeking from its edge. I crawl out from under Frank, who slept curled up on my legs like a giant cat. On the note, I find square, precise handwriting:

AUTO SHOP WILL GIVE DRIVING LESSON—B

I turn over the bowl to find two apples, a hardboiled egg that's still warm, and a Clif bar. When I realize it's the kind with chocolate chips, I get so excited I almost drop it on the floor, then eat it in three bites. A gurgling pain quickly follows, and I sprint to the latrines; my digestion system has been on vacation too long. But the walk down to the Auto Shop afterward, with sugar in my bloodstream, is what I imagine taking Molly must be like. The cherry trees are like pastel fireworks in the morning sun, the cook fires smell delicious instead of alarming, and the laughter ringing down the halls makes me giggle.

Coming into the Auto Shop from the hallway lets me appreciate how well their mirror system works. The large mirror from yesterday sends diffused beams of daylight zigzagging across the whole shop, through a network of smaller mirrors and other reflectors, so the mechanics can work around oil without torches.

A mechanic races over as I step through the door: "Hey, need some help?"

"I came for a driving lesson?"

"You got a car?"

"No, but—"

"So, you need to *buy* a car. Let me show you what we got. This way."

He nods, confidently misunderstanding me, and I follow him outside to their parking lot. Brick must have forgotten to arrange lessons, and I have nothing to trade. Well, except my locket, but I'm not trading that for anything.

"We got this Camry here." The guy slaps a rusted red vehicle, both of us squinting in the bright sun. "It runs, but brake pads are shot, so that'd be additional." I try to cut in, to explain there's been a mistake, but he goes on cheerfully, "And this old hoopty—someone did a lot of weird mod work, but you know, it runs. I think."

He throws a sheet off an old station wagon, its windows boarded up with plywood, a bright green Jefferson Senators sticker on its bumper. It's a punch in the gut—I actually stagger back a step, then blink hard, sure I'm wrong. But no. I know this car, all right.

It's Kyle's Volvo.

✝HE LESSON

KAY

The mechanic flops the cover back over Kyle's car, the vehicle everyone in Jefferson is dying to see, and moves on: "And we got one of those VW bugs from the 2000s, remember those?"

My mouth has gone dry, but I force the words out: "Can I see the Volvo again?"

He shrugs but uncovers it. The ground tilts underfoot as I inspect it. The tires are all intact. No dents, no claw marks. I lean into the window: the radio is still hooked up, the curly cord of the mic hanging from the cup holder.

It's like Kyle drove up to this very spot, parked the car, and walked off.

"How did you get this?" I try to keep my voice steady.

The mechanic shrugs, face scrunched up against the sunshine. "Don't know. You want to trade for it or what?"

"Someone has to know. I need to talk to them, right now—"

"You must be Kay." A familiar voice breaks in, and I turn to see the beautiful guy from the mirror. "I'm Leo." He offers a handshake; it goes on half a beat longer than I expect as he regards me. But in the shadow of his slanting eyebrows, his eyes are friendly. Pieces of sunny sky. "You need lessons, right?"

I nod.

"Okay," Leo says. "Follow me."

He turns, leading me to a black Chevy Tracker, his pain perfectly concealed until he opens the passenger-side door for me. The motion makes him wince, and I note the faint purple blur of a bruise above the black V of his speed suit. But his expression is neutral as he gets behind the wheel.

"How much driving have you done?" Leo asks.

"Two lessons Before."

It's hard to focus; it's like an alarm is going off only I can hear. *Kyle's Volvo is at Moore. What does it mean? Can I ask Leo about it? Can I ask anyone about it?*

Leo takes us along a narrow outlet from the parking lot, then down a short dirt road across a lawn and into the tree-lined neighborhood. And just like that, we're driving down a street where there are no Growns, at normal speed, like it's Before.

When was the last time I did this? The ride to school that last morning in October, in Reese's car, my long hair piled in a coil on top of my head. We'd gone through Dunkin' Donuts on the way to school; we were howling about a reality dating show we both followed, two glamorous women of the world sipping milkshakes.

"Looks like we hit the morning rush." Leo nods toward a herd of deer milling across the road and up into the lawns, peering through the shattered windows of a nearby house. The herd watches us pull over with unworried expressions. Leo slows to a stop and has us switch places. I grip the wheel and stare forward.

"You nervous?" he asks, kindly.

"No, yeah, I'm just—I just . . ." I have to know. "That Volvo I was looking at back there, do know where it came from?"

"They didn't tell you?" he says. "That guy from Jefferson drove it over. Kyle."

Something fast and thin arcs over the car; the deer scatter into the woods before it lands, white tails flashing. Left behind is a tiny fawn, who turns to see what's coming.

In my rearview are five guys on bikes. One of them sits back on his seat, no hands on the handlebars, a bow in his outstretched arm. He's drawing another arrow from his JanSport backpack but has to reach down to straighten the bike before he can aim again.

I punch the horn as the arrow flies; the curious fawn bolts into the woods. And as the bikes race past us and into the trees, I turn on Leo.

"Kyle was here?!"

"Let's go farther down the road," Leo says, scanning around us. "Somewhere quieter."

I bumble down another street and into a cul-de-sac before parking with a lurch, wrenching the brake in a way that makes Leo wince.

"Kyle was here?" I repeat. "And he met Max?"

"Yeah, they hung out the whole time."

"And Brick? Brick met him, too?"

Leo nods. "They all had dinner every night, him and the King and Merlin and Slayer."

Every night? "How long was he here? And when?"

"I'm not sure exactly when, but at least a couple weeks back. He stayed for, like, three or four days, I think?" Leo's eyes flash to the rearview mirror, as though making sure we haven't been followed. "Then he just took off. One of the King's guards told a couple of my guys to strip the car, without telling me. But they told me, of course." A flicker of pride. "So I told them to leave it the way it was, just cover it up and siphon the gas."

I rest my forehead on the steering wheel and burst into tears.

So Kyle hasn't called in for weeks. He couldn't have, without the radio. Both Nirali and Simon have been pretending to talk to him? Have been *enforcing the Rule*, when he could be—

Kyle could be dead. Is most likely dead. And if Kyle's not coming back with help, then everyone I know at Jefferson is doomed.

"You want to talk about it?" Leo asks gently.

Can I? Or will I get dragged out of here, too, if I tell the wrong person what I've figured out? Max and Brick and Merlin are lying to me, acting like they never met Kyle. Simon is covering it up back at Jefferson. Is there even one honest person in this whole town?

"I can't tell if this place is crazy or if I am," I splutter at last. "Some dude in a red fur coat told me he was my liege lord yesterday." I look up at Leo, face streaming. "And shit, man, *I bowed to him.*"

A laugh, sharp as broken glass, somehow makes Leo even more handsome. We laugh together for a moment, nervously at first, then letting it break through. It's a small crime, laughing at the King. But the harder we laugh, the safer we are with each other.

"Like, yesterday I met a wizard?" I go on. "And she was *making an important potion.*" He rocks forward and I crack up fully; we laugh until we're breathless.

"Wow," Leo gasps at last. "Yeah, no, I've gotten used to it, but this place is nucking futs, okay." He grinds his palms over his eyes; his gaze is warm when it returns to me. "How about Jefferson? You guys manage to hold on to your sanity a little bit better, I hope?"

"I don't know about *that.*" I sigh. "But at least we don't *bow* to anybody. And we got to vote for the people in charge and—" But then I bite my lip.

That's not exactly true. When we voted on the Student Council Before, the biggest decisions were whether or not the vending machines should offer gum. Now Student Council holds the power of life and death. And Simon is lying to the whole school to keep hold of that power.

So why would Max and the others lie about Kyle coming here? What could *they* possibly lose by telling me the truth?

"I'm just confused," I go on carefully, rubbing my locket until it's warm between my fingers. "Why would they act like I was the first kid from Jefferson?"

"I don't know what game His Highness is playing," Leo says darkly. "But you should play along until you decide what you want to do."

"*Want* to do? There's no way to go back."

"No, you shouldn't go back. That's not what I'm saying, I—" Leo ducks his head, tries again. "You should talk to Artemis. That Kyle guy spent a lot of time in the music wing. And she's one of us."

"Who's 'us'?"

Leo turns stiffly toward me in his seat, framed by the meadow of wildflowers and butterflies that's grown up in the cul-de-sac just outside our window. A halo of morning light rings his perfect face with gold. "People who are sick of living under a tyrant. People who remember we still live in the *United States of America* and not some—cut scene in a video game. People who want a free Moore."

". . . How do I talk to Artemis?"

"I can arrange a meetup," he says. "But it's dangerous. King Max takes treason seriously. If Brick or 'His Majesty' find out, you'll be kicked out of Moore. Hell, we both will."

My stomach twists at the thought. But something happened to Kyle that both schools are hiding. If he's not coming back, Jefferson deserves to know the truth. And I'm the only one who can uncover it now.

"Okay," I tell Leo, "but Max is making me live with Brick, so finding a place to meet might be tricky."

His smile is cutting. "Yeah, Slayer will be *thrilled* we're friends. Don't worry, driving lessons are a perfect excuse. See that house right there?"

Across the cul-de-sac meadow is a white colonial with an old red brick chimney running down its front.

"That's 1776 School Hill Road," Leo says. "We can meet Artemis there during our lesson tomorrow. If you're sure it's worth the risk."

I picture Kyle waving up at our school, his confident smile.

"I am," I tell Leo.

"All right. *All right!*" He claps excitedly, then insists on a high five, and I realize I'm smiling again. "And don't worry, Kay, I'll also get you driving. Why don't you go ahead and start the engine again."

He has me go around the neighborhood a couple times, then

insists I learn how to use a tire jack. "We get about ten flats every Expansion," he explains. Once he's watched me raise the car and lower it back down safely twice, we head back up the road toward the school.

"Easy there!" he says dryly as I crawl past a herd of deer, waiting for one to jump out at me. "We're clocking what, fifteen miles an hour?"

"It feels fast," I grumble.

He grins. "Next time I'll show you how going fast really feels."

I give him the side-eye, sure I'm interpreting this wrong, and his grin downshifts to a smile as he directs me to a space in the Auto Shop parking lot.

"Great first lesson," Leo says. "And next time—"

"*KAY!*"

Leo rolls his eyes at the voice, and we both get out of the car. Frank races up to me, and I scratch behind his ears. Brick, striding after him, is less enthusiastic. He glares at Leo, who's standing as tall as he can, like he won't let Brick see he's hurt.

"*You're* teaching her?" Brick scowls.

"I am the best driver." Leo smiles.

"She won't be doing *stunts*." Brick is actually mad. "You have enough to do in the shop for Expansion."

"I'll find the time." Leo looks at me. "In fact, I was about to have lunch if you want to join?"

"She can't," Brick says before I can answer. "Her training starts at noon."

"My training?" I blink at him.

"Dragon-killing lessons," Brick says, like that explains it.

". . . You signed me up for dragon-killing lessons."

"Yes, because we have a dragon to kill in three days, remember?" he snaps. "We have to be at the library in ten minutes. You can eat on the way."

I'm about to protest when Brick holds out a bread roll wrapped in wax paper, and I swear I smell bacon.

"Let's go." I snatch the roll and follow after him and Frank. Just before we step back into Moore, I glance over my shoulder. Leo is leaned against the Tracker, hands in his pockets, staring after me. He winks one electric-blue eye, and I hide my smile.

+ + +

"So what is a dragon-killing lesson?" I ask Brick, my mouth full of sandwich.

"Today is sort of a placement test. The rest of the training depends on how you do."

"Oh." A placement test at the library. For killing dragons. "Like . . . multiple-choice?"

Brick snorts, then shakes his hair in front of his face to hide what this does to his scars. "No. It is definitely not multiple choice." The way he says this makes my stomach go sour.

"What is it then?" The words come out squeezed and small.

"State secret," he sniffs, and though this is a joke, I've run into enough secrets the last twenty-four hours that it effectively kills my appetite. Brick clocks me wrapping the last bite up. "You don't like the sandwich?"

"No, I love it. It's the best thing I've eaten since Before. Where did you get it?"

"Morning market. Most days I go down and get some hot bread, ketchup, and deer bacon, and slap a couple of those together. But they've got other stuff, too, if you want." He speeds up as we hit the hall around the Flower Aquarium, ducking his head even lower as girls start catcalling:

"We're playing truth or dare in our room tonight!"

"I dare you to come, hottie!"

He hurries past them, rounds the far corner into a paneled hallway, and stops in front of a recessed set of double doors.

"Okay. Good luck," Brick says, not quite looking at me.

As he turns away, I blurt out: "Wait, Brick?"

"Yes, Kay?"

He's probably going to roll his eyes and tell me to stop stalling, but I'm shaking now.

"Will I—can I get hurt?"

He gives me a long look through his hair.

"Yes," Brick says at last. "But not badly." He starts to head off again, but then for some reason turns and walks back to me, his expression softer. He stands where he was before but feels closer, his voice kind. "It's going to be scary. It has to be, for it to work. But it *does* work. You'll be fine, Kay. You've already been through a lot worse."

I nod, heart pounding, and knock on the doors.

THE PRIESTESS

KAY

It's dark inside the library; they've boarded up the windows so it's more like Jefferson than anywhere else at Moore. But burning torches along the stacks give the darkness height and breadth, and I can make out two levels of bookshelves opening onto a central staircase as I pass through the shoulder-high book-detecting scanners that flank the doors.

Stokes climbs over the old library checkout counter, holding a long rifle, which she hands to me.

"This is an air rifle. It only shoots BBs, but you can put your eye out if you're not careful. Ever shoot one?"

I shake my head, so she shows me, twice. Slow the first time and quick the second. I imitate her, fingers fumbling, then she helps me put on lab glasses and an orange vest with a reflective stripe.

"Try and get all the light bulbs you can," she says. "Don't get tagged. See you at the top of the stairs."

Then she lets out an earsplitting whistle and thunder rolls down from above. Timpani drums? Are there people in the dark playing timpani drums?

More arms grab me, all three cheerleaders spinning me in a

circle as the drums pound. They push me toward the staircase as the drums cut short. All I hear is my own breath and then a high, almost insect-like rattle as the shadowy shape of a Grown snakes down the stairs.

They keep one in here?!

I run for the doors, but the cheerleaders are ready, lined up between the walk-through scanners. They push me back, yelling: "TOP FLOOR! YOU GET OUT AT THE TOP FLOOR!"

I curse them out with all my heart, then dash over a tabletop as the Grown turns toward me, skull yawning. I hoist myself to the top of the nearest bookshelf, hardly realizing what I'm doing until I'm crouched, panting, on top and looking down at what is *not* a captive Grown. It's the skeleton of one, mounted on cardboard and puppeted like a paper dragon at Chinese New Year by hidden people.

I'm lost, staring at the claw that extends toward me. At the way the white bones that used to live in human arms knit into one joint, like many forks of lightning branching from one bolt.

The Grown skull yawns wide. Its surface is pocked with the blurred eye sockets of the human skulls it's melded from. How many? Is there someone I know in the silent bone mask staring up at me?

Something glitters in those dark sockets: little light bulbs. Dozens of them have been taped where the Grown's eyes used to be. Those are my targets. I hoist the air rifle with shaking hands and fire down. A small pellet ricochets off bone and buries itself in carpet.

The bone puppet angles its massive skull closer. There's a hiss from inside its jaws and the sharp smell of spray paint. No! I'm not supposed to get tagged! I turn and scuttle down the back of the bookcase, as the skeleton puppet heaves back and rears around.

Either the drums have started again or it's just my heart, as I dive under a table and scramble to the stairs. The puppeteers barrel after me; another hiss, and cold wetness tingles at the back of my scalp just as I reach the landing. I clamber up onto the handrail on all fours like a monkey and scurry up along the banister just ahead of the beast, when my air rifle slips from under my arm and clatters to the ground, at least thirty feet below.

But I'm almost out. The doorway is glowing ahead, through the stacks. I clumsily rise to standing and run up the last four feet of the handrail like it's a balance beam, piloted by pure adrenaline. I leap to the ground so hard I roll forward, then I'm up again and sprinting, shrieking, for the door. When I break through back into the bright light of the hallway, the cheerleaders are clapping for me.

I bend over and heave up hot bread, ketchup, and deer bacon all over the floor.

+ + +

Once I've recovered and helped clean up the mess, Leila counts my spray marks: a cloud of silver on my ankle and shoe, neon green across the back of my head.

"One maim, one kill, no light bulbs." Leila frowns at a clipboard. "*And* you dropped your gun."

"But you're a climber!" Amy's eyebrows are all the way up. "That's huge!"

"A climber?" Brick strides toward us, Frank at his heels, all half smile and sun-kissed muscle. Has he been lying out in the sun this whole time? Because he's actually glowing. "We always need climbers, that's great."

He pats my shoulder. Part of me wants to swat him away; part of me wants to reach up and palm his smooth, broad shoulder. See how he likes a condescending pat on the back.

"So?" He scans me, clocking the flecks of vomit and spray paint. "How're you feeling now, Kay?"

"Like I need a shower."

"That," Amy says, "we can help you with."

+ + +

Brick lets the cheerleaders take me to get cleaned up. We go across the overgrown football field and through the chain-link fence surrounding it, down a well-worn trail along a grassy stream that grows and swells in a ravine until it lets out at Mill Pond.

I find myself completely submerged in water for the first time since Before, deep emerald water that turns gold when I look up at the sky from the silence below.

The winter Before, my family skated up there. My dad on the bench with a thermos of tea, my mom spinning around with Artie, both of them laughing so hard, their smiles so alike—a bubble wobbles out of my mouth and floats over my head at the thought, and I don't want the silence anymore. I surface among the lily pads, a dragonfly careening by my ear, then glide back toward the shore until my feet drag the mud and I can hobble out onto the smooth, uncertain stones of the bank.

"Nice trunks!" Stokes calls. I pull at the clinging fabric of Brick's plaid boxers, looking very chic under Amy's borrowed sports bra. Stokes is in a gold bikini, sunning herself on a hot-pink pool float shaped like a slice of watermelon.

"Thanks. What's on the other side of the pond?" I ask her. "Has Moore expanded out that far?"

"Nope. But dragons can't swim!" she says, eyes closed. "Don't Jefferson people know *anything* about them?"

"Hey, Kay!" Amy calls. Her hair is a soap mohawk, and she's holding out a weathered Suave bottle. "You want some shampoo? Get that paint off your scalp?"

"I kind of like the neon green with the buzz cut." Leila sits on a broad rock just above Stokes. She's elected to wear a T-shirt over her swimsuit, and her braids are pinned carefully on top of her head. She leans forward over one straightened leg, like a ballerina, to paint her toenails bright red. "Are buzz cuts a Jefferson thing?"

"No, they're a me thing," I say, and breathe in the pink gel Amy squirts in my palm: strawberries. "I had really long hair Before, but it got all matted and weird. So my friends staged an intervention."

Reese had plied the best hairdresser in Jefferson with extra food from the kitchen. When he asked what I wanted, I told him to shave it all off. My friends watched, horrified, their nervous laughter trickling into silence as the clippers buzzed. But when he was done, the bald girl who looked back from the mirror didn't look like me at all, and that helped. This life wasn't so bad if it was happening to someone else.

"What does it mean that I'm a climber?" I ask, raking flakes of neon green from the back of my head.

"Like the name says," Leila drawls, "climbers climb when they're attacked. Everybody wants climbers because you need someone covering from above. It's way better than being a runner, which most people are. Fighters are the rarest, the people who stay where they are and attack. And there's only one person I know of who actually went running *toward* a dragon."

"King MAX!" Stokes hoots. "Let's GOOOO."

"I feel like more of a barfer," I confess to Amy.

"That's why you keep training," she says. "You can get used to being scared."

"And then on the actual day, we all take Lucid anyway." Stokes shrugs.

"Lucid?"

Leila and Amy exchange a glance. "It's something that . . . helps," Amy says.

"Like a drug?"

"A potion," Leila corrects me, focusing back on her toenails, when a *whoosh* of flame makes us all look farther down the rocky bank, where people are lighting up chunks of Sterno suspended from wire. The flames are pale in the daylight.

"Here we go," Leila mutters, and Stokes sits up on her elbows to watch as two lines of dancers start moving in sync, little leashed fire balls whirling around them.

"Is *that* a Moore thing?" I make a face.

"Hell no," Leila snorts. "That's an Artemis thing."

Artemis. The other one of "us" at Moore. I watch the dancers until someone's burning chunk of Sterno goes flying, and they all break apart, laughing. The one clapping out the beat makes them start from the top: *five, six, seven, eight!*

"Who's Artemis?" I ask.

"Well, for starters, her real name is Heather." Stokes scowls.

"She was a theater kid Before," Leila goes on. "You know the type. Busting out singing in the hallway, going on and on about sopranos and mezzo sopranos and being just, you know. Just too *much*. 'Ohmigod, auditions are coming! Ohmigod, I have a sore throat!' Like *that*, all the time."

"A big dramatic dork," Stokes clarifies.

"But she put together King Max's coronation, and off that, she got put in charge of the *whole auditorium*."

"It was a really good coronation," Stokes admits.

"And sure, she's talented or whatever. But she's still too much. Like renaming herself *Artemis*? And now she's trying to upgrade it to High Priestess Artemis? I can't!"

The fire dancers finish their routine, and all the people watching them clap. One of the guy dancers makes a big dramatic bow before rushing with the others to get their towels and go back down the trail, back to Moore.

"I should head back, too," I tell the cheerleaders, catching up Brick's huge, borrowed flannel.

"Don't forget! We're training again tomorrow at noon!" Amy waves, and I step into my old Keds and hurry down the trail after the theater kids.

I'm still shivering from my swim, but Leo's voice rings in my head: *That Kyle guy spent a lot of time in the music wing.*

The theater kids chatter loudly the whole way back to the school. I keep a careful distance at first, but by the time we're climbing an echoing staircase to the second floor of the music wing, I'm right behind them and no one seems to notice. They slip through the choir room, around a grand piano, and into a large dressing room, where they change shoes, grab water bottles, and deposit their smoldering

Sterno chunks in a low sink before hurrying down a narrow back stair, joking and laughing the whole time.

I cross the dressing room to the door they all disappeared through, avoiding my own gaze in the mirror that covers one wall. A cheery plonk of piano rises from the stage below, echoing strangely along the dim, empty back hall. At its other end, across from the stairs, a strip of pale green buzzes and glows. Like someone left a light on.

I move soundlessly toward the light, up a shorter set of stairs to a narrow door left slightly ajar. I knock: no answer. I step inside, and the smell from the back of a thrift store hits me hard. The small room is packed with old clothes and props: fancy gowns and calico dresses, military coats and clown suits, plastic wands and rubber swords. Above the crammed racks hang posters: *My Fair Lady, Camelot, The Pirates of Penzance.*

Why would anyone leave a precious camping lantern on in here?

"I have it all set up, Your Majesty!" a froggy female voice echoes up the stairs, and multiple sets of footsteps climb toward me.

Your Majesty? I spin around, looking for another exit. There is none. Panicked, I slip between a clothes rack and the wall just as three figures come through the costume room door.

"I've pulled everything even *vaguely* medieval," the froggy voice continues. The shadows tilt and roll across the floor like she's plucked the lantern off the rack. Between the hangers I can just make out her face, and it's too much: lips too pursed, eyes too protruding, makeup too heavy. She makes me think of Judy Garland, though it could just be her throaty, theatrical voice. This must be Artemis.

"*Camelot.*" She sets her hand on one section of the rack. "*Pippin. Once Upon a Mattress.*" I hear the scritch of metal hangers pulled along a metal rack, and then the clatter of one being pulled free.

"I like this cloth," Max says.

"Gold lamé? We'll pull all the gold we've got. Stacey!"

"Yes, Artemis?"

"Pull all the metallic fabrics. All of them! If it shimmers, I want to see it."

Stacey, I guess, makes her way to the far end of the rack I'm hiding behind and starts going through the hangers: *scritch, scritch, scritch.*

"I want lots of light onstage," Max goes on.

"Well, that goes perfectly with my concept!" Artemis cries. "Picture the new Duke—or High Lady—kneeling center stage."

Scritch, scritch, scritch! Stacey is ten feet away. There's no escape. I'm trapped between a cement support in the middle of the wall and a cluster of peacoats marked *Fiddler on the Roof '09.*

"We have the chorus doing the 'Miserere' very soft," Artemis goes on, "as you enter holding aloft your sword. We turn a mirror, lit up by three, four torches—"

"No mirrors. I don't want anybody thinking we borrowed ideas from the Auto Shop."

"But it could be diff—"

"I don't want anyone associating Los Martillos with a royal ceremony."

Stacey is just three feet away. *Scritch! Scritch! Scritch!*

"Got it! Totally!" Artemis says. "Ooh! What about candelabras? Or the candles like in the holiday concerts Before?"

The clothes in front of me start to tremble.

Scritch! Scritch! Scritch!

"Stacey! Where did Ms. Pettibone keep the holiday concert candles?"

Stacey stops directly across from me. "On the other side of the auditorium."

"Can you go get those please? Right now," Artemis says. Stacey moves away, and I sag with relief.

Then I hear the dog paws coming straight for me.

"Brick!" Max cries. "I wanted to ask you about the Duke's helmet—"

And now Frank is jumping up, whining with joy, knocking the costumes in front of me to the floor in his excitement.

Artemis wails: *"There's someone hiding! Behind the peacoats!"*

"Seize them!" Max yells, and a massive hand closes on my collar, the room spinning around me as Brick hauls me out and throws me to the floor.

THE LIE

KAY

"I'm so sorry!" I stammer, on my hands and knees in front of King Max, face inches from the matted carpet. "I'm so sorry, I just wandered in here and then I heard voices and hid behind the rack!"

"She's a spy," Max says coldly. "I knew it."

"NO!" I shake my head frantically. "I'm not a spy—"

"Then why are you hiding?" he demands, a vein pulsing hard in his throat. *"What are you doing in here?"*

My heart races. Even if I come up with some plausible excuse, I'll start blushing and grinning. I'm done. They're going to drive me outside again. *I'm going to die.*

Brick's deep voice cuts through the heavy silence: "I told her to come here."

I stare up at him, not sure I heard that right.

"She doesn't fit in my stuff." He shrugs, ducks his chin as everyone turns to look at him. "I told her to try and find some clothes."

"Well!" Artemis's hand is still clutching at her heart. "Just so you know, Brick? No one may take costume pieces from the Theater Department without asking me first."

Brick looks at me, widening his eyes meaningfully. "Well? Did you find anything?"

"N-no, your lordship," I stammer.

"Okay, don't call him your lordship." King Max rolls his eyes, but the rage is gone. "He's not a lord, okay, he's Captain of the Guards. And sneaking around spying on people is a good way to get your butt sent right back where we found you."

"I'm sorry," I start. Cold sweat breaks out under my clothes. "I was just so intimidated when I realized it was Your Majesty coming up the stairs, and the longer I didn't say anything the worse it got, and well, I'm . . . just awkward, I guess."

"No *shit*." King Max laughs. Now that he's decided this situation can be funny, everyone else joins in. He turns to Artemis. "This is the Exile I was telling you about."

"I am High Priestess Artemis." She seems to expand a bit when she says this, extending her hand. She is dressed in layered lacy slips and skirts and some kind of brocade corset, with jewels pasted around her eyes and a fake flower crown to top it off. It's the kind of look that announces she doesn't have to do her own chores. Leo said Artemis is one of us, and I doubt there are two girls named Artemis at Moore. But it's hard to imagine her leading any revolution against Max; this girl seems like she's got a pretty good seat at the old post-apocalypse Round Table.

"Brick, why don't you take your guest back to the Cage?" King Max says. "Artemis, let's see those candles."

+ + +

Brick is silent all the way to his room, walking just slightly ahead of me so I can't see his face. He just saved my life, but why? What does he want from me? I have no power, no leverage. Information on Leo? Or something more personal?

Like, does he think I owe him something now?

When we get to the tiny cell, I turn to face him, bracing myself for anything. But he just walks right past me, up the ladder, and out through the skylight without a glance in my direction.

I sink down onto the cot.

Frank jumps up beside me, claiming the majority of the bed again. I smell the charcoal smoke before I see it rise through the soft blue square of the skylight. Brick is starting dinner.

I collapse forward with relief, grabbing my locket with both hands and squeezing my eyes shut. But what if Brick hadn't covered for me? What if they'd driven me back out, into another night running blind from falling trees? What if—

Coldest Lakes starts playing.

I climb up the ladder. Brick kneels beside a little hibachi grill, the late evening sun setting off the deep tan of his shirtless back, gold muscles carved by blue shadow. There's a small Igloo cooler of vegetables next to him. He glances at me, then angles his head, just a little, so his face is more hidden.

"That's 'Homebound,' from *Kite Weather*," I say stupidly when the song ends.

"You know Coldest Lakes?"

"*Know them?* They're the greatest band of all time." I cut myself off because the next song is starting. Brick gestures to a low beach chair between the boom box and grill, and I climb out onto the roof and sink into it. The tendons of his forearms stand out as he cuts the vegetables precisely, then lays them beside two thick venison steaks. Is he going to eat both of them?

"How do you like your steak?" he asks, answering my unspoken question.

"However I can get it."

"Good." He chuckles, flipping them over. "Because no matter what I do, they usually end up medium rare."

The sky above us is shifting from blue to pink, a strip of creamy clouds gone gold at the edges blocking the fading sun. Fat drips from the meat and sizzles in the coals, and the smell makes Frank whine below us. Brick expertly flicks a piece of gristle through the skylight, and we both smile at the gobbling sound that follows.

"Where did you get a Coldest Lakes CD?" I ask. "I thought they only released digital albums."

"I burned it." Brick laughs. "My truck is so old it wouldn't play music off my phone Before. I had to burn everything on CDs." He gestures to a fat CD holder with a zipper up the side.

"You realize this ancient artifact is, like, priceless now, right?" I joke, flipping through it. He's got all the albums and the B-sides, including one I haven't even heard of. "I've never met anyone in real life who's even *heard* of Coldest Lakes."

"Me neither." He squints at me. "I'm shocked you like them."

"Yeah?" I make a face. "What'd you think I'd be into?"

"I don't know . . ." He considers me then, shaking his hair back from the unscarred part of his face as he assesses. "I've never seen you in Before clothes. My first guess would be . . . battle drums."

I rub my palm self-consciously over my scalp, pleased by the answer but wondering how he got to it. How I must look to him.

"So how'd you get into them?" he asks.

"My mom has a flower shop. Had a flower shop." I stop, blink, start again. "One time I helped bring this really big order of flowers into the greenroom of this tiny place in South Brockton—"

"The South Brockton Amphitheatre?"

I almost jump out of my chair. "Yeah! You ever go there?"

"A couple times during off-season. I play—*played* baseball. I couldn't do a lot of late nights," Brick says, eyebrows coming together, "but it was a really cool place. So, you found out about it doing a flower delivery?"

"Yeah, then I made a point of dragging my friends there the next weekend, and then right before the band goes on, this *song* comes on the house music. And I'm like, 'Who put the heroin in my ear?' Then it cuts out, because the band is about to start. But I'm like, '*No!* I need. To know. That song!'" I slap my hands together. "I booked it to the lobby, looked up the lyrics, and found the song. And it was 'Curiouser.'"

"That's their best one," he says quietly.

"Absolutely." I nod. "I sat in the lobby the rest of the show listening to Coldest Lakes on my phone. My friends were furious, but . . ."

"Worth it."

"Honestly, still one of my favorite shows!" I laugh. "I was hooked. I got to where I couldn't go to sleep without listening to *Kite Weather*."

"You know Coldest Lakes was supposed to play Brockton Amphitheatre the weekend after it happened?"

"Oh, I had tickets. Were you—"

"Yup." We look at each other for a beat.

We would have been at the same show. Lined up in the amphitheater's cramped, maroon-painted lobby, or milling around by the scuffed-up stage. Me with my long hair, him with an unscarred face, two more strangers in the crowd.

He tilts his head, still assessing. "Let me guess. You would've been dancing down by the speakers."

"Um, no. More like middle of the house with my noise-canceling headphones on."

"*Yes.*" Brick salutes me with his tongs. "Only amateurs don't wear earplugs!"

"I know, believe me! I'm not a mosh pit person, at all. I had, like, waist-length hair Before, actually."

I don't know why it's so important that he know this. But I really want him to know.

"Waist length?" He is gratifyingly impressed. "Like a mermaid?"

It's so not what I expected him to reference that I start laughing. "Oh yeah. Totally covered my boobs."

He laughs too loud, and I realize he's blushing. A strange flutter goes through me as he ducks his head and moves things around on the grill, face suddenly solemn like he's remembered something important.

"What are those drawings?" I ask after a beat. "The ones on the walls downstairs?"

He shrugs. "They used to be like posters and stuff. I turned them around and drew on the back."

"Wait, *you* drew those plans? What are they for?"

"Eh, just some different ideas." He shrugs again. "I like to tinker around."

"Just a regular old Tinkerbell."

"I prefer Tinkerbeau," he says with mock seriousness.

"Ho ho ho!" I give him an appreciative eyebrow raise. "He's got jokes!"

"Stop calling me names and hand me some plates," he says, and this surprises a laugh out of me as I reach for the stack of paper plates beside the cooler. He's still smiling as he divvies up the food.

Is this the first normal conversation I've had since Before? Normal the way it used to be, when it was normal to drive across town and spend a night out with my friends without thinking, even once, about any of us dying.

The sun is going down. Brick throws some stripped twigs on the coals for light and pops open another beach chair a few feet away from mine, facing out toward the labyrinth of fences and the woods beyond. He pulls a fleece blanket around his bare shoulders, and we eat and listen to the music and stare at the sea of treetops.

And then one goes down in the distance with a burst of screaming blackbirds, and my food sticks in my throat.

Brick leans forward to watch.

"I don't know how you stand it," I say, shielding my eyes with my hand. Waves of panicked birdsong radiate out from the fallen tree, like rings in a pond after you throw a stone in.

"You need to see how they behave if you want to kill them," he says in a low, tense voice. "Two of them are probably fighting, but I can never figure out over what."

"Food?"

He's silent long enough I bring my hand down and see his shocked expression. "I thought you said you had people studying them at Jefferson. They don't need food—they don't eat anything. You don't know that, at Jefferson?"

I shake my head. "So why do they kill us?"

"Because they want to," he says. The treetops stop shuddering around the hole that's been gouged in the canopy, a last few leaves drift down, and then there's a distant but unmistakable glow of blue. Brick rockets forward, and I hear people yelling from the windows below us:

"*BLUE!*"

"YO, IT'S BLUE! IT'S HIM!"

"Who is Blue?" I whisper to Brick, whose veins are standing out from his jaw to his shoulder, his hands gripping the aluminum armrests of his chair.

"It's so stupid." Brick keeps staring, stricken, at where the glow was. "There's a rumor going around that there's a lone Knight out there, fighting the dragons on his own, with some kind of burning blue sword."

"*What?!*"

Brick shakes his head. "More likely, the Growns are hitting generators and causing small electrical fires or something . . ." He frowns. "That did look *blue*, though."

"Yeah, it was blue. Do you think it's possible? That someone could fight the Gr—the dragons alone?"

"Anything is possible, these days." Brick's voice is low in his throat.

We sit forward on our chairs, both of us watching out for more blue flashes, cozy in the dark. It feels like waiting for fireworks on the Fourth of July, exciting and safe at the same time, and we share a quick smile.

"Brick," I ask after a beat. "Why did you cover for me?"

"I didn't want you to get in trouble." He stretches his long legs straight out in front of him, one bare foot balanced on the other. "We all get on edge before an Expansion. But we shouldn't take that out on you. And what can you really do in the costume shop?" He sounds amused. "What were you doing in there, anyway?"

"I don't know. I just followed the fire dancers up there from the lake and started . . . snooping."

"Well." He shrugs his heavily muscled shoulders and pulls the corner of the blanket farther over his face, like a hoodie. "Snoop all you want, ma'am. We've got nothing to hide."

A long beat of silence follows. Like we'll leave it at that. Like I owe him nothing.

"Are you sure about that?" I blurt, and his head jerks toward me in surprise.

I know I shouldn't pop off. But Brick defended me for no apparent reason other than it's the right thing to do. *And* he's a Coldest Lakes fan. The music you love is the measure of your soul. I can't help it; I trust him.

"I saw Kyle's car in the Auto Shop," I say with a lurch in my chest like I've stepped onto slick ice.

A look of exasperation crosses the undamaged side of his face. "I *told* him you'd find out."

"Find out what?"

"That your president guy came through here." He leans forward and throws more strips of bark on the fire so it flares brighter, eyes hard on my face. "He stayed a few days—he and King Max hit it off. The King made him switch out the Volvo for one of his Escalades. They're higher up off the road. You can see farther. It's safer."

"Then why didn't you guys tell me that last night? Why pretend I was the first new kid?"

"You said you were dragged out of Jefferson. We would never do that to one of our people, not unless they did something *fucked up*." His tone is calm and reasonable, but his jaw tightens in the firelight. "King Max wanted to see what you would say about Jefferson. If it would be consistent with what we knew from Kyle."

"Well! So, have I passed your test?"

"You're doing great. Except for the spying."

"I wasn't—" I swallow. "When was Kyle here?"

"A month and a half ago."

I pull my knees up to my chest on the beach chair and try to hold still as I ride out the anger. But I don't want to be still. I want to pick up the grill and fling it off the roof, I want to dig my nails into my arms until they break my skin, I want to scream at Jefferson so my voice rings out through the trees until all the birds are shrieking along. But I stay still.

"What's wrong?" Brick asks.

". . . I had hoped there was some way this was just Simon. But Simon *and* Nirali have been lying to us . . . pretty much the whole time Kyle has been gone." A tear glides down the side of my nose. "Kyle wasn't calling in *before* they proposed the Rule! A couple weeks enforcing the Rule, without knowing if it's true—like, that's bad enough! But Nirali wasn't talking to Kyle *when she made the Rule*."

". . . What's the Rule?"

"A lie," I admit. "A total, complete lie. One that we have to believe, or else."

Ob-lo-quy:
Strong Public Criticism

NIRALI

I pause to plaster on my smile before walking into the Jefferson cafeteria. It takes some effort to keep up a confident façade across from the huddled masses in line for their meager dinner: *We've got this, guys!* But I've managed it this long. Though every day, in that last moment before I walk through the cafeteria doors, the same thought rings through my head:

I'm not supposed to be here.

I am Nirali Chaudri, damn it. Jefferson's homecoming queen and shoo-in for valedictorian.

I'm supposed to be waking up in my Yale dorm, my roommate teasing me for studying late the night before. Pulling my freshly washed hair out from under the collar of my beautiful new wool Burberry pea coat—the one hanging in my closet right now, that my mother said would last me "forever"—before I sashay out into the crisp air of Yale's immaculate campus.

I would meet my father for lunch between his surgeries at Yale New Haven Hospital. He would take me to some hidden Indian restaurant with the softest rotis and then slip me an advance on my allowance. I'd promise to come back home to Brockton the next weekend. *You know, I actually miss that place sometimes?* I'd say. And I'd mean it. It's amazing how cute a town can be when you aren't trapped in it forever.

That was the future I was promised. I was told if I worked hard enough, I would make it out in the "real world," so I've worked my ass off since eighth grade. Waking up at five for PSAT prep; my math was solid, so I spent hours training my vocabulary. Skipping summer trips to Kyle's lake house for MediCamp. Sacrificing afternoon drives with Tiana for Student Council meetings.

No one could have predicted what happened. But that doesn't change the fact that I was cheated. That the "real world" I worked so hard for vanished before I even got to see it.

And every time I enter this cafeteria, I know the only thing waiting is hunger and misery. No matter how hard I work.

People in the lunch line stiffen and then curse under their breath as I walk by, skipping the line. I have to get back to my patients; I can't stand in line for an hour like they can. But the cafeteria has been running out before everyone's served. Every bite we take comes out of someone else's mouth now.

And this slop is barely edible. When I get to the counter, I cringe at the steaming trays of mushed-up chickpeas and expired barley flour. There's some kind of sourdough breadsticks, too, but they haven't risen correctly; they look like pale broken fingers.

Reese silently portions this sludge directly onto the trays handed her. She's supposed to be chatting and joking to defuse the tension; that's why she got this job, because she's funny and charming. But today her eyes are swollen from crying, and when they rise from my red tray to my face, they narrow.

"Nirali." Reese's voice carries farther than it needs to. "What happened to Kay?"

Someone down the line sucks their teeth.

"How does someone 'disappear' from a birthday room?" Reese's voice gets louder. "The gate locks to the floor. The fire doors are chained on the outside. If they turn, they burn—that's the phrase, right?"

"Reese, I am so sorry about Kay," I begin. "She was my friend as well, and I promise, we are doing everything we can to—"

"Simon's been telling people she walked out," Reese interrupts me. One of the cooks tries to pull her back, but she whips away from him and snaps, "No, if they're going to say that about Kay, I'm going to say something back! You know she didn't walk out!"

"Kay did walk out." Simon is suddenly at my side. "Nirali missed council this morning, so she didn't hear about Kay's letter."

Her letter?!

I stare at him. The absolute fathead. She didn't leave a note. He's fabricating a suicide, when everyone is on the brink? And it's too late to fix it; they've all heard.

"Kay left a note that we've posted on the gym doors," Simon goes on solemnly, his deep voice as awkward and stiff as the rest of him. "I'm sorry, Reese, but Kay—"

"No! NO!" Reese's fellow workers are barely able to contain her as she tries to claw her way over the counter. "It's not true! Kay had a plan! Kay was going to make changes! She would never walk out!"

And then it happens. A male voice audible from far down the line, bold enough to break through Reese's wails:

"She figured out Kyle's never coming back."

A hiss runs through the crowd, fire through dry grass. People suck their teeth and look around, scanning the line for the source.

No one believes the statement, of course. That's not what they're reacting to. They are shocked someone just broke the Rule, in public, out loud. Our most important rule: No one may say, imply, or believe that Kyle will not return.

Rule breakers are reported for whispering less, even to their closest friends. So for some troll to shout out the edgiest thing possible, in front of Student Council members?

We have to come down on this right now, as hard as we can.

"Who said that?" Simon yells, neck going blotchy red. "Who just broke the Rule?"

Total silence, air suddenly heavy, the moment before a storm breaks.

Then a girl down the line, in sight of the remaining food but not at the counter, shrieks, "Right here! This guy!" She pushes a guy in a faded camo hat in front of her.

I know him; that's Ajay. There aren't a ton of Hindu families in Brockton, and we went to the same temple. He'd gotten a terrible upper respiratory infection in February, and once he got better, he stuck around the hospital to help out. His nursing skills have bought me many extra hours of sleep.

So it really shocks me when Ajay turns and yells, "Shut up, bitch! I didn't say shit! It was that guy with the bags." He wheels around and points out an underclassman standing alone and slightly apart from the others. Plastic bags are knotted at both his wrists, like a true outcast: he doesn't have a place or person safe enough to leave them with.

"What are you talking about? I didn't say that!" the outcast shouts. He obviously wasn't the one who broke the Rule; the register of his voice is too high, and it climbs higher now with panic: "I know Kyle is coming back! He could drive up any minute! That's what I've always said!"

Scattered applause along the line. The outcast goes red at the support and bumbles on, eager for more: "We just gotta make sure the school's still standing when he gets here! We all gotta stay positive and support each other!"

"'Support each other, y'all!'" a mocking voice calls from down the line, and my hands fist. We don't need outcasts coming out too hard in favor of the Rule. It would actually be better if the outcast *had* broken it. If his voice weren't such a mismatch, I'd declare him the Rule breaker to get this over with and make it clear that cool kids follow the Rule and losers do not.

The first girl stabs a bony finger toward Ajay's face. "How dare you accuse him, just because he has no friends! You're disgusting! You're the breaker!" Her expression is terrible, tendons standing out under fish-belly white skin, thin lips trembling over exposed teeth as she turns to me, hand still flailing at his face. "Nirali, this guy is lying. He broke the Rule. He should get out of line!" Her eyes flash to the almost-empty tray of breadsticks.

Did she hear Ajay? Or does she just want one less person between her and the food?

"Get your hand out of my face!" Ajay, who I've seen tenderly hold a stranger over a steaming tray of hot water to help them through a coughing fit, shoves her hard.

"Hey, man, not cool!" Her gangly boyfriend moves to intercede, but Ajay's friends block him, telling him to get his girlfriend to shut up already.

"No fighting!" Simon claps for their attention, and there are scattered chuckles at the dorky gesture. "The last thing we need is a physical altercation. Control yourselves!"

I cut a look to the Scavenging Team members on lunch line security, Tyler and Antonin. They nod in response and start moving in.

"You in the hat!" Simon sounds like a substitute teacher losing control of the class. "And you with the bags! You'll both be considered Rule breakers unless another witness comes forward, right now!"

"I'm gonna starve because she's lying?!" Ajay shouts. His friends are holding him back now, watching Tyler and Antonin. The Scavenging Team always eat first because they go get the food. This has the unintended consequence of keeping them slightly bigger than the rest of the students, which is quite helpful when they're needed as security.

"Stay positive!" the outcast weeps, turning on anyone who will make eye contact. "I've stayed positive! I know Kyle is coming back, and if I thought he wasn't, I'd walk out, too—"

"Please." I shoot the outcast a hard look: *You're not helping.* "Can we all just take a breath here."

I slow my words, keep them loud but calm.

"Nobody else heard the Rule breaker?" I meet each gaze as I walk down the line; almost all of them have been my patients. "We all know covering for a Rule breaker is as bad as breaking the Rule yourself. Words have power." I sweep a hand to the first girl, who's sobbing hysterically now. "You're hurting vulnerable people. Pushing them past their limits."

Or maybe she just wanted one less person ahead of her in line. But that's not the point right now.

The point is, without the Rule, we will break down. There will be panic attacks and night terrors. No sleep and no food will turn into fights. Fights in a closed space get out of control fast. We are under siege. One big release of fear, one lapse in morale that escalates into a mob, could break our barricades from the inside out. Let in the circling Growns at last.

And then it will be all over, for all of us.

That's why the punishment for breaking the Rule is three days of no food. Harsh, but I have no problem being harsh if it keeps us alive.

"I talked to Kyle this morning," I go on, and a hush falls over the line. They love Kyle; I make sure of it. "He's hungry, too. His rations are small, but he feels guilty taking detours to scavenge when he knows we're waiting on him. All Kyle ever asks is, 'Are you guys all right?'"

The Kyle outside of my stories would never ask this question. Kyle's focus was always on material advantages and protecting his own morale. That's why he pitched his trip out into the world to the council in the first place: *We need food, we need soap, and I need some goddamn fresh air.*

"I told him you are all holding strong," I go on slowly, and several of them nod back. "That he could take as long as he needed to return safely. Was I wrong?"

A hand darts up farther down the line, indicating a tall guy who looks suspiciously bored. As I approach, the tall guy clocks the gesture and turns slightly, muttering something in a voice that was unmistakably the one.

"Thank you," I tell the person who pointed him out, granting them my most dazzling smile. "Please go to the head of the line."

Simon is right behind me now, and Antonin and Tyler make a pincer movement toward our Rule breaker. He's tall, and I can tell he used to be athletically built, but he's not a team player because he's obviously not on the Scavenging Team. His muscles have gone stringy, his eyes hollow. Guys like him get hungry fast, and then they snap.

"No food for three days," Simon tells him.

The guy's jaw clenches, but he says nothing. So he's not a total fathead; he's figured out there's no defense he can make that doesn't break the Rule further.

"And no food today," Simon goes on, "for the people around him who said nothing."

"Hey, man!" a scrawny girl yells. "That's not part of the Rule—"

"Enough," I cut her off. "Keep complaining, and you'll miss all three days, too. The three people in front of the Rule breaker and the three people behind him—all of you are missing lunch today. Isn't that right, Simon?"

"Escort them out of the cafeteria," Simon tells Tyler and Antonin.

But before they can get to them, the job is practically done. The people behind them in line violently shove the Rule breaker and his accomplices out. A gob of spit lands on the Rule breaker's shoulder. The outcast spat on him; thrilled not to be at the bottom of the pile for once.

I suppress my cringe at the sight and return to the start of the line, where I make a show of letting the informer go first. Then a new server finally gives me my food.

I take it out of the cafeteria, up the stairs, and to the gym doors, where I read the curling page of legal pad paper tacked up at eye level.

Simon spelled her name right in the signature. That's the only good thing I can say for it.

+ + +

Simon and I sit on either side of the radio that night, static filling the room. We always keep it going, in case someone comes in.

"What were you thinking?" I ask him. "That letter doesn't read like Kay at all. Her friends are going to know the second they see it—"

"Friends?" Simon sneers. "All four of them, you mean?"

"Reese is enough. What do you think she's going to tell the lunch line tomorrow?"

"She will be working somewhere else."

"Simon . . ."

"What was I supposed to do?!" Simon pitches forward in his chair. "You weren't exactly overflowing with answers, Nirali."

I glare at him. "We both know the answer. It was someone on the Scavenging Team—"

"Would you shut up?!" he hisses.

"Why else would her birthday room guards not show up? Who else would have the balls to drive out into town?" I go on flatly. "Tyler told the whole team about Kay's Costco proposal, so it could be any of them. Or all of them."

"We are not launching an investigation into the people who manage our crowd control, Nirali. That would be suicide."

"I know, Simon! Believe me, I know! But it's one thing to not ask questions. It's quite another to fabricate three paragraphs that don't match our secretary's handwriting!"

"It will blow over. We just hold the line," Simon says. "Kay walked out."

"What we need to hold is elections."

"You know I would hold elections tomorrow, except what would we tell the new president about Kyle?"

"Like I keep saying, Simon," I say for what feels like the six thousandth time, "the first morning when we show the new president the radio, we act like it's the first time we've lost contact."

Simon laughs and shakes his head like I've said the stupidest thing imaginable. "Let's play that out, Nirali. Let's travel that road, shall we? The new president finds out Kyle isn't calling in. Maybe he believes that it's really the first time, or maybe he has two brain cells and doesn't; that's the least of our concerns. He'll end the Rule. And if you think the night terrors were bad *before* Kyle left, I want you to picture every single person in that gym, screaming all night long. And then you tell me what happens when this school realizes they have no help coming, no food, and no sleep, and half the school is done with Student Council—"

"Done with *you*, you mean," I say, just loud enough to make him stumble over his words.

Simon can make fun of Kay not having friends, but his own reserves of social capital are vanishingly small. If he wasn't Student Council vice president, he'd have plastic bags tied around his wrists, too. That's why he's fighting so hard against elections.

He knows he'll be voted out.

"You're not safe, either. You get that, right?" Simon's voice is cold. "No amount of 'good' you do offsets your princess attitude. You've always thought you were better than everyone else. Now that it's official, guess what, Nirali? It doesn't make people like you, it makes them hate you. Even on Student Council, everyone is fed up with your supercilious attitude—"

"Only a supercilious person says 'supercilious,' Simon."

"But you figure you can always go jump on a bigger dick, right—"

"Shut up!" I'm on my feet now. "Kyle is coming back, you jackass, and I will never be with another man while there is the possibility he is alive, let alone a worm like you. And if you keep it up with your creepy little come-ons—"

"Would you shut up?! This is not about you and me!" Simon leaps to his feet, his voice dropping down to a hiss: "We have days until we run out of food, and when we do, people are going to lose their fucking minds. And then how is anyone—elected or not—supposed to keep control? On top of which, people are saying Kay turned, and that's all we need to really set things off in this hellhole—" He recovers himself. His shoulders twitch under the layers of sweatshirt and corduroy jacket; he adjusts his glasses and clears his throat. "We needed a reason for Kay to be gone that wasn't her turning into a Grown," he says, voice almost apologetic. "I came up with the cleanest excuse I could on short notice. All right?"

Reluctantly, I nod. He's right, and I hate when he's right, but there it is. We're almost out of time.

"If there was just some way to get food . . ." I sigh.

"Food? Wow, you think food would help? Why didn't I think of that?" Simon says sarcastically, settling heavily back into his chair. "'Some way to get food.' Great idea. Great leadership, Nirali."

I take a deep breath then, steeple my hands, and put into words what I've been debating the past two days.

"Kay's Costco trip," I say slowly. "*That* is a great idea."

"I know," Simon fumes. "Are you volunteering to propose it?"

And the room fills with the static of Kyle's signal again.

THE KISS

KAY

Frank sits up, jolting me awake. It's dim, almost dark—like when school used to start Before. Brick's steps creak; he's halfway down the ladder and desperately trying to shush Frank. It doesn't work. Frank whines and hops down with a clatter of claws on the vinyl flooring, almost tipping the cot over.

"It's cool, I'm up!" I announce, sitting upright like I can convince us both. I knead at my face, tight and swollen around my eyes from crying myself to sleep. I made a fool out of myself, weeping about the Rule and Nirali and everything at Jefferson. But Brick let me take his CD player down so I could fall asleep to *Kite Weather* for the first time since Before, so I can't feel too bad.

"I'm going to get breakfast," Brick says, voice gruff like he just woke up.

"I'll come with," I say.

He opens and closes his mouth, as though unsure how to object, then shrugs, and I follow after him, alongside Frank.

The air is soft, and already getting warm. Brick skirts the Auto Shop lot without comment. I follow him down the incline of the hill, off school property, through the trees toward Mill Creek Road.

Once we're in the neighborhood, I'm surprised at how many other Moore kids are out as well, setting up white folding tables along the sidewalks. Bleary-eyed but smiling, they wave to Brick and scan me, openly curious.

Brick leads me through a maze of backyard fences to a small one-story bungalow, the last house before the wall. I'm sure it was an old person's house Before—something about the dusty blue color and its old-fashioned mailbox. We walk down the side of the fence to a gate, blanketed in thick flowered vines, that goes up just past Brick's head. Dozens of pollen-drunk bees roll off its door once Brick spins the padlock open and swings it wide for me.

Frank goes bounding ahead of us into a no-nonsense vegetable garden. Three raised beds of dark soil hold plants tented with plastic bags and rows of seedlings cuddled into toilet paper cores. The tall fence that encloses the yard is one buzzing green bower of honeysuckle and snap peas, leaves so thick I can't tell if it's wood or chain-link underneath. Brick hands me a plastic bag, opens one for himself, then gestures to the vines.

"Now, the fun part," he says.

"We're having peas for breakfast?"

"No, we're going to take two big bags of fresh peas back to the market tables and trade them. But if you want to eat some, go for it."

The smell is fresh and strangely clean, almost soapy, as I snap the peas from their curly vines. They taste sweet, and crisp, and green somehow.

"Is this your garden?" I ask Brick.

"It's shared by all the guards."

"A guard-den?" I try, and he shakes his head in feigned disappointment, then laughs.

I can tell he's good at it, at gardening. He touches things so carefully, harvesting each pea so neatly their leaves barely rustle. We stand side by side in comfortable silence, the bees bumbling with increasing fervor as the sun crawls higher.

Brick pulls his T-shirt off and wraps it around his head to keep the sun off his face. The golden curve of his shoulder pulls my focus; it keeps, like, gleaming. He glances over at me, and my eyes dart away before he asks, "Did *Kite Weather* help?"

"Oh! Yeah, totally! Best sleep I've had in a long time."

". . . 'Cause it sounded like maybe you were still crying or something."

"Well, I was," I admit. "Talking about the Rule brought a lot of feelings up." I swallow, hard. "I just can't believe that we were ready to sell each other out so fast. Like, people were afraid to even say things to their best friends about Kyle. Afraid to even think things. Things that were probably true."

"Ah," Brick says.

"And the whole time, the Rule was the lie! And I'm not surprised *Simon* would lie to get what he needed. But Nirali?" The thought is a splinter I have to push out. "There are two things I would've bet my life on. One, that Nirali is a good person. And two, that lying is evil."

"But Kay . . ." Brick's voice is almost gentle. "People lie all the time, Before and now. And not because they're evil. Just to make life easier. Like I did in the costume room."

Our bags swish in the silence.

"I still don't understand why you did that."

"I could tell you weren't lying about why you were up there." Brick shrugs. "You got tells."

"Tells?" I peer at him.

"Like in poker. Ways to tell you're lying. You smile all weird and go bright red. Here, I'll show you." He turns to me and lifts the T-shirt covering his face. "Rate my looks," he says, "on a scale of one to ten."

I haven't seen him full-on since that first time on the front steps; he's always so careful. And the morning sunlight is pitiless. As the downturned eye circled in scar tissue rolls to meet mine, I'm speechless.

"Come on, Miss Integrity. One to ten, let's go."

He thinks I will lie to save his feelings, turn red, and prove myself a hypocrite. So instead, I lift my chin and look him in the eye.

"One. You're a one."

He nods, then gets back to picking peas. And the corner of my mouth jerks.

Uh . . . what was that, mouth? He's very much a one. Yet my chin is buckling, and there's a telltale burning creeping up my face.

Luckily, he doesn't notice. He's tearing peas off the vine so fast leaves are shuddering to the ground. I bite the inside of my cheek.

"Well"—he clears his throat—"my bag is pretty full. How's yours looking?"

"Almost." I squeeze the word out, the corners of my mouth twitching wildly. I need him to not look at me for the next five minutes, but he's walking over to inspect my snap pea haul. When I try to turn away, he freezes, then steps so close I can smell his sunscreen.

"Dude . . ." Brick says. "Why are you a cranberry right now?"

"Don't know what you're talking about." I turn; he sidles left. I turn again; he sidles right. So I bulldoze straight toward him, refusing eye contact, just head down plowing forward. He lunges out of my way with a short, confused laugh. Then he follows after me, into the shadow of the house.

"Look at me," Brick says. "What are you lying about? What, am I a *negative* one?"

"No." I cannot and will not look at him. "You're a five." A traitorous grin stretches my face. "Six. Six point five." Why is my life hell? "You're a seven, a solid seven, okay? Look, leave me alone!"

He bursts out laughing again as I try to hide my maniacally grinning face with my hands.

"Kay." I can hear his smile. "Even your neck is red right now."

"Fine! Fine!" I glare up at him at last. "You're a nine, okay? On a scale of one to ten I think you're a nine. Happy, asshole?!"

And not knowing where else to hide, I flee into the house.

It's completely scavenged inside. Even the walls are gone, the slats and struts stripped bare. The floor is covered in sawdust, and two sawhorses brace what looks like half a circular ladder. I'm trying to figure out what you'd even need a circular ladder for when I see a larger version of the drawing from Brick's wall, with the same blue Bic lines and all-caps writing. My jaw drops.

Footsteps scrape through the door, and I turn, my own embarrassment momentarily unimportant. "This is a water wheel, right?" I ask before he can say anything, and he wobbles a little on his back foot, as though about to turn and leave. But I push: "Will it work?"

"If I ever finish it." Brick frowns. The unscarred half of his face is going pink. "Stuff like this takes a lot longer without power tools. Just getting this far took me all winter."

"Right, you did this by hand, right." I leave his carefully drawn plan and circle the half wheel again. "So you're, like . . . a genius?"

"I didn't invent *the wheel*, Kay." He rolls his eyes. "Coach—my baseball coach—got me construction jobs in the summer, so I saw a blueprint or two Before. That's all."

I don't think one in one hundred people who'd seen a blueprint Before could make something like this. The precision needed to make the joints that interlock the larger pieces, the way he's straightened and planed the repurposed wood . . . all by hand, through the freezing winter months. I've certainly boosted his ego enough for one day, but someone needs to tell him this is incredible, because he doesn't seem to get it.

"This is not tinkering," I tell Brick. "This is amazing and important."

"Thank you." He says it like he's conceding a point in a fight.

The air feels so tight between us now; every gesture, every swallow, is too large, too loud. I bunch up the top of my bag of peas, then tilt away from him.

"Sorry if I made it weird by rating you a nine."

"Are you kidding?" Brick's laugh is so earnest it releases me. "You're the first new girl I met since my face got scraped off. I just figured you were . . . vomiting in the back of your mouth this whole time."

"Well, I—am not!" I laugh awkwardly.

"That's . . . very nice to hear," he says, staring at the floor.

My heart is going so hard. Like I'm right at the edge of some dizzyingly great height, here in this closed dark space.

"Let's get breakfast," he says, and he turns and walks out the front door.

+ + +

The market tables are humming when we get back to the street, with crowds collecting over the wares. A large group in white T-shirts and flower crowns are hawking bread and tortillas at one end of the line of tables; a clique of mostly shirtless guys in sunglasses are cooking deer meat on a grill rigged out of shopping carts at the other. Along the way, people offer all kinds of things to trade: bushels of fresh herbs, canned goods, arrowheads. But only one stall stops me in my tracks: a table covered in handsewn booklets of printer paper, with brightly colored hand-drawn covers. They feature mash-ups of characters from Before—Marvel, DC, and anime heroes all sharing panels. There's also a couple of prominently displayed booklets starring Max, but the most popular character is definitely the Blue Knight.

He's depicted in full armor and haloed in blue flame on the cover of an entire row of booklets—a run twice as long as Max's series.

I really hope Max knows this.

Brick offers to get me one. I shake my head, figuring it would cost a ton of peas. But Brick could have anything he wanted for free, it seems—the vendors claim whatever he asks for is on the house. Brick refuses all discounts in the friendliest way possible, and the vendors all capitulate, relieved and obviously grateful. One of the bakers, a girl wearing a daisy crown, even winks and makes a cringey joke about how much Brick likes her buns.

"Come on now," I mutter, once we've assembled our breakfast sandwiches. We're sitting on a low wall that runs across from the market, at the edge of school property, its stones cool in the shade of several sycamore trees. "That baker girl was flirting with you, Brick.

And every time we go past the Flower Aquarium—"

"The what?" Brick laughs.

"—the hall by the cherry trees, all those girls, like, beg you to notice them." I lean over and give the staring Frank a piece of my bacon. "This isn't a me thing. Every girl at Moore thinks you're hot."

"It's a joke. Because I'm so messed up. Get it?" He flexes his hand nervously, looking around like he's trying to find a way out of this conversation.

"Hey, Brick?" I lean forward, fixing him with a concerned stare. He freezes, as though bracing for impact, and I say, "Can we *please* talk about something besides your looks for five minutes, you *raging narcissist*?"

Brick bursts out in a relieved laugh. His full face turns to me, like he doesn't need to hide it, both of us smiling as I change the subject: "Because you're really onto something with this 'Brickwich'—"

"The what now?" He is still grinning.

"The Brickwich. We need to start our own stall. Maybe we can work something out with your fans in the baking world, because we're going to need a lot of that bread. The crust is perfect—"

"Better than Jefferson's?"

A heaviness falls over me at the word.

"There's no bread at Jefferson." I stare out at the heaped market tables. "They'll be completely out of food by the end of the week."

"I'll talk to Max," Brick says, clapping crumbs off his hands and rising to his feet. "I'll tell him I want to take on getting the food to Jefferson as an engineering challenge. Like, can we catapult them hot dogs or something. He'll be into that."

"Really?!" My voice breaks. "Brick, thank you. Thank you so much, you have no idea how grateful I—"

"Look," Brick puts up a hand. "I got a lot to do today, and you have a driving lesson. We need to get back."

I nod quickly. But as we head up the hill, the relief is so intense I can't keep it in.

"Brick, seriously," I say, and stand still until he turns and looks me full in the face again. Then I smile at him with my whole heart. "Thank you."

"Yeah, well." He gives me a wry half smile back. "Flattery will get you everywhere."

+ + +

When we reach the music hall, Amy runs up to me and pushes a bag of toiletries into my hands, including deodorant, tampons, a toothbrush and toothpaste, a razor, and a sealed tube of brand-new strawberry Chapstick.

"I can't," I protest. "Amy, this is too much!"

"Uh, soap is a necessity. I don't know what y'all are doing at Jefferson, but . . ." Amy winks. "Oh, and this, too—" She pulls a small multitool out of her back pocket, the kind of thing they'd have at the counter of a gas station Before: like a Swiss army knife, but for screwdrivers. "I always carry one of these on me. This completes your official Moore welcome kit."

I give her a huge hug before running my treasure up to Brick's room. Between the Teen Spirit deodorant and the Chapstick, I'm feeling downright glamorous when I walk into the Auto Shop.

A couple of Los Martillos nod in welcome, then wave me out to the parking lot. Leo is waiting in the sunshine by the Tracker with two travel mugs of coffee.

"Can't let Brick show me up in terms of hospitality." He smiles, handing one to me. "Ready?"

For our secret meeting with Artemis.

My smile falters. Suddenly I feel like I'm betraying Brick. He's been so kind, and his explanation for why Kyle would take an Escalade instead of the Volvo makes sense.

Except . . . why wouldn't Kyle take the radio? Maybe he couldn't? *I* wouldn't know how to uninstall and reinstall a radio. But that's just it. I don't know what I *don't know*. And I have no idea what Artemis could tell me about Kyle's time here. What's the harm in asking?

This meeting is just three people getting together to share information about a missing person. How can that be a betrayal of anyone? What rule are we even breaking? There are no rules at Moore, right?

Only Max's commands.

Like how Max must have commanded Brick not to tell me about Kyle coming here. And Brick followed his orders.

And now I don't feel guilty anymore.

"Let's go," I tell Leo, and he grins.

+ + +

Inside the 1776 house, even the Sheetrock has been scavenged from the walls, and daylight leaks through the wood slats in between pebbles of old plaster and horsehair. Dominating the interior is a massive picture window, glass and screen gone. It looks out on the backyard garden below, a jungle of goldenrod and morning glories and fiery red azaleas. Standing at the center of the window, her rounded figure framed by the flowers like a stained-glass halo, is High Priestess Artemis.

"Leo!" She smiles. A ribbon of wine-colored lipstick floats across her teeth; beads rustle in the folds of her gauzy sundress as she steps toward us. "And Kay. We met yesterday, though it wasn't under the best of circumstances." Then, to Leo, "The King was ready to throw her out!"

"I got caught 'spying' on her and Max," I explain. Leo looks impressed.

"I hope the Slayer wasn't too hard on you?" Artemis asks.

"Not at all," I say loyally. Then, "Why do some people call him Slayer?"

"To remind King Max that he's not actually King," Leo says darkly.

"King Max has always said he has the right to be King because he was the first to kill a dragon," Artemis goes on. "But he *didn't* kill the dragon. The *Slayer* did. The dragon was still alive when Brick got to him, that's why half his face is missing. Brick is the *true* King of Moore, by King Max's own logic."

That's why he said his friends call him Brick.

"Lucky for him, Slayer is loyal as a damn dog." Artemis rolls her eyes. "But Merlin knows the royal claim is all smoke and mirrors. That's why she wants to create more royals. Get more people invested in King Max staying on his throne."

"*Merlin* is creating more royals?" I ask, and they both look at me.

"Merlin's the one in charge," Leo says, like he's surprised I haven't noticed. "Max runs around in his costume and has his orgies in the principal's office, but every meaningful decision comes from her."

"I'm confused . . ." I say. "I thought you wanted to get rid of Max because he's a bully."

"We want to get rid of anyone who isn't *voted in*," Leo says. "Moore deserves a vote. The *rooms* should decide who gets to be in charge. Whether that's Brick, or King Max, or someone else completely."

"You don't think people would vote for Merlin?"

"She doesn't have a room."

"Her friends were all online playing *Echellion*, not at Moore," Artemis adds, hands on her hips.

"But she figured out the fences, right? I mean, that's kind of amazing." They exchange a tired look, but I can't help adding, "Like, whoever's in charge would probably want her around to chime in with stuff like that. I'd hope."

"Figuring out who runs in our first election is a problem I'd love to have," Leo says. "But we don't have a ton of time, and we came here to ask Artemis about Kyle."

"Yes." I nod quickly. "Do you remember him?"

"Do I *remember* him?" Artemis smirks. "Honey, he was new and gorgeous. I was obsessed! He made everybody swoon, then hit the road without saying goodbye. Or that was the story . . ." She looks from Leo to me, and digs into the purse pouch at her waist, beads rustling. "But then yesterday, after you left with Brick, I sort of went through the costume room. To make sure you hadn't taken anything—"

"Heather!" Leo laughs.

"I didn't know she was one of *us*!" Artemis fishes a little metal-and-plastic canister out of the purse. "Here." She hands it to me. "It was in one of the shoe bins in the costume room."

I look down at its label, and see it in black and white:

MEYER, KYLE. ALBUTEROL SULFATE INHALATION AEROSOL.

Kyle's inhaler. His asthma was infrequent but severe enough he had to keep this inhaler on him at all times. In their first outing, the Scavenging Team made a point of going to his house so they could get his backup and travel inhalers. I was in charge of inventory. We triple-checked that Kyle took a full inhaler when he left.

I had almost pretzeled my brain into accepting the Volvo. But there is *no way* Kyle would have left this behind.

I pocket the inhaler in Brick's giant, borrowed hoodie, then grip Artemis's shoulders. "You have to tell me everything you remember about Kyle's visit. From when he first got to Moore to the last time you saw him."

"Oh, like, a police statement or something?" Artemis backs slowly away from me and sits hard on the windowsill. "Feels like I'm back in *Mousetrap* sophomore year! Well, I wasn't out front when he drove up. But I heard about it. How the King came out with his crown on and made Kyle bow before he came in. Kyle laughed, but he did it. He was a good sport. And he and the King really clicked—that I saw myself. They went out raiding together, had long dinners every night with Merlin. Then the night before Kyle left, there was a big party in the principal's office. That was the last time I saw him, walking into that party with all my dancing girls running after him."

Leo abruptly walks into the other room. Artemis looks after him, worried, but goes on, "When the girls came back, they said it was a very wild party, and that Kyle had gotten really drunk and eventually hooked up with—"

"Wait. Hooked up?" I interrupt. "You mean like—"

"Mm-hmm. In the King's own bed."

"No way. Kyle has a girlfriend."

"Well, I feel bad for her." Artemis is trying not to laugh. "But this is coming from several firsthand witnesses and the *actual girl he hooked up with*, so . . ."

A crash in the next room; wood splinters onto the floor. Leo has kicked the baseboard of the stripped wall, hard enough to dent it inward. Artemis looks back to me, face flushing, and mouths:

"*Jessica.*"

I know I've heard the name, but I don't remember when. I'm still stuck on this timeline. After Kyle's big emotional goodbye to Nirali, after promising to go find help before we all *starved*, Kyle hung out at Moore for days and hooked up with some rando?

Nirali lied, and Kyle cheated. These cool seniors I'd always looked up to were just people, and not particularly good ones. Sure, Kyle had always done the right thing with everybody watching. But this was a situation where no matter what he did, no one at Jefferson would ever find out.

"Okay . . ." I exhale slowly. "Got it. He hooked up with your— dancing girl. Then what?"

"That's all I know." Artemis shrugs. "The next day we were supposed to put on a big send-off service, but the King canceled last minute. Said Kyle already left." Her eyes cut to the other room. "You okay in there?" she calls.

"Fine," Leo calls back, not fine.

"Here's a thought." Artemis fans a hand toward me, still talking to him, watching him pace through the slats. "We could have Kay confront King Max with the inhaler. Tell him she found it in the costume room."

My jaw drops. "*Are you kidding?* You found it—why don't *you* confront him?"

"Me?!" Artemis lets out a shocked laugh. "I'm not going to accuse the King of murder!"

"Whoa—hold on now." My face heats, and suddenly I'm aware how dangerous this meeting really is. There are lines being crossed that even I, a person who does not believe in the monarchy, understand to be treason. "You think *Max murdered Kyle*?"

"Well, I mean—" She gestures, shrugs, eyes bulging, blinking very fast now. "He's covering the car up. He tucked away that inhaler. Something's going on! Maybe—" Her gaze, never long away from him, cuts back to Leo again. "Maybe he had an issue with *who* Kyle hooked up with. Slayer is enough of a Boy Scout that if we raise the right questions, he'd make the King answer them. And like you always say"—she is addressing Leo fully now—"without Slayer, King Max is done."

"Not like this." Leo walks out of the shadows, shaking his head. I feel a moment's relief until he says, "It has to be cleaner."

Neither of them care about what happened to Kyle. They just want to take Max down. I'm about to protest when a deer leaps through the front window. Its long shivery legs scrape at the floor as it snorts at us in alarm.

"Cellar, *now!*" Leo orders, and Artemis hustles, beads jangling, through the picture window and into the backyard below. Before I can follow her, an arrow buries itself in the floor just beside my foot.

The frightened deer bounds past me, so close its warm side brushes my arm as it leaps through the open picture window. Bikes are thrown down by the steps and feet land on the porch, the hunters yelling:

"The house! It went in the house!"

Leo grabs me by the shoulder, turns me to face him.

"Sorry about this," he says, and kisses me.

✝ THE LOVERS

KAY

I flinch in surprise as his arms wrap around my waist and his mouth presses into me, tongue working against mine as the hunters burst through the door.

Bless you, Amy, for the toothpaste and Chapstick.

"The new girl?! Damn, Leo works fast!" a hunter laughs.

Another whistles, the third yells "LET'S GOOO!" and they're gone.

Leo's cool face lifts from mine, and we stare out the front window after the hunters, now running through the flowers, one of them inexplicably wearing a Dr. Seuss–style felt hat that bobs over the tall grass.

"I'm so, so sorry," Leo pants.

"No worries." I make a great effort to sound casual. "Should we get Artemis?"

"She can't be seen with me. She'll hide in the cellar until it's safe to go back." He points out the back window to the slanting doors of a storm cellar almost hidden by lavender. "And you should try and get some driving in, before your other lesson."

I nod and stumble after him back toward the cul-de-sac meadow, lips tingling as I slide behind the wheel. I pull the brake up, hoping he doesn't notice my hands are shaking.

"Your hands are shaking," Leo says. "Did I *fluster you*, Kay?"

"Too much coffee," I say. "Also, a deer shrieked at me, and I almost got shot by an arrow. I mean, it's been a *whirlwind*."

I pull away from the curb. He directs me down the block. Three guys leisurely open the fence for us. We pull into another neighborhood, and he shows me where to turn before asking, seriously, "Was that your first kiss?"

"Uh, no!" I laugh, offended. I've kissed guys before, why would he think that was my first time? "You caught me off guard. Do *not* judge my kissing skills off that experience."

"How *should* I judge your kissing, then?" he asks innocently, then grins.

"Back to what we were talking about before." I widen my eyes. "The girl Artemis was talking about, Jessica . . ." When I say the name, he looks out the window. "Were you two . . . together or something?"

Leo sighs. "It's complicated. But we sure as hell aren't together now."

"And she's with the Theater Department?"

"Why? Are you going to talk to her?" he asks quickly.

"Seems like the best way to get the whole story."

"I'd, uh, appreciate it if I could talk to her first." Leo frowns. "Considering what she might hear about you and me after—" He brushes his mouth with his knuckles, still looking out the window, then turns to me with a guilty smile.

"Oh." My face heats. "You really think those hunters will, like, go around telling people they saw us?"

"In case they do. I should talk to her first."

"Okay," I say, not sure exactly what he's going to tell her—*I fake-kissed the bald girl?*—when I hear a short honk.

Up ahead, the cheerleaders are waiting in their Jeep, Leila sitting on the hood, Stokes chomping venison jerky. Amy stands up in the passenger seat to wave us down.

"You know," Leo goes on, dropping his voice as I park, "if the

King has his eye on you after the costume room, you might want to tap the brakes on your investigation. And you probably shouldn't be carrying Kyle's inhaler around. I could keep it for you, if you want."

"It's cool," I tell him. "I'll be careful."

+ + +

The cheerleaders have prepped this block for my "dry run." Amy is climbing with me; Leila and Stokes are drivers. When Leila calls time, Amy and I sprint for the tallest vantage point: the roof of the nearest house. We get there by climbing in the window on the stripped first floor, racing up the stairs and through the patchy second floor, and finding a window on the almost intact third floor, its cream wallpaper still dotted with family portraits.

Amy struggles to open the third-story window, all overgrown with ivy. After a couple good shoves, it flies free, and we climb out onto the roof. I peer over its edge at the tilting ground below.

I spot the Grown skeleton shambling at us from behind the garage across the street then. The bones are somehow worse in the daylight. The skull alone is the length of a car hood.

"DRAGON—TWELVE O'CLOCK!" I scream, and Amy gives me a thumbs-up, then points to her eyes. I get a Grown eye socket in my air rifle's sights, but the skeleton puppet shifts course. Barrel still raised, I try and stay trained on my target, but as I pivot, my worn Keds slip on the ivy covering the shingle. It all happens so fast: I slam backward and slide down the steep roof before I can even yell. Suddenly my shirt strains hard against my chest, sleeves cutting under my arms like a harness as I jerk to a stop. Amy has caught the back of my T-shirt and caught me just short of falling off the roof. There is only birdsong between my dangling Keds and the lawn.

"*Kay*," Amy whispers, barely audible over the blood pounding in my ears. "*Take the shot.*"

My arms are locking up, fingers stiff and shaking, but Amy calmly directs me: *Breathe. Focus.* I line up the air rifle, squeeze the trigger, and glass shatters.

Stokes runs out of the front door, screaming, "Car! Let's go!"

"Now we get back to the car as fast as we can," Amy says coolly, helping me back to my feet. I cling to her all the way back to the window and follow her down through the house on jelly legs, out to Stokes's car, Leila yelling for the puppet to reset for the next run.

This is just the first of five houses we're going to train on today. Brick has asked them to cram in all the practice they can ahead of the real thing.

Just the thought of the real thing makes my gorge rise.

But by the third house, the pukey feeling goes away. By the fifth house, it's actually sort of fun. I shatter glass on three consecutive shots from the roof of a one-story bungalow.

"That's all the light bulbs!" comes a muffled voice from the skull.

"Amazing!" Leila hops down from the car hood where she's been watching. "Your aim just keeps getting better, Kay. A climber with an eye? You're gonna be some room's MVP." She high-fives the puppeteers as they get out from under their bones. The Grown disassembles into two girls and three guys in all black, all wearing bicycle helmets and goggles.

"This was really helpful," I tell the cheerleaders as we circle up on the porch, Stokes pulling sandwiches out of her backpack for our lunch. Peanut butter on homemade hamburger buns.

"I'm impressed, Kay. You picked this stuff up quick!" Leila's smile deepens. "You moving that fast in your driving lessons?"

Stokes snorts.

I look around the circle. ". . . I guess?"

"Leo teach you stick yet?" Stokes asks, and they all burst out laughing.

My jaw drops.

"That's right, girl! We heard about your little make-out session!" Leila grins. "Details, let's hear 'em!"

"*How?*" I gasp. "That was like, *an hour ago—*"

Amy grins. "You're the new girl, people notice you."

"And you know we *all* keep one eye out for Leo!" Leila says.

"How, Kay?" Stokes demands. "How'd *you* pull the hottest guy in school?"

"First of all, rude," I laugh at Stokes. "Secondly, I didn't."

"Stop. Lying!" Leila points in my face. "You and Leo were at his hookup spot! What else would you be doing in there?"

Attending a secret revolutionary meeting, of course. I duck my head and cover my reddening face, trying to buy time, my guilty smile ready to go if I lie.

"Yeah. They made out," Stokes says.

"*Damn.*" Leila shakes her head. "Just damn! Maybe he's into buzz cuts? Have I been going about this all wrong?"

"Leo doesn't like me," I tell them honestly. "He's hung up on some girl from the Theater Department."

"He told her about Jessica! See, he's being straight up," Amy says triumphantly. Leila and Stokes scooch in, and this is actually perfect: I can be as nosy as I want about Jessica, without raising any suspicion, if they think I really like Leo.

"I mean, he didn't say much . . ." I bite my lip. "Could you guys tell me, like, everything about her real quick?"

They all laugh knowingly.

"Jessica is . . . a freshman?" Amy begins, looking to Leila.

"No, no, she *was* a sophomore Before, so she's a junior age-wise, but school's out forever, so . . ."

"All the guys think she's hot," Stokes says flatly. "Just because she's thin with big boobs. I don't see it, personally."

"She's beautiful, Tiffany! Come on, now. Let's be real—Jess is stunning, okay." Leila waves a hand. "But the point is, Leo never had an actual girlfriend Before, just hookups. Then after the dragons, he and Jessica were like this, right—" She holds up crossed fingers.

"They were so cute," Amy sighs.

"They were either making out or yelling at each other. Seemed like hell to me." Stokes's eyebrows arch cruelly. "And I heard someone saw Leo push her by the shoulder against a wall outside the Auto

Shop, screaming, 'You want to go be a whore, go be a whore!'"

"Leo would *never*," Leila says. "Who said that? Give me a name."

"I heard it from a reliable source, after one of the office parties."

"Reliable source! Every time you say that, it's bullshit. Don't spread rumors unless you have receipts, Tiffany."

"Wait," I cut in. "What are office parties?"

"The King hosts private parties in the principal's office," Amy says.

"We were invited a couple times, but we stopped going," Leila adds.

"Why?"

"Because they're shady." Stokes sniffs.

"They're kinda gross." Amy tilts her head back and forth. "All the drinks you want, but it's thirty girls and maybe ten guys who are all being dicks."

"The Theater Department has, like, a standing invitation to the principal's office. To come fire dance and do black light stuff and hype up the party or whatever," Leila goes on. "But apparently Jessica was turning up to every single one of these parties. And that pissed Leo off." Leila looks around, then leans in farther. "But what *I* heard, is that Heather *made her go*."

"Heather meaning Artemis?" I confirm, and off Leila's nod: "Why would she make her go?"

"Because Heather has liked Leo her entire life!" Leila stabs the porch with one finger.

"It's true." Amy nods seriously. "I was at the slumber party, in fifth grade, where she literally *carved his name into her arm* with a razor blade."

"Whoa!" I flinch.

"It's three letters," Stokes says, unimpressed.

"And it wasn't, like, super deep," Amy admits. "But it was a big deal in fifth grade."

"Ugh, Heather." Leila rolls her eyes, then shakes her head at me. "She's always doing too damn much. But you can see how, like, if it's making their, uh, extremely volatile relationship fracture, Heather might have had a hand in making Jess go party it up."

"Or—" Amy points a finger. "King Max could have insisted she be there."

My stomach twists; I remember Leo's anger before. "You mean, like, maybe Max was—hooking up with Jess?"

"*King* Max," Leila corrects me gently.

"I seriously doubt it." Amy gives me a nervous smile. "Jess and Brick are really close."

There is a strange sensation at the base of my belly, as though it were a fishbowl and the fish just jumped out.

I try to sound only slightly interested. "Like . . . they dated?"

"No, no no no." Leila rolls her eyes. "Just friends. But *really* good friends."

"Didn't Cassie, like, offer herself to Brick before she joined our room?" Stokes asks her.

"There you go talking shit again. Was this from a reliable source, too?" Leila snaps.

"She did, though! She offered to spend the night with him for a bag of rice—" Stokes's face is screwed up with laughter. "And he just gave her the rice and told her to go."

A helpless laugh escapes Leila.

"YOU GUYS." Amy smacks Stokes's knee. "Stop! Brick is a gentleman, and Cassie . . . was hungry."

"Cured her hunger, not her thirst," Leila says, and then we all crack up.

"I was telling him!" I start excitedly. "All these girls seriously like him, but he doesn't believe it—"

"Yeah, duh, he's hot." Leila rolls her eyes. "Not *Leo* hot, but who is. Let me tell you, if I was Jess? I would've bunked up with Leo like *that*." She snaps her fingers. "Sorry, ladies. The very idea of turning him down to stick around the *Theater Department*—I can't!"

"But that would have put a huge target on her back with King Max," Amy points out. "It would be such a declaration that she was *with* Leo."

"I'm confused by all the 'with' stuff," I cut in again. "Was Jess 'with' Brick, is that—"

"Oh no!" Amy bursts out laughing. "I guess we do use it a couple different ways, but it boils down to what room you're with. Like, everybody has a room, every room has a leader. I'm 'with' the cheerleaders, so I'm 'with' Leila. But if you're in a relationship and it gets so serious you want to switch rooms, then you're in that room *with* your boyfriend or girlfriend."

"But it looks like Leo and Jess weren't that serious after all!" Stokes shrugs. "So there's hope for you yet, Baldy."

Leila's tone becomes elaborately casual. ". . . Have you been invited to a room yet, Kay?"

I shake my head. The others fall silent as she continues: "We really wanted to invite you to ours, but we can't, Kay. I'm so sorry."

My stomach drops. Leila explains some logistical issue with fitting another bunk in the space while I stay silent, face tight. I had really just assumed they would take me in. Now I have no idea where I'll live. Amy looks like she's worried I might cry. Stokes is no doubt hoping I will.

"I totally get it, no worries." I nod, a little too quickly. "Thanks for the heads-up."

"Hey!" Brick's voice calls out. We turn to see him coming down the sidewalk, Frank at his side. "How'd she do?"

"Amazing! Five houses and no falls!" Leila calls. "She's all yours!" And then she leans forward and whispers, *"Except for your heart, which we all know is Leo's."*

I widen my eyes at her, panicked Brick will hear.

"I'm heading up to the school." Brick leans on the fence across from us. "Kay, you want to walk back with me?"

"Yeah, sure." I hop up and give each cheerleader a hug goodbye, so they know there's no hard feelings.

"Lucid," Stokes says in my ear. "Get some from Merlin before she runs out."

I nod, then join Brick on the sidewalk, giving Frank a hello scratch. The late afternoon sun is gold as honey; it turns Brick into a glowing god of amber light at the corner of my eye. Like hell he doesn't know he's hot. But he's something else, too. He's tense.

Has he heard about the kiss with Leo?

"What's wrong?" I warble.

"Well, Kay, I don't know how to tell you this." Brick frowns. "I pitched the King on catapulting food to Jefferson. But he's decided no food can be sent until you've officially joined a room at Moore."

"Oh." There's no way I'll make a group of friends ready to take me in before Jefferson runs out of food. My throat feels tight. "Couldn't I just . . . stay with you?"

A long moment passes. Then Brick says: "It's not *my* room. It's the Captain of the Guard's room. You're in it because I'm guarding you."

"Got it."

"No, you don't understand, it's not up to me—" He breaks off and starts again: "Max would have to be the one to invite you. King Max," he corrects himself.

"King Max. Of course." King Max, who was probably forcing Jess to come to his nasty parties just to torture Leo. "Why do you give him so much control over you?" It comes out too loud. Brick stiffens, but I can't stop myself. "What if, like, a girl wants to sleep over? Do you have to run down and check with him first?"

"Uh, there's a big difference between a girl sleeping over and a girl *moving in*."

"How do you know? Have you *had* sleepovers before?"

"Kay . . ." Brick looks uncomfortable. "What are you getting at here?"

I flush. "I'm just trying to draw your attention to how much control your best friend has over your life. Coming from an outside perspective, it's *weird*."

"Maybe the 'outside perspective' is your problem," Brick says calmly. "He isn't just my best friend, he's *our King*. The sooner you get that, the sooner you'll fit in around here."

"Um, I fit in *fine*." I lift my chin, stung. "I'll find a room, okay? You won't have to worry about me hanging around much longer."

"Great," he says, annoyed.

A block ahead, a group of guys have a freshly carved deer to trade, bundles of wrapped meat set out on a card table, their bicycles piled by the curb. One of them wears the red-and-white Dr. Seuss hat. They're the hunters from the 1776 house. I quickly turn around, hoping they don't recognize me. Brick stops with an exasperated gesture.

"Look, I have to go see Merlin," I tell him. "Can I meet you back on the roof for dinner?"

Brick nods, and I hurry away from the table, but a sharp wolf-whistle rings out behind me. They've spotted me, they remembered me, and no doubt they're going to tell Brick they saw me making out with Leo.

Great. Let him hear just how well I'm fitting in.

+ + +

Merlin's "Cavern" is quiet, except for a decadent thread of music coming from a battery-powered tape player, and the quiet bubbling of beakers and test tubes. A thin girl in an oversized hoodie and lab glasses springs up when I come in.

"Can I help you?" she cries, and I hear a drawer shutting as Merlin emerges from her private office.

"Kay! Marissa, can you file the rest of those?" Merlin nods to the girl, who picks up a cardboard box and retreats to the office, leaving us alone. "How's training going?"

"Intense," I tell her. "I don't think I'll ever get used to the Gro— the dragon skeleton."

"You shouldn't. They are powerful creatures. Even when they're just bones."

I nod, feeling suddenly shy. "Right. Well, uh, the cheerleaders mentioned that you make something that can help? Called Lucid?"

"A potion that makes you fearless, yes, for half a day."

"I don't know how much it costs—"

"Costs?" She gives me a heavy look, then turns and wheels to the teacher's desk, where she pulls open the deep bottom drawer. It clinks heavily, and I watch her shuffle around cans of Sterno, flat bottles of lighter fluid, packages of Firestarter, and *several* 64-battery packs of AA Duracells: an almost unfathomable display of wealth.

"Why would I charge my people? Everything I want is for them." Merlin pulls a baggie of pink powder from the bottom of the drawer. She holds it out to me, but when I reach for it, she pulls it back again. "But you're not one of my people yet. And you have something I want."

I freeze, maintaining what I hope is a neutral expression, though cold sweat is breaking out across my back.

"Kyle's inhaler," Merlin says impatiently. "Give it up, Kay."

The Invitation

KAY

How does she know I have the inhaler? I didn't tell anyone. I didn't have the chance to! Does she know about the 1776 house? Is it bugged? *Can* you bug a place where there's no electricity? My face goes red before I can even start denying that I have it.

"I could make the guards search you." Merlin leans back in her chair, relaxing into her total control over the situation like it's a hot bath. "But I'd rather you give it to me as a show of good faith."

I dig the small device out of my pocket and clench it in my fist, feeling like I'm slipping on the roof again, sliding out of control. She reaches out her hand, and I put it in her palm, helpless. She delicately tucks the inhaler inside her jacket.

"Kay, whoever gave you this is not your friend. If I were you, I'd think long and hard about why they're trying to get you all worked up against a King who's on the edge of kicking your butt out as it is."

"How did you—"

"Magic." Merlin tosses the baggie of Lucid at me. I fumble it and have to stoop to pick it off the floor, then hurry out of her sight before I burst into tears.

When I get to Brick's room, I fully intend on balling up in the bed with Frank and weeping myself to sleep, but Brick calls down through the skylight:

"Kay!"

The second I hear his voice, I know he's heard about the stupid kiss. I climb up the ladder, hands cold, feet heavy.

Brick is leaned back in his chair, Frank piled in his lap. He must have carried him up, and picturing this in any other mood would make me smile. My beach chair from last night has a plate on it, with two roasted ears of corn and a skewer of chargrilled deer meat. So maybe he's not mad. Maybe he doesn't care who I kiss.

Somehow that doesn't cheer me up.

I take my seat, balance the plate on my lap. When I look over at Brick, he's staring straight ahead, jaw clenched, his own food uneaten. I can't take it.

"What's up, Brick?"

"I will do everything in my power to get Jefferson food, but damn . . ." He shakes his head. "It's going to be so much harder when the King finds out you're with Leo."

"I'm *not* with Leo." Deep breath, stay cool. "I'm guessing you heard Leo and I kissed or whatever today." I can feel my face heating. "It meant nothing, we were just . . . sucking face to kill time, I guess—"

"Generally, during a driving lesson, you kill time by driving." He gives me a hard look, and my face gets hotter. "You're all red." He looks away again. "So it didn't mean nothing, Kay."

I should be grateful that Leo's cover worked. It's not like I can tell Brick why I really went to the house with him.

So why do I feel sick?

"*Even if I liked Leo,*" I say with great effort, "how is that Max's business? What, he's willing to let thousands of people at Jefferson starve over some high school dating drama?"

"This isn't about dating. It's about loyalty. Leo is trying to take down the King."

"And why is that?" I pop off. "Is it because he made Leo's friends beat him up? Or because he forces Leo's girlfriend to party with him?"

"Hold on . . ." Brick squints at me. "So you *are* a spy?"

"No!"

"You're supposed to be learning how to drive down at the Auto Shop, not digging up rumors about King Max and Leo's 'girlfriend.' *What* girlfriend? Leo doesn't *do* girlfriends. If you mean a girl he's hooked up with, that's practically every girl in school—"

"I didn't have to dig anything up!" I cry. "Everyone at school talks about Max's *orgies* in the principal's office, which I'm sure are lots of fun for you and your bros—"

"I don't go to the office parties."

"Right."

"*I don't.*"

"Why not?" I lean toward him. "What happens at those parties?"

"'Sucking face,'" his deep voice booms. "Gotta kill time somehow, right?" I practically choke, and he storms on: "You've been here forty-eight hours. I've known Max since Little League. My mom used to work for his mom, his dad was my coach, he got me my scholarship, and—"

"Cool!" I cry. "How does that qualify him to be King?"

"Who do you think qualifies? Leo? Leo! Of all the guys in this school—" Brick shakes his head and rocks forward in his chair, his face pained. "Two days before Expansion, and he's spending *your driving lessons* crying his way into your pants, of course. That's his style. If that fool were King? He would be way, *way* worse. And he'll *never* be King because *he didn't kill the dragon.*"

"Neither did Max!" I explode. "*You* did! You're the only person with the right to stand up to Max, and you don't! *You should be King.* That's the truth—"

"Oh my God, Kay." Brick is enraged. "You go on and on about the truth, but what does that even mean? What about being true to your friends? Keeping the faith with them, keeping your word? There's nothing else now, do you get that? The people around us, right now, are *all we're ever going to have*, for the rest of our lives! All we are, is what we mean to our friends!"

I'm stunned into silence for a moment.

"You know that Rule you told me about? Everyone snitching at Jefferson? That's *sick*. That is the sickest, saddest, most cowardly ass shit I've ever heard!" He sits up in his chair, eyes blazing through the wild carvings of his scars. "At Moore, we go out and we kill dragons together. Do you understand the *trust* you have to have in your team to face one of *those things*?"

He points with deadly understanding toward the woods, his blanket slipping down from his bare shoulder.

"People believe in King Max here. And he believes in us, and that makes us believe in each other. And if we keep that faith and work very, *very* hard, we *will* get this whole town back. From the dam to the beach, Brockton will be free."

I can see it, the beautiful golden street we walked down this afternoon, unfolding the length of town. Can picture my friends biking from house to house, faces rounded from deer meat and brown from so much sunshine, can imagine taking off my shoes and stepping into the cool sand of Calf Pasture Beach. I can see it so clearly it hurts.

"Getting us to that point is all I care about." Brick settles back in his chair. "Because *that's* what really matters. Not who's wearing a crown when it happens."

"But now matters, too, Brick," I tell him quietly. "For some of us, now is all we get. Kyle is dead." It's a struggle to say it out loud. Because even if Kyle was not who I thought, even if he was a cheater and a faker, he was still Jefferson's last hope. "He left his inhaler here, and he's always supposed to keep it with him. And when I went to see Merlin, she *made me give it to her*. Someone here knows something, okay? And if Moore knows what happened to Kyle, they need to let Jefferson know *now*. Or else all my friends are going to die, waiting for him."

Brick doesn't blink; he's watching me for tells. I hold his gaze aggressively, stare back straight in his face. His gaze softens, and after a moment, he looks away, his expression troubled.

"Here's what we'll do," he says at last. "After the Expansion, I will take you to speak with Merlin and King Max privately about the inhaler—"

"Oh, after the Expansion!" I nod sarcastically. "Yeah, I'm sure after I'm dead or sleeping in the football field, it'll be a real *pressing issue*—"

"You'll be in the Auto Shop."

"I told you, Brick, I'm not *with* Leo—"

"I don't care," he cuts me off. The fire crackles, spits. Then, "Why did you go see Merlin?"

"To get some Lucid."

"Oh yeah? How much did you get?"

I hand him the bag, and he gets up and walks to the edge of the roof.

"No! No *no no NO!!!*" I'm on my feet, grabbing at his arm, but I'm too late: the powder sails soundlessly into the dark. "What the hell is wrong with you?!" I yell, shoving him in a rage. "Do you *want* me to die? I needed that! *I needed that!*"

"No one needs that."

"*Bullshit!*" I push him, hard, and he grips my shoulder to stop me. The contact is like lightning, searing up and down my arm. I grab his wrist, meaning to thrust his hand away, but once my fingers circle it, I can't let go. It's like we've completed some inner circuit and now lightning is racing through us, circling from him to me and back again. We stare at each other in the electrified silence, and I wish so much that he had tells. Because it must be as plain on my face as dawn through a window, what I feel right now.

Frank's barking breaks us apart. He's bristling at the skylight; someone is knocking at the room door. Brick hurries down the ladder, and I collapse beside Frank, ruffling his neck, furious at the interruption.

"What are *you* doing here?" Brick says.

I look down just as Leo looks up, the moon bathing his perfect face in silver, turning his pale eyes to stars.

"There you are." He smiles, and Brick looks up at me as well, their faces framed by the skylight into a stark comparison: Leo all boyish smile and glowing light, Brick all ruined and rageful. "Can I talk to you for a minute?" Leo asks. "Outside?"

"I'll ask my guard." I look hard at Brick. "Can I go?"

"What's it about?" Brick crosses his arms over his chest.

"Well . . ." Leo's smile widens. "I wanted to ask Kay if she'd join my room."

I stare down at him, stunned.

"You better go then," Brick snaps, not looking at me. The moment I land on the desk, he lunges past me up the ladder. An amber flicker from the fire catches his face, head hanging like a surrender flag. I hear Frank whining softly, hear the two of them pile up in one chair.

I want so badly to climb up after him. But he's told me enough times that I'm not welcome.

So I follow Leo down the stairs, skin still ringing where Brick and I touched.

We go down past the Flower Aquarium and out into the spring air, to a side courtyard ringed with heavy benches. There's a group clustered nearby: four guys listening to a girl pick out a song on guitar, her voice dancing through the notes, one of them taking down her chord changes by candlelight.

"I need to tell you something," I say before Leo can start. "Merlin knew I had the inhaler somehow and took it from me."

His perfect smile flattens into a grim line.

"I didn't tell her. I didn't tell anyone," I go on. "I have no idea how she even knew."

"Someone in the Theater Department is reporting on Artemis."

"Yeah, well, I understand if that changes whatever you were going to ask me about—joining your room, or whatever."

But Leo shakes his head. "That's not why I want you to join my room, at all. I just thought that kiss was pretty hot."

There is no way I heard that right. "I'm sorry. What?"

"I was going to wait for our next lesson, but the moon was nice." He looks up, and the moon beams back as though returning the compliment. "I wanted to ask if you'd move into the Auto Shop and be with me, as my girlfriend."

If I'd had a long shower or even a cute pair of earrings, I might entertain the notion he's serious. But I don't buy Leo is *that* blown away by my cherry Chapstick.

"Is this . . . to get even with Jessica? Like . . . she got with the new guy, so you're getting with the new girl?"

"That's what I like about you." Leo smiles. "You cut right through the bullshit." He shakes his head. "I'm not over Jessica. I won't lie to you. But the relationship is over. I won't stay with someone who cheats on me."

"Okay . . ." I squint at him. "So why jump into a new relationship?"

"Well, I like that you're not *brainwashed*." He widens his eyes. "That's a breath of fresh air. And I think you joining the Auto Shop, as the first new kid, would be a huge vote of confidence in Los Martillos. Which would make King Max . . . extremely nervous."

"Well, when you put it like that." I smile at him, relieved that he's leveling with me. "So, we could be, like, a pretend couple?"

"Sure." His beautiful face moves a little closer to mine, his arm sweeping behind me. "Want to pretend make out?"

My answer should be yes, but all I feel is panic. And thankfully, a familiar voice interrupts:

"*Exile Kay?* And . . . El Martillo?" Max looms over us, flanked by Nunchucks and Golf Club. Leo and I stand to make perfunctory bows.

"Your Majesty." Leo makes it sound like an insult. "Having a good evening?"

"Always." Max grins. "Yourself?"

"Kay and I were just talking about her joining the Auto Shop."

Max lifts a wine bottle, half-concealed by his swim coat, and swigs from it. Then he rubs his broad mouth with the back of his hand, staring at me.

"Didn't know you were a mechanic, Kay," he says at last.

Leo drapes an arm around my shoulders. "She'd be with us as my girlfriend."

"It's something we're talking about," I add primly.

Max wags a finger at me. "Be sure you really kick his tires first. Leo can pull chicks all right, but he has a hell of a time keeping them around." The guards behind Max chuckle as he throws back more wine. "Well! We needed to find Kay a car for Expansion, so you can put her in one of yours. Glad we got that straightened out! Now, I was about to pay my respects to the heroes. Kay, why don't you come with me."

It's not a question.

"Go ahead," Leo says, like I need his permission, then pecks me on the lips before I fall in beside the King of Moore High, the guards just out of earshot.

"You and Leo, huh?" Max looks at me, dead-eyed, then drawls: "He's *cuuuute*."

"I need to be in a room before I can make petitions, right?"

"Yes, but Los Martillos isn't just any room." Max frowns. "It's a whole . . . thing. Sort of like a cult that can change your oil."

"Well, to tell you the truth . . ." Why not take the chance? What do I have to lose? "If it were up to me, I'd rather just stay with Brick."

"Yeah?" Max scans my face. "Why?"

"I've gotten attached," I say, "to Frank."

"That's no good." Max gives me a crooked smile. "He already has a master."

It takes all my strength not to fire back, and Max laughs, a strange sparkle in his eyes, then reaches out and pinches my cheek. I twist my head away.

"What the hell are—"

"Watch your language, Kay," he scolds. "Get a hold of yourself. We're about to enter a memorial service. Show some respect."

I'm choking on rage as Max lands before the center set of double doors to the auditorium. He hands his wine bottle to the guards, straightens his crown, and then nods. They throw the doors open, and he steps ahead of me down the aisle.

Moore's auditorium is almost identical to Jefferson's: dingy theater seats, a broad balcony hanging over the back quarter of the house, muted carpet. But the sensibility could not be more different. Whereas Jefferson's auditorium is now our courthouse, filled with harried whispers and shuffling papers, Moore has made theirs a cathedral. The chandeliers are filled with burning torches, and brass incense burners hang every few feet from the walls. Over the stage is a cross, a Star of David, and a moon and star beaten in brass and polished to a gleaming shine, radiating in the flickering light of hundreds of pillar candles covering the black stage.

A line of hundreds fills the central aisle and snakes along the edge of the stage, and for once everyone is being respectful. No one is fighting or eating a squirrel drumstick or twerking against a wall. The Moore students make silent reverences along the stage, at each of the twelve music stands towering over them. Each music stand has a row of tea lights along its ledge and supports a large portrait of a smiling face. The portraits are drawn in photo-realistic style in tight, careful pencil, as though the artist didn't want to lose a single detail. But the tightness makes the smiles stiff and cold. At the foot of each stand, students pile flowers, stuffed animals, and folded notes. Like roadside memorials from Before.

"We bring the heroes out before each Expansion," Max says, as we move down the central aisle. "They died killing dragons so we could live in freedom. Our gratitude is eternal, and they will live forever in our memory." When I look back over my shoulder to the rows of seats, the people behind me are all crying.

As we move along the edge of the stage, Max names each of the portraits in my ear: ". . . Jameel Wilson, a senior. Lisa Stroff, she was a fighter. So rare. Jorge Gonzalez, we had homeroom together Before. His little sister is with the Star Sailors now. That's Tara Smith, she has a twin brother . . ."

"So many," I say when he finishes the litany.

"Too many. All different ages, all different positions. But they all had one thing in common." He turns to me. "They all went out in the first heat."

I blink at him. First heat? It's a racing term, I think.

"Los Martillos are the first heat of this Expansion," he adds after a moment, cold eyes squarely on mine. "So, uh, if you have any other room offers, I'd say take them."

I drop into a seat, my knees too weak to hold me any longer.

I would give anything to be back at Jefferson.

Hec-a-tomb:
Extensive Loss of Life

NIRALI

Every time I wake up, I expect to be back in my own bed, to smell my mother's cooking and stumble downstairs and tell her about the hideous nightmare I just had.

But every time I wake up, I'm still here. On the floor of the supply closet off the biology lab, in a sleeping bag, across from forty-seven jarred pig fetuses we can't eat because they're soaked in formaldehyde.

This morning, night nurses shake me awake. The patient is vomiting loud enough I know what's happened before they tell me. It's nothing serious. People just keep trying to eat things they can't because we're all starving.

I rush to the radio room just short of dawn, to sit next to Simon and bicker over the static. Roaches the size of Medjool dates zigzag across the wall and under our chairs because his lantern has run out of batteries and all we have is my flashlight.

When we finish, one of my staff is waiting just outside the door—someone's suture tore. They've brought rations up for me so I don't have to go down to the cafeteria. Chickpea mush with even more barley flour. It smells less appetizing than the predawn vomit, but I still wish there was more of it.

Repairing the suture takes just long enough to make me late for the council meeting. I trade my filthy lab coat for Kyle's even filthier varsity jacket and sprint down the stairs to the gym with my flashlight off to save batteries. I've done this run so many times I can do it with my eyes closed, but it does make it harder to avoid the roaches.

For the first time since Student Council meetings started, there are people in front of the gym doors, about twenty of them. Antonin, posted at the doors as security and wearing a varsity jacket, gestures to me.

"Reese's friends have been asking if the door can be open today during the council meeting," Antonin says, "while she testifies and whatnot."

I recognize Reese's clique among the crowd, but it's not just them. It's not any one social circle, but a motley crew of grim-faced individuals from different grades and social strata. Looming in the back is the Rule breaker from yesterday's lunch line.

"Absolutely not," I tell Antonin coolly. "Student Council meetings are for elected officials only. If they want a Tribunal, they can start a petition." I sweep through the doors. He closes them after me; they fall on muffled protests.

A torch sputters at the far end of the basketball court, held aloft by a microphone stand, its smoke curling up through the basketball hoop. The Student Council sits in a ring of folding chairs inside the three-point line; the rest of the scuffed floor is piled with rolled-up sleeping bags, filling the room with the dirty-sock smell of unwashed bedding.

Simon is standing, and across the torch from him is Reese. She's still in her rubber gloves, like the Scavenging Team pulled her out of work. Her hair, as long as Kay's was Before, is in a double French braid, the trailing pigtails pinned on top of her head like a crown. This is the opposite of the outcast with the bags tied around his wrists: proof she has friends who take care of her.

"Nice of you to finally join us, Nirali," Simon snipes at me. "I call this meeting to order. First on the agenda: Reese." He cuts a look at her; she straightens her narrow shoulders. "You are here because your job, a job which guarantees you get to eat every day, is to lighten the mood in the lunch line." He looks around the circle of chairs at the other student representatives. Eight in total, two from each grade. "But instead, you started a scene yesterday and attempted to discredit this council."

"I just asked a question." Reese shakes her head. "It's not my fault you can't answer it."

"Reese. Please," Simon snaps. "Do not speak out of turn again. You will have a chance to make a statement when I'm through with the allegations—"

"Allegations?!" Reese cries, voice carrying through the gym.

"Which are," Simon steamrolls, "that you endangered the student body by willfully spreading disinformation about the suicide of Kay Kim."

"Kay has been my best friend since first grade. I know her. She would never walk out on her friends or this school—"

"Whatever your private speculations may be, the lunch line is not the place for you to air them. You will be moved to back of house in the kitchen until you understand that." Reese starts to protest, but Simon cuts her off: "Fine, bathroom duty it is! If you can't keep your mouth shut while cleaning toilets, at least no one will stay around long enough to hear your ranting—"

"Nothing you do will convince me that Kay killed herself," Reese interrupts him. "Punishing me like this only makes you look worse. I know Kay better than anyone. She was excited about the birthday room, about working on her proposal. She had big plans—"

"Can you be more specific about these plans?" Simon says.

This, I wasn't expecting.

"Just, you know . . ." Reese seems momentarily thrown, then rallies. "Her whole Costco pitch. She was going to work on it overnight, in the birthday room. She said we could get as much from one trip to Costco as twelve neighborhood raids."

Simon's eyes leap to my face. The weasel has found a way to propose it. I look to Tyler, standing outside our circle, by the doors that lead to the athletic hall. Tyler is shifting his weight from one foot to the other and staring hard at Simon. His supratrochlear vein makes a ridge straight down his forehead, like a crack in a dam.

But the idea is out, and the council is murmuring excitedly.

"What do you think, Nirali?" Yashpal, the other senior representative, leans into me. "You think the Scavenging Team would go for it?"

"No." Tyler shoots forward, addressing Yashpal directly as he cuts into our circle of chairs. "No way. The Scavenging Team has never driven out that far—"

"They'd have so much food!" a junior representative says.

"And soap. And new clothes. Deodorant. Medicine!" one of the sophomore reps chimes in.

"It doesn't matter what Costco has," Tyler pleads, "because none of us would make it back! You're tryna send us to our deaths right now!"

"So the only guy who drives around town doesn't think he can go ten miles, but Kyle's supposed to be halfway across the state?" Reese yells.

SNAP!

The double doors across the gym buckle sharply. As though someone has just tried to kick them open.

"Order, please!" Simon adjusts his round glasses with a shaking hand. "Reese, focus. I am asking you to either publicly correct your dangerous statements or join janitorial staff. What will it be?"

"What"—her face screws up—"you want me to say Kay killed herself?"

"At lunch, today." He nods.

"No." Reese's voice is small and almost a question, but then she lifts her chin and repeats, louder: "No. I won't. I won't say what I don't believe."

Simon looks to Tyler. "Tyler, please remove Reese from council."

"No way." Tyler shakes his head. "Not until you veto this Costco thing. Right now."

And then I know. From the way Tyler demands it from Simon, like a payment he's owed. It wasn't just the Scavenging Team that threw Kay out.

It was Simon, too.

CRACK!

The double doors across the court fly open, Reese's supporters crowding the doorway. Antonin is yelling something, but there's just one of him.

"Tyler, could you go see what the issue is?" Yashpal says with authority.

But Tyler just stares Simon down, openly defying Yashpal.

"Veto the Costco trip," Tyler says through clenched teeth. "Now."

Reese starts yelling: "Scavenging Team won't drive out past two miles! But you're telling us Kyle is hundreds of miles away, no problem?"

"Not hundreds," a junior rep says. Another fathead. You don't argue details on fine points, you tell her to *shut up*.

"This is out of order," I cut in.

"How far is it, then?" Reese turns on me, projecting her voice even louder. "You talk to Kyle twice a day, right? Don't you ask where the hell he is?"

"How far does the radio range go?" someone yells from the open doorway, and there is scattered applause from the crowd in the hall.

Tyler needs to shut the doors. But he's locked in some primal exchange with Simon, and I'm terrified of what he will say next, afraid of what the faction at the door will do if I command Tyler and he ignores me.

So I turn on Reese, my voice dropping:

"The penalty for breaking the Rule is three days without food." Practically a death sentence. I hold her gaze: *Don't make me do this.* "The more you talk, the closer you come to breaking the Rule. Be very careful what you say next. Because I don't think you want to do that, Reese."

"I don't want to break the Rule." Reese's voice echoes through the gym. "We want to *destroy* it."

The faction at the door bursts into cheers.

"You're not eating for three days," I tell Reese, getting to my feet. My voice doesn't shake. My eyes don't blink. The angrier I get, the colder I get; my look freezes her in place. I move across the court, closer to the far doors. "Freshman Representative Carl," I call over my shoulder. "Take down the names of everyone who just clapped. For the next three days, none of them will be eating."

This is meant to send them running, to scatter them when physical force will not.

But none of the people at the door moves.

The large guy at the back calls out, his sardonic voice carrying down the hall: "Eating? Who's eating? I'm not eating! Are *you* eating?"

"Who's eating?" The faction picks it up. "You eating?"

I back away from the door as the faction finds a rhythm and turns this into a chant, barging right past Antonin, straight into the gym, trespassing on the Student Council meeting as they repeat:

"WHO'S EATING? YOU EATING? WHO'S EATING? YOU EATING?"

The sound of running steps echoes down the hall, a nightmare within a nightmare. More people, drawn by the chant, by the word *eating*. People who think the Student Council has opened its doors to make some happy announcement about food, and are about to be bitterly disappointed. Then dragged into a very large, very public discussion about Kyle's whereabouts.

This is turning into a worst-case scenario. Unless . . .

I turn. I reach up and tighten my ponytail. Then I stride back to the circle of chairs, head high, face composed, voice calm but carrying:

"Council. I would like to propose a bold but necessary motion, to be voted on immediately, to both honor our secretary's memory and ensure every student at Jefferson is ready to move forward when Kyle gets back—"

"Not a chance!" Tyler snaps, but there are footsteps pouring through the dark into the gym. If I do this right, they will be enough to protect me.

"The Scavenging Team could recover enough food from the Costco to last the entire winter," I go on. "Yes, it's a risk. But if we don't do something bold, we will suffer casualties in our very halls. I have faith in our Scavenging Team. They've had plenty of practice." I am at full volume, but taking care to keep my face pleasant. "I vote we send the Scavenging Team out to scavenge the Costco, as soon as possible."

"No." Tyler's whole face is red; there are tears in his eyes. He appeals to the circle of representatives. "You want blood on your hands? You'd be sending us out to die!"

"Who is eating, I continue to ask," I cry, and the growing crowd shushes each other to hear this explanation of the chant. "Are *you* eating, Tyler? The Scavenging Team's duty is to bring in food. But *who* is eating?"

The initial crowd of Reese-supporting intruders seem confused as the people who just came down the hall pick up their cheer and start shouting it even louder. But that's all right, because it means what I want it to mean now.

Reese turns back to the council, brow furrowed, uncertain where she stands.

"Destroy the Rule!" she tries, but the words are drowned out by the chanting.

"Order, please. We are in the middle of an important proposal," I snap at Reese, and the crowd grows quiet at my voice. I look hard at Simon. "Who will second my motion?"

He leans forward on his elbows, staring at the floor.

"*I'll* second the motion, Nirali. We need food, no two ways about it." Yashpal raises his hand, and there is raucous applause from the ragged crowd that keeps leaking in from the hall, pooling in the shadows beyond the torch's reach.

"Let's vote now!" I nod to Yashpal. "We don't need to spend days debating our survival. Jefferson needs food, and we know how to get it!"

Wild cries of approval echo up the bleachers.

"All for?" Freshman Representative Carl calls. No need to count twice: every hand goes up but Simon's. Our eyes catch; he looks away. The coward.

"All against?" Carl hollers, though the crowd is already cheering the motion passing when Simon gives him a small wave.

"The ayes have it!" Carl announces, and the crowd joyfully stomps and chants: "WHO'S EATING? WE'RE EATING!"

"You can't make us!" Tyler screams. I smile wide, walk past the torch in the microphone stand, and pat him on the back, leaning in close.

"I know what you did to Kay," I whisper in his ear, not dropping my smile. "It's this or a murder trial." I pull back and raise my eyebrows: *Well?*

Tyler's slack face goes pale. After a long beat, he gives me one defeated nod. I raise our joined fists, as though announcing a prizefighter, and cry:

"The Scavenging Team is going to Costco!"

THE TORCH

KAY

I put everything into my final training session, my last chance to practice before failure means death. I rub violin rosin on my hands to help my grip the way Amy shows me, put the strap of the air rifle over my chest like Stokes says. We're on our fourth dry run when a black El Camino pulls up and Leo leans out: "Kay!"

I jog through the overgrown lawn toward the car.

"Don't use up all that energy now!" Leila calls after me, and Stokes stifles a laugh. I flip them off over the top of the car, then get into the passenger seat.

"Hey." Leo smiles, but his eyes are bloodshot.

"Hey yourself. You okay?"

He steers with one hand and kneads his face with the other. "I was up late. I shouldn't even be here right now. The Auto Shop lines up the cars, so I'll be working till late again tonight. But I wanted to let you know about tomorrow."

He pulls up to the 1776 house and hands me a folded-up piece of notebook paper: a sketch of the parking lot, dozens of rows of rectangles representing vehicles. The first three are circled in red.

"You're in the third row, with Seth. Black Honda Civic with gold detailing. I put you as far back as I could."

So this is what first heat means: the first fifteen cars to hit the streets and face the Growns. No wonder all the "heroes" were in the first heat. More like martyrs.

"Leo, how many Expansions have there been?"

"Nine Expansions. Six blocks recovered."

Twelve people lost.

"Seth is my best driver," he says quickly. "And with the Dukedom up for grabs, everyone is going to be hauling ass to get at the dragon. You'll be lucky if you even see it alive."

The paper starts to flutter. Leo puts it aside and takes my hands.

"It's going to be all right," he says gently. "If I were you, I'd be more worried about crossing paths with Artemis than a dragon. She's pissed."

"Because I lost the inhaler?"

"For a lot of reasons." He releases my hands, sits back.

". . . Would she be less mad if we told her we're just friends?"

He rolls his eyes. "Probably. But we *can't* tell her, because someone's spying on her. And I don't want to give the King an excuse to keep you out of my room."

"Ugh." I bite my knuckle. "So she's just going to, like, always be mad at me?"

"Aren't I *worth it*?" he says sarcastically, then: "It's not like she can do anything to you. You're not in the Theater Department, thank God." He turns to the back seat and fishes up a pair of black coveralls. "Here. We'll all be wearing these tomorrow. They might be a little big."

"Thanks, Leo," I say, taking them. "For everything. I really appreciate having a place to, uh, live."

"My pleasure." He offers his hand, and then laughs. "This seems weird. You sure you don't want to—"

"We need to goose this handshake up," I say quickly. "Maybe we do a snap, then a bump . . . oh, I see, you can't snap . . ."

"I can snap!"

"Sure, sure you can, champ." He really can't. We end up with a simplified secret handshake consisting of a bump followed by us saying "kaboom!" and doing jazz fingers. By the time we can do it in sync, his eyes are bright and his real smile is back.

"We ride at dawn," he says as I get out of the car. "I can drive you back to where the cheerleaders—"

"No, no, it's cool!" I wave. "I want to walk."

I need to think.

I follow a footpath worn through the high grass between yards, sun warm on my shoulders. I have to join a room now if Jefferson is going to get food while it still matters. My only offer is Los Martillos, which means being in the first heat and also signing up for some silent war against Brick and Max. Which is fine as far as Max is concerned, but *Brick* . . . if I could choose to be *with* someone at Moore, it would be him. But Brick will never choose me over Max. So what choice do I have?

A metallic bang and a scream make me whip around to a driveway I just passed, half-hidden behind an overgrown hedge. Long legs scramble desperately under a car propped up on a jack stand. The stand has proved stronger than the frame it was supporting; the metal has bent around it, bringing the car down fast enough to push the jack out of place.

"*I got you!*" I scream, sprinting for the car. The sunshine, so pleasant a moment ago, is smothering as I fall to my knees beside the front tire. Gritty asphalt bites through my sweatpants while I feel for a ridge along the side of the frame, like the one Leo made me find on the Tracker.

"You okay?" I ask the guy, maneuvering the jack into place with a clatter. The car has pinned his arm so it blocks my view of his face, but his breathing comes short and fast from the deep shadow of the sedan.

"Fine, fine, just hurry up!" he cries back.

Fair enough. I focus on getting the handle of the jack in place and then rotate it as fast as I can manage. As soon as the car is a couple of inches higher, he scrambles from beneath it with a gasp, then stands, shaking. There's an angry red notch on his dark brown wrist, but his long, thoughtful face seems unhurt. He bowls forward, hands on knees, laughing almost hysterically with relief.

"Do you need to see Merlin?" I ask him.

"Merlin?" He blinks up at me, then shakes his head. "No, I'm fine. Really. Just gave me a scare."

"Let me go find someone with a car, you should get checked out—"

"No!" he says too fast, then seems to cover: "I'm fine. Really, it's cool."

He's backing away from me though, moving warily toward the house behind us. Probably he's just rattled from almost getting crushed. Or he's wondering why he doesn't recognize me.

"I'm the new girl, by the way, if you're wondering why you haven't seen me before," I explain. "I came here a couple days ago, from Jefferson. My name's Kay."

"The new girl?" His face clears; his smile becomes radiant. "Right, the new girl. Nice to meet you! I'm Starr."

"Well, if you're sure you're not hurt, Starr . . ." Would this be an awkward time to ask if I could join his room? Probably.

"Yeah, yeah, I'm great! And glad you came through here, let me tell you!" He waves me off, moving quickly up the porch steps toward the door. "I owe you one, new girl."

+ + +

Frank lifts his head when I come in that evening, but the skylight is still closed. I bang around the drawers of the desk, hoping to get Brick's attention. Nothing.

I climb up the ladder all the way to the closed skylight and listen for movement overhead, then finally push it open, announcing myself with: "Got any medium-rare steaks up here?"

The only answer is wind. The rooftop is empty.

But there's a bag of groceries, and new charcoals in the grill.

Okay. He's just not home yet. He's probably doing stuff for Expansion. I start the coals for dinner as distant laughter floats up from the front of the school. Hammering, rusty brakes, and tire squeals reverberate from the Auto Shop and its lot. My brain tries to turn the sounds into Brick opening the door, Brick climbing up the ladder.

But as many times as I turn to see him, he's never there.

I wrap Brick's giant navy fleece around me and flip through his old CD Trapper Keeper as the sun goes down, hating how much I like his music. Frank whines below until I climb down the ladder and give him a squirrel drumstick, but for once he seems more interested in the door.

"Fine, since you insist," I say, hoisting the torch off the wall. "Let's go find him."

+ + +

The throne room is dark when we get down to the music hall, the auditorium dim and heavy with crying and incense. Frank and I move quickly along the Flower Aquarium hall, where a rapt crowd is watching Artemis, expression hidden by a mask of dramatic eye makeup, as she lays out tarot cards. Her eyes find mine and she seems to stop midsentence, as though she's seen a bad omen.

I duck my head and hurry on.

We make our way to Moore's front lobby: the tiled space between the principal's office and the five sets of double doors that open onto its broad front steps and lawn. Beyond that is the parking lot, where Los Martillos have the first three heats lined up, the asphalt a grid of fresh chalk lines, the air tinged with exhaust. I turn away, stomach twisting, and find myself facing Moore's trophy case.

The trophies from Before are gone; now the case holds Grown teeth bolted on wooden mounts. I bring my torch closer in the darkening lobby to see them. The teeth have five roots, gnarled and thick as carrots. The base of each tooth is huge, a pool ball made of bone. The crown rises almost two feet, curving like a scythe to a tapered point fine as a needle.

I think of the red slug of muscle unspooling from Jermaine's sleeve, across the lab table in the Jefferson hospital. How far his eyes stared, even after he could no longer see me.

The door to the principal's office opens. A guard darts out with a box of beer empties, a low trap beat pulsing after him. Through the office doorway, a shirtless Max bounces effortlessly in and out of sight, like he's crossing a trampoline, shouting along with the music. Then Frank barks.

Brick comes to the door, and our eyes meet. He doesn't look back for Max's approval. He crosses the hall to me, bows his head to whisper in my ear:

"I'll be home soon."

"Promise?" My voice breaks.

"Yeah," Brick says. "Promise."

+ + +

When Brick comes in half an hour later, he finds me lying on the cot with Coldest Lakes playing. I watch him closely, wondering if he's been drinking, but nothing about him is unsteady. His eyes are almost too focused on me, as he moves to put out the torch in the flag stand.

"Don't," I say from the bed, flattened against the wall by the sleeping Frank. "I don't want to be in the dark."

"No?" His voice scrapes low in his throat. "What do you want, then?"

He sits on the floor, back to the wall, right across from me. He puts his hand up to shield his face, so the torchlight falls down his long, muscular forearm instead, tracing from the notch of his wrist, along the prominent veins, to the point of his elbow.

"I thought you never went to office parties?" My voice comes out small.

"It wasn't a party. It was more of a preparty. I left when the girls showed up."

"Poor things," I say, and he half smiles. "Come up here?"

He springs off the floor, whistling for Frank to get down. I turn and scooch to the wall so Brick can fit onto the narrow cot behind me, unseen. He's close enough I can feel the warmth radiating from his chest on my back, and his breath stirs the baby hairs at the nape of my neck. But he keeps a distance, a single inch of space between us.

In the space I imagine threads of lightning snapping back and forth, like a Tesla coil.

"Brick?"

"Yeah?"

I try to turn around to face him, but he says quickly:

"Could you stay like you are?"

"I want to see you." I turn and look at him.

"Feast your eyes."

The scarred half of his face is buried in our shared pillow, his muscled shoulder haloed by torchlight. His eye is half closed but misses nothing.

I imagine him Before, a guy who looks slightly too old for high school, forehead starting to line from so many practices in the sun. A guy I would've been way too intimidated to talk to. His chest is rising and falling like he's just won a race.

"The King gave me hell for leaving early," Brick says.

"Are you not supposed to hang out with me now?"

"We're not hanging out," he says. "I'm *guarding you*."

"Oh, right." I swallow. "Because I'm such a threat to the school and everything."

"It doesn't help that you're with Leo." A loaded pause, then: "The King said he caught you two making out."

"We weren't *making out*." I roll my eyes. "We were *talking*."

"About how you're with him now," he says, and after a moment I nod. "You really like that guy?"

"Why wouldn't I?" Technically not a lie, but the corner of my mouth jerks and he's watching for it.

"Say it. Say 'I like Leo.'"

I give Brick a hard look.

"You'll move in with him, but you won't say you like him?"

". . . I like Leo," I say carefully, and the corner of my mouth twists up hard. He starts laughing, and I try to turn away but he gently grips my shoulder so I can't, the lightning that lives in his hands instantly pinwheeling through me. He shifts so he's right over me. The shadows mask his face, but I can still feel him staring. I cover my face with one hand, but he pins it by my head, his own smile growing with mine.

"You're *bright red*." He laughs.

"Shut up."

"You are *a cranberry* right now."

I try and cover my smile with my other hand, but he pins that one the same way. Not rough, it's just play wrestling; it's frustrating how restrained he is. I find myself straining against him to make him hold me tighter, the unseen threads of energy between us growing brighter. He smells like summer, and he's shaped like a young god. He's laughing so hard: "Come on, Cranberry! Tell the truth! Let's hear it!"

"Okay, fine! I said yes! I'm *with* Leo now." I say it the way they do, and he releases me, returning to his side, his smile fading along with mine. I pick at the sleeping bag below us. "I don't want to be. I asked Max if I could stay with you, but he refused. He said—"

"Don't," he cuts me off.

"Don't *what*?"

"He's the King. He can say no for whatever reason he wants."

I turn my back on him then, stung. "How can you be such a good friend to such a bad guy?"

"How can you move in with someone you don't like?"

"I don't have any other options."

"It's warm now." Brick's voice stays very neutral. "Lots of people will be living out in the neighborhood houses for the summer. You could stay in my workshop, in the house with the garden. Take as long as you want finding a room."

I think of the little house surrounded by clumsy bees and honeysuckle. I could sweep aside some of the sawdust. I could set up a hammock for the warm months and have the whole place to myself.

It would be quiet, though. Completely outside of "court," out of sight of Max and everyone else. Unable to advocate for Jefferson, no excuse to talk with the people who think for themselves. Is Brick offering to keep *my* options open, or his?

"While Jefferson starves?" I say at last. "No. I need to be in a room to get my friends food. By order of the King."

A long silence. Broken at last by a loud, annoyed sigh from Frank against the wall. He gets up, turns around, and flops down again, impatient to have his bed back.

"So when are you moving out?" Brick asks.

"Tomorrow night." I fight to keep my voice from wobbling. "Assuming I come back, of course." That's the abyss of dread underneath all this: it's not just our last night together, it's possibly our last night. Brick's big warm hand rests comfortingly on my shoulder, and I cover my face.

Would it be weird if I begged him to wrestle me again?

Brick would think I was a cheater on top of a liar. And I can't tell him Leo knows we're just fake dating. He would have to tell Max, and then we'd all be in trouble.

"Everything's going to be all right," Brick says, voice low and deep.

"When, in all of human history, has everything been all right?" I say, my voice eerily calm. "If my face is on a music stand next time around, you better light a candle for me, okay? Because no one else will know who the hell I was."

His heavy arm sweeps around my waist and pulls me into him tight, my head resting in the curve of his throat, my back right against his chest, so close I can feel his heart between my shoulder blades.

It's *racing*. Just like mine.

I stare down at his rough knuckles grazing the inside of my arm.

The way they glance my skin with the rise and fall of our breath is the most intense thing I've ever felt.

I turn around to face him again, and if this is too far, then I'll have messed everything up. But, also, I might die tomorrow.

My hand goes up toward the unmarked side of his face as I lean in toward him.

He flinches back. A slight movement, but clear.

All feeling sweeps away from me, like when the tide goes out and everything from down deep gets laid out in the sun. I see everything that's wrong with me at once, with bright clarity: I am bald and pitiful and awkward. And stupid, *so stupid*. I turn around again to face the wall.

I just have to get through tonight, and then I can move in with Leo and never talk to Brick again.

"Well." Brick sits up, the word almost a sob. "We have to go kill a dragon tomorrow. We should get some sleep."

Yes, go, get out of here so I can cry in peace.

His weight shifts off the cot, and my hot tears streak down to the pillow. But he doesn't climb the ladder. His steps travel to the corner, there's a mechanical whir, and then "Curiouser" starts playing. I hear the hiss of him dropping the torch into a bucket, and the room goes dark.

Brick comes back. He gets on the bed again and hugs me to him, harder and closer than before. His lower arm wraps around me, spanning my waist. His other hand drifts, so carefully, from the curve below my ear to the top of my shoulder, and halts there. His breath feels faster on the side of my neck.

I don't understand. He doesn't want to kiss, but he likes cuddling? Are we friend-cuddling? *What is happening?*

"Turn back around?" he asks, his voice so deep, the thunder before the lightning.

But I can only shake my head. I don't want him to see I'm crying, and I don't understand what he wants from me. His weight shifts away—he's getting up? *No.* I clutch his arm—I won't let him. Now he's as confused as I am. But then his shoulders release, and both arms wrap around me, heavy and loose and comforting. And between the song and the weight of him around me, somehow I fall asleep.

"Hey, wake up," Brick says in the dark, what feels like a minute later. "It's time."

THE DRAGONS

KAY

When we pass the Cage on our way out, me in my coverall, Brick with his shield and crossbow, I stop. I fumble with the tight clasp of my locket, left closed for so long.

"Would you put this in the Cage for me?" I ask, holding it out to him. "Just in case."

He rubs his thumb over the flowers engraved on the pendant.

"Forget-me-nots," I say. He opens it to see my brother's eighth-grade portrait, and I add, "That's my brother, Arthur. He stayed home sick that day." I don't have to explain what day.

"I'm sorry."

"It was fast, at least." That's as close as I've gotten to admitting he's gone out loud. "Will you keep it for me?"

"You're going to tell me all about him tonight," Brick promises, then reaches through the bars and sets the locket on top of a box of paper towels, and we walk out to the parking lot.

Several of the cars have their headlights on, long white lines cutting through blue dark. The birds are starting to wake up, their calls describing the hidden galaxy of branches suspended above our town. I'm shivering hard as we make our way past row after row of vehicles to the first heat. When I stop at the third row, Brick turns to me, looks me straight in the eyes.

"I'll see you soon," he says. And then he continues on, to a souped-up white pickup truck in the first row.

The first row!

Beside Brick's car is Leo's black El Camino. The rest of the first heat are all Los Martillos; they're hard to miss in their black cars and black coveralls.

I find the Honda Civic. The guys nod to me, and the driver, Seth, shakes my hand. The guys go back to some detailed debate, and I hover at the edge of their circle.

"Yo, butthead!" Stokes yells. The cheerleaders are loading into the Jeep next to us. "You feeling that Lucid?" She grins. They're in their cheerleader uniforms and knee pads, faces freshly painted with red skulls. I give her a tight-lipped smile. I don't want to ask for her share of the potion, not after she warned me so many times to get my own.

Behind us the sky is starting to pale, the rooms gathering at their cars in full regalia: people in anime sailor dresses, cave man furs, and ghillie suits. The jumpiness builds with the crowd, some unseen pheromone ricocheting through the grid of cars; it's a million times as intense as the morning of the SATs, but with everyone dressed for Halloween.

The other climber in my car turns and offers me some rosin. I rub the plug of amber pitch between my hands, but it slips through my fingers and shatters on the pavement. I get down on the rough asphalt, grabbing for the pieces, the exhaust so thick I start to cough. Still on all fours, I see paint-spattered Converse sneakers pass by and hear Max's voice boom through a megaphone:

"Glory lies ahead, brothers and sisters! Glory and danger! Life and death! Nature, red in tooth and claw! That is the nature of Expansion! But *what* glory! For whoever kills the dragon this day will be crowned tonight as my High Duke! *Or* High Lady! And earn the *third Royal Crossbow*—"

"You gotta get in!" Seth calls. Everyone else is in the car now. It's time.

"I can't do this," I say, sliding into the back seat. All I want is out. I don't care what happens after that, I just want out. "I can't do this," I repeat. They look at me like I'm speaking gibberish, all of them with thick black lines of paint under their eyes like football players. These are the people I'm going to die with? I don't even know them!

"Here." Seth pulls a worn Altoids tin out of his coverall, flips the lid, and holds it out to me. The chalky pale green pills inside must be homemade, they're so irregularly shaped. "Put one under your tongue."

"What is it?"

"Something to get your shit together," the raider on the other side of me grumbles.

"It's like Lucid?" I ask warily.

"Hell no, we don't do magic, we're mechanics!" Seth says proudly. "That's not Lucid, it's Drive, and it's for Los Martillos, by Los Martillos, only. Welcome to the family." I take a pill from the tin, then hesitate.

"Right under the tongue, come on!" Seth says, and the guys all start drumming on their knees: "MAR-TEE-YO! MAR-TEE-YO!"

I put it under my tongue, cringing at the bitter metallic taste, and the car whoops.

"You're a Martillo now, girl!" The guy in the passenger seat turns around, reaching out with one fingertip to paint a pair of black stripes under my eyes. Then he hands me a pellet gun shaped like a pistol. The rest of the guys pull on balaclavas, the engine revs below us, and the car shoots forward.

I wanted calm, but that's not what I get as the pill dissolves. Instead, there is a sudden awareness of my whole body, down to my capillaries, down to the individual blood cells flowing through them. The guys play thrashing metal music, and I look out on the tree branches rolling overhead and the fences we speed through with a disembodied lightness, like I'm flying through them. The three guys needed to open each fence and close it after us as we drive by scream at the car, at the top of their lungs: *"GET SOME!"*

We roar through the last fence and out into the town, *my* town, my *hometown*. This is my town. Riding around in a car full of kids my age is what I should have been doing all this time, and these goddamn monsters robbed us of that, of everything. Our futures, our lives, our parents. Hunting them down and hanging up their heads is the only thing that makes sense.

SKRRREEEE-BANG!

A wheel of red sparks fills the dim sky ahead: one of the drivers has spotted a Grown to the east. Seth leans on the wheel, all of us shouting for him to hurry up, the car screeching toward trees that shudder and shiver as they come down. The trailing firework smoke hangs over a horde of cars racing down both lanes of the suburban street toward the beast.

It comes into sight all at once, framed in the center of the windshield: a Grown as long as a school bus. It's scuttling through the broken front window of the Quiznos across from Brockton Library. I am face-to-face with a dozen staring eyes rolling along the side of a long grinning head. The gray skin is warped and dimpled with the screaming, grown-over skulls of the people it's made from. *Our* people. Our teachers, our neighbors, our parents.

The Grown opens its mouth and becomes a hellgate of jaw and teeth. It strains like it's making some sound, but not one we're built to hear. The windshield of a dusty car cracks as the Grown's tail slaps against it, its pale underbelly vibrating with its soundless roar.

Brick's truck and Leo's low-rider almost graze each other racing toward it, but Seth pulls away toward Kiddytown, the local toy store I used to beg my mom to take me to, at the other end of the block. We passengers spill out into the unfenced Brockton. The other climber and I race toward Kiddytown's doors so we can get up on the roof, but they're locked. The Growns happened midmorning, so the doors of stores and houses around town are usually open. But Kiddytown, I realize, staring at its faded EVERYTHING MUST GO sign, had been closed a long time.

"We gotta go back!" the other climber says. We turn and almost slam into Amy, who's just climbed out of the cheerleader's Jeep.

"It's locked!" I scream.

"Leila!" Amy's face goes red as she calls for the Jeep, but she's too late. Both drivers are careening down the block, joining the other cars herding the Grown to the end of the street. "Tree!" Amy orders us, pivoting, and we follow her to a tall oak beside Kiddytown. There's a wrought iron enclosure around its trunk that helps us get to the higher branches. I throw my hands down to the Martillo climber.

"We could get over to the roof?" the Martillo calls over my head to Amy, hoisting herself up the tree ahead of us.

"No, we need to cover the cars!" Amy yells, and crawls out on a thick branch that extends past the sidewalk and into the street. If she can get just a couple feet farther, she'll have a perfect position. Down at the end of the street, the Grown is batting at the cars circling it, a cat playing with mice. Sparks fly and tires tear each time it makes contact. The drivers can steer it toward the power lines once we blind it. Until then, they're not safe, not even in their cars.

Amy, now in position at the low end of the thick branch, braces herself with one hand and lines up the shot. She takes a deep breath, and I hold in mine as well, and then she goes flying forward in a cloud of leaves.

A second Grown has her in its teeth. She jolts forward and backward as the Grown's massive head snaps side to side, the thick branch tearing like paper.

We never even saw it coming.

"Get up higher!" the Martillo climber wails as Amy drops from the Grown's mouth.

"We can't leave her!" I tell him, and he takes off, scrambling past me, making for the roof. The thick branch was torn in half when the Grown took Amy; the Grown itself has moved out of view. Heart thrashing, sweating and shivering, I crawl toward the fresh stump.

Below me, Amy's arms and legs all bend in the wrong direction. She is completely still, except for her hair. The wind pulls its strands across her staring eyes and unhinged jaw.

Shrieking axles pull my gaze to the end of the block.

Brick's truck moves directly across from the first Grown, and he revs his engine until it fixes its rolling eyes on him. Its huge jaws yawn open.

No. *No.*

A chemical calm takes hold as I extend my arm.

Focus, Amy says in my head.

I take a deep breath, then shoot. Then I shoot again, and again, a sob of hate and fear rising out of me.

The Grown rears back, two of its eyes streaming black blood, and wheels away from Brick's truck. It lurches to the other side of the street, where another fleet of cars has just arrived. Arrows and pellets fly into the other side of its unspeakable face, and it turns again, shuffling through two narrow buildings so stone molding breaks off and crashes to the ground below.

The cars swerve and stall in front of this avalanche, except for Leo's. The black El Camino wheels around 180 degrees, so hard I smell burning rubber. He speeds to the closest intersection, and all the other cars throw themselves into three-point turns and chase after him.

I look down at Amy's red hair, the angle of her neck. She's past helping.

"What the hell are we supposed to do?" the other climber hisses down to me from the roof. "All the cars are gone!"

Before I can answer, the tree heaves beneath me so hard I'm almost knocked off the branch, my pellet gun flying from my hand and spinning across the street below. The second Grown, the one that just killed Amy, is battering the base of my tree, trying to bring it down.

The Martillo climber disappears. This second Grown is relatively small, about the size of an SUV. The smell of rotting flesh radiates from its socket-pocked face as it shudders with a soundless roar. Then it rears back and batters the metal enclosure, hard. This tree is coming down. The enclosure has bought me time, but only seconds. *Think, Kay.* What part of the tree will hit the street hardest when it falls? The side facing the street. I need to get to the other side of the tree, while staying high enough that the Grown can't rake me off the branches.

So climb.

I reach for the branch above me and haul myself upward through the tree branches, which jounce harder every moment around me, feeling like I'm watching myself on a delay. As if everything I do, I've already done, and all I can think is, *How weird, how weird that I did that.*

And then the tree goes still, and I know this is the last moment. With a high shriek, the trunk gives, splits, and tilts, and the street comes flying up to meet me.

The jolt and recoil of impact almost throws me clear, but I cling to the branches with frozen hands. My breath is knocked out of me, but nothing is broken as far as I can tell. I'm alive, but I need to get clear of the fallen tree and on my feet. I wrestle my way through the now-vertical branches, broken glass under my knees, my hands, something warm and wet soaking through my pants. Amy's blood? Or my own? The smell of rot surrounds me, its breath so close. This is the last moment.

I turn around to look death in the face as an engine accelerates.

Brick's truck rams the Grown with a blistering crunch of metal, hard enough to knock it off its feet, and then Brick stands up out of the truck cab's sunroof and sends bolt after bolt at the Grown before flinging open the passenger door.

"COME ON!"

I hurtle toward the cab, flinging myself in as Brick wheels the car around, past the Grown still trying to get upright, and we fly through the intersection and around the next block.

He doesn't take his eyes off the road. But his hand moves to the middle of the truck's bench seat, searching until it finds mine, and our fingers interlink, tight as we can get them. The wind roars through the truck cab, so hard it feels like we're lifting off the ground, into the radiant sky ahead, and leaving the ruined world behind.

Ahead of us, dozens of tricked-out cars surround the Grown that came out of Quiznos, now lying on its side. Even horizontal, it's taller than all the cars and people warily approaching. Every one of its eyes is extinguished, its side peppered with pellets and arrows and even a pitchfork, different colored ribbons and streamers fluttering at their ends to claim the shots. Brick parks and we get out, walking to the edge of the crowd.

In its center, Leo is kneeling on the Grown's shoulder, pulling at a deep-set arrowhead buried where the Grown's heart must be. Blood thick and black as crude oil spurts up, bathing his arms, spattering his face. He sets his jaw, then yanks the arrow out with both hands, the blood rushing up like a fountainhead briefly before flowing freely down its side. Leo, bathed in iridescent black, stands and holds the arrow over his head, eyes brighter than ever with his face smeared in blood.

"The Grown is dead, and I killed it! For Los Martillos!" Leo yells. A cheer answers him from the guys and girls in black, but everyone else seems uncertain. Whispers leak through the crowd, spreading fast and wide as water running downhill.

"He drove it into the power lines, I saw," a guy in a ghillie suit says to a girl in a bikini and raver boots.

"The King won't allow it." She frowns.

"But Leo got the heart shot, we all saw!"

Brick looks down at me. "I need your help."

"Anything."

He jerks his head toward his truck bed, and I follow him over. He throws a tarp back to reveal a chain saw.

"After I congratulate Leo," Brick says, "I want you to walk this over to him." I start to protest, but he goes on: "Loyalty during Expansions is everything. People will remember you showed up for your room when it counted."

"Okay . . ." I'm worried what this will mean, but before I can find the words, he climbs up into the truck bed and whistles piercingly, again and again, cutting through the hubbub until the crowd turns.

"Congratulations!" Brick hollers to Leo. "Leo and Los Martillos! I recognize your kill on behalf of King Max!" He carefully hands down the chain saw to me, a mass of oily gears and teeth. I walk unsteadily, straining under its weight, toward Leo. The crowd parts, every face turned to watch me, none of them smiling.

"*Leo* gets to be the freaking *Duke*?"

"And he's with that new girl?"

"So she's Duchess now or something?"

"Haaaa, yeah right."

When I get to the hideous mass of the Grown, Leo leans forward, wraps an arm around my neck, and kisses me. His lips are hot and dry, and he flutters with full-body excitement after his big kill, but the dragon blood is all I register: it tastes like death, like rotten milk and stagnant water, and I just want away from him. I feel myself go red, but Leo doesn't notice; his eyes are on the crowd as he turns from me. He lifts the chain saw over his head, and they all cheer now.

I look around for Leila, see her and Stokes, and silverfish to where they stand.

Stokes knows as soon as she sees my face. She bursts into tears. Leila looks from her to me, panic setting in: "Where's Amy?"

"I'm sorry." My voice breaks, and then we're all crying, as the applause from the crowd builds around us. "I'm so sorry. It took her right out of the tree."

"We have to go get her! We can't just leave her!" Stokes sobs to Leila. I start to follow them, but Stokes shoves me back. "Not you!" she yells in my face. "Just her friends!"

"I *was* her friend—" The sputter of the chain saw engine cuts me off as Stokes and Leila slip away, and the crowd surges forward, pulling me along with it. I turn around to see Leo lower the chain saw blade to the throat of the Grown. Black blood splatters up and bathes him, and then flesh flies from the ripping chain in thin, papery flakes like ash. Everyone around me starts screaming and dancing in the falling flakes like they're snow. Something in me snaps. I hear myself screaming, too, hands raised over my head, like our voices are proof: We're still here, doing what living things do. Going on.

+ + +

"Don't!" Seth shouts. We're in the middle of the house El Martillo gets to scavenge, and I had stepped aside to wash the dragon blood off my arm and face, left by Leo's kiss. But Seth knocks the bottle of water out of my hands, takes my arm, and firmly kneads the blood into my skin, like it's lotion. It's dark and thick as molasses, and I gag on the smell.

"Water on dragon blood makes it burn, makes your skin bubble up. It hurts like hell," Seth says, releasing me. "Just rub it in. And don't go for a swim for a day or so."

I am learning a lot about dragons today. Like, they stay about three hundred feet from dead bodies of their kind until all the flesh flakes from the bone. That usually takes a week, so the last heats work night and day to fence in the new territory.

The rest of us ransack the empty houses, left untouched by human hands since Before. We go from room to room, throwing open windows to get rid of the smell. Teeth grinding, head pounding, I snatch food from the kitchen, metal cutlery from the drawers, batteries and paper towels from the hall closet. I still feel like I'm not here, like I'm sitting in the back of my head watching a movie of my own hands ripping the sheets from a bed, slamming a family photo against the wall, shaking the glass out so we can take the gold frame.

The sun is low in the sky by the time we're done, having stripped everything in the house but the walls, which will be ripped out by the fence crew. Then we load into the car and head back with the windows down, evening breeze rolling through, in hollow silence, draped in whatever spoils caught our eye.

Back at Moore, torches and road flares mark a path from the parking lot to the auditorium, and people walk along it with their arms linked, holding each other in a weary ecstasy of relief. I find myself clasped by strangers who tell me good job, and I hug them back hard. I end up sitting between more strangers but feel somehow completely at home.

A lush red velvet curtain hangs across the stage, and as the auditorium fills, the torches along the walls are extinguished, one by one, until everything goes black.

A line of theater kids walks onstage holding tall unlit candles. They make a semicircle and pass a flame, one to the other, gold altar robes glimmering, voices swelling, building to a hallelujah chorus. And just as they crescendo to a high note, Artemis takes center stage.

For once she is not too much. Onstage, her gestures, her makeup, her personality fit. She is magnificent in white and red, and her huge, darkly lined eyes are mesmerizing.

"Tonight, we honor the sacrifice of hero Amy Hall, of the Cheerleaders!" she calls out into the dark. "And of hero Omar Khan, of the Lone Stars! We love you, Amy! We love you, Omar!"

A muffled sob rises from the back, but nothing else breaks the silence of the dark auditorium.

"Our heroes are surrounded in light and glory. Their sacrifice gives us our future, and their names will live on, in Brockton's future, forever!" Artemis cries. "And now, please rise for our great King Max!"

I stand with the rest as Max enters, wearing the red swimmer's coat, steel crown, and an expression of total solemnity. He launches into a speech, but he doesn't project as well as Artemis; he sort of has to scream. I find myself tuning out until he says, "I come to knight the new Duke, and declare him and his line to be royal . . ."

Knight the Duke? The choir starts singing again, some ancient hymn I recognize from a dozen different movies but have never heard live. It was meant to be heard live.

"*Miserere mei, Deus: secundum magnam misericordiam tuam . . .*"

The harmony of the voices is unearthly. Their sadness washes over me, and everything I thought bounced off me this afternoon breaks through now: the family's smiling faces in their photo, fluttering to the floor. The way the Grown looked at me, wanting me to die. And Amy. Amy's perfect form as she braced herself to take the shot. Her excitement when she gave me the bag of toiletries. Her hand closing on my shirt before I slid off the roof. Her body on the ground.

A sob rises from the pit of my stomach. Why am I here when she's not? I am so guilty, and so painfully grateful; it is astonishing to be safe again, to be at all. A perfect high note pierces through the music, and through my haze of tears Leo enters stage right.

His face was made to be surrounded by red and gold. The pure sculpted lines of his jaw and cheek, the lift of his chin and well-earned weariness of his shoulders. He looks like a figure from a legend, cut out from the glittering gold chorus by his spotless black coverall.

Wait. Spotless? How?

Last time I saw him, he was covered head to toe with Grown remains. This is a new coverall, with no evidence of gray Grown flakes. But his face has been artfully smudged with ash in a way that calls out his sculpted cheekbones, and his hair is perfectly tousled. We're supposed to think he came straight from the Grown, but that coverall isn't just spotless, it's *tailored*. This isn't a uniform; it's a costume.

Artemis, onstage, is watching Leo with a look that hurts, an artist in love with her own creation. She tailored the suit; she probably knows his measurements by heart. I realize she planned the red and gold to set off his black figure. And she did it all right under Max's nose!

Merlin sweeps in from stage left in a navy men's suit. There's a glistening sword resting on her wheelchair's arms, and a crossbow on a cushion in her lap. The sword she hands to Max, her expression solemn. Max nods to Leo, who walks over and, after a moment's hesitation, kneels before him. Max stares down at Leo's bowed head, sword in hand, like he is considering lopping it off. But instead, he taps Leo with the polished blade on each shoulder. He gives the sword back to Merlin, then takes up the crossbow—his father's, or his, from Before—and offers it to Leo.

The gold helmet comes last, brought out on a red cushion by a tall, scrawny guy who reminds me somehow of an asparagus, his hair short on the sides and long and curly up top. The helmet extends in panels that frame the eyes and shield the face. Max holds it up, letting the gold metal catch the light, and the audience murmurs appreciatively. Then he sets it on Leo's head, his voice ringing to the back of the auditorium:

"I command you rise, Leo Gutierrez of Los Martillos, right royal Duke of Moore!"

Leo rises, and they shake hands, like the captains of two rival teams making a show of sportsmanship; though whether this is the shake before or after the game is hard to say. The chorus cuts abruptly into the part of "Ode to Joy" that even I recognize as the audience shoots out of their seats in a standing ovation.

"*PARTY TIME!!!*" someone howls from the upper balcony, and the bubble of reverence breaks as the doors to the lobby fly open.

A path of flares leads us all to the gym, where a band set up on a platform goes absolutely wild. An entire scoreboard of sparklers lights up behind them, filling the gym with frenetic white light. The theater kid dancers are lined up at the tops of the bleachers, trails of swirling Sterno making figure eights through the dark. Moore must have expanded through the Party City at some point because everyone has at least one glow stick necklace around their throat, and handfuls of them are being offered up, along with cups of warm beer from several kegs in the corner.

I'm pressing myself against the gym wall, intimidated by the crowd and scanning for Brick, when a gold flash streams through the double doors with a scream of:

"MAKE WAY FOR THE DUKE!"

Leo is carried in by Los Martillos, all of them bellowing "*MAR-TEE-YO, MAR-TEE-YO!*" and swinging their fists over their heads. It quickly becomes a faster "DUKE! DUKE! DUKE!" as everyone on the gym floor starts jumping in unison, Leo beaming through his helmet, crossbow lifted overhead. I can't believe Max actually gave it to him, but there it is. A sea of hands reaches out to touch him as the band tears through a punk cover of "Hail to the Chief."

For a split second our eyes lock. Then a wave of people crashes between us. I slide against the gym wall until I feel the cool breeze of the exit and duck out. When every girl in the place is trying to get at your fake boyfriend, the place of a good fake girlfriend is outside the room.

I drink in the cool evening air and look out on the dark lawn, where the only light comes from the neon glow sticks strewn in the damp grass and the cold stars in the black sky. The lawn is lousy with couples cuddled up on blankets and groups of friends slapping each other's backs and laughing at nothing. I attended maybe two keggers in all of Before, and I remember people hanging on each other then, but this is deeper somehow. Like no one can quite believe they're still here. Like the flip side of unbearable terror is unbearable relief.

One of Max's guards, Nunchucks, is nearby. I give him a wave. "You know where Brick is?"

"Fence!" he calls back. "Why? Need something?"

"Just need to ask him something." I shrug. "He does first heat *and* fence? Geez!"

"He stays until the second building crew comes through at sunset. So he should be back soon."

"Are they sure it's safe?" I ask as he turns back to his friends. They chime in:

"Totally. It's completely safe now!"

"You made it. Relax!" A girl smiles at me. "You want a beer?"

I shake my head. I'm still wrung out from whatever the hell Drive was; it's burned through my energy but not my anxiety, which is returning at full volume. At last, I spot Frank, sitting at the curb before the broad expanse of the parking lot. I go over and sink down beside him, getting out the dog treats I pocketed for him while scavenging. He eats them out of my hands with gratifying smacks.

Deep bass from the gym throbs behind me, the lyrics getting

picked up by the crowd, cheers building and surfacing like rip tides within the sound: "*LEE-OH, LEE-OH!*"

I feel a physical pang of hope each time new headlights wash over the parking lot, and a sinking dread when they're not him. Car after car trickles in, but never Brick. Frank whines and presses close to me.

"Hey!" Nunchucks's friend yells. "Kay, right? You're with Leo? He's looking for you!"

"What?" I call back.

"My friend said all of Los Martillos are looking for Kay. Leo wants to see you!"

Frank is on his feet, though. A tall pair of headlights sweeps up the long dark field, the rumble of an engine makes Frank whine, then he runs off before I see where the truck has parked.

As I chase after Frank, the girl shouts: "Wrong way! Leo's in the gym!"

Brick lopes across the lawn from the parking lot, broad shoulders slumped, chin ducked, heading straight for the music wing entrance. Like he's skipping the dance altogether.

"Hey!" I call, running toward him. "Brick!"

"Cranberry!" Brick slows to a stop before pivoting toward me. He takes a small step in my direction, then pauses. I do the same, like we're gauging how far we can go out on new ice. We land about three feet apart.

"There's a dance going on in the gym," Brick says stiffly.

"I hadn't heard!" I call over the throbbing drums. Brick does his half smile, then looks down at the ground, thick neck tensed like he's straining against some invisible leash. "Brick, I wanted to ask you something—"

"HEY! KAY!" the girl from the field calls, staggering toward us. "YOUR BOY LEO! HE WANTS YOU! RIGHT NOW!"

Brick's head falls back. For once, in the moonlight, it's the unscarred half of his face that seems pained.

"What?" he says sharply, not looking at me, and I falter. But he saved me today. His fingers were so tight in mine, I could feel his heartbeat in my palm. He asked me to turn to him last night. I either tell the truth, or I live a lie.

"I'm sorry if this is too much." I am talking too fast. "And I'm sorry if it makes it weird, but I really need to ask if—"

The shriek of a breaking tree right at the edge of the parking lot cuts me off. Birds rush overhead, a wild scream from the lawn becomes a cascade of panicked howls, and I turn to see three massive Growns running straight for the open doors of Moore's gym.

THE WOUND

KAY

Brick strong-arms me to his truck. He gets his crossbow from the cab, then lights up a torch from a stash in the back and hands it to me.

"Take this, and stay behind me. If I say run, you go straight to Merlin's." His hand is on my neck, his eyes intent. "You understand?"

I nod and hurry alongside him toward the screaming and wailing.

As we enter the gym, glimpses of hell are caught in the halo of my torch: a rolling eye, not a Grown's but a girl's. The flash of bared, scythe-shaped teeth drooling blood overhead. Max, holding up a crossbow, with blood streaming down his arm. The screams and moans are drowned out by the splintering crash of the bleachers breaking under the weight of the monsters. Bodies are strewn across the floor, drunk or fainted or dead, I don't know. I slip on what feels like a hand and look up in time to see a crossbow bolt hitting Brick in the leg.

"*NO!*"

He rocks forward, almost the entire bolt buried in his upper thigh.

"*BRICK!*" I grab Brick's arm with my free hand and tuck under his shoulder. He collapses against me, almost sending us both to the floor, but I keep upright. I swing my torch in an arc, looking for any help, and see Nunchucks. "HELP ME WITH BRICK!" I scream. He blinks back at me, dazed, and I yell louder: "I *ORDER* you in the name of the *KING* to help me get your *CAPTAIN* up to Merlin's room *NOW!*"

That gets through. He helps hoist Brick up between us, Brick's struck leg all red, his whole body seizing with anguish. We drag him into the moonlit hallway, people practically running up our backs to get away from the stench of the Growns.

"Hold on, just hold on," I whisper as we race for the stairs.

+ + +

Merlin's assistant will only open the door once she hears we have Brick. By then he's passed out.

"Bring him in!" Merlin says. "Marissa, make a pallet in between the lab tables—"

Merlin cuts his gray sweatpants away. The crossbow bolt, a black carbon rod the width of a bullet and length of an arrow, is half-buried in the powerful muscle of his thigh. The yellow flare at its end twitches with his involuntary spasms.

"Should we pull it out?" Marissa says, snapping on gloves.

"*No!*" I cry.

"Absolutely not," Merlin says almost at the same time. "Right now, it's like a plug. We pull it out, he could start bleeding internally." She shoots a glance at her books. "That much I know at least."

She doesn't know how to take the bolt out. Neither do I. What, we're going to learn on Brick?! This can't be happening. He'll die without someone who can do this properly.

Like Nirali. But she's all the way across town.

Someone pounds on the Cavern door.

"OPEN IN THE NAME OF THE KING!" Max screams. Then, soft and panicked: "*Nia?! You in there?*"

Merlin throws open the door. "What the hell is going on down there?" she hisses, and I sit up, peering over the lab table.

"The dragons are taken care of," Max says, dark circles around his eyes. His crown and coat are missing; his shirt is bunched up and held tight around his left arm.

"How many dead?"

"We won't know till sunrise." Max leans against the lab table, eyes burning into Merlin's. "They're setting the wounded out in the gym. The worst ones will come here, but I need to talk to you first." He ducks his head toward his arm, voice dropping to a panicked whisper: "I can't feel it. Why can't I feel it?"

Merlin peels the shirt away from the arm and looks at the wound. I can't see it from this angle, but from the hiss she makes, I know it's not good.

"That looks serious, Max," she says in a low voice.

"Why can't I move it?"

"I don't know! I'm not a doctor!"

"But Nirali is." I stand, and both of them turn to me.

"No, she's not," Merlin snaps.

"If Nirali were here, she would know what to do. She could fix his arm." And more importantly, she could fix Brick.

Merlin is glaring, but Max's eyes are hopeful. She turns on him angrily.

"She's at Jefferson. Even if she could help, how would we even—"

"We can call them at dawn," I say, staring Max down. "On Kyle's radio."

†RA-VERSE:
†O †RAVEL ACROSS

NIRALI

Tyler is crying as he starts the van. It's a disturbing kind of cry. Just tears streaming around his big, thick, grimacing features, face slack, eyes staring, as the engine warms below us.

"I hope the Growns take us out, I really do." Tyler turns to me. "You know that? Just so you can see what you put us through."

Every other Scavenging Team member that came back from Costco yesterday is in critical condition right now—and not that many of them made it back. Losing so many of the people who provide our food, and getting absolutely no food in return, hit Jefferson hard. Simon locked himself up in the radio room, anticipating a full-scale mutiny. When the call from Moore came in at dawn, it was like a miracle. They offered food for the whole school, if "that one surgeon's kid who went to MediCamp" would come help them out.

But since Tyler is the only Scavenging Team member capable of driving right now, I am making this outing in the worst possible circumstances. Leaving the shelter of our barricades for the first time since Before with a guy who despises me. The back seat of his van is soaked through with blood, the smell so strong it stings the back of my throat like a nosebleed. I have spent the night managing four different amputations. I know exactly what Growns are capable of. And now I am being openly threatened.

"Sometimes," Tyler goes on, "I think Kyle took off just to get you off his back for a while. You always got to run things, you always think you know better. And you don't." He shakes his head, tears still streaming. Then he clears his throat, and pulls out of park. "So here's how this is going to work."

Tyler turns the nose of the van down the driveway toward the street.

"You will have to be spotter, which means if you see or hear a tree go down, you tell me. You see a group of deer running or birds flying, you tell me. You see a Grown—" His voice goes thick with sarcasm. "You know what they look like, right?"

"Yes. I'll tell you." I keep my voice neutral. I am not going to distract him by arguing. There's no point. He's always hated me, and frankly I'd be more offended by his approval. I turn to the window, reach up, and tighten my ponytail.

We're a couple of intersections out when Tyler does a double take in the rearview mirror. Behind us, a gray shape beyond the trees that I had mistaken for a shed sidles closer to the street.

"Is that—?"

Tyler takes the corner hard enough to snap me side to side, and the shape lunges.

My orbital bone cracks against the passenger door as the van's frame crumples around us, the grass and sky spinning with me as their axis as we slide off the road and down, at an angle a van can't go. Blood-soaked rags thump from floor to ceiling as the van rolls. I cling to the armrests as gravity shifts and the ceiling of the van bulges toward me, and then everything goes still and silent except for a monotone *ding, ding, ding*.

I'm upside down in a ravine, body barely held in place by the seat belt. Tyler's already gone, the driver's-side door wide open to the blue sky. And then the van lurches forward, the Grown not done with me yet, and I grab at my seat belt with trembling hands. I have to get out.

I get the belt undone and drop hard onto the ceiling below, then frantically knock out the spiderweb of shattered windshield before crawling on hands and knees through the gravel and broken glass at the side of the road. A Grown the size of a tree has wrapped itself around the car, its head disappearing into the driver's-side window as I get to my feet and break into a sprint.

"*NIRALI!*" Tyler screams from across the road. I can just see him, hidden behind a garage door that he's bracing one foot off the ground. I run up the drive and roll through the gap, warm, pebbly asphalt swiping my cheek. I catch a dim glimpse of messy garage as I get to my feet, just before the door rattles shut behind me and everything goes black.

"*We need to find the keys!*" Tyler hisses.

Yes, of course. How? We blindly grope the walls. I knock my shin against a lawn mower. Then my hand lands in a bowl of clinking metal, and my fingers close on a thick key fob, a button. The headlights of an old minivan flash behind us.

The garage door cracks inward with a sound like a gunshot, a thread of light splitting its main panel.

"Get in the back and lie down!" Tyler yells, grabbing the keys from me. I scramble into the back seat footwell, burrowing under a pile of old gym clothes until my face is pressed to the floor mat, hiding like a child. The Grown batters at the garage door as Tyler begs the cold motor to turn over.

The garage door comes apart in a burst of blinding daylight just as the engine comes to life. Tires shriek as Tyler skillfully maneuvers around the Grown, just slipping past it. I peek from under the clothes up at the rearview window, and seven of the Grown's rolling eyes meet mine through a fog of its steaming breath. The thing slams its hideous head straight into the glass, which showers down on me as the axles whine and a back tire explodes. The minivan fishtails, tires shrieking as the Grown tries to mount the roof, the corner of the car sinking so far white sparks leap off the road.

"Damn it all to HELL!" Tyler weeps. He punches the gas and swerves hard enough the Grown slides off, but now we're riding the rim and zigzagging wildly down the street. Smoke burns my throat. I sit up to see black fumes rolling off the windshield.

"What if it explodes?" I grab Tyler's shoulder.

"At least we die fast!"

And then the engine stutters, shrieks, and stalls, sending me tumbling forward.

"COME ON!" Tyler throws back the sliding minivan door. "COME ON, IT'S GONNA CATCH UP—"

I scramble down into the street and run alongside him. There's the rush of water below us, the green lamp posts that line Brockton Bridge above us.

"Downtown?" I gasp, looking around. "We're downtown?"

The Growns coalesced from crowds of adults. The larger the crowd, the larger the Grown. So here, on the busiest street in Brockton, the largest Growns formed. Out of crowded restaurants and bustling shops, monsters exploded. Now it looks like a war zone, every glass front blown out across the sidewalk, trampled cars rusted out from the winter snows, mangled mannequins from the Urban Outfitters strewn up and down for blocks. Weeds wave limply from the rooftops above, like surrender flags: *We lost.*

"We're almost at the halfway point!" Tyler says. "Come on, come on!"

He grabs my sleeve and yanks me along. I don't just hear the Grown behind us, I can feel it approaching, like an 18-wheeler crawling by in the next lane on the highway as we race toward the intersection.

Ahead of us, a Grown twice the size of the one chasing us has its horrible face upraised, tilted blindly toward the sky, as though staring straight at the sun.

And as our footsteps fall still, it cranes its terrible head and fixes its eyes on us.

Wordless, nauseous, I pull Tyler down a small side street, toward a tiny Indian grocery my mom used to visit, with two Growns now after us.

We run past the brightly painted orange storefront and down its narrow brick side alley when something stranger than a Grown stops us short: a person, out here, all alone.

The tall, handsome Black guy stands astride a motocross motorcycle at the end of the alley, wearing a bizarre metal backpack and a face shield he has raised in one gloved hand. He stares at us through a shower of tiny yellow leaves, looking so stricken that for a moment I think he's going to say my name.

A car alarm goes off on the other side of the grocery.

"*Let's go!*" Tyler yanks me forward as the rotten smell of Growns fills the alleyway. The guy on the motorbike pulls down the face shield, guns his motor, then shoots right past us—so close Tyler and I have to flatten ourselves against opposite walls—charging right for the monsters. There's a sustained rush, like the sound of a fire hose, and strange blue light bounces across the brick in front of me. But before I can look back, Tyler drags me forward, bawling over the motorbike engine: "*LET'S GO LET'S GO LET'S GO!*"

Bursting out of the alleyway, we turn the corner toward Kiddytown, and almost run into the towering struts of a fence under construction. Hands reach through, voices yelling encouragement as they pull us between the fence posts, to safety. I collapse onto the asphalt—for a minute or ten I don't know. But I'm helped to my feet by a ring of concerned strangers.

Tyler is standing apart, weeping again. But this time his tears wind around a beatific smile. He stares with a lovestruck expression at the headless body of a Grown. Bits of it blow away in the warm spring wind, harmless as gray confetti. Tyler looks at me, eyes still streaming, and for a moment all our enmity is forgotten in silent understanding: *They can die.*

Nothing has ever been so beautiful.

+ + +

A couple "Motorheads" drive us the rest of the way to Moore while explaining "dragons" won't come near their own dead. They've brought us rounds of fresh bread, so I put that in my mouth instead of laughing out loud. *Dragons . . .* they're losing it out here.

They drive us to a towering wall, a crazy quilt of bone and Sheetrock and raw lumber. As three guys open a concealed panel, the Motorheads proudly explain their wall system keeps Moore "free."

Until last night, I almost say, but swallow the words with my bread.

The guys are far more impressive than their walls. They're muscled like serious athletes, skin tan and hair gleaming. And when we get to the school, everyone there radiates health. Even the nurses waiting for me in the gym hospital, who were AP Biology students Before, look like they've picked up bodybuilding since. They are handling general first aid, blunt trauma, and sprains for about fifty patients. A smaller group of more serious cases are upstairs with someone called Merlin. So I leave Tyler to talk shop with the Motorheads, who seem like Scavenging Team types. Then I go up to inspect their so-called ICU, preparing myself for the worst.

Instead, I find another miracle: Kay Kim. Alive. Alive and *well*: her heart-shaped face slightly sun-kissed, her buzz cut long enough it's gone from a blue shadow against her pale scalp to a shining black sheen. She rises between two lab tables as I enter, her eyes going wide, then she practically runs toward me. We meet in a hug.

"*Kay?*" I choke. She smells so clean. I pull away, scanning her face: "Did you—are you—" *Tyler tried to kill you. Do you know that? Because he's downstairs right now.* "What happened to you?"

"We'll go over all the Jefferson stuff later, but right now you need to see Brick. Please." Kay's fingers dig into my arms. "He was shot in the leg last night. You have to tell us what to do—"

She pulls me back between the two lab tables before I can protest. And when I see the patient she's taking me to, I stop resisting and stare.

I've never seen someone who's survived such extreme trauma. Half his face is gone: the zygomaticus almost completely severed, nose sheared away on one side almost to the skull; the tube of oxygen leading to a tank has been taped to exposed cartilage. Even Before, damage this severe would've required the talents of a brilliant plastic surgeon and multiple grafts and surgeries. But it speaks to their level of care that he's still alive. For now.

Because the bolt in his leg is no picnic, either. The injuries I deal with when the Scavenging Team comes back are teeth punctures or traumatic amputations. I don't have to remove missiles, usually. I know *technically* how to do it, but I've never done this kind of operation and I have not slept in almost twenty-four hours.

With any luck, I can put this off until I've had some rest.

Kay is staring at me so hard she looks like she's praying to me inside her head.

"Good job not removing the bolt," I tell her. "Since he's stable for now, let me check in with the other patients, and then we'll prep him for surgery. It'd be amazing if we had proper scalpels and some kind of anesthesia, but they won't have—"

"Sure we do," comes a soft, deep voice, and I turn to see a Black girl in a wheelchair and royal-blue hoodie coming up behind us. "We scored an ambulance on our third Expansion. And captured a CVS and a medical supply store on our fourth." Her smile is girlish, and she has very large, thickly lashed feminine eyes, but her stare has all the arrogance of the hottest guy in the room.

"I'm Merlin." She looks me up and down. "You must be 'Doctor' Nirali."

". . . Just Nirali is fine. Nice to meet you."

"Merlin is in charge of Moore's hospital," Kay says.

"Let me take you around to see the patients," Merlin says, and I squeeze Kay's hand before following after her. I have to warn Kay that Tyler is here, but he won't come help with the wounded anytime soon, and these patients have no time to lose.

There are four beds going, camping cots set up between the lab tables, and all the patients in them are unconscious. But Merlin's diagnoses are impressive, and she's kept things relatively sterile and is managing twenty-four-hour care—no small feat.

"Marissa can get you whatever you need," Merlin says, before sweeping away to another patient.

"I'll show you the supply closet." Marissa smiles.

I follow her across the hall and through a door marked *Physics Library*. Its bookshelves have been cleared of books and stocked instead with massive blue Tupperware bins. I take one down, pull off its lid. Inside are zippered pouches, neatly labeled and alphabetized. This first bin is Advil through amoxycillin.

After my winter spent scrounging for basic disinfectants, I'm speechless. If we'd had even that *one* bin, half the people this winter—I can't even finish the thought.

"Do you organize it differently at Jefferson?" Marissa asks.

I would laugh, except it could turn to tears. "This is fine," I manage. "Thank you. I'll gather some things and join you in a moment." She nods and hurries back to their ICU.

For just a moment I cup my face in my hands, overwhelmed.

"Everything alright, 'doctor'?" Merlin's voice again. She smoothly wheels past me to the shelves.

"Yes! A little tired, that's all." I give her a tight-lipped smile. "And you really don't have to call me doctor. Just Nirali is fine."

"I'm confused. Kay said you called yourself a doctor at Jefferson. Isn't that true?"

I don't like her tone.

I reach up and tighten my ponytail. "They call me a doctor at Jefferson as a shorthand for what I do. Which is treat the wounded, and the sick, and save lives. Which is why *you* asked me to come here and help your school."

"The King asked you," Merlin corrects me, "after Kay told him all about your candy-striping and whatnot. But I've spent a lot of time in hospitals myself, and it's never occurred to me to call myself *a doctor*." She looks at me sharply, a look like a shove. "Lots of power in that word. But maybe I take that a little more seriously than you do."

My jaw falls open, and she's about to go on with her tirade, when sharp static interrupts. A muffled whine of feedback comes from behind her chair, and then a tinny voice:

"Wizard Merlin? Wizard Merlin, do you copy?"

Her eyes flash to me as my hand drifts up to my mouth.

"Wizard Merlin?" the voice repeats, and with a grumbled curse, she pulls a walkie-talkie out of her wheelchair backpack. The voice says, clearer now: "Wizard Merlin, do you read me?"

"Ten-four, Chris. What's up?" she answers.

"Will you need the elevator this next hour? I was going to help in the gym."

"No, Chris, not until dinner."

"Okay, cool. Chris out."

The static fills the small library; he's waiting on her to end the call. At last, she says: "Wizard Merlin out."

The walkie-talkie drifts down from her mouth, the silence very loud.

". . . I'm sorry." I smile at her coldly. "But did you just call yourself—"

"Look." Merlin holds up a hand. "I know that sounded bad, but to be fair, there is no degree involved in—"

"*Bad* isn't the word. *Delusional* might be more accurate. *Hypocritical*, for sure." I walk toward her. "You call me out for pretending to be a doctor, and you're pretending to be a *wizard*?"

"I'm not pretending anything," she says, like she means it. "I practice magic."

I cross my arms over my chest, lean back, and fix her with my hardest stare: *You have thirty seconds to walk that back before you lose my respect.*

Merlin lifts her chin. "How can you live in a world with dragons and not believe in magic?"

"Because I believe in *empirical logic*?" My voice is ice. "I'm sorry, Harry Potter, but the things that just came through here are *not* dragons, and you had better have a plan for keeping them out that doesn't involve the words 'hocus pocus'—"

"Moore has an advanced fence system—"

"That just failed spectacularly," I cut her off. I haven't been this openly bitchy all year. I've missed it.

"Okay. I wasn't going to go there, but okay." Merlin redirects herself so she's straight across from me. "You want to talk about *failing spectacularly*, then let's talk about Jefferson."

"Excuse me?"

"You are starving," she says, matter-of-fact. "You're up to your eyeballs in roaches, you make people spend their birthdays in jail, and Kay was low-key assassinated. If *anyone* is failing here, it's Jefferson's leadership."

My jaw drops again.

"We did an investigation. We know how the dragons got in," she goes on, her expression harder with every word. "The panel in our west fence was closed incorrectly. It's secured now, and dragon remains have been scattered along the west wall as backup—"

"Dragon remains? How did you get dragon remains?"

"We killed the ones that came in." Her eyes are steady on mine. I fight not to look impressed, but it must reach my face because her expression turns smug. "You want to make fun of magic, but all of Jefferson is sitting around waiting for a miracle to save them instead of going out and dealing with how the world is now. Jefferson hasn't killed one dragon since Before. You don't even know how."

My hands make fists.

"So don't you dare stand there and sneer at us, when by your own 'empirical logic,' you're the ones who have failed."

I'm choking with rage, but what can I say? I'm desperately trying to come up with some counter, when the door flies open and Kay rushes in.

"Brick is bleeding out!"

+   +   +

The patient had rolled on his side in his sleep, twisting the crossbolt deeper. The wound is now pouring blood. His blue sheets are purple with it; blood pools on the floor, sloshes under my shoes as we run to the bed. *Exsanguinate* is the vocabulary word. An artery must have been hit, and *please* not severed, but either way the clock has started, and I have to operate now. I hunch over the gloves station they've set up and wring my hands with sanitizer. Kay, at my side, is no help. She's frantically sobbing and tugging at me like she's drowning. I need her out of here.

"Get Kay out right now," Merlin tells a helper, before taking Kay's place beside me. She offers a hospital mask; she has one on already. "What do you need?" she asks as I put it on, gaze neutral, all emotion wiped from her voice.

Cold steals through me, the kind of cold I need.

"Scalpels," I tell her. "And people to hold him. Two—three sets of artery forceps. They're about this big, they look like a steel crab claw." I pinch the air with gloved fingers. "And a retractor. Like scissors, but with fork tines. Do you know what I mean?"

"All the disinfected surgical clamps will be in the fourth bin, left shelf," Merlin tells Marissa. Then, to another helper: "Reggie, we're going to need that oximeter from the ambulance. It's on the cart by bed three—wheel it over here."

Someone rushes forward with a steel tray. There's alcohol and gauze swabs and tweezers and three scalpels.

Merlin's eyes rise to mine. "I believe in you," she says firmly, and I startle.

I know she doesn't, but it's strangely heartening to hear. I take a scalpel and turn back to the patient, then cut a red line between life and death.

There is so much blood. It leaks inside my gloves and starts to itch into the fine lines of my palms as I open his leg and the crossbow bolt falls out. Someone wipes the sweat from my brow before it falls, at Merlin's direction. Thick muscle twitches as I pull it back and fix it in place with the retractor. Merlin will have to hold the artery still once I clear the blood from the femoral sheath and find it.

The amount of blood is terrifying. So much, so fast. *My father did this every day*, I tell myself. But *his* patients were out, *they* didn't whimper and flinch like the boy under my hands. Three helpers keep him still, but his screams tear through the room as I direct Merlin where to clamp the pearlescent artery to stanch the flow. When he goes quiet, it's worse. But the artery is only nicked, not severed, and Merlin holds the clamp perfectly still.

"Pulse?" I can't see the oximeter; someone is standing on a chair with a Maglite trained on the patient's leg. Everything that isn't bleeding is a haze of white.

"Still in a safe range." Merlin's voice is calm. "You've got this."

She has a needle threaded and waiting. My icy fingers move precisely, though the rest of my body is bathed in nervous sweat. The fine sutures I make are small and even, my best work forever inside him, and at last the blood ebbs. I return each part to its place, pull the fat and skin back together, such feeble armor. I make another set of sutures that will scar, but he will run and walk and not remember this. And Kay Kim will finally stop crying and have to forgive me.

"Pulse?" I ask again, stepping back from the table.

"Eighty-nine BPM," Merlin says. "Eight-eight. Eighty-seven."

We all watch the orange square letters of the oximeter together, my heart dropping with each one: eighty-six, eight-five . . . but there, it holds. Eighty-five. I feel them all staring at me. I stare at the numbers, willing them to hold.

Eighty-five, still.

"Okay . . ." I step back, sawing my forearm across my brow. "Okay. Thank you, everyone. Let's get him an IV—antibiotics, fluids— and a clean bed."

I feel Merlin's hand gripping my arm. I grip her hand back.

+ + +

"It's almost sunset." Marissa ducks beside me. I'm re-dressing the bandage of a finger amputation. "The King has arranged a welcome dinner in your honor. I've gotten some nurses to cover while you go to the royal feast, but I thought you might want to get ready first in your room."

The King? A feast? My room? I'm too grateful for a break to question it, but I scan the room as she leads me out. "Do you know where Kay is?"

She points to Kay, passed out in a chair next to Brick. I still need to talk to Kay about Simon and Tyler's "low-key assassination." But she needs the sleep, and Tyler won't come up here, so I follow Marissa to the door beside the physics library.

It opens with a whoosh and crackle that tells me there's a torch inside. And then the smell of perfume hits me. *Redolent,* that's the word. The air is redolent with steam that smells like flowers. And in the corner, past the queen-sized bed freshly turned down for me, is an *actual tub,* full of hot, perfumed water. Marissa shows me where I can find soap and towels, and points out a rack of formal dresses. The moment she closes the door behind her, I inspect the bath, desperate to know if they have plumbing.

No, they must have ripped the tub out of a house, carried it up all these stairs, and fitted a crystal doorknob into the plug before filling it with hot water and scattering the surface with flower petals. I could cry at how lovely it smells.

I haven't taken a real shower or bath since Before. Settling back into that water is the best thing to happen to me in months. I want nothing more than to follow my real bath up with a night in a real bed, and fall asleep to a view of something besides jarred pig fetuses. But the choice of dresses suggest a formal event is at hand.

I put on the simplest one—a pale pink strapless A-line—then hang Kyle's letterman jacket on my shoulders. At Jefferson, it became a symbol that I know he will return, that I'm keeping it safe for him until he comes back. And I feel it's more significant than ever to carry his banner here at Moore.

But it does smell *putrid*.

When I step out into the hallway, a shape speeds by. For a moment I think a prowling wolf has gotten loose in the school. Then I realize it's the "wizard," wheeling herself back and forth impatiently down the hall, changed into a fresh black jacket over a royal-blue hoodie. She sees me and slows, hands pulling at her wheels until she goes still.

". . . Nice dress."

There it is again, that undercurrent of arrogant assessment. The glance the hottest guy in the room gives you right before he asks if you have a boyfriend. But it's undercut by her sincere, dimpled smile. She points a thumb over her shoulder. "I'll take you down. It's this way," she says, taking out her walkie-talkie. "How much do you weigh, Nirali?"

"Oh, I don't really know." I do, roughly, but I don't want to tell her. It's so low, it'll just make Jefferson look even worse.

"The guard who helps with the counterweight needs to know how much weight we're adding." She scans me and speaks into the walkie-talkie: "Chris, Wizard Merlin heading down with guest. I'd put guest at a buck, buck ten at most."

The walkie-talkie crackles back: "Ten-four, all hands on deck, clear for descent. Chris out."

"Wizard Merlin out."

"So this is, like, a homemade elevator?" My steps slow as we approach the darkness of what I would have sworn was an open elevator shaft. "Should I be concerned?"

"Not at all." She rolls easily into the darkness and smacks an LED light stuck to the wall, illuminating a tiny cell of particleboard.

I hesitate. "How does it work? I thought there was no electricity?"

"The pulley runs on a diesel engine our Captain of the Guard rigged up. Come on in."

I step in gingerly, expecting the floor to tilt. It doesn't. I take my place beside her, and she yanks a black nylon strap threaded through a hole in the ceiling. An engine wakes up high overhead. The particleboard cell oscillates, and I gasp and almost run out again. She puts out her arm and I halt, just short of making contact.

"Now, now." Merlin's eyes twinkle. "The engine's loud because it's right above us in the North Tower. But we're fine. I do this every day."

We start to descend, smoothly enough, and in the small cab I become aware of an amazing smell: girly shampoo and really nice men's cologne at once. It makes me think of the most exciting parties Before, of prom photos and the limo to homecoming. "Still afraid?" she asks, and I shake my head.

"Okay. Well." She takes a deep breath. "Nirali, I wanted to escort you to the feast so I could take a moment and apologize. For what I said before, about the whole doctor thing. I . . . could not have done what you did. You saved my friend's life, and I am . . . really glad you're here."

"Well, you set me up for success," I admit. "Your staff, your supplies, your help. I couldn't have done it without you." I widen my eyes. "And we were lucky that the artery wasn't severed."

"Oh, man, I know, right?" She shakes her head, wide-eyed. "It takes everything, doesn't it?" And I nod, holding her gaze with the same sense of terrified wonder. All our skill and effort and supplies, matched against the million things that could have possibly gone wrong and didn't. This time.

"So this dinner is where I'll finally meet the King?" I say after a moment. "Do I bow?"

"No, no, I don't think so." She frowns. "Bowing is required for subjects, but you're a guest from Jefferson. You *should* call him King Max or Your Majesty, though. Like, you can make your little wizard jokes about me"—she gives me a wry look—"but don't play around with the King. He holds dominion over everyone who lives at Moore, and his room leaders take that seriously."

Dominion: supreme authority, command, or sway.

"So he can say 'off with her head' if he doesn't like me?" I tease.

"Oh . . ." She leans her head back, her features lit up by the second-story elevator opening now rising from the floor. A trellis nailed across the opening captures us in a net of shadow. Diamonds of amber light illuminate the reddish brown of her doe eyes, the scimitar sweep of her long eyelashes. ". . . He'll like you."

Some pang goes through me, faint but unmistakable, like the start of a sore throat. I'm not sick, I'm just startled. She said the words almost unwillingly, as though I'd compelled the compliment. Her eyes return to the dark in front of us as the diamonds of light slide away, and she says: "Kay tells me you elect presidents at Jefferson?"

"Yes." I nod quickly, though it feels like prevarication, the prettiest word for a lie that I know. "Well, we had an election, Before. And, hopefully, another one soon. And the King . . . ?"

She turns to me, eyebrows up.

"How was he—crowned?" I bite the inside of my cheek at the word.

"After he killed that first dragon," she says, her tone dead serious, "I told him what I'd figured out, about dragons staying away from their own dead. And about a vision I'd had."

"A vision?"

"A vision of Max, a crown burning over his head, driving the rest of the dragons from Brockton."

I blink at her, stunned. "So *you* made him King?"

"He knew what he was. The whole school did, after the dragon fell." She won't look back at me. "I just helped him figure out the right word for it."

I give it a beat, then ask as innocently as I can: "Were you and Max friends Before?"

"Not really. I'm sort of a loner. Most wizards are." Her jaw works a little. "But we did play video games together." Those doe eyes flash up at me again, their expression hard to name. "You much of a gamer, Nirali?"

"Not at all."

"But Kay said you play chess?"

"Yes! Do you? Should we play a match, while I'm here?"

"Depends." She's not kidding. "How good are you?"

"Um, the best. I've won every game I ever played at Jefferson."

"Same for me. At Moore." She lifts her chin slightly. "And other schools, when I played on a team."

"You were on a chess team?! Okay, now we have to play—"

The first-story opening rises from the floor, and my words cut off at the sight of two girls leaned against the lockers, their glowing faces pressed together, an arm around a waist, a burning red cheek. It's genuinely shocking. I can't remember the last time I saw any kind of couple making out at Jefferson; we have different priorities now. But these two want nothing else. They're so lost in each other they don't even notice a wizard in a sports coat and a doctor in a ball gown, sinking through the floor.

"We better not," Merlin says as the couple rises out of view.

"What?"

". . . Play chess."

I clear my throat. "Why?"

"Because you would pitch such a fit when I won."

"No, I wouldn't," I promise. "Because you would never beat me."

We both look at each other then, at exactly the same time, and she breaks into such an unwilling laugh that I can't help it—I crack, and smile my real smile.

My stomach turns over as we come to rest in front of a heavy tarp curtain. It's immediately parted by waiting guards, who then *bow* to her. And then they bow to *me*, and I follow her down a narrow hallway.

The windows of the cafeteria doors glow amber straight ahead, and they fly open as we approach, held by waiting servers.

Moore's cafeteria stops me in my tracks.

It's like something out of *Vogue*, Before: a spring meadow by candlelight. Every long cafeteria table has been set up in a huge circle, and the space they ring is packed with blooming wildflowers, yellow and red and orange and blue and those tiny little white ones that look like mist from far away. Above the flowers hang hundreds of tea lights in little glass jars, suspended at different lengths by thin wires, their floating bubbles of light casting the artificial meadow in a golden haze. They're baby food jars, I realize. Someone with longer nails and more patience than me must have picked away every sticky bit of label.

Even more stunning are the platters and platters of hot food. Grilled meat, dressed salad, warm bread. Though I'm a lifelong vegetarian, the sheer abundance comforts me.

I'm so entranced by the meal it takes me a moment to notice the crowd waiting to eat it: At least fifty people sit at the tables, silently staring at me. They're wearing a mishmash of formalwear and outrageous costume pieces—cat ears and mohawks and homemade armor—but they make it look cool, because they're all in fantastic shape.

A guy wearing a long red coat stands, and everyone else stands rippling out from him, as if they've been watching him for a cue. And as he starts pounding on the table in rhythm, they all join in.

Merlin turns her chair to face me and joins them by clapping, and I realize they're *thanking me*: their eyes are gleaming as the tables rattle under their fists, and I'm so overwhelmed I let myself tear up a little, to show I understand.

I follow Merlin to the guy in the coat, who also wears a weird crown of welded-together nails. He's pulling this dubious look off with pure personal enthusiasm, like a frat guy in a last-minute Halloween costume.

"Doctor Nirali of Jefferson," Merlin says quietly, and the table immediately falls silent. "May I present His Majesty, King Max of Moore High."

Honestly, I'm surprised. He's tall but probably the least jacked guy at the table, with a smile that is too wide for his narrow face but enormously assured. I offer a professional handshake, and his smile goes even wider, exposing perfectly even white teeth.

King Max takes my hand and lifts it to his lips, then inclines his head to me. There's another round of pounding on the table.

"I can bow to you, because you're, like, a Queen," he says just to me, like he's checking the math.

"No, not even close." I give him a quizzical look. "I'm a senior representative."

"Well, here, you're a Queen," he says, and then continues louder, in a presentational voice: "We are joined tonight by a leader from every room at Moore. To give you a royal welcome, and our total thanks, Queen Nirali!"

I offer my best smile.

"It's the least I can do to help!" I cry, my voice wavering across the distance of the table.

The King pulls out my chair for me. Once we've sat, the room leaders take their seats and start passing food and cracking open bottles of beer and soda. I pass on the tray of venison steaks Merlin offers me with a pang of guilt.

There are so many people who need these back at home.

"The food delivery arrived safely at Jefferson," King Max says confidentially, leaning closer. He smells clean and minty, like highly effective mouthwash. "I talked to Simon over the radio before I came down."

"Thank you."

"It's the least we can do."

"And this beautiful dinner! Everything is so gorgeous."

He nods toward a chubby girl with long wavy hair. "Our Priestess, Artemis, put it together."

She was already staring at me, and when I look up, she smiles reflexively: *You caught me!* There's a smear of burgundy lipstick across her teeth. In a room of hard bodies, she is conspicuously soft and pale.

"And the mural?" I point to the wall behind King Max, where a map of Brockton with Moore at its center has been painted in black and white. Golden lines encircle several blocks around the school, their intersections strangely organic, more a web than a grid. The spaces held by the golden lines are filled in with red.

"The lines are the fences we've put up. The red is all the territory we've taken back," King Max says proudly, "in what we call Expansions."

He gives me the full breakdown of what that is, which is terrifying but exhilarating. He tells me how he *killed a freaking Grown*, and that as of last night they've killed ten altogether and mean to kill all of them. This brings us to the recent attack, and he asks after the patients. He knows all of them by name and, broadly, their injuries.

"Did you help with the wounded?" I ask, surprised.

"Of course," he says: *How could I not?*

It's another unflattering comparison to Jefferson. Kyle never set foot in our hospital, claiming he would faint at the sight of blood.

King Max leans in closer. "The big guy with the scarred face, how is he? Why—why hasn't he woken up?"

"He's lost a lot of blood."

"I could give him some of mine."

I shake my head and explain I don't know their blood types, and he looks so stricken I smile reassuringly and add, "But Kay's been looking after him, and she's a great nurse. I think she's still up there—"

"Sorry, I forgot to invite her."

"It's fine, she's getting some much-needed sleep. I doubt she'd leave his side even if she was awake."

"Don't tell her boyfriend that!" King Max laughs, cutting a glance across the table to a guy all in black. I look over, then do a double take.

"Her boyfriend? *Him?*" I point as discreetly as I can. "*That* guy? The one next to your Priestess? *That's* Kay's boyfriend?"

King Max wiggles his eyebrows. "Yup. And the Duke can't keep his hands off her, from what I've seen. She's supposed to move in with him tonight."

No offense, but *what?*

The "Duke" is completely out of Kay's league. I love Kay; she's a sweet girl with almost too much integrity, and cute enough, sure. But this Duke looks like a male model from Before. What is happening there?

"—he put down his welder's mask and drove straight for the Grown," I hear Tyler saying to Merlin, on the other side of me.

"You mean the guy in the alley?" I chime in. King Max asks what we're talking about, and I explain how the guy on the motorbike chased off the Grown.

"The Blue Knight!" he says, his eyes connecting with Merlin's.

"The Blue Knight?" I say, confused.

"There've been all these stories about a guy who *wields blue fire* going and fighting the dragons one-on-one and whatnot, but holy shit." King Max laughs uncertainly. "It's *true*?!"

I look around. Everyone is hanging on my words now. "Well, he had some kind of weapon that lit up. And the light was definitely blue. And he had a face mask he pulled down, made of metal."

"Like armor?! Wild! This guy is wild!" King Max shakes his head at Merlin, then looks back at me. "And you didn't recognize him?"

"No, I'd never seen him before. But he's our age, obviously. Maybe he went to that prep school?"

"Sharpe Academy?" Merlin frowns. "But they're up in the hills, way above town by the dam. More likely he's from Briggs—it's the closest."

Briggs, farther west, by the middle school. I seem to remember it being affiliated with the correctional system.

"We have to find this dude," King Max insists to Merlin. "I'm making it a royal edict. Seriously, I got to know what this dude is up to."

A kid who's wearing a Puerto Rican flag as a cape leans in. "We've seen him *inside* the fence, too, Your Majesty."

"How though, Armando? Our lookouts always signal strangers." King Max frowns. "How would he get through?"

And then King Max does something strange: He reaches across

his body for a Heineken bottle with his right hand, keeping his left arm against his side. It's only then I notice the slight purple depressions under his eyes, the pinpoints of sweat on his forehead.

He's hurt. Seriously hurt.

I wait for a natural pause in the conversation, then when the others seem engaged with each other, I lean forward to whisper, "Are you injured?"

King Max makes the smallest possible nod, scanning the table as he answers under his breath, "But we can't talk about it here."

"Maybe we can go into another room for a moment? I can say I'm tired or something—"

Heartbreaking relief washes over his face: *You would do that for me?*

But a chair scrapes across the floor, and the gorgeous Duke stands as Kay walks in. Beside the built, tanned Moore room leaders, she looks like an unfriendly little ghost. But the Duke hurries to meet her. She stiffens then goes still as he whispers in her ear, her eyes flashing to me.

My gaze moves helplessly to Tyler, catching him mid-laugh. I need to get him out of the room before there's a confrontation, but before I can stand, King Max calls out:

"Kay! Over here, girl! Your Queen wants you!"

"Please, don't interrupt her if she's talking to her boyfriend," I protest, but she's already headed our way. I'm between the King and Merlin, and neither of them budge to welcome or accommodate her. So I spring out of my seat and give her a long hug to show them she means a lot to me.

"Kay, so glad you're up!" I cry, but her eyes cut past me to Tyler. "Could we go talk for a moment? Not here, but—"

"Hi, Tyler!" Kay says over my shoulder, voice too bright, eyes blazing. "Surprised to see me?"

Tyler's thick features twist into a scowl as a hush spreads around the table. I can feel Merlin staring at me, so I hold my face carefully.

"Tyler can join us, or not, if he makes you uncomfortable,"

I whisper to Kay. "But let's please discuss this out in the hall."

"Who ordered my murder?" Kay's bloodshot eyes lock with Tyler's. "Her or Simon?"

The whole room goes dead silent. Everyone has heard, and my heartbeat seems to stutter to a stop as my brain races to catch up.

"Simon ordered it," Tyler says flatly. "Nirali had nothing to do with it."

"I am shocked and grieved." I keep my voice concerned but controlled. "If this is true, Simon has broken our laws and will be held accountable. You can't just order people off to *die* at Jefferson."

"Unless they're on the Scavenging Team, right?" Tyler's voice booms through the cafeteria. The absolute fathead. I squeeze my eyes closed as he goes on: "Because of the stupid Costco trip Kay came up with, seven of my friends are dead."

"Costco trip?" Merlin cuts in at my elbow.

"The Costco trip?!" Kay bursts out in wild laughter, punch-drunk from lost sleep and grief.

I grip her shoulders and try to physically pull her away from the table before she can do more damage, but she pushes me away and starts railing at Tyler.

"The Costco trip had nothing to do with it! Simon told you it was about Costco so you would try and *kill me*! Because I found out Kyle wasn't calling in! And now I know Kyle's car has been parked at Moore for the last six weeks!" She turns on me, furious. "You have no idea where he is! You've been punishing people for saying Kyle might not come back, when the whole time Kyle has been *dead*!"

An image of Kyle on homecoming night, bright as a photograph flash: turning to me just after we were announced homecoming king and queen. Reaching up to adjust my hair, pulled out of place by the crown, before the spotlight swirling around the room found us.

Kyle was *here*?

"How do you think they called in to get you, Nirali?" she goes on. "We used Kyle's radio! I'm sorry to tell you like this, I'm sorry, but Kyle is *gone*. He's gone, all right?"

I have to remember where I am right now. Everyone is watching. Everyone is listening. I have to get her out of here and find out what she knows.

But then Kay wheels on our host and yells:

"And King Max has been covering it up this whole time!"

Re-al-po-li-tik:
practical politics

NIRALI

"TREASON!" King Max leaps to his feet, chair clapping to the floor. "Seize her!"

A guard rushes forward, wraps a large hand over Kay's mouth, and pulls her away from the glow of the table and into the shadows.

I want to tear the guy off her, but we're outnumbered. King Max isn't just wearing a costume, not the way guards are appearing from the corners of the room at his command. And right now, surrounded by every leader in the school, all King Max is going to care about is what they say to their rooms afterward.

The better I make him look, the better things will go for Kay.

I turn to King Max and speak with careful deference, loud enough so everyone can hear: "I'm so sorry, Your Majesty. I'm sure there's been a misunderstanding."

"Yes, Queen Nirali, a terrible misunderstanding." King Max

raises his voice for the benefit of the table: "Kyle came to Moore six weeks ago. We were excited about his mission. We hosted him for a few days. We offered him a safer vehicle. He took it and left the old one here. What's to cover up? I didn't *brag* about it to Kay because, well"—he makes an elaborately casual shrug—"why would I? She was some random Jefferson reject. But now she's my subject. And I *do not* tolerate this kind of disrespect from my subjects."

Low sounds of approval come from around the table, and then the beautiful Duke in black, Kay's improbable boyfriend, steps forward.

"Kay is *with* me," he says, addressing the room. "As the Duke of Moore, I demand she be allowed to speak her piece."

I am surrounded by fatheads. If the King lets Kay speak now, it will look like the Duke is the one who's really in charge. He's just condemned her with this direct challenge.

"Take her to the dungeon," King Max tells his guard.

"The *dungeon*?" A needlepoint of pain pushes through my temple. "Hold on, HOLD ON! Kay Kim is from Jefferson!" I look around the table: *Help me out here.* "I'm the Queen of Jefferson, right? She's my—citizen. You can't just *throw her in a dungeon!*"

"Queen Nirali." King Max's tone is respectful, but imperative. "Kay is no longer *with* Jefferson. She *begged* to join Moore after she was dragged into the middle of town by her own people." He waves at Tyler, whose face goes red.

"She was about to propose a plan *I knew* would kill my friends. It was her or them!" Tyler gets to his feet. The guards hover, but they let him finish. "And you still did it." Tyler looks at me, and I realize he's weeping again. "Twenty Scavengers were sent out, thirteen came back. Seven of my friends died at the Costco!"

"I would like to hear about this Costco plan." Merlin doesn't raise her voice, but it silences the room. She stares at Tyler, her expression inscrutable. "When was the Jefferson raid on Costco?"

"We set out yesterday midmorning and got there just before sunset."

Merlin sweeps her chair toward the mural of Brockton on the wall, taking a diamond-top cane from one of the more ludicrously dressed room leaders as she goes. "So last night. And the Costco was locked up?"

"Yes, ma'am. We opened the doors and out came three of the biggest—dragons I've ever seen. And I've seen plenty, ma'am."

Merlin taps at a point on the mural with the borrowed cane. "You're telling me Jefferson raiders unleashed three huge dragons from this Costco, the one off I-10 going west. Correct?"

"Yes, ma'am."

Merlin drags the tip of the cane in a straight line from the Costco, down across the highway, and through the single fence the dragons came in. Straight to Moore High School.

"If Tyler is right," Merlin says coolly, "then Kay's Costco trip is why we got attacked last night."

Guilt spiders through me. My skin crawls with it. All the injuries I've been healing today . . . did I cause them? But what was I supposed to do? Let the whole school tear itself apart?

The table behind me convulses with outrage:

"A Jefferson plot!"

"Why would they do this!?"

"There was no plot." I turn to the table. "Please, listen to me. We sent our Scavenging Team to Costco because we had no food. We were desperate. We thought any dragons formed inside the Costco would've surely starved by now—"

"They don't eat!" someone shouts. "Haven't you watched them at all?"

Failing spectacularly rings in my head.

King Max walks past Kay, past me, and lands beside stocky Tyler. He puts his hand on Tyler's shoulder.

"What's your name again, man?"

"Tyler. I'm the Captain of the Scavenging Team."

"What is that, exactly?" King Max asks gently.

"We go out and get food for the rest of the school. We started as a group of eighty." Tyler's shoulders collapse. "Now thirteen. Thirteen Scavengers are left."

"Scavengers?" King Max shakes his head. "Nah, man. You go out and you face dragons. You are a warrior. A hero. At Moore, we don't call you Scavengers. We call you Knights."

Tyler's head bows, his chest swelling as low sounds of approval rise from the table, and I burn with shame. We sacrificed the Scavenging Team's lives for the greater good, and what did they get in return? Not even a grave. No one is brave enough to go outside for the time it would take to dig one.

King Max addresses the table. "Jefferson's problems aren't our business. But the attack last night, that took so many of our friends, that sure as hell is. It's *my* business, as Moore's Liege Lord and Protector." His tone has changed, all boyishness gone. "This Knight says Kay's Costco plan killed his people and our own. And though Queen Nirali says this plan arose from ignorance, not malice, either way justice must be done. I hereby declare a Trial by Combat."

Gasps and murmurs tear through the cafeteria, but nothing as loud as the hysterical laugh that rises from my own throat.

"Trial by Combat?" I sound shrill. "That's not a thing, that hasn't *been* a thing since the Middle Ages! You expect Kay to get in a ring and fight *for her life*?"

"That's how we do it at Moore!" a guy with barbed wire drawn all over his arms in Sharpie yells. The people around him are nodding. "You guys do it your way, we do it ours."

"She came to Moore." A girl in a cheerleader dress and micro braids half-rises out of her chair. "She ate our food, she trained in our cars, she *moved in with our Duke*, but when she kills our friends, suddenly she's from Jefferson?"

"Kay chose Moore. So she must defend herself in a Trial by Combat," King Max concludes. "Or a champion can step forward to defend her."

"I will." The words shoot out of the hot Duke like they're spring-loaded. "I will be her champion."

The air goes tight, some subtext I don't know filling the darting glances around the table with dark excitement.

"Perfect!" King Max says, just as fast, a menacing smile spreading across his face. "The day after tomorrow. A champion of my choosing will represent Moore, versus our new Duke, Leo of Los Martillos, on behalf of Kay Kim. May justice prevail."

The table rocks, glass bottles falling to the floor and shattering, as all the leaders drum their fists excitedly. I glance back at Tyler. He isn't looking at me; he's staring at the King in the same lovestruck way he looked at the fallen Grown. Like everything is possible.

"And now, if you'll excuse me." King Max walks to my side. "I would like to spend some time with this beautiful Queen in private."

The others cheer, but I can see the sheen of sweat across his face. And when he takes my hand in his, it's ice cold. His eyes are dilated. He's pulling me at first, but by the time we walk the length of the table, I'm practically holding him up. So though the guards are dragging Kay the other way, I stay with King Max until we're swallowed by the dark of the hall.

Once we're out of the cafeteria, he stops. His long hand slaps the wall and clutches for a moment before going limp, and then the King of Moore High collapses at my feet.

The guard who followed us out makes a move to go back for help, but I grab his sleeve.

"Let's you and I get him to his room," I say in a low voice. He hesitates. I give him my most appealing expression. "Please, can you show me the way?"

He melts and helps me with the unconscious King.

King Max's weight dragging between us, the guard and I clumsily navigate the halls, rowdier at midnight than Jefferson gets at noon. People are milling everywhere, fires and torches blazing up and down the hall. Several doorways are hazy with pot smoke, air ringing with the profligate use of boom boxes. Half of one hall is taken up by a cardboard corral in which a crowd of drunks are racing wild rabbits. And in a moonlit courtyard, ringed by silent onlookers, two bare-chested guys are circling each other with broken glass bottles and laughing like maniacs.

But everyone we pass has some cheerful, heartfelt greeting for their unconscious leader.

"Passed out already? That's our boy!"

"My King knows how to PARTY!"

At last, the guard guides us past a front reception desk and in through an office door marked *Principal*. Inside, the guard snaps on a camping lantern beside a giant mattress laid directly on the floor.

Across from the mattress is the principal's desk, strangely preserved: it still has a brass placard engraved with *Principal Bone*. The desk's surface is scattered with bongs and pipes and blackened mesh filters. Behind it, an oil painting of Moore hangs beside an American flag. The carpet is spotted with singe marks and dark stains. There's a pyramid of empty beer cans in the corner, neat rows of full liquor bottles on the emptied bookshelf, and torn condom packages peeking out from under heaps of clothes on the floor and around the bed.

I sweep the clothes away and help the guard lay King Max down.

"What's your name?" I ask the guard.

"Chris."

"Chris, I'm going to make a list of supplies I'll need from the gym, if you'd be so kind as to get them for me."

He balks. "And leave you alone with King Max?"

"The King is entitled to a private examination."

He shifts his weight uneasily.

"And I demand it as a—Queen, or whatever," I add.

He immediately bows, relieved. "Oh! Okay, cool, Your Majesty."

I write my list on the margin of an old *Playboy*, and Chris takes it with another bow and hurries off to the gym.

Then I circle the bed with every lantern in the room, before carefully extending King Max's arm and removing the swimmer's coat. He hisses back to life, his face creasing with pain.

"They saw me fall," he weeps. "They saw, they all saw—"

"No one saw," I promise. "We made it out of the cafeteria before you collapsed. I sent the guard out before I took off your coat. No one knows how bad it is."

His eyes meet mine with cautious understanding, and he lets out a long shaky breath. I kneel beside the bed and carefully peel back his bloodied bandage.

The wound is deep and jagged, and wraps all the way up and around his dislocated elbow joint. By all logic he should have passed out from the pain a long time ago. He could have had Merlin send me to him first. But he waited until I had treated everyone else.

The guard knocks.

"Medical supplies," I explain.

"Leave it by the door!" King Max yells hoarsely. The steps retreat. After a moment's pause, I get up and bring in a small plastic bin of requested supplies, then sanitize my hands with clear gel before putting on the latex gloves.

"It's bad?" he asks.

"It's not good."

"You can't tell anyone," King Max says, a fine crease in his forehead. I nod, more focused on cleaning the wound, but he grabs me with his good hand. "I mean it," he says through his teeth. "That Duke dude wants my throne. He thinks I'm weak, 'cause Brick is in a coma, 'cause of the attack—" He tries to sit up. I gently push him back, but he goes on with frightening urgency. "If he knows about my arm, he and his whole crew will come for blood. The rooms will try to defend me, and it will be *bad*, okay?"

"I understand. I won't tell anyone, I promise." I hold his stare. "But you must promise me that Kay and Tyler can leave this school with me, unharmed."

"Yeah, sure." He lets out a sigh of relief and falls back against his pillow. "Of course."

"Is it 'of course'?" I carefully swab alcohol around the site of the wound. "Because you just announced a Trial by Combat."

"Not a chance that's happening." His eyelids are shiny when they close. "Believe me, the last thing I want is more of a spotlight on that piece of shit Duke. I just have to figure out a bigger show to put on instead . . ."

"And you'll get Kay out of the dungeon?"

He shakes his head. "She's safer there, if people blame her for the attack."

". . . I see." I probe his arm as gently as I can, feel the bone, its displacement. "I need to pop your elbow back into place. It will be painful." I clear my throat. "I assume you don't want to be heard screaming. Is there something in here that you can bite down on?"

"Just do it."

"On three, then. One, two—"

He should scream. But he doesn't. His head strains back, the cords in his neck and shoulders standing out in sharp relief, but he doesn't make a sound.

"Okay," I breathe, and gently fold his arm against his chest. "Now we'll need to do stitches, but I want you to take these first." I hold out a gloved handful of pills.

"What are they?"

"Broad-spectrum antibiotics." He pushes them into his mouth, and I find a bottle of water on the floor to help wash them down. "So. What happened to your arm?"

It's hard to follow his description of the melee in the gym, but when he describes the stab of pain inside his elbow, my heart sinks.

"The UCL is badly inflamed. You'll need to wear a sling for a while. Then you should start on physical therapy, if you want to keep doing strenuous activity with that arm."

"If?! It's my sword arm!" He sounds agonized. "How long will it take to heal?"

I keep my voice neutral. "Three, maybe four months."

He crosses a tan forearm over his face, but his total despair is clear.

"I'm going to start stitches now," I explain. "I'll be as careful as I can, but it will hurt."

He barely moves. He keeps his eyes on the ceiling and bites his lip but holds the arm perfectly still.

"You have a high pain threshold," I tell him. "Most people would've passed out from this kind of injury way before the feast."

"You got me out just in time, Nirali. I don't know what I would've done if it was just me."

And though he was surrounded by friends and guards, I know what he means. People who've never been in charge have no idea how lonely it is. How in the end you only have your faith in yourself, and most days you barely have that.

But my empathy is intruded upon by the realization that King Max is staring at me. That sort of momentous stare guys do while telepathically commanding you to look back at them.

I finally relent, and as our eyes meet he says:

"Nirali, will you marry me?"

I shush him and start a neat knot at the end of fourteen stitches.

"I'm serious. If I have to do months of therapy with you, I won't be able to keep it a secret." He tries to sit up again. I push him back down.

"Easy, don't—"

"*Unless there's another reason the doctor needs to be with me,*" he continues. "Because she's not my doctor. She's my Queen!"

I brusquely pull each of his eyelids up to inspect his pupils. They're no longer dilated; his smooth forehead is cool. He's not completely delirious.

"I'm not a Queen," I remind him, snipping the ends of the knot. "And this is no time for a royal wedding. Please calm yourself."

"*That's the show!*" he cries happily, sitting up again, and when I try to push him back down, he covers my hand with his. He clutches it to his chest so I can feel his heart rate accelerating. "A royal wedding! It's perfect! Way bigger and better than a Trial! Uniting Jefferson and Moore to take on Brockton!"

I shake him off, biting the inside of my cheek.

"We've had enough death. We need a big party, you know? And

you're so insanely gorgeous, the whole school will fall in love with you. Who cares about a new Duke when there's a new *Queen*?"

"You need to rest now. And I want you to take these." I hold up an orange vial with three pills inside. "Take all of them as soon as you wake up, with some water. Understand?"

"Nirali." His eyes are feverish. "Do you remember meeting me? That time at Harvey Goodwill's party?"

If I weren't so tired, I would burst out laughing. He's gone from planning a royal wedding to referencing the worst night of my life. Who is this guy? I slip out of the office, shaking my head, and find Chris in the lobby. He offers to escort me back to my room, and I want nothing more than to pass out on a real bed.

But once we get there, Merlin is waiting outside my door.

"Hey!" she cries as we approach, eyes huge, voice low. "Chris, man." She reaches out to give a quick and secret-looking handshake to the guard. "Thanks for walking her up. You're dismissed."

"Can *I* be dismissed?" I cross my arms. "I'm exhausted."

"I know, I know. But we need to talk." She looks down the hall, makes sure the guard has turned the corner. "Can I come in for a minute?"

Confused, I hold open the door for her before carefully closing it behind us, then pull out my hair tie so the tight ponytail releases me. I sigh with relief as my hair falls in waves around my face, my one little sensory luxury. I turn back to find her staring.

"So?" I comb my hands through my hair.

"Yes." Her eyes cut away. She clears her throat. "I need to tell you why Kay thinks we're covering something up with Kyle." Her shoulders are creeping up to her ears, her graceful hands kneading each other. "It's because she got hold of an inhaler he left behind."

A shiver shoots up my back. But I keep my face tightly composed.

"I can see why that would alarm her," I say. "He would never leave an inhaler behind. Unless it was empty?"

"That's what I figured. I assumed he replaced it from my supply bins. We told him to take whatever he needed for the trip. But Marissa wasn't sure if one was missing."

"We should get it back from Kay and see if it's empty," I suggest.

"I already got it back from her." Merlin looks right in my eyes. "And I destroyed it."

The shiver rolls through me again, deeper, but I don't let it show. Maintaining authority is about not relinquishing control, and that starts with control over yourself. I sink onto my bed across from her, tucking my clenched fists under my elbows.

". . . Why would you do that?"

"To protect Kay." Merlin doesn't blink. "Whoever gave her that inhaler was setting her up to do their dirty work, to accuse the King. Tonight they made their move. Pushing her to accuse him like that, in front of all the room leaders."

"Why would someone want Kay to accuse King Max?"

"They want a war." Merlin's face is cool, but her eyes burn. "And I'll be damned if I let them start one in my school."

She said King Max holds dominion at Moore. But she says it like the school is hers.

"Taking the inhaler cost me Kay's trust," she goes on. "I don't want to lose yours, too."

"I appreciate you telling me," I say after a beat. "I can handle just about anything if I'm given the information openly and honestly. So. I appreciate the transparency."

"And I appreciate you keeping a cool head at dinner. And getting the King out of there when you did. It means a lot." She glances up at me, tilting her head and rubbing her neck in a boyish gesture. "Okay. Okay, I'll go." She turns for the door, and as I open it for her, a dimple flashes in her cheek. "But before I do: What's your opening move?"

". . . What?"

"For chess."

"I never make the first move," I say, and it's true. "Secret to my success."

"Really?" she says, surprised. "Maybe we *should* play. What if we were an even match?" She nods good night and sweeps down the hall.

+ + +

I do morning rounds in the lab and then the gym, and on my way out hear thrashing music and animal screeching bouncing down the athletic hall. I follow the sounds to Moore's pool, or what was formerly a pool and is now an Olympic-length porcelain hole. It's unnerving to see a diving board over twelve feet of air and tile, but the shallow end is worse. Tyler is there, bludgeoning the rubber shoulder of a football tackle dummy with a wooden sword, a crowd of guys egging him on.

"Tyler?!" I strain to be heard over the music reverberating throughout the pool. The five guys hanging around the boom box give me tight-lipped smiles and lower the volume. Tyler, soaked through with sweat, turns to face me like I'm next.

"What's up?" he barks.

"Can I speak to you for a second?"

There's a beat of squirmy silence as he looks over his shoulder. Then he says, "Anything you have to say to me, you can say in front of them."

"Okay." I walk down through the bleachers to the edge of the pool. "I've got some concerns about our return trip to Jefferson I'd like to run by y—"

"Nope." He scrubs his thick forehead with the back of his hand and crosses the tile of the shallow end to meet me. "I'm not going back. I am staying at Moore and as proof of loyalty, I'm going to champion the King's cause."

"Tyler, you can't be serious."

"King Max chose the Motorheads to provide his champion. I asked them if they'd give me a shot." He lifts his chin, like he's proud of his homicidal tendencies. "Now, if you'll excuse me, I have to fight someone to the death in twenty-four hours, so . . ."

"You're really embarrassing yourself here, Tyler." I cross my arms and duck down, dropping my voice so the others can't hear me. "Because there's not going to be a Trial. I'm working on a diplomatic solution. When we get back to Jefferson, we can handle things between you and Kay. I know Simon played a role, and if you testify against him to Student Council—"

"Fuck Student Council," he says, so close now I can smell old coffee on his breath. "My friends are dead because of Student Council. I'd rather fight for a King than get killed by a bunch of nerds too scared to get their own food."

"I am brokenhearted about the Costco trip, Tyler, okay?" I hiss. "But when I sent you out, there was *a chance you all could come back*. And if we didn't try to get food, everyone would starve. But you dragged Kay out hoping she would die! And now you're ready to kill a guy you just met? You're a *murderer*, Tyler!"

"Kay's still alive, Your Majesty," he says sarcastically. "You have a hell of a lot more blood on your hands than I do. And you can't boss me around here because I serve King Max!" he yells, glancing over his shoulder for approval.

"King Max!" the Motorheads chorus.

"KING MAX!" Tyler yells, right in my face.

"King Max!" someone calls from the bleachers, and we all look up to see a guard at the top of the concrete steps, holding a sheaf of wildflowers. "His Majesty sent me to find you, Queen Nirali, to give you a message. And these."

He holds out the massive bouquet and a tightly folded square of lined notebook paper. The Motorheads make impressed sounds: low whistles, soft laughing curses. One of them puts his hand over his mouth and stage-whispers, "Yoooo. Straight *simping*."

Tyler looks queasy as I take King Max's message. I unfold it leisurely, enjoying his discomfiture. I make a point of smiling as I read it, laughing a little to myself as though over some private joke, though all it says is:

Follow this guy to lunch—Maximus Rex

I fold the note back up with a coy look, then tilt my head back and stare down at Tyler. "Well, it was fun chatting," I say frostily. "But I shouldn't keep His Majesty waiting."

"Nirali—"

"*Queen* Nirali," I cut him off, and the way he shrinks back is deeply satisfying. "You will address me as Queen Nirali from now on. Because that's what *your King* said." And I turn, smiling, and follow the guard back up the steps, Tyler's eyes burning a hole in my back.

Af-fi-ance:
To bind in a promise of marriage

NIRALI

The guard leads me through the lobby, out the front doors, and across the lawn, where almost the entire school is milling around. The half-naked Moore kids are drunkenly cavorting around *burning hibachi grills*, until someone cries, "That's that Queen!"

This sets off a murmuration of turned heads in my direction. I clutch my flowers and cross the lawn to an idling Escalade, which has MAXIMUS REX stenciled on its side. What felt triumphant in front of Tyler now feels like the walk to the "make-out room" in the middle of a house party.

The drive is long. We cross under three of Moore's towering fences before turning down a winding wooded drive I recognize with muddied apprehension. We're having lunch at Harvey Goodwill's house?

I haven't been here since the night Kyle and I almost broke up. It was the end of last summer, the start of our senior year, and a rumor was going around that he'd hooked up with a sophomore while I was at MediCamp. I'd gotten ready for the party with my friend Tiana, who vowed to stay by my side the whole night if I wanted to ice out Kyle, and insisted I borrow her tight red bustier dress. We sang Taylor Swift as we drove down the Goodwills' long, manicured drive that night forever ago.

The same driveway is now a tunnel of rampant hedges, branches so overgrown the leaves press against my window, trapping fat bumblebees momentarily against the glass.

Tiana had turned off in front of the house and gotten out an Arrowhead bottle full of vodka and orange juice for us to preparty with. Which normally I never did, but with the prospect of facing Kyle in front of a crowd, I was desperate to appear more at ease. We half emptied the bottle, then walked arm in arm through the dark, toward the drifting laughter from the Goodwills' back deck. Almost our entire grade was congregated around the salt pool, sparkling under strings of outdoor Edison bulbs.

Now the deck is bleached and cracked, and empty except for King Max. He's shirtless, lying out on a faded yellow lawn chair in cutoff sweatpants and sunglasses, smoke curling up from the joint in his good hand. The midday sun carves dark shadows along lines of wiry muscle, more muscle than I would've guessed. When he hears my steps, he curls upward, grinning and stamping the joint out on the aluminum armrest.

"Hey, Queen!" He rises, a wink in his voice. "Thanks for coming out!" He closes in with a one-armed hug that lasts just a fraction of a moment too long.

"We have to make this quick," I say, pulling back. "I have patients I have to check in on."

"I won't keep you. But you gotta eat. *And* . . ." He takes my arm with his good hand and gently positions me close to the pool, then goes back about eight feet. He walks by me holding a phantom drink, then knocks my arm and rears back.

"Whoa, did I get you?"

I smile, confused.

"And then *you said*," he goes on, like we're rehearsing a scene, "'No, I'm good' with this crazy gorgeous smile. You were in a red dress. I'll never forget it." Tiana's dress. He *was* at Harv's party. "We talked for like twenty minutes about Jefferson being a magnet school, and how people had to, like, test to get in. And how you were applying for early decision at Yale, remember?"

I don't remember him *at all*.

"Oh right!" I smile, eyes wide. "Wow, what are the odds! Such a great party. Were you and Harv close?"

"Harv knew Brick through baseball. Brick didn't want to go alone, so he brought me." King Max gestures to a table heaped with food under a frayed sun umbrella, then pulls back a chair for me, wrought iron feet scraping against wood. "But I wasn't tight with Harvey. I wasn't really a sports guy. And definitely not a magnet school kid."

"So what were you?"

"A King waiting for his kingdom to appear." He smiles and grabs something like a cheesesteak sandwich. There's one on my plate as well.

"I'm actually a vegetarian?" I say with my most charming smile, and his smile drops.

"Oh! Wow, okay, my bad—here, I also had them do like a charcuterie thing." He pushes a cutting board covered in cut apples, peanut butter, and fresh cookies toward me. "And I can send someone over to the market for whatever you want. Anything you want, just tell me."

I can't resist testing this assertion.

"Could I get a veggie burger?"

Max whistles for one of his guards, then communicates my order. I give him another smile.

"You thought any more about what I asked you last night?" he asks.

I inject some confusion into my expression: *Not sure what you mean?* Though I'm afraid I do.

He wolfs down his sandwich before I've gotten through half an apple, wipes his hand on his shorts, then takes a ring out of his pocket. It's a four-carat solitaire, with more diamonds on the band. He holds it just outside the shadow of the umbrella, so rainbow sparks wheel across the table between us.

"I'm just starting out." His half-joking demeanor vanishes. "But I'm headed places, Nirali. I'm going to take back the town."

Oh boy. I cover my mouth, hurrying to swallow before I protest.

"And if you don't like that one, you've got options. Hey, *Chris*!" He whistles again, and another guard pushes over a wheelbarrow that tinkles like a chandelier. When Chris lands in front of us, its contents are blinding: tennis bracelets and gold chains and jewel earrings, jumbled together in a sparkling heap.

"The thing is . . ." I have to close my eyes against the glitter. "I have a boyfriend. You hung out with him, remember?"

He hesitates, then says, "Yes. Kyle was very cool. He and I clicked right away. That's why I told him to take one of the Escalades. And he told me he'd bring it back on his way home, and he'd be home soon because he had a beautiful girl waiting for him."

This is abject gallantry. Kyle didn't talk like that. I'd be shocked if Kyle mentioned he had a girlfriend at all.

"But that was a long time ago," King Max continues. "He's been out there"—he gestures grandly, as though everything outside of Moore is outer space—"for a while now, Nirali."

"That doesn't mean he's not coming back."

"Well, okay, but . . ." He scratches the back of his head for a moment, then says, "I think even if he did, he would understand this as a *practical thing*." He taps his bandaged arm. "I need you to fix me."

But it isn't just a practical thing.

Guys start looking at you a certain way, as they develop feelings. Like a dog when they hear you opening their food. Like the way King Max hangs over me now, hungry for my next sentence.

But I feel more hopeful about Kyle than I have in a long time.

There's a good, rational excuse for him not calling in. He took a safer car, which makes sense. I don't want or need another boyfriend. So this burgeoning royal crush has to be deflated.

As diplomatically as possible.

"You don't have to *marry me* to get medical care." I smile encouragingly. "I will help you no matter what. Give your 'subjects' some credit. You really think your room leaders will reject you because you need a little physical therapy?"

He's already shaking his head. "Not the rooms. It's like I told you. There's a small faction behind the Duke that wants me dead. They don't have the numbers to challenge me openly, but with everyone so freaked out, if they know I can't defend myself?" He stares at me intently. "I need to bring the school back together. A big show of strength that's also a good time, with a big star. And you aren't just a star. You're a Queen."

"I am not a Queen."

"A *born Queen*." He leans forward, matching my insistence. He takes my hand and slips the ring onto my finger.

It looks all wrong. Not the ring, but the ring on my hand. My knuckles are calloused, the nails broken short. How much money is a ring like this worth? What can we even use money for now? Starting fires?

"I'm flattered, really, but—"

He holds up three fingers and leans forward, sunglasses sliding down his narrow nose to reveal a self-deprecating twinkle in his eye: *I know, but hear me out.*

"Here's my offer to you, Nirali: I will feed all of Jefferson, indefinitely. No problem." He says it with an easy shrug, like he's offered me the rest of his sandwich. "I can justify sending the food a lot longer if we're married. Because then Jefferson is family, right? Which leads me to point number two: we can have the schools connected in six months."

I nearly laugh at his audacity, but he is completely earnest.

"We've been expanding east this whole time, toward the beach, which is also toward you guys. Six months from now, you could *walk* back to Jefferson. Three months after that, I'll have the hospital back on our map." He counts off the third finger. "Finally, with three more months expanding out from Jefferson as our base, we will take the power plant. I can have electricity running again before the end of next year."

I'm struck by the magnitude of his plan. He's aiming for further and higher targets than anyone on Student Council has even imagined. *A hospital with electricity by next year?* I wouldn't have believed it until I saw Moore, but now . . . who knows. Maybe he and Merlin could do it.

"Tell me what you want," he says. "I can make it happen for you. Anything, Nirali, just ask."

"All right." I stare for a long beat. "I want to talk to Kay. Alone."

"*That.* That right there." He grins, pointing at me. "That is *exactly* what a born Queen would say. Born Queen!" He whistles over his shoulder. The guard who took my order jogs up to the table, holding something wrapped in wax paper. The King takes it, dismisses him and the guy with the wheelbarrow of jewelry, then hands it to me.

It's a fresh veggie burger.

"I had to send them off to tell you this, because it's technically very against the rules, so keep it, like—" He puts a finger over his lips. "But yes. I will arrange it so you can see Kay."

"Thank you," I say from my heart.

"No problem," he says.

I inspect my order: The bun is homemade, the patty perfectly grilled. It's hot and fresh and the first food I've chosen for myself in almost a year.

"Thank you for joining me for lunch." He grins, rising from the table.

"It was a pleasure," I admit, getting to my feet.

He takes my hand to shake, then keeps it in his. Turns it over, as though to admire his ring on it again.

"Just do me a favor?" King Max says. "Don't come up with an

answer to the big question yet. Just . . . think about it." He smiles, and I think he might be sort of flexing as he walks back to the lawn chair, but I concede he has plenty to flex.

+ + +

On my return to Moore, I find the nurses in the gym and lab are handling things beautifully, and after putting out some false alarms, I find myself with free time on my hands. So I make my way to the Auto Shop to inspect the Volvo.

Fifty grease-smeared mechanics in black coveralls do double takes when I walk in. The Duke is announced by a rooster tail of sparks shooting up from some kind of metal grinder just as he strides in from the glaring sunlight, five people talking to him at once. He deftly parses the chatter and is giving each a clear answer when one of them points toward me, and our eyes connect. The Duke sends them on their way and wrings his hands with a rag before offering me a handshake.

"Your Majesty." He nods. "To what do I owe the honor?"

"Please, your—Dukeship." I give him my most charming smile. "It's just Nirali."

"Same," he grins. "I mean, call me Leo. Not Nirali. Though it's a prettier name, for sure."

Guys as hot as Leo either never flirt or flirt with everyone to keep a friendly distance. Leo seems to be the latter. I will be a relief to him as I'm immune to hot guys. It's sort of my superpower. Kyle told me once it was why he went after me so hard freshman year. Because I "didn't even know" he was alive when all the other girls were memorizing his schedule.

Now I tell Leo, "I'd like to see Kyle's car, if that's possible."

"Right this way. We owe you some tires—someone stripped 'em before the last Expansion—but I can have them replaced by the end of the day."

I follow him out to the farthest corner of the parking lot, through yards of brilliant sunshine. My skin practically purrs from the bright, wholesome heat.

But as Leo stops at the last row of cars in the lot and pulls a canvas cover off a hidden vehicle, an inner shadow swallows me.

That's Kyle's Volvo all right. I don't want to touch it, but he comes around and opens the driver's-side door for me. "We should make sure it runs," he says.

So I get in.

The smell of upholstery cleaner is still heavy on the seats, along with that summer smell of sunbaked plastic and nylon. My knuckles go white on the steering wheel.

Leo nods toward the blocked-out rear windshield and boarded-up back seat windows. "If you wanted to radio back home for a bit, I can leave."

"Thank you. But there won't be anyone on the other end until sunset."

I hit the button that ejects the radio faceplate. To remove the rest of it would be what, twenty minutes? Why would Kyle leave it behind? If the radio couldn't transfer to a new vehicle, why not at least call us one last time, and let us know?

"Leo, if you have a minute, I'd like to talk to you."

"I figured." He widens his eyes slightly.

"I wanted to thank you for stepping up as Kay's champion—"

"Of course. She's my girlfriend."

"—and I wanted to assure you no one will be fighting tomorrow," I go on. "I'm working on a diplomatic solution."

"Please," Leo says. "Don't."

I give him a hard look. "You're *okay* with killing someone you just met?"

Leo puts an arm on his headrest and leans forward confidingly. He *exudes* charm—it's overpowering, like too much cologne (though he smells more like orange cleaner).

"I don't plan on killing anybody," Leo says, slowly and clearly. "But I need to make Kay's accusation in front of the whole school."

I raise my eyebrows: *Go on.*

"Last night Kay accused King Max of covering up Kyle's disappearance. And they spun it so fast. So fast!" He shakes his handsome head. "It was incredible. Now everyone thinks the Trial is about whether or not Kay caused the attack on the gym. That was *never* what it was about." He stabs the air between us with one finger. "This is about holding a tyrant accountable for his actions."

"A tyrant?"

"We never voted for him. No one asked him to be King. He has absolute power in this school, and anyone who remembers we have, like, *constitutional rights* is a dissident."

I look at him a long moment. "So what would you do differently?"

"What?"

"If you were in charge. Would you take down the fences? Would you stop expanding, or expand in a different direction? What's your goal in rising up against him?"

"The goal *all humanity* has *always fought for.*" He raises his chin. "To be free."

"That's a T-shirt slogan, not a plan," I snap. "I'm sympathetic about wanting to hold elections, believe me. But I'd vote for King Max starting a hospital over the—the abstract concept of freedom any day! How much 'freer' can it get around here? There are no rules that I've seen!"

". . . You're upset," he says gently, as though this invalidates what I've said without him having to refute it. "I'm sure this car is bringing up memories of Kyle."

Before I can tell him it's not that at all, he reaches out and pulls down the visor, and my own junior class picture somersaults into my lap. Kyle had taped it up before he'd driven out.

"I need to talk to you, too," Leo says after a long beat. "Some things went down while Kyle was here. Things that you deserve to know."

I look down at my own tiny smiling face, upside down in my lap: hair and makeup perfect, eyes hopeful. A lamb to the slaughter.

"... Go on."

"The night before Kyle was supposed to leave, that wise, responsible King you would vote for threw one of his trademark orgies in the principal's office." Leo's charm has given way to something colder and more honest. Now we're getting somewhere. "He has one or two a week. He keeps a stash of liquor and drugs in the Cage for his guests."

I'm not surprised Kyle partied with King Max. It would be an opportunity to backchannel support for Jefferson. But I don't interrupt.

"My—my girlfriend, at the time, Jessica. She was at the party. And she said Kyle came on to her really strongly. And they ended up hooking up."

"... They slept together."

He nods. "If you want details—"

I shake my head, then lean forward, a wave of nausea washing over me, and cover my face completely.

In the dark of my hands, Harvey Goodwill's finished basement glows. The faint bass and muffled laughter of the party overhead. The aquarium I stared into, dizzy drunk, as Kyle told me yes: He had hooked up with that sophomore. And he wasn't sorry.

"Why do you even care what I did with her? It's not like *we're* doing anything."

He'd been so completely understanding when we first started dating. My parents were very strict, and I didn't want to deceive them. But over time, that had become incomprehensible. His new go-to response was: "You're almost eighteen, Nirali, what do *you* want?"

The unsaid corollary being, what *could* I possibly want, if I didn't want *him*, the hottest guy in school.

What I wanted, Before, was to be *Nirali Chaudri*. Valedictorian, homecoming queen, half of the most popular couple at Jefferson. A total success.

What I did not want was to go back upstairs and begin senior year alone.

"We could . . . try doing stuff," I wept, using his term for the things he wanted that I didn't.

Kyle's stare was cold: *Prove it.*

So right then and there, in the Goodwills' basement, the party still going, I proved it. I "did stuff" to Kyle, half pretending it was some sort of unorthodox anatomy lesson to get through it. We went back upstairs hand in hand and word went around that we'd made up, and he said in front of all our friends that the sophomore girl was crazy and he had no interest in her. Kyle drove me home, and I let him keep his hand on my knee—a promise I would submit to further incursions. I went up to my room without looking either of my parents in the face. I brushed my teeth until I retched, then washed my face long and hard without once meeting my own eyes in the mirror. I shut myself in my room and didn't come out the rest of the weekend.

Of course, once you get on that escalator, it only goes up. Anatomy lessons became full intercourse, and I hated that even more. I hated sex, and I hated Kyle for demanding it.

But when the Growns happened, all of that stopped. I was working night shifts up in the hospital; he was sleeping in the gym with everyone else. And for that one aspect of our new world, I was truly grateful.

No, I do not want another boyfriend. I don't even want the one I have.

So why is this still painful?

"Her telling me that . . . was the worst I've ever felt," Leo says, agonized. "It still hurts like hell. It probably always will. Because I loved her, I *really* loved her." He leans back, still not looking at me, voice strained. "And things are so . . . we're so limited to each other now, there's no going off to meet people in another town, right. But she still threw away our whole relationship, our whole future, for one night with some guy she'll never see again." He looks at me quickly and adds, "Most likely."

I swallow hard, pivot: "There's no chance you two will work

things out?"

"No way!" He looks shocked. "What, you'd take Kyle back, knowing what I just told you?"

"I have before." I don't know why I say it. Maybe because it's something I could never tell anyone at Jefferson.

Leo lets out a low whistle. "How?"

I shrug again. "Like you said, we're limited now. And he is the best guy at Jefferson by far."

Leo looks sick. "Yeah, well, no thanks. I could never be with someone who cheated. It would drive me out of my mind."

I think of Kay, hanging over Brick's hospital bed. I turn the keys in the ignition, anxious to get the hell out of here.

The Volvo stalls at first, but then the engine turns over and Leo claps, satisfied. We both get out of the stuffy car to circle it again. Leo is suggesting some other minor repairs, when a thin guy with a mop of curly hair and jazz shoes drifts uncertainly across the parking lot. He looks a bit like a worried asparagus, scratching at his neck as he hovers alongside us, waiting to be recognized.

"Hey, uh, Leo?" he interrupts at last.

"Damon. What's up?"

"Have you seen Jessica recently?"

Leo shakes his head.

"She hasn't slept in the theater room since Expansion," Damon says nervously. "Has she been here?"

"She's not with me," Leo says crisply.

"She said she was meeting up with you the night before Expansion."

Leo nods. "Yeah, we met up for a minute. Then she took off early to go to an office party. You know how Jess is." He doesn't make it sound like a compliment. "Look, let me finish up with the Queen here, and then we'll talk. I'll ask around the shop."

Damon nods and moves quickly back toward the school. Leo turns to me, slightly impatient now, his dazzling flirtatious affect discarded.

"Anything else you want for the car?"

I drop my voice. "Well, I don't know how to fix this, but I'm short a driver. For my return trip. Tyler has told me he's going to stay here."

"And you're letting him?"

"It's his decision." I clear my throat, then add, "But I'm inexperienced with driving, the way you have to drive now. And I'm concerned if I have to leave in a hurry for some reason . . ."

"I will drive you myself," Leo says solemnly. "I promise."

I nod, turn, and hurry out of the Auto Shop, heart hammering in my chest.

+ + +

When I get back to the Cavern, Marissa tells me Merlin is waiting to see me on the roof.

I take the narrow back stairs at the end of the hall all the way up, and step out into afternoon sunshine, the sun slanting heavy and honey gold across the broad white roof. There's a greenhouse in one corner, windows sweating from the enclosed wealth of plants, with a shade sail cutting from its topmost eave to the ground. In its shadow are several bird cages: fancy brass ones, pink and green plastic cartons, and a few rustic chicken coops, all housing pigeons.

Merlin, in a threadbare white T-shirt and purple hoodie, is holding a pigeon close, apparently whispering to it. Its flat, iridescent eye flashes, and she tucks it back into its home before coming over to meet me.

"I know, I know, they should be owls." She rolls her eyes, suppressing a smile. "They found me a baby owl from one of the neighborhoods, and I tried, I really did. But he took off the first time I sent him to a wall guard."

"Those are messenger pigeons?"

"Eventually. I'm working on it." She shrugs, gives me a sheepish smile. "So far I've only gotten them to go as far as the West Rocks wall and back again. But I want to try Briggs next. Then maybe Jefferson."

People are too scared to go out on the roof at Jefferson. But before I can admit this, I notice she's staring at my hand. At the King's ring, sparkling ostentatiously. I nervously tighten my ponytail.

"Congratulations," she says. She doesn't sound happy.

"I haven't accepted anything," I inform her. "The King asked me to wear it while I'm considering his proposal. Which I guess he already told you about?"

"Are you kidding?" She comes forward in a rush, then politely extends her hand: *May I?* "I picked out the ring."

I put my hand in hers. She holds it gingerly, thumb just twitching the stone, and the insides of my fingers buzz.

She drops my hand abruptly. "I just never thought you'd actually accept it."

"I was trying to be diplomatic. Ever heard of it?" I say acidly. "But my boyfriend is still out there, and Jefferson would not appreciate me marrying some guy I just met."

"Don't *you* have any feelings on the subject?"

"I am used to considering Jefferson first."

Merlin tilts her head. "Our food truck driver said people at Jefferson were too weak to carry our donations in. I don't think they'll give a damn who you're with if you cut them in on the wedding cake. Do you?"

"Do I what?"

"Give a damn about who you're with. Or is this just a promotion? You liked being first lady, so now you'll be Queen." She stares up at me. "I mean, considering how Kyle acted when he was here, I just figured you two were open."

Open? Like an open relationship? Like I wanted him to cheat on me? I hesitate, heart rate accelerating, unsure what would make me look worse: admitting I knew or claiming ignorance. I reach up and almost tighten my ponytail again, then shake my head. "My relationship with Kyle is none of your business."

"But your relationship with King Max is."

"Well, as the King could tell you himself, there is no relationship.

He's not interested in me that way." I roll my eyes. "He wants to marry me because I'm a doctor—"

"I know what he said," Merlin cuts me off. "He was practicing the whole 'walk to Jefferson' speech on me all morning. But the truth is, he doesn't want to marry you because you're some great surgeon—"

I start to object, but she goes on:

"He wants to marry you because you're beautiful." Merlin's voice is pained. "The most beautiful girl I've ever seen in real life. The kind of beautiful that makes smart people stupid, the kind where once you walk in the room, no one else counts. That's what you are, Nirali." She glares at me. "You're perfect."

A surprising twinge, like a piece of ice slipping down my spine, makes me shiver at the words. I've been told this sort of thing before. Softly, seductively, by guys who wanted something from me. But she says it like a declaration of surrender. Like she is helpless against my power.

"And King Max? He doesn't stand a chance, being across from that every day. Who does? He will fall in love with you. He won't be able to help it." Her face is wrung by frustration, her shoulders high and tense; she pulls the cuffs of her hoodie sleeves over her restless hands. "The King is . . . a romantic. He wouldn't be like Kyle. He doesn't want to be half of a power couple—he thinks he can make you fall in love with him. And when it clicks that you can't, he will feel deceived. And you really don't want him to feel that way. King Max can be the greatest friend you ever have, or your worst enemy."

"Why would you think I can't love him?" I ask.

She looks at me like I know the answer: *Come on, now.*

I shake my head again. "The King made a practical proposal. You're the one getting emotional." I mean, he definitely has a crush on me, but why does she have a problem with that? "You don't want me around—you've made that clear since I got here. You think I'm a fraud and a—"

"You are a great doctor," Merlin says gravely. "I've learned more from you in a couple shifts than from every book in this school."

Warmth, unwelcome, floods me at her words.

"And I like working here, with you," I blurt out. "Back at Jefferson, I don't . . . there's not the same kind of . . ." I struggle for the right words. "I thought we were an even match."

She bites her full bottom lip: I've hit a nerve. She's threatened. Is that what this is? She thinks I'll take her place, is that it?

"Well. It doesn't matter anyway since I'm not staying," I go on quickly. "You can have the King all to yourself. I'll take Kay back to Jefferson as soon as I can, and you'll never have to see me again."

But her shoulders don't relax. If anything, Merlin looks tenser.

"That's no good, either," she says morosely. "He needs you. Moore needs you. But I . . ." Her mouth jerks down on one side. ". . . I didn't see you coming."

She takes her wheels, pivots. For a moment, I'm sure she's going to leave me on the roof without another word. I wish, more than I have since those first months, that I had my phone. So I could take a picture of her in this moment, in the amber light of the afternoon sun. The filigree of gold along the fine curls of her braids and down the long line of her neck, the controlled expression below the wild storm of her eyes. I wish I could look at her as much as I want.

She turns her head, catches me staring, and her shoulders drop.

"Aw, hell." She lifts her chin, almost defiant, that cocky flash back in her eye. ". . . You want to play chess tonight?"

"Tonight?" My heart hammers. ". . . Okay."

There's a loud crack as the fire door flies open behind me. I turn, half expecting to see my father, furious: *What are you girls doing?*

But it's Marissa, panting like she ran all the way up the stairs.

"Queen Nirali!" She holds out a tightly folded square of lined paper. "It's a direct message from the King!"

Merlin waves her hand: *Read it.* I unfold the note:

The thing you wanted? You have half an hour. Go.

†HE DUᑎGEOᑎ

KAY

I bet actual medieval dungeons smelled better than the Moore boys' locker room. Generations of mildew and body odor and fear pheromones from kids who didn't want to publicly disrobe leak from the walls, and bright, too-close eyes skittered around the floor all last night. Rats come up from the drains, big and bold and fast.

I stayed balled up on the camping cot all night, my back against the sheet of dented steel that separates my quadrant of the shower from the rest of the circular stall, too scared to sleep. Even worse than the rats was the yelling from Jimmy's stall, two over from mine. His rattling chain, going taut as he tried to break loose; the tumble and splash of his "necessities" bucket; the harsh smell of his urine seeping toward me along the grid of grout between the small gray tiles.

"Hey, bitch," Jimmy kept calling. "I'm going to set you on fire."

Then his lighter would click and fizzle. I was cold enough that this started to sound less and less like a threat. But his chatter became crass and personal. I didn't let myself cry until I heard him snore.

The guards came in after what felt like one hundred years with food: a big bowl of pasta, no complaints there. I can hear their echoing steps now, down the bank of lockers between the shower room and the hall doors. More food?

"Champion incoming!" one yells. "Kay, look sharp! You have a visit from your lawful and true champion!"

The guard is warning me in case I'm on the bucket. Luckily, I'd rather die than use it. And though it's empty, I slide it under the cot, then shuffle my chained leg back under me just as Leo appears, haloed like an angel by the flashlight he carries.

"Dear God." Leo's flashlight swoops from my face to the thick chain leashing me to the stall, to the hunched figure of a rat darting across the floor. He sets the flashlight down with a curse, his black Carhartt hoodie and dark hair cut out against the gray of the diffused light, and hugs me close.

I keep my face slightly turned away in case he tries to kiss me. But of course he doesn't. I'm completely gross right now; I haven't changed or bathed since the night of the attack. I'm wearing the same coverall I wore during Expansion, stiff in places from Brick's blood. Leo leans back and surveys me with evident distaste.

"He will pay for this, Kay, I promise you," he says grimly. We listen to the guards' steps retreating back out to the hall. Once the door falls closed and the echo fades, the only sound is Jimmy's snoring.

"Who's that?" Leo mouths.

"Jimmy." My voice comes out hoarse. "He should be out for a while. He was up all night. Have you heard about Brick? Has he woken up yet?"

"I hope not." Leo's frown deepens. "It would make things a lot more difficult tomorrow if he did. Artemis—" Leo stops, considers, then continues. "She said something about you being involved with him."

The side of my mouth jerks. "With Brick?"

Face, stop—please, for both of us, please stop.

"Yeah." Leo stares at me. "When I was looking for you in the gym after Expansion, she said she saw the two of you meeting up by the Theater Department."

It had felt like a kiss, locking eyes with Brick that night.

But we hadn't touched.

"She said that?" My voice is too high.

"Is it true?"

"We were talking, yeah. I had to talk to him." That is true. "But I'm not with him." Also true. "He came back really late, and I met him coming from his truck. We hadn't planned to meet up or anything." All of this is literally true. I can say it without smiling. Just barely.

"See?" Leo calls over his shoulder, and a hooded figure moves out of the shadows. An emerald velveteen hood falls back, and Artemis's heavily lined eyes glare at me through the dark. "She's cool, I told you."

"I don't know." Artemis crosses her arms. "There was really a vibe between them."

I look from her to Leo. "What is happening right now?"

Artemis rolls her eyes. "Calm down. We're just trying to get some clarity. Did you really think Brick could wake up soon?" Artemis searches my face, then cuts a look to Leo. "Because if that's even a possibility, I should talk to my friend."

"Talk to your friend. Better safe than sorry." Leo nods.

"What friend? What is going on?" I cry.

Leo puts his hand on my shoulder. "Tomorrow, I am going to accuse King Max of Kyle's murder in front of the whole school. I'll either fight Tyler, or I'll fight King Max, but either way I'll win. The only risk is if Slayer wakes up before then."

"Why would that matter?"

"Because he's the Captain of the Guard." Artemis rolls her eyes. "If someone challenges King Max, they have to go through Brick. But if he's out of commission, the King has to defend himself."

"King Max is a joke as a fighter. I'd destroy him," Leo says confidently, then frowns. "But a fight with Slayer? I don't know how that would end."

"So wait, I don't understand. You're accusing him of *murder*?" I look from Leo to Artemis. "You have evidence that Max killed Kyle?"

"That's the beauty of the Trial by Combat!" Artemis smiles. "We don't need evidence! We just have to make sure Brick stays down for the count."

I turn on her. "You're going to *kill Brick*?!"

Artemis's eyes bulge as she shushes me, jerking her head in the direction of Jimmy. "Would you calm down! No one is killing Brick! My friend will just slip him some Nyquil or something to make sure there's no surprises."

"You can't mess with him right now!" My chest is so tight. "He's not in a stable condition. He lost *a lot* of blood, okay? You could kill him! Just leave him alone, please, I'm begging you."

"See?" Artemis turns to Leo. "She's in love with Slayer."

They'll kill him. *They'll kill Brick if I don't fix this right now.*

"Yeah, right, Heather!" I choke out. My face is burning, but my smile is in check. I can do this, I can do this for him. "Look at Leo. You really think any girl would choose Brick over *him*?"

I'm blushing so hard, but Leo isn't Brick; he's never bothered to learn my tells. He is convinced. Artemis is not.

"So why were you so anxious to talk with him the other night?" she pushes.

"My locket is in the Cage." Also a true statement. The more I focus on the truth, the easier it is to control my face. "I had him put it there in case I didn't make it back. It has a picture of my little brother in it." The thought of Arthur vanishes any trace of a smile. "I hadn't taken it off since Before, and I wanted it back. I still do."

"I'll get it back for you," Leo promises. "Tomorrow will be a big day. Things are going to change, and they might change very fast, once I make the challenge, so be ready. We're going to give the crowd a couple they can really root for." He looks me up and down and says to Artemis, "She should be in a dress."

"Play up the damsel in distress bit, sure," Artemis agrees.

"Would you mind, Kay, wearing a dress for tomorrow?" Leo asks.

"Whatever you need." I nod.

"And we'll kiss, after I win."

"Of course." I nod again.

The doors clap open in the distance. A rough voice yells, "Time's up, champion!" and Leo's face flickers with annoyance.

He reaches out, squeezes my hand. "I'll leave you the flashlight."

"And you won't mess with Brick?" I hiss as they turn to go. It's pushing things, but I need to hear them say it, or I will lose my mind once I'm alone.

"We'll do what needs to be done." Artemis raises an eyebrow, then pulls Leo's arm. "Come on—"

They sweep past the stall divider, past the range of my chain, Artemis's steps vanishing up the pool stairs as Leo calls out to the guards, "All set. Let's go."

I can't do this. I can't just stay down here if Brick is in danger. Maybe I can get the chain loose somehow? I hop onto my cot to reach the end tethered to the shower stall, but it collapses instantly. I crash to the floor with a yelp.

"Kay! Are you all right?" Nirali helps me to my feet.

"Nirali?" I whisper. "It's you! You have to go back to the Cavern. They're going to hurt Brick." I am close to hyperventilating. "Artemis is—she has—she said her friend—"

"I heard. I snuck down the pool stairs right about the time Leo came in. It's all right, Kay. I won't let anyone touch Brick. Just calm down." The flashlight catches her shiny black hair in its beam, makes her large liquid eyes glitter. "It's going to be all right."

I bury my face in my hands and burst into tears. She watches me helplessly. She's not a hugger, and I said some terrible things at the feast. Worse, I said terrible things that were true.

"I don't know what to do," I say, voice all high.

"Here is what we know." Nirali's voice is cool, efficient. "Leo wants a fight. And King Max does not. He's willing to do anything he can to prevent it. I know he came down on you hard, but he's just trying to keep things under control—"

"Is that how you justified the Rule?" I ask dully. "'Keeping things under control'?"

Nirali gives me a look of utter contempt. "Kay. You are in a dungeon right now. Your life is on trial tomorrow. I am the only person in this school you can trust, and you want to *pick a fight with me*—"

"Trust you?" I wipe at my face. "I don't trust you. There's no one I can trust anymore, that's my whole problem. All of you just lie and lie whenever you—"

Nirali seizes my arm and leans in.

"There are things more important than the truth. I lied to *save lives* at Jefferson. And I will say whatever it takes here at Moore to get you out safe. You can trust me to do what's best for you, Kay. But first you need to grow up and stop questioning every decision I make because, the fact is, I know better than you do!"

Her hand gripping my arm catches the beam of the flashlight; it sparkles almost audibly.

". . . Where'd you get that ring?"

Nirali pulls the hand back like I've burned her. "King Max proposed."

"And you said yes?!"

"I didn't say *no*." Off my horrified reaction, she goes on, defensively, "So he would let me come see you! Aren't you glad I did?"

I start crying again.

"I don't have a ton of options here. Tyler is staying at Moore. He made that *very* clear," Nirali goes on. "Leo offered to give us a ride home if we need one, but it sounds like he might be busy tomorrow. King Max says if we announce our marriage ahead of the Trial we can skip the combat. And that's the best plan I've heard so far."

"You wouldn't." I shake my head, but she just stares at me. "You *cannot* marry Max," I insist. "I don't know how to tell you this, Nirali, but I found—"

"Kyle's inhaler," she finishes for me. "I know. Merlin told me."

". . . Oh."

Her hands float up to her ponytail, her nervous habit: she tightens it with a painful wrench. "And I know about Kyle hooking up with *Leo's girlfriend* at the King's party. Maybe that's where Leo's antagonism is coming from, that she was off partying with the King."

"*Leo's* antagonism? Max is the one antagonizing Leo!" I object.

"Leo is willing to kill King Max, and Brick too if he has to," Nirali says coldly. "King Max is trying to unite the school, and Leo is trying to tear it apart. This place—" She shakes her head; her eyes soften with admiration. "What Merlin and King Max have built here is incredible. I don't think you or Leo appreciate how hard it is. To make something like this and then keep it going."

"I don't think you or Max appreciate how much better you have it than everyone else!" I stand, and the chain on my leg clatters ominously. I kick my leg, rattling my leash against the tile. "Your comfort comes at the cost of everyone else being afraid *all the time.*"

"They have all the food they want, Kay. And he's willing to share with us." She rubs under her eyes, weary. "If that means marrying him, fine."

"Even if he killed Kyle?"

She flounders, about to sputter a response, and I go on: "Why would Kyle leave without calling in one last time? Without taking the radio and supplies? Without *one of his inhalers*—"

"I don't know."

"But Jessica might," I push. "Leo's girlfriend, from Max's party."

". . . You think I should go and talk with her?"

"It can't hurt, right?" But of course it will hurt, talking to the girl her beloved boyfriend cheated with. "If I could go find her myself, I would. I'm sorry to ask you to do this, Nirali, but—"

"I can handle it. It's not a problem," she says quickly. "But I don't actually know who I'm looking for. Do you know what she looks like?"

"Just that she's beautiful."

Nirali sighs. "Well. Whatever happens, we have a way out tomorrow that doesn't involve anyone getting hurt. You only have to make it through one more night down here."

"I can handle being down here if I know you're keeping Brick safe."

Nirali nods. "You have my word. No one will touch Brick."

"Thank you," I whisper, and the door from the hall to the locker room opens, voices echoing down the tile.

Nirali squeezes my arm before disappearing between the showers.

Then she cries out, the sound arcing sharply down to the floor.

Jimmy's manic laughter rings through my skull:

"Well, well, well, what have we here?"

İL-Lİ-Cİt:
FORBİDDEN

NIRALI

"You smell good . . ." the unseen assailant says. He grabbed my ankle as I ran by, and now he's crawling on top of me. He smells like urine, and there's a strange chemical sting to his breath; his fingers twitch up my body, toward my chest, and his jittering eyes are dilated. I bite back a scream as the guards approach.

"What you got hold of, Jimmy?" one of them calls.

"He's so strung out on Drive he's probably making out with his foot!" Kay calls back.

I scuffle to my feet, then kick out hard, my foot connecting with his hip. His laughter twists into a sharp whine. My running steps ring through the tiled space, and the guards hurry after me, racing me to the back door. I sprint up the stairs to the pool.

"Stop! Stop in the name of the King!"

I run, gasping, out into the vast white space of the pool room. I'll be seen if I run for the doors, so I turn and hop down into the empty pool itself, the point right before it angles toward the deep end. I land hard, impact ringing through my shins, then press myself up against the tile wall and fight to hold my breath.

The guards' sneakers squeak across the tile just overhead.

"Those doors are supposed to be *locked*, Chris."

"I didn't unlock them! You hear that? In the hall—"

They take the steep bleachers two at a time, steps fading out into the athletic hall, and I exhale.

I cross the empty pool, clamber out the other side, and exit the school. I lean against the warm concrete exterior wall, safe, and for just a moment let myself enjoy the sunlight.

I'm not the only one. The lawn is blanketed with beautiful girls sunbathing. Most are in bikinis, some with the back strings pulled down or completely undone so they don't leave tan lines. More bikini girls run, laughing, across the parking lot, damp skin gleaming in the sunlight.

I remember an SAT lesson that said *paradise* comes from an ancient Iranian word meaning "walled garden." Moore has its fences, and these girls are the flowers. Kyle must have loved it here; he probably thanked his lucky stars the moment he saw this lawn.

The mystery is why he ever left.

Where are you, Kyle? What happened?

Trudging several feet behind the laughing bikini girls is the boy with the bad haircut, the one who approached Leo in the Auto Shop, a towel knotted around his hips like a skirt. I cut across the parking lot toward him. He's so lost in his thoughts he doesn't notice me walking alongside him until I finally tap on his shoulder.

"Damon, right?"

"Yes!" He adjusts his glasses, looks down at me from his droopy asparagus height. "Your Majesty, uh, hello. How can I help you?"

"It's just Nirali. I recognized you from before." I slow our pace so we fall farther behind the girls, out of earshot. "Any luck finding your friend Jessica?"

"No, actually." He winces. "Everyone I talk to is like, 'Oh, she must have got hurt in the attack.' But I've checked the gym, I've checked the lab, I even checked the lists outside." He means the lists identifying those who died during the Grown attack. He brushes under his glasses quickly with the side of his hand. "And I can't find her anywhere."

We land in front of the concrete steps to the musical wing doors. His friends pause, waiting for him. He nods their way: *Just a second.*

"But you thought Leo might know, because . . . ?"

He shakes his head, looks around, and says, "Why don't we go up to the dressing room?"

He leads me into the music hall, the bikini girls darting curious looks at us. Most of them break off and lope down the hall into the school, but two of them, a tall redhead and a short brunette, travel ahead of us around the corner and up an echoing set of stairs.

"Usually, when Jess isn't sleeping in the theater wing, she's with him. They're together. Not 'really,' but *really*, you know?" Damon continues fretfully. "The last time I saw her, she was on her way to meet him before she went to the office party before this last Expansion—"

"Wait. The office party the night before the gym attack?" the redhead interrupts, unapologetically eavesdropping. "Jess didn't go to that party. I was there pretty much all night, and I didn't see her."

"No?" I frown, my eyes cutting to Damon. "Didn't Leo say she left him early to go?"

Damon scans our surroundings as we get to the top of the stairs, then motions for me to follow him. The redhead widens her eyes at me: *Some big secret, huh?*

We careen around an old baby grand in front of a whiteboard in a sunny chorus room; the room has been converted into something between a laundry and a dressmaker's shop, with dress forms draped in outrageous formal wear and long clotheslines of drying clothes. We duck under a gold lame choir robe and hurry into a dressing room scattered with cheap club clothes and crumpled bedding.

The dressing room is long and narrow and lit entirely with camping lanterns so it feels like the middle of the night. A mirror runs the entire length of one wall, over a thick Formica counter on which all kinds of makeup, hairbrushes, and snacks are jumbled. A back door opens out onto a black hall; a dead smartphone is wedged under it for a doorstop.

Damon collapses onto an old couch, fake leather seats patched with duct tape; the redhead hovers beside us as I perch on its arm. By the mirror, the short brunette girl adjusts her bikini top. And in the corner is a pale guy with dyed black hair. He wears a black bikini top, a knee-length black skirt, and clunky boots. He keeps shuffling shabby cards around and tiling them on the floor.

"Hey, Andi," the redhead calls to the brunette. "Jess didn't go to that last office party, right?"

Andi takes a bag of gummy worms from the counter beside her and tears it open, considering.

"Before this last Expansion? If she did, I didn't see her. And she *definitely* missed the crowning ceremony—we had an extra candle and it messed with our blocking. Guess Jess had better things to do, if you know what I mean." Andi rolls her hips suggestively, face deadpan.

"*Andi*," Damon snaps. "How does it feel to be the saltiest, most shameful bitch to walk the face of this earth? Or should I ask your mom?"

They all laugh then. Andi bites one end of a gummy worm and pulls it until it snaps, holding Damon's eyes, unfazed.

"Wasn't she staying with that one guard, Chris?" the redhead asks.

"Aren't *all* the guards named Chris?" Andi laughs.

"Could you go check?" Damon grabs the redhead's hand. "Like, could you go ask that guard if she's been staying with him, while I talk to this visiting royal? *Please*, Zoe, I beg of you?"

"Yeah, sure, no problem."

She turns for the back door, and Damon calls after her, "AND HURRY BACK!" before reaching out with one long, impatient hand to Andi: "Can I get some gummy worms, please?"

Andi hauls them over like she's carrying a block of cement.

"Why are you looking for Jess?" asks a low deep voice from the corner: the boy with the dyed black hair. He turns giant pale eyes on me; he has a surprisingly sweet expression.

"I have a couple questions for her. About my boyfriend, Kyle."

The air goes tense.

I take a gummy worm from Andi with a smile: *I know, but I won't freak out.*

"Jess didn't know Kyle had a girlfriend," Damon says quickly.

"But *she* had a boyfriend, didn't she?" I keep smiling.

"Damn!" Andi puts her hand over her mouth. "They don't call it the Drama Department for nothing!"

"No. They were not official, because Jess wanted to do her own thing," Damon insists. "She liked working the royal parties, and he thought she should sit around in his Auto Shop and just look at him instead."

"What does it mean, to 'work' a royal party?" My skin is starting to crawl. What is King Max asking these girls to do?

"Okay, so—" Andi sounds like this isn't the first time she's had to explain this. "King Max has these parties that are *very* VIP. Because only so many people can fit in the office area, right? But he always reserves spots on the list for the Theater Department. We have to dress up, like you would for a nice club night, or come in costume if it's a theme night—Before movies, that was fun, angels and devils, and—"

"But only the girls get invited," Damon cuts in, giving me a look. "He wants to make sure there are more girls than guys. So it's not a bunch of straight bros standing around staring at their shoes."

I cringe. "Right. Frat party rules."

"That's what Moore *is*, right?" the boy in the corner adds sarcastically. "An eternal frat party you can never leave."

I bite my lip. "So how do you decide which girls go? Does Artemis choose?"

"It sorts itself out." Andi shrugs. "Because some people *really* don't like to go, and some people *really* do. Jess would always go, because she likes to get wasted."

"Andi, you are actually a trash can." Damon throws a gummy worm at her. She catches it with a big smile and eats it.

"Jessica is a lot smarter than people realize." The boy in the corner looks up at me again. "People think she's so hot she must be dumb. She's not. She's so smart I think it makes her kind of sad. These days, she likes to turn her brain down a bit. And I don't blame her."

Andi rolls her eyes. "Yeah, well, seems like she's been turning her brain all the way off, since that Jefferson guy came through." Her tone is not charitable. "Guess she thought he'd stay for her, or something. But he dipped, and Leo won't take her back. And now *he's* hooking up with a new girl at *their* old hookup spot and the whole school knows about it."

Hell yes, Kay, I think grimly.

"You think Jess confronted Leo about Kay?" I ask Damon.

"No, it was his idea to meet up. He wanted to set the record straight, the night before Expansion." Damon absently plucks at his hair. "And I haven't seen her since."

"And now Leo's going to fight to the death for the new girl, but like, what?" Andi rolls her eyes. "I don't get it. That new girl's such a bowl of plain oatmeal."

"Um, that bowl of plain oatmeal is *her best friend*!" Damon gasps, gesturing at me.

"I was a little surprised they got together myself." I smile conspiratorially: *Keep talking, Andi*. "So Jess wasn't going to all those parties because there was something between her and King Max?"

They all gasp.

"Oh no no no." Damon shakes his head. "*No*. King Max has always been hands off with her, because of Brick."

"Jess and Brick were together?"

Damon shakes his head. "You know that condominium behind Cumberland Farms?"

Cumberland Farms is—was?—a shabby liquor store right by the train tracks. I seem to remember dogs barking a lot in the building behind it.

"Their moms lived on the same floor and were friends. Jess's mom worked days, Brick's mom worked nights, so they traded off babysitting. Brick and Jess basically grew up together. Jess always says Brick is like her brother."

Of course, that awful sophomore girl Kyle hooked up with used to claim the same thing about Kyle.

"Though, if you want to know what *I* think—" Damon leans in confidentially, as though reading my face, when the chorus room door flies open, and the High Priestess herself comes in.

Down in the dungeon, after she'd stepped from the shadows in her cape, I had felt a thrill of repulsion at Artemis. At the way she'd casually referenced giving Brick, already unconscious, a sedative; at how she'd sneered that she and Leo didn't need evidence, they could just kill King Max with impunity. Her large, unblinking eyes, with no question behind them about the crimes she was suggesting, had truly frightened me.

I jump at her entrance now, as she strides in with a garment bag draped over one arm, barking orders like a sergeant:

"Andi! I need something hemmed for the Trial, right now, so make it snappy."

Andi claps gummy-worm sugar off her hands and takes the offered garment bag.

"Use the Singer in my office. Can I get some gummy worms? Thanks. Damon!" Artemis, mouth full of candy, turns to Damon, then clocks me.

Her face erupts in a smile that doesn't reach her bulging eyes. She bows with surprising grace. "Your *Majesty*! To what do we owe the honor?"

I'm at a total loss. I didn't prepare an excuse, and I certainly can't tell her the truth.

"She wanted someone to read her tarot," the boy with black hair covers for me, tone perfectly bored.

"Very cool!" Artemis smiles wider. Lipstick is smeared across her teeth again. Does she not have a single real friend who will show her how to blot correctly? "That's actually perfect, because I'm working on *your* dress right now and I was kind of guessing at your measurements. Maybe we could sneak in a quick fitting?"

I'm getting a Trial dress, too?

"Of course." I nod, stiff, and Artemis points a finger gun at me, bangles clanking, before hurrying back into the chorus room. The moment the door falls closed, the redhead comes in the back door from the hall. She's slightly breathless and eating a roasted squirrel leg.

"Chris hasn't seen Jess," she says, and Damon deflates into the couch.

"I can see why you're worried," I tell Damon. "I'll ask the King to search for her."

"If you could do that," Damon says eagerly, "I would *really* appreciate it. Like, you have no idea."

"Of course," I say, and there's a beat of awkward silence. "What were you about to tell me, before Artemis came in?"

"Nothing, nothing." Damon shakes his head quickly. "I forgot already."

He's watching the chorus room door now, tensed. Is he afraid of Artemis overhearing?

"Let me read your tarot," the boy in the corner says, that deep voice so startling.

"Oh! Thank you, that's very kind. But I don't really believe in all that stuff."

"Come on," he insists. "Someone wants to communicate with you. I can feel it."

The room has gone silent. Everyone watches me stand and cross over to him. I don't like this kind of stuff, fortune tellers or Ouija boards. But not wanting to kill the fragile rapport in the room, I settle down on my knees across from him and force a quick smile.

"Hi, Nirali," he says. "I'm Kelly."

"Hi, Kelly."

Up close, he has golden eyelashes with lots of kohl around them, and shiny blue-black polish on his nails. They flash as he handles the cards, fanning them out and collecting them with practiced gestures.

"Why don't we go back to what brought you here," he says. "What do you really want to know about Kyle?"

"I guess I want to know if he's okay," I say, feeling foolish. "And when I'll see him again."

Kelly nods. But instead of having me select the cards, he turns the images to face him and rifles through like he's arranging notes for a speech. Then he tiles them, face down in rows of three, with a last card at the end.

He flips over the first row: the Lovers, the Hanged Man, and the Wheel of Fortune. The pictures are strangely old and wildly colorful, each one a sinister fairy tale.

"These cards are saying you should *definitely* hang on to Kyle. He's the best, a prince, your love is perfect and true." He flips the cards in the next row. "The World, the Star, the Fool. These tell me that, after he hooked up at the party, he realized it was time to hit the road and get back to his mission. He's far away now, miles and miles, for sure."

If he thinks this is comforting, it's not. Honestly, it's sort of offensive. But his eyes bore into mine like he's speaking some kind of code, as he turns over the final three cards: Death, the Chariot, and the Emperor.

"These tell me you will see him again soon, and live happily ever after."

He holds up the last card, a woman on a throne holding a sword. "This is the most important one, understand?"

He throws it on top of the other ones, the lady upside down so her sword points toward me.

"*Understand?*" he repeats. I feel suddenly queasy.

The door bangs open, and Artemis sweeps back in, arms full of billowing white silk; she looks like she's wrestling a parachute.

"Ta-da!" She hangs the white bundle on the mirror frame. "Your dress is ready to try on, Your Highness!"

"Wow." I stand uneasily. "This must be a very fancy Trial."

Artemis gives me a puzzled look as the massive skirt drops down from a sweetheart bodice and . . . a veil?

"This isn't for the Trial," Artemis says. "This is your wedding dress."

✝HE FOOL

KAY

"Kay!"

I stir on my narrow cot. I must be dreaming. There's no way that voice is who I think it is.

"Kaaaay," Max calls again. He sounds like he's smiling. The amber halo of his torch blooms past the edge of my shower stall, and then he's right across from me in the small space, two guards flanking him. One has a wire shopping basket over his arm, full of food. The other sets up a camping chair for Max, then helps me to my feet.

I watch in disbelief as they layer my cot with down blankets and pillows. Max waits until they're finished, then, seeing my flashlight, commands them to take his torch and dismisses them. He gestures to a garment bag, laid out on top of the puffy new bedding.

"From my High Priestess," he says.

The "damsel in distress" dress Leo wanted. Artemis found a way to get *Max* to deliver it? I immediately unzip my coverall and shuck the stiff sleeves off my arms.

"What are you doing?!" Max laughs.

"Getting dressed. I haven't changed since Expansion. Don't look."

"Don't look? At what?" He shields his face with his hand. "Your bones? You look like a Halloween decoration, get over yourself."

Still hotter than your Ren-faire reject ass is my kneejerk response, but I bite my tongue and unzip the garment bag.

The dress inside is a strange A-line shift with a deep scoop neck. A tag on the hanger reads: MHS 97 CAMELOT / CH: GUINEVERE / EXECUTION. The material is scratchy and smells like mothballs, but I don't care. It feels so good to get the bloody coverall off.

"That was a joke." Max's chair squeaks as he leans back, nervously bouncing one leg.

"Oh yeah?" I say flatly. "Warn me next time, so I can fake laugh like the rest of your friends."

A tense silence, then: "I feel like you and I got off on the wrong foot, Kay."

"You mean when you made me bow to you?" I pull the dress over my head.

"Very weird of you to take that personally. I make everyone do that." Max drops his hand from his face. I don't ask how he knew I was done dressing; I can guess. "Because I am King, whether you like it or not. But right now, I am also your potential friend."

If looks could kill, he would be a pile on the floor right now.

"Nirali values you a lot," he goes on, his tone uncharacteristically reverent. "And she is such a *special person*. I've never met anyone like her before in my life. We've become so close, so fast—"

"Uh-huh." He thinks she's hot, I get it.

"But I can sense she has reservations about my proposal—I'm sure she told you about it?"

"Yup." I cut a glance to the food, the bed. Now it makes sense.

"Well. I would *really appreciate it*, Kay, if you could put in a good word for me."

I burst out laughing. He smiles at first, but his smile eventually sours when I don't stop. I can't help it—it's laugh or cry at this point. He is out of his mind. *He is absolutely unhinged.*

"Now *that* was hilarious," I manage at last. "Look, Max? You had me thrown in a dungeon—"

"For your own safety."

"It's not safe in here! I had to deal with Jimmy all night—"

"He's out." Max throws an arm over the back of the chair, leans past the shower partition, and whistles, a piercing taxi-summoning whistle, then yells: "Chris?! CHRIS! Hey—take Jimmy in the other locker room. Now, yeah, right now."

There is a wheeze and a few belligerent protests from Jimmy as the guard rousts him to his feet and unchains him. But in a matter of moments, the pool doors are banging closed and Jimmy's shouts are silenced by the layers of concrete between him and me.

The relief is physical. I drop down onto my soft, fluffy cot and bury my face in my hands.

Everything that was bothering me has so easily been taken care of. Just because Max said so. I live or die because Max says so. And we both know it.

"What else do you want?" Max taps his fingers on his knee and surveys my semicircle cell. "That's kind of a flimsy dress. Maybe you'd like a hoodie as well? Keep that bald little head of yours cozy, or—"

"Why would I help you?" I cut him off. "Why in the world would I talk anyone into marrying you, let alone someone I consider a *dear* friend?"

"You could be with Brick."

He says it so casually, but everything I was going to say I forget.

"We could go on double dates," he adds with a smirk. "You and him, and me and Nirali. The four of us getting dinner, doing brunch, how fun would *that* be, Kay?"

He offers this now, of course. When I don't know if Brick will even wake up. When Leo is my "champion" and I'm supposed to move into the Auto Shop if I live through tomorrow. When it's too late. Of course.

"And you were just keeping us apart before because . . . what? Because you don't want someone taking up his time, is that—"

"Because I don't trust you." Max shrugs. "I don't think you're really into Brick."

I blink at him. "You think I like Leo?"

"I think you like power," Max says simply. "And that's why Simon kicked you out of Jefferson. Because he saw that, too. Your little Costco plot was a strong play for the crown—"

"We don't have crowns at Jefferson."

"For 'president,' whatever you want to call it. Costco was a good idea! But you didn't have the guts to just go for it, *you asked permission*, and that's why you failed. You tell everyone you can't lie, but what I see is someone who can't be honest with herself. About what she wants, and why."

I am stunned silent for a moment, then shake my head. "You don't know me at all."

"I know if I proposed to you right now, you'd say yes." Max stares at me, on the edge of a smile, so perfectly confident. "You want power. It's easy to tell. Because the people who don't want it—and there are very, very few—*don't get any*."

"If getting power is how you can tell someone wants power, maybe look around!" I gesture at the "dungeon" surrounding us. "What power do I have here, Max?"

"Look who's across from you!" His tone is truly resentful, eyes snapping under his thick dark eyebrows. "Do you have any idea how valuable my time is? Yet here I am, in my own damn dungeon, negotiating with a lousy little traitor. Look at it from my perspective." Max leans forward, his features sharpened by his focus. "You just got here, and you're with the leader of the largest and only opposing room. Then you try to trade him in for my best friend. Who, by all rights—I'll say it! I'll say it!—who by all rights, should be the King of Moore. Brick should be King! I told him that first day: 'You killed the dragon, man.' *But he doesn't want it*." Max glares at me. "But you would. You would come up with something, you would make it seem like Brick just *had* to 'make the sacrifice' and be King for everybody else's sake and—"

"No." I shake my head. "I would never want Brick to be anything but himself."

"Which is why you're with Leo," Max goes on. I start to protest, but he waves a hand in my face as he steamrolls on: "Then, at my first sign of weakness, you bring in Nirali to be Moore's new savior. And at our historic first meeting with Jefferson, in front of all my rooms, you turn around and *accuse me of murder*! With Leo just *waiting* to pounce. That was an attempted coup, Kay! *Not cool.*"

"No, it wasn't—"

"Yes, it was, *yes, it was*, enough!" He laughs in my face. "You had a strong play, but you fumbled the ball. *Just like at Jefferson.*"

"You're out of your mind."

"And you're in denial! Do I have to spell it out for you? You spend all winter starving, but you don't put forward your Costco idea until you hear there might be elections. *What do you think that was?*" He sits back, shaking his head at me. "You want power, Kay, and you keep getting *thiiiiis* close." He pinches his fingers together in front of his eye. "But not quite."

"All I want is to keep my friends alive."

"Yeah? Cool. That's all I want, too." Max puts out his hands, shrugs, and smiles. "But, like, I can actually do it."

I shake my head, fighting to hold back tears.

"I'm sorry to break it to you, Kay." He leans in, voice gentle, like a kindergarten teacher explaining something painful to a child. "But no matter how hard you stomp your bony little feet and yell how things aren't fair and poor little you, none of that is going to get you where you want to be. Which is Queen." His smile gets broader. "But Nirali gets it. She *gets it*. So if you play your cards right, you could be the Queen's best friend. Which is one hell of an upgrade from where you're sitting."

What I want is to slap him across his face, knock his chair backward, and kick him while he's down.

But I have to focus, I have a very small window of opportunity here. He doesn't know Nirali is ready to marry him. And no thanks to me—I've tried my best to talk her out of it. But she's ready to announce their engagement so everyone will forget the Trial tomorrow in all the excitement over a royal wedding.

Unless I can show Nirali he's been covering up Kyle's death. That, she would not forgive. And I know he's covering up *something*. Otherwise, why would Merlin take the inhaler? So how do I make Max think it's in his best interest to tip his hand? If he wants to be with Nirali so bad, is there a way to use that, to make him tell on himself? I think there is.

If I can just keep a straight face. Please, just this once, you stupid face, be cool.

I let my head drop, as though I'm mustering strength to tell him a secret. Then I lift my chin and say, as earnestly as I can, "Nirali will not be with someone else while she believes Kyle is alive." All true. "But if she knew for a fact he were dead, she would be more . . . practical." She's a very practical person. This is a fact.

"I see." The weight of his stare is terrible. "But if I can't prove—"

"Are you sure you can't?"

Max holds very still, and I go on:

"Nirali is going to find out what happened to Kyle. She's asking around right now. *She is going to find out.* All you can do now is try to beat her to the punch. Tell her yourself."

He sits back in the chair. His knee starts going again, bouncing on the ball of his foot, while he stares at me. "Why are you so sure that I killed him?"

"Because maybe I can't lie"—it is a white-knuckled fight to keep my voice calm—"but lying is *all* you do. Everything about you is a goddamn fiction, from your crown to your friendship with Brick to your dickheaded proposals. The fact that you keep insisting Kyle is fine is all I need to know that you probably *strangled him yourself*. And I would *never* make any kind of deal with you, Max—"

"That's *King* Ma—"

"I will never call you King again as long as I live."

He bursts out laughing, leaning forward so fast I flinch. But he doesn't strike me. He just stares, wide-eyed, then shakes his head, teeth bared in an angry smile.

"Well! I won't keep you from the rest of your night." He gestures toward the rat-infested shower room. "I've got to get back to my throne room and people I actually like. But remember, Kay: when I stand to leave, you have to kneel."

"Fuck you."

He leans in farther, smile straining like he's keeping in a yell, and rises to his feet. "Get on your knees. Or I'll have them bring Jimmy back. And handcuff you two together for the rest of the night."

I spill forward off the cot, the tile cold and hard under my knees, and bow my head forward so I don't have to look at him. I wish I could hurt him. I wish there was any way in this world I could even threaten him. There's only one thing I can think of.

"When Brick wakes up," I say through clenched teeth, "and finds out how you've treated me, he'll never forgive you."

My face is burning, and I bite my lip to try and control my facial tic. But Max leans down, grabs my chin, and wrenches my head back so we're face-to-face.

"Aww, so red." He grins. "You're so red right now, Kay. It's *pathetic*. You know what, Kay? Here's a tip." He runs his thumb slowly from the corner of my mouth to my ear, as though gauging the heat of my blush. "The best liars know the truth is whatever the most people will agree to. So, stop worrying about telling the truth. Worry about saying things *people like*."

His hand drops away, and he grabs the flashlight on his way out, leaving me in the dark.

Con-script:
to force to join

NIRALI

How do I ask my royal patient if he plans on forcing me to marry him?
I perch on the ergonomic principal's chair in front of the desk where
I've laid out my medical supplies, considering. Artemis had seemed
shaken when I refused to let her take my measurements. I told her
the dress would not be necessary. I couldn't even look at the cloud
of white fabric, hovering over us like a ghost. *My wedding dress?* My
wedding dress would be a red lehenga choli, and I, Nirali Chaudri,
Jefferson valedictorian and Yale-admitted student, was still deciding
whether I wanted to honor their "King" with my hand, thank you
very much.

Unless this was never my choice at all.

My father always said the most important decision I'd make
in life is the man I marry. My father only permitted me to date
Kyle because he was the most promising young man in town. The
handsome, wealthy Student Council president, from the best family
in Brockton, who unfailingly got me home by curfew.

My father would not have let King Max in the house. And I've spent the day debating whether or not to sell myself to him, *for food.* Now I know he's planning the wedding without waiting for my decision. Am I his doctor, or his captive?

I'm not supposed to be here. I'M NOT SUPPOSED—

"You're not supposed to be here." The King of Moore High steps into the principal's office. He looks more pained than I've ever seen him, even during stitches. But he forces a smile and adds, "Not that I mind! But I thought we were doing doctor stuff *after* dinner?"

"I've been to the Theater Department." I lean back in the chair, Kyle's jacket hanging off the back of it like a protective shield, and fold my arms across my chest. "I know, okay?"

He takes a step back, almost bouncing against the closed door, and stares at me.

"About the wedding dress?" I add sharply.

"Oh, right! Right." He nods quickly, then gives me a broad, excited smile. "Do you like it? I haven't seen it yet."

"*Do I like it?*" I throw my arms out wide: *Somebody help me explain to this man!* "You could have waited to see if I *said yes*?"

"Just hedging my bets." He shrugs and unzips his hoodie with his good hand, throwing it to the bed with a thoughtless gesture. Then he pulls off his T-shirt so he's unnecessarily half-naked when he adds, "That way, if you say yes, I have everything ready to go."

If he thinks he's going to soften me up with some hard abs, he's in for a disappointment.

"And if I say no? What happens then? The Trial happens, is that it? I marry you or one of my friends dies, is that it?"

He puts up his hand: *Easy, easy.*

"No. Nirali, I told you. The Trial is not happening. I'm not giving Leo a stage. My thought was, we proceed as planned at first. Everybody goes to the Trial—" I give him a look: *Excuse me?* But he keeps his uninjured hand up as he sits at the end of the bed near me, still smiling. He smells like weed and expensive cologne. "*But then,* before it starts, you come forward, looking beautiful, all dressed up for the Trial, and beg me to show Kay mercy."

"Beg?" I cock my eyebrow, though I'm starting to relax a little, his tone is so playful and unserious. "Oh, I don't like the sound of that at all."

"Remember. We're putting on a show. We need some drama." He smiles wider. "Maybe you even sink to your knees?"

"I am not begging anyone for anything on my knees. Ever."

"'Oh, great King Max,' that would be a good way to start." He's teasing now, and I can't help laughing and smacking his good shoulder. "But then I stop you, of course. I take your hand and raise you from your knees, and I say"—and he takes my hand now, his expression so earnest—"'Queen Nirali, if you will grant me the honor of promising me your hand, I will grant your friend pardon, as a sign of my everlasting fidelity.'"

We sit for a moment, hand in hand, staring at each other.

"And then we have the raddest wedding ever." He laughs.

". . . And then?"

He lifts his chin to indicate the room. "You'd live in here with me, but I'll sleep on the floor if you want. Not that you'd want me to for long." He grins. "I'm pretty irresistible. You're warming up to me already."

I roll my eyes and move to smack him again. He dodges me with another laugh. I sit back in my chair, cross my arms across my chest, and feel his stare, heavier each moment.

"I appreciate that," I say at last. "But there's still the issue that everyone at Jefferson will see me getting married as proof Kyle is not coming back. When for all we know, he could drive up here tomorrow."

"Right." King Max gets up with a small hiss of pain, walks over to the desk, and leans against the edge of it, staring somberly at the floor. "But you don't doubt I can do what I said?"

"No," I admit. "After seeing Moore, I believe you could take Brockton back. I really do."

And I mean it. The same guy my father would have dismissed as a loser cares about his subjects and fights by their side. Whereas Kyle took off at the first opportunity to go party while we starved. King Max is a better man than Kyle in this new world.

But why, Before and now, have I been compelled to attach myself to a man? With everything I have to offer, why is sex what they want me to trade on?

How long until he gets tired of sleeping on the floor?

"So if I'm hearing you right, you *would* marry me if Kyle wasn't an issue," he says slowly. I don't contradict him, and the silence between us expands, solidifies, becomes almost an animal presence. Then he says: "What if I could promise you that Kyle is not coming back?"

A shiver spills down my spine. "I don't see how you could."

"There's something I haven't told you." His voice is strained, like he is forcing each word out. "I should have, but I wasn't sure how you'd take it."

". . . Tell me what?"

"It's fucked up." King Max pushes away from the desk, starts to pace the carpet beside his bed. "It's all just so fucked up."

"What is?"

He looks at me then, eyes wild in his otherwise controlled face. "Listen. You proved I could trust you right from the start, when you covered for me at dinner. I want you to know you can trust me, too. I don't want any secrets between us. Just—just don't hate me, okay? Promise you won't hate me?"

I can make no such promise. "Tell me."

"The night before Kyle left, I threw him a party, right." He leans against the wall, staring down at the floor, good hand drifting up to sweep his coarse bleached hair out of his dark eyes. "The party was, like, in the whole front office area, from the copiers to the mailboxes. I had a keg brought in and invited a bunch of rooms. I had the generator going so we could do black light stuff—you know, where you draw on yourself with highlighter? It's so stupid, but I like the stupid party stuff. It makes it feel like Before, for a little while, you know?" He stares at me until I nod, then looks away again. "We had beer pong on top of the mailboxes, and I was doing that for a long time, but things were winding down, and as people said goodbye, they kept joking about avoiding the black light room—in here, you know?"

I nod again. He slides down the wall, the knobby elbow of his good arm balancing on his knee, the bandaged one hugged to his narrow, bare chest. He still avoids eye contact.

"They were all saying Kyle and one of the girls were getting down in here, basically. In *my* bedroom. Hell, in *my* bed." He looks awkward, flicks at his nose. "I was *not* thrilled, obviously, but what am I going to do? Pull them apart? He's my guest or whatever."

"I get it."

"By the end of the night I tell the guards to go ahead, go to sleep, I'm just waiting for them to get out of my room." He shakes his head. "Then Jess comes out, and she's crying and shaking, and she says Kyle is . . ." He closes his eyes. "She says she can't wake him up, he drank a lot and had some Lucid but—"

"Lucid? What the hell is Lucid?"

"Everybody takes it. It's not a big deal, and he didn't even take that much, she said—"

"*And he died?*" My voice sounds like a stranger's, a stranger out of my control. "He died, and you hid it? Kay Kim was right, and you *put her in the dungeon?*"

"No! No! Let me finish, okay? Let me finish!" King Max presses the heels of his hands to his eyes. "Please!" His hands slide away, bloodshot eyes streaming tears. "He woke up, all right? But not before Leo had seen them."

". . . Leo?" I knew it.

"So when Kyle wouldn't wake up, I went to get some medicine, some Ifipac—"

"Ipecac?" I whisper.

"Yeah, the stuff to make him throw up. Then as I was coming back to the office, when I was out there in the hall, I heard screams, right?" Finally he looks at me, eyes ringed with broken red veins, and gets to his feet. "And Leo is in here, right, shouting at Jess and Kyle—"

"How did he know?"

He shrugs. "Maybe someone coming back from the party told one of his guys or something, I don't know. Things get around pretty fast now. But Leo just barged right in, comes in and punches the mattress right by Kyle's head—" King Max leans over and punches the bed with his good hand for emphasis, eyes not leaving mine, though tears stream continually down the narrow olive planes of his face. "Well, that woke Kyle up, I guess. He was totally out of it, and Leo was all yelling in his face. And my guards were gone for the night. So I had to push Leo out of the office myself, and he was *losing it*. He's all, 'I'm coming back with twenty guys! He's dead, he's so dead!' And he goes to get some of his Auto Shop dickheads, and Kyle is like, 'I should just go.' And I told him not to, okay, I told him to just sleep it off but—"

"He drove off while he was still drunk?" *Oh no.*

"I tried to make him stay, Nirali, I tried so hard." King Max sobs, crouching down beside the bed, staring at the rumpled covers like he can still see him there. "I would have let him stay as long as he wanted. I really liked him, we were friends, okay? But Leo messed it up."

That's why he left the radio. He was truly out of it. Kyle drank enough to know his limits, but whatever Lucid was, it pushed him past them. I think of Jimmy in the dungeon, his twitching hands and chemical breath. Kyle must have taken some kind of amphetamine.

"Kyle's dead," I say, trying to believe it.

Kyle grieved with me when I realized I would never see my parents again. Now he is gone, too. I'm the only one left who really knew any of them. What happens to your past, when all the people from it are gone? They take the future you planned with them, and all you have is what you are. My parents will never see me succeed, despite all my hard work. And if I can't pull Jefferson through to the other side of this winter, Kyle will not come back to help.

Jefferson!

How do I tell them that the Rule, the Rule above all our Laws, was wrong? That *I* was wrong? How do I bring back this news to people who were starved and spat on and beaten for telling the truth? How do I face any of them, ever again?

King Max pulls himself across the floor and rises up to his knees in front of me. "I should have told you. But I thought it was my fault. You think that too now, huh? You think it's my fault?"

He's begging me for absolution, begging on his knees.

"It's not your fault," I say, though my voice is still a stranger's.

King Max's head falls into my lap, his shoulders release, and he sobs. Big shuddering sobs, and I find myself comforting him, petting the head of bleached hair and dark roots like I'm soothing a child.

"That's why I can't give Leo any opening tomorrow," he says, large hand turning into a fist at the top of my hip. "He's making this big play with being Kay's champion because I cut down his room. He wants power, and he'll start a war to get it—"

"We'll announce our engagement before the Trial," I tell him. Yes. That's the solution. "In front of the whole school before Leo can even speak. Order him to drive Kay back to Jefferson while we have our wedding."

Kay can explain to Jefferson. She'll tell them everything, that's her whole problem. I won't try to stop her. She can let the council piece together the timeline and question Simon about why we made the Rule and why she was dragged out. I'll weather the fallout here, as Queen of the school with all the supplies and food.

"You'll do it?" King Max looks up at me, eyes glistening, mouth agape. "You'll marry me tomorrow?"

A flash of me and Merlin beside a fire in winter, discussing some solvable problem over mugs of tea. King Max coming in and announcing some holiday scheme, the three of us laughing. Not the worst outcome for me.

But certainly the worst outcome for Kyle. Whatever his faults, he didn't deserve this. A senseless death at the height of his youth, after everything we survived. Because of some *drug dealer*, some witless creep, no doubt skulking through the halls right now. One chemical miscalculation took Kyle's life, and very nearly took the rest of Jefferson with him.

Fine. I won't sell myself for just food. Let my bride price be revenge.

"Yes. I will marry you tomorrow," I tell King Max. "If you tell me who makes Lucid. Right now."

+ + +

She stuns me, when I pull back the door to my room: Merlin, in a black tank top, sitting at a desk with a minimalist crystal candelabra, an ornate gold vase full of candy, and a carefully laid out marble chessboard.

She places her knight with a *clink*.

"All right, Nirali," she says. "Your move."

Ice. I must be ice right now. I take the chair across from her. I pull out the bag of Lucid King Max gave me and set it in the middle of the board. The marble knight falls to its side with a clatter.

"What the hell have you been giving the people at this school?" I say.

The knight makes a long rolling circle across the board.

"Some kind of methamphetamine?" I ask, louder.

I can practically feel her temperature rise across the table.

"You think . . . I would give my people . . . *meth*?" The disgust in her voice is palpable. She grabs at her wheels, muscles standing out along her shoulders and arms, and in a heartbeat, she's swooped past me. She's out of the room before I can get up and retrieve the baggie from the table. By the time I'm at the door, she's halfway down the hall, rushing toward the biology lab, yelling over her shoulder, "Come on! Let's go, Your Majesty. I'll take you to my *drug den*!"

I follow after her, through her Cavern. There are only three patients left; the others have been transferred to the gym. I had Brick moved to the physics lab after meeting Kay; I am the only one with a key, and to be doubly safe, I plan on sleeping on a cot at the foot of his bed.

Merlin is in the teacher's office at the back of the lab, impatiently hauling a massive Tupperware container from under a desk. On its lid, in Sharpie gothic lettering, is written KEEP OUT.

"Open it," she commands me.

I give her a dark look and pull off the lid to see row upon row of caffeine pills, one of those big Spalter scales from chemistry class with the metal plate and the sliding scale, a battery-operated food processor, and several bags of pink C&H sugar.

"Lucid is caffeine and sugar. Marissa and I grind it up fine and add food coloring. It's about as harmful as powdered Mountain Dew."

". . . But you tell people it's a drug."

"I tell them it's a *potion*," Merlin corrects me.

"It doesn't matter what you call it, people would only take it if it works!"

"It does work. But not because it's a drug. It works because *they believe in it*."

I open one of the baggies in the box, wet my pinkie, and fish out some powder. It tastes like Pixy Stix.

"People just need something to work a little bit to start believing. But the belief? That does everything else. That's the power, that's what *magic is*."

"I'm sorry," I say at last. "But *someone* at Moore is making some kind of amphetamine." I'm about to mention the guy in the dungeon, then remember I wasn't supposed to be there. "I've seen people . . . tweaking, all right?"

"No. Absolutely not." Merlin shakes her head. "No room has the setup to make meth, and if they did, I'd shut them down."

There's a strange crackle from the big metal desk drawer, which is slightly open. Her hand flashes over and slams it shut. Her walkie-talkie?

"Well, if the interrogation is over, Your Majesty," Merlin says, "you can see yourself out."

I turn and walk back down the hall, feeling hollow. I should go back to Brick's room, but I stop in mine first, to take in the scene she'd prepared. The vase, the candles—she went all out for our match. And I ruined it. Tears roll down my face, like that will help. I don't even know what I'm so sad about, it's just sad, it's all so sad. Then there's a knock at the door. I wipe my face hurriedly, take a deep breath.

On the other side is Merlin.

"You thought the Lucid killed Kyle." Her voice breaks; her hand darts up to her eyes. "The King just called me on the walkie-talkie. Nirali, I'm so sorry. Is there anything I can do?"

"Can we reset the board?" I squeak, and swing the door open a little more.

"Of course." She glides back to her side of the table, puts our opposing forces in neat lines, and then looks up at me, her eyes soft. "And congratulations. For real, this time."

"He told you."

She nods.

"I get you don't want me here." She starts to speak, but I hold up my hand to stop her. "Please, just let me clear the air. Whatever your reservations, I know we can work together, if we keep communicating openly. I'll admit, I try to avoid confrontations—"

"Yeah right! The way you threw down that bag of Lucid? If looks could kill!"

She seems almost impressed.

"Well, I misunderstood things. But now I know how Lucid works, I . . . I could help you formulate other potions. Multivitamin elixirs. Antibiotic salves."

She looks skeptical. "You'll support my magic?"

"Hey, when in Rome! I got my *tarot* read today!" I widen my eyes sarcastically, then add, "I don't like magic, but belief I can handle. Belief doesn't sound so bad. Especially compared to skepticism." I think of the faction that stormed the gym that day, when Reese was called into Student Council. All the anger and blame. "I would like to believe what King Max promised me. That I could walk to Jefferson in six months. That we could have the electric plant back up . . ." I watch her face as I ask: "Is that possible? Isn't there some larger state grid the town pulls from?"

"Brockton draws most of its power from the dam," Merlin tells me. "And with our smaller population, we could easily be self-sustaining. That's the basis of our five-year plan. We already met our first milestone early: becoming allies with another school." She gestures to me.

"So if we—" I pause, but it's right. It's *we* now. "If we expand the fences to surround the whole town and draw power from the dam, Brockton could be as close to normal as any place in the world *can* be now. I believe that, for sure."

"Then you believe the dragons are all over the world?" she asks quietly.

I nod after a long moment. "I've spent . . . a lot of hours listening to dead air waiting for Kyle." I take a deep breath and say out loud what I have never dared tell anyone else. "If there were any adults left, we would know by now."

"Agreed." Merlin nods, just as quiet. "We are the adults now."

I let out a shaky laugh. "Not that I *feel* like an adult."

"But neither did the adults Before!" Merlin rolls her eyes. "All the grown-ups I knew were faking it, are you kidding me?" Then she adds: "Wait . . . is that why you called them Growns? Because they're *made of grown-ups*?"

I bite my lip and nod, and she breaks out laughing and rolling her eyes.

"Well, hey." Merlin breathes at last, shrugging. "Historically, the world has been run by people our age, okay? Younger people make better leaders because they have more future to lose! Alexander the Great, Queen Elizabeth, King Tut—I know we're used to modern leaders being like *ninety years old*, but—"

"How much worse can we do."

"Exactly!"

"I can *believe* in *us*," I say sincerely. "In Moore and Jefferson, together. We have . . . complementary strengths."

"The cool kids and the nerds," she adds.

"The jocks and the geniuses, sure," I correct. I'm rewarded by a flash of the tiny gap between her perfectly straight teeth. "I believe if we get the power on and slay all the—dragons—"

Her smile gets gratifyingly wider at the word.

"We could, in the process, become the kind of grown-ups who *aren't* faking," I finish. "Does that count as a magical vision?"

"You've got a little magic to you, Nirali. You know that," Merlin says. I can't help thinking about what she said earlier. About me being perfect. We both lean back at the same time.

She clears her throat. "So what did your tarot reading say?"

I reach up to tighten my ponytail, but then find myself pulling out the elastic instead, so my hair falls in glossy waves. I shake it past my shoulders, very aware she is watching me. The same way Max does, but not the same. His gaze is a leash I can pull. With her, when our eyes meet, it feels like she's the one pulling.

"It was sort of vague." I fix my eyes on the board, send forward my black pawn. "Do you know what the Queen of Swords means?"

Merlin laughs. "Of course *you* would get the Queen of Swords."

"Why? What does she mean?"

"She represents looking at things honestly and intellectually. Avoiding emotion to get to the truth." Merlin raises an eyebrow, leans forward, and slides her queen into the bishop's place. "Being *practical* about your romantic partner, for example."

I don't let the hurt reach my face.

"Of *course* you would know all about tarot." I take her knight with a sharp *clink*. "Can't say the same about chess." Then, inspecting the small red marble horse I've just claimed: "Does a card mean something different, if it's upside down?"

"Oh yes." Merlin nods. "Reversal means the card should be read in the opposite way. So a reversed Queen of Swords would stand for treachery and deception. Whatever you *think* you know isn't true."

She slides her queen to where my pawn just stood.

"Check," Merlin says. My heart hammers. She can take my king away. Another move, and the game is over.

"*Wait.*" I pick up the king protectively, scan the board.

"Chess team. You were warned."

"It's still my move." I raise a finger. It's so early on there aren't a lot of places open; she has him pretty cornered. I look up at her. "It's not like we're doing timed turns, right?"

"We didn't establish all the rules before we started playing. That's on me," she says, then: "So here's what you have to know: If you make him look like a fool, I can't protect you."

I set the piece down. We're done with the game.

"I told him I wouldn't sleep with him," I say, "and he agreed to those terms."

"Because he believes he can *win you over*," Merlin says. "He's planning a huge wedding. He wants to make you his Queen in front of the whole school. It will be a very public relationship, like I'm sure it was with Kyle. So if things go badly, the King will act to protect his reputation by framing you in the worst possible way."

"Go badly how?"

She holds my gaze. "Like if you were to get involved with someone else."

"Not an issue." I shrug easily, relieved, and when she scoffs, I insist: "Honestly. Don't worry about it."

"You said you don't want to sleep with Max. You're going to, what, live like a nun?"

"Sure. I'm not a very sexual person." Then, with a wobble in my voice I can't control: "Why do you think Kyle cheated on me so much?"

I think of the tarot reader saying Kyle was my soulmate. That we'd get back together and it would be happily ever after. And how I had known none of that was true.

"I hate sex," I confess, face growing hot. "I don't want to sleep with a guy ever again. It ruined things between me and Kyle. It made me—I think it made me hate him."

The room seems to ring with the words. Merlin stares so long I cover my face. I don't know what I should look like.

I hear her push back from the table and come around to my side.

"I mean, we were friends of course, he—he was a very important person in my life," I go on. "I'll miss him. I've *missed him* as a person for a long time. But I . . . am also relieved, that . . . I don't have to see him again?" I knead at my face, lean back, and widen my eyes, embarrassed. "And I know I'm a horrible bitch for that. He was so handsome and charming; everybody loved him. *I* was the one they couldn't stand. But being with him, you know, they call it like, the 'halo effect'—like I was *tolerable* as Kyle's girlfriend. But I never . . . and I *kept trying*, because if I could just make this one thing *work*, then it would be perfect. But . . ." I shake my head, the tears mounting behind my eyes. "I couldn't! It never worked. And I started to think . . . maybe I don't even like guys, like that, at all? So. It's fine. It's just . . ."

She's right next to me, just listening.

"Like, my parents? If they knew? What I did with Kyle?" And the sob I'm holding back breaks through. "They would have been ashamed of me. And I never even *wanted to*—"

Her arms go around me then, surrounding me with her gorgeous smell, boy's cologne and girl's shampoo. I lean back to see her face. There is nothing but understanding in those large eyes.

"And girls?" she asks gently.

"Yeah right." I roll my eyes. "I have no idea what to do with girls. And they all think I'm completely straight, so no one has ever made or will ever make the first—"

She tucks my hair behind my ear, and the room tilts.

That strange pang goes through me, that dull ache like a sore throat but everywhere at once. I look at the full oval of her mouth, so close, then back up at her eyes: *Please help.*

She takes my hand, hers so steady, and raises it to her mouth. She kisses the back of it, an almost courtly gesture. She gently opens my hand and sets my palm against her cheek. Her pulse must be accelerating, like mine, because her cheek is so warm. But she is so perfectly calm, perfectly confident, as her other hand lifts my puffy, tear-streaked face. She looks at me like I'm the first girl she's ever seen.

"Okay?" she asks. I feel like I'm in a dream as I nod, and then she kisses me.

I thought kisses were about mouths. My first year dating Kyle, I kept waiting for something to happen while he kissed me, searching his mouth for what I was missing. Then I just started waiting for it to be over.

But Merlin's kiss doesn't happen in my mouth. It happens all over, the dull ache that's been building catalyzed by her contact into pure adrenaline. All my synapses light up at once, nerves throughout my body going off like fireworks. And one thought connects as I kiss her back: *Maybe there is magic.* If a feeling this big hid in me so long, maybe anything is possible.

Then the door comes flying open.

I leap to my feet as Marissa steps into the room, her smile dropping. She flinches back, and I call her name to keep her from actually leaving, trying desperately to play it off like she's read the moment wrong:

"Marissa! Hey! Everything all right in the Cavern?"

"Yes, I'm sorry, I should have knocked, Your Majesty. You told me to remind you about Brick before I went off shift, so. Here I am." Marissa stares at the floor.

"Oh, no worries, no worries!" My voice is breathless and wild. "I'm so sorry, Merlin." I turn to her. Her hand is in front of her mouth; her eyes are stars. "I totally forgot. I have to go check on Brick. But this was fun! This was so fun."

"Of course you'd say that," Merlin says with some difficulty. "You won." And she shoots me one piercing look, an arrow straight through my heart, before slipping out into the hall.

+ + +

"WHERE'S KAY?!"

I startle awake to see Kyle's broad shoulders and thick neck looming over me; his large rough hands shake my cot. My reaction is instinctive: I rocket to my feet and push him away with all my strength. *"Get away from me!"*

The nightmare Kyle's face catches the lantern light and seems to disintegrate: one wide exposed eyeball barely tethered by the remains of an eyelid, back teeth glinting through a torn cheek. It's not Kyle at all—it's Brick.

I'm in the physics lab, where I slept last night. Brick is finally up, or *was*. Now he's flying backward, the IV stand clattering heavily to the floor as the bed catches him. I freeze, terrified I've hurt him, but he sits right back up again and continues:

"You tell me right now where Kay is, so help me, or I'll break that door down and—"

"Kay is *fine!*" I snap. I let out a deep, shaky breath, one hand at my chest, trying to avoid looking at him as he yanks the oxygen tube from his face. "You almost gave me a heart attack, okay!"

"Same." He glares. "Who the hell are you?"

"I'm your *doctor*. Nirali Chaudri, the senior representative from Jefferson. I operated on your leg, the one that was shot by a crossbow a couple days ago."

His gaze drifts down to his hospital robe and bandaged leg, then back to me. "So why are we locked in here?"

"You missed a lot." I lower myself back onto my cot across from him. "And I will catch you up, if you promise to *stay calm*."

He tries to listen calmly, and to give him credit, he makes it through the feast. Through Kay's wild accusation and the Trial, and Leo stepping forward as her champion. But when I tell him Kay is currently in the dungeon, he springs to his feet.

"With Jimmy? He seriously put her down there with Jimmy?"

Jimmy, that was the tweaker who felt me up. Could Jimmy's room be making the drugs? "What room is Jimmy from, Brick?"

"He *was* with the Auto Shop, but they threw him out."

Drive. That's what Kay said to the guards, that Jimmy was *strung out on Drive.* Of course. They have chemicals, they have space, and they have enough acrimony with the crown that they'd hide it from Merlin. And if there's an amphetamine in the Auto Shop, Jess could have gotten a stash from Leo. If Lucid wasn't enough to make Kyle think he could drive past the fence with impunity, homemade meth would.

I grab Brick's arm. I can't leave him here now that he's up. Leo's and Artemis's minions will be after him.

"You're coming with me," I tell him. "Right now."

He looks down at his hospital gown. "Could I at least put on some pants?"

"If your pants are on the way to the Auto Shop, then yes."

I have a Duke to confront.

WHAT THE HELL, MAN

BRICK

It turns out, you really need all your blood. Whatsherface, Nirali, said I lost maybe twenty percent. That's why I feel heavy and floaty and not really here, except for my leg. My leg is a chunk of burning meat. I knew the pain was coming. I felt it looming, hovering at the edge of my consciousness like the sun overhead when you're trying to doze off at the beach. It was like that the first time I almost died, days of dreading what would be waiting when I woke up.

Nirali is going on and on about how I shouldn't strain myself, a half step behind me. If that makes her feel better, sure. We don't live in a time and place where you can take a little vacation whenever you want. Especially not when your best friend has your crush locked in a dungeon, awaiting a Trial by Combat everybody's real hyped about. You'd think it's Super Bowl Sunday or something. The hell, man.

Every room I pass has a handmade banner hanging on the door, black or red, and the halls are packed even though the windows are bright blue with the start of a good day. This kid Francisco yells from his doorway as I pass: "Leo's going to cut that dude in HALF!"

"Nah, man," Larry Orr fires back. "Tyler was center at Jefferson, dude. He's no joke, man."

Then they do a double take as I walk by, and girls openly snicker as I stagger past them down the stairs. I clutch the back of my hospital gown.

"You go get your pants," Nirali says when I turn toward the music hall, like I need her permission. "I'm going ahead to the Auto Shop. You can come find me there."

"Find you? Why?"

"Because you need your vitals checked, and I need to see you eat something before I can officially discharge you from care."

"Right." I can't tell if she's condescending to all her patients, or just me. She says King Max wants to marry her. Personally, I'd rather slam a car door on my balls.

The hall in front of the theater is a mob of people in formal gowns and tuxes, getting their hair specially braided and jewels stuck on their face by theater kids. The air is thick with hair spray. I throw an arm over my mouth and duck into the music hall. If the guys upstairs were treating this like the Super Bowl, the Theater Department is turning it into prom.

It's neither of those things. It's a fight to the death.

And Max's favorite part of *Echellion*. I can picture him playing it, Before.

"Hey, hey, check this out." Max leaned back in his desk chair. His mom had given him an insane computer budget, and he'd poured it all into a gaming rig. It was one of his last days before shipping out to military school, and I was practically living in his room, my books all over his bed, finishing my homework. "I got to the Trial by Combat level!"

"Oh yeah?" I didn't look up from my physics packet.

"No, seriously, check this out. If you try to leave the ring before the fight's over, look what happens."

His knight, all in white and red, ran for the bales of hay that ringed the composited arena. A guard immediately glitched into frame and pushed him back.

"So if you try to leave three times—watch this, watch this!"

"What is that, an axe?"

"Naw, man, that's a halberd."

The guard pulled back the halberd and clipped Max's knight across the neck with a thunderous sound effect, the camera jouncing. The knight's head flew upright, a plume of blood spurting as the armored figure fell to his knees and the screen went red. White gothic lettering faded in:

EXEUNT SIR BUTT

"You named him Sir Butt?" I laughed.

"This is my mess-around game. The real guy I'm playing through to king is Sir Jordayne."

"Jordayne? That's even worse."

"What ho, whoreson! Darest you make light with the name of Sir Jordayne?" Max cried in a kingly *Echellion* voice. "A gentleman and a scholar, he be!"

"You're slipping into pirate territory."

Max rocked forward, laughing, but was cut short by the yelling from downstairs. I recognized Coach's voice, cursing out Max's mom. Then she told him to just get out, the front door slamming hard enough to shake the walls. Coach's car started, then peeled down the road. And then everything was quiet except for Max's mom faintly sobbing.

Max loaded a new game.

"Are you going to like . . ." I nodded toward the floor. He shook his head, his face pale.

"Every time I try to comfort her, she starts telling me stuff, that like . . ." Max got a one hitter out of his desk drawer. "That she wouldn't tell me if she were not half out of her mind. Like shit that actually messes with my life?" He looked through the drawer for his lighter.

His mom had been in a weird mood since announcing the divorce, that was for sure. Every time she saw me, she'd turn and walk straight out of the room.

"Like what? What'd she tell you?"

He just shook his head and put the pipe to his mouth, flicked the lighter.

"You're going to smoke with your mom in the house?"

"What's she going to do, send me to military school."

"Yeah, well, don't do that shit around me." I swatted his elbow. "They do drug tests during playoffs."

"*That's* the kind of thing that would set her off." Max threw the pipe back into the drawer. "She keeps saying my dad is more concerned about your baseball scholarship than 'being present with his own son.'"

It felt like he was asking me a question. I hurried to answer without exactly knowing what it was: "Well, I was leaning on Coach pretty hard last year to get my stats up. It's a real competitive field this year, but he almost went pro, and he thinks I have a real shot at—"

"Could you please shut up," Max cut me off, reaching for his controller. "Goddamn, I hate baseball. Talk about the most stupid, boring, weak-ass sport on earth. Bunch of dudes knocking balls around a field, like, who cares?" He gestured at the screen, the Trial by Combat level fading in. "*This* is what sports should be, this is what *life* should be! Men fighting hand to hand, in contests of strength and honor!"

"Like your scrawny ass could even walk with armor on." I grinned, and that got him out of his chair. He leapt at me, playfully throwing punches until I twisted his arm behind him and made him cry uncle.

In my room now, I carefully pull on my oldest, softest pair of jeans over my bandage, as well as a cutoff sweatshirt. It takes what feels like forever, but I get on my duck boots from winter, some gut instinct telling me I'll need them, though the one on the injured leg I don't bother trying to lace up. Then I reach into the way back of the top drawer and retrieve a box cutter as well.

Something tells me I'll need it, too.

+ + +

No one's in the first-floor hall that leads to the Auto Shop, so every word Jimmy says is clear as I approach:

"Sorry about tripping you before. I was messed up. But nobody's home in the Auto Shop. Los Martillos didn't sleep here last night."

"Where are they?" Nirali's voice, trying not to sound small.

"Somewhere just for Los Martillos. Not me, they kicked me out. You ever find Jessica?"

I hate the sound of her name coming out of his mouth.

"'Cause I heard you talking to the Exile," he goes on, "and I heard what Leo said to her. Dude is full of shit. Making like he's sprung on some ugly bald bitch? When he curved her the night before Expansion to meet up with Jess? I saw them, man. I saw her go out there with him. And he came back. But I never seen her since."

I run through the last few days in my mind, trying to think of the last time I saw Jess. I've been so worried about Kay, and busy with the Expansion. And Jess and I have been sort of avoiding each other anyway.

The day before Kay arrived, Jess had come to my workshop, fully drunk. I started in on her about the drinking and Lucid, and she kept saying "Okay, Dad" until I snapped.

"Why are you so hellbent on killing yourself?"

"Why are you so hellbent on staying alive?" she yelled. "It's the end of the world, dumbass, chill out! I like drinking! I like drugs! If they kill me, so what?"

"If my mom, or your mom, were alive right now, they would be so disappointed in what you've become."

"I'm the disappointment? *I'm* the disappointment?" she screamed. "You dropped her—you dropped all of us!—for Coach!"

"Not this again—"

"All through high school, all that mattered was your little boys' club. Hunting every weekend and practice after school with Coach. Hell, Brick, you spent the last three Thanksgivings at Max's house! How do you think your mom felt? After the way he treated her?"

"Treated her? What are you talking about? Mom loved Coach! She was grateful for everything he did for me."

"Sooo grateful! Because he did sooo much, because he felt sooo bad for you, right?" Her eyes were glazed over; she was ranting. "Because we were all trashy, and our home was trash, so you better get that scholarship and get the hell away from us—"

"You need a nap." I steered her toward my bedroll.

"You don't want to live with a bunch of trash, so throw it away! Brick, I'm doing you a favor. I'm taking out the trash *for* you, the trash is burning itself up!"

"*Enough,* Jess."

"*Let . . . me . . . burn . . . up.*"

I got her some water. She chugged it down, then I made sure she fell asleep on her side. The next morning, she was so normal I could tell she didn't remember anything she'd said, that she had been black-out drunk.

We hadn't talked since.

"I can take you where he met up with her?" Jimmy is saying. "Leo's little make-out spot?"

I hear Nirali step back from him.

"You think I can't keep my hands to myself around you? Yeah, I'm a little worried about that, too."

Enough. I turn the corner, box cutter out, and say:

"Sure, you could, Jimmy! Sure, you could."

His eyes break from her face and flash to me in a look of pure annoyance. Nirali turns to me with a grateful smile. Now I understand why Max is marrying her: She's quite pretty when she's not sneering at you in disgust.

"Slayer! Hey! Let's be cool, we're all friends here!" Jimmy backs away, hands up. His teeth, never the cleanest, are coated with a milky film. "She wants to go to Leo's make-out spot. I'm just trying to help her out. It's *of the Spur*, you know?"

The phrase makes my stomach turn. How does he know it? He can't, unless Max told him. What the hell is going on?

"Would you come with us?" Nirali asks me, desperate.

"Yeah, sure."

Jimmy grins his milky grin. "Hey, if the lady prefers a threesome, that's cool with me. Car's this way." Jimmy walks backward down the hall, still grinning. Nirali and I give each other a wary look, then follow after him.

+ + +

The pain in my leg has somehow taken over my head. I'm so desperate for water I'm considering drinking the full bottle rolling around in the passenger footwell of Jimmy's car, among all the wax-paper food wrappers and squirrel bones. Nirali, behind us, says nothing. We glide through the silent neighborhoods. Everyone's getting ready back at Moore, I guess, because the streets are empty except for clouds of butterflies.

Jimmy's car lurches to a stop in front of a white colonial-style house, and when we get out, the cicadas are so loud the air sounds like it's deep-frying. Nirali looks at me expectantly, so I hang back until we're side by side.

"What did he mean by the Spur comment?" she whispers.

I shrug because I can't tell her. All guards are under oath not to reveal this secret phrase, a password that tells other guards they are on orders direct from King Max. Jimmy shouldn't know the phrase, either, unless he's trying to claim King Max made him a guard while I was out, which is unthinkable. But so is the Trial by Combat, and Leo as Kay's champion, and King Max marrying someone. I've had to think a lot of unthinkable things today.

Jimmy is walking around the side of the house to a bank of lavender. Whiteheads stand out along his red temple as he shoots us a look. Then he stoops down, brushes the purple flowers aside from two slanted cellar doors. Weathered gray paint flakes off it in patches the size of my palm as he lifts one.

"When Leo wants to keep it secret, they meet down there." Jimmy lets the door drop open. It falls with a rusted scream, and cold breathes up from the cellar. Nirali goes still beside me.

"I'll go down with you," I tell her, and she nods eagerly. As we move down the steep stone steps and out of the sunlight, the temperature changes. The pool of shadow at the bottom of the stairs swallows us like cold water.

"Jess?" I call. The dirt walls muffle my voice. There's no way she's in here still unless she's . . . "JESS!"

Like the house above, the basement has been stripped. What remains is either useless or too heavy to move: the headless torso of a dressmaker's dummy, an ancient coal-burning furnace in the corner, a—

CREAK! CREAK! CREAK!

Nirali has bumped into an old rocking horse, which knocks merrily into my good leg now, and we both let out nervous laughs.

"You okay?" I ask.

"Fine," she says through clenched teeth. "I just can't see anything."

We're past the light floating down through the doors. Nirali shuffles ahead of me, hands outstretched, groping blindly at the air. A few tentative steps, then she lets out a cry.

"What?"

"I tripped over a . . . rolled-up rug, I think."

"Usually they take the rugs." I frown, and the rug moans.

No.

I'm on my knees next to her. She feels so cool.

Shit, shit, shit.

Nirali gets between us, feels for a pulse.

Jimmy yells excitedly from above: "Did you find her?"

"We need to get her out into the open air," Nirali says.

I pick her up, and black ants race over my eyes as I stand. As we move toward the light coming down the stairs, for one brief moment I think she's someone else. Jess is blond; this girl's hair is almost black.

Then I realize it's black from her blood.

"Get out of my way!" I call out, swaying up the stairs.

"She's dead, ain't she?" Jimmy says as I push past him, a cloud of ants sweeping between me and the world. I head for the deep green grass, find the cool shadow of the house so she'll be out of the sun, and set her down as carefully as I can.

Unconscious, she looks like she did when we both stayed home with strep throat in third grade. Eventually Mom had to take her to the emergency room. I was left on the couch with solemn instructions to watch *Wheel of Fortune* and not answer the door if anybody knocked, and I cried until they got home, the same prayer running through my head then as it does now:

Let her be all right just let her be all right.

Nirali is on it, straightening Jessica carefully, holding up one wrist, popping open some kind of plastic tube to wave under Jess's nose.

"Ammonia inhalant," she explains coolly, eyes not leaving Jess, long narrow fingers steady and efficient as she probes the blood-soaked hair. "Her pulse is strong, but there's a contusion at the back of her head. Maybe there's some water in the car?"

I stand up; the ants go wild. I duck my head and hurry, half-blind, back through the lavender.

"She's *alive*?" I hear Jimmy yell, and clench my teeth.

Then, when I bend over to get the water bottle from the car, the ants swarm. It all goes black, and I grip the top of the car. The cicadas bubble and hiss so loud all around me, like I'm being submerged in hot oil. I can't see. I can't see anything.

Then I hear Nirali scream.

I turn in the direction I think the house is. I uncap the water bottle, and take a swig, then lean forward with my hands on my knees until the ant swarm thins. Then I stumble toward Nirali's screams, and miraculously the ants start to retreat. I run for the backyard, covered in goose bumps and cold all the way through, when Jimmy screams:

"*How is this bitch still alive!*"

Jessica is on her stomach, trying to crawl through the sunlit part of the grass, head bowed forward like a broken doll. Jimmy's shadow falls across her back.

"YOU LEAVE HER ALONE!" Nirali throws her small, starved body at Jimmy, clawing at his throat. He shakes her off; she lands hard in the grass. He turns like he's going to step on her face, but I get his arm and twist it behind him so hard I can practically feel his shoulder slide out of joint.

"Don't. Move," I tell him.

I wrestle the keys out of his hoodie pocket and toss them to Nirali. "Drive the car closer. We'll get Jess in and get back to school."

Nirali, eyes like saucers, scrambles to her feet and runs off. Jess rolls onto her side, and when her eyes meet mine, she collapses into the grass like she's touched home base.

"He did this?" I ask her, wrenching Jimmy's arm tighter.

"Brick, come on," Jimmy says through gritted teeth. "This is Spur business. You are interfering—"

I bring my knee up through his legs and connect right in the balls. When he rocks forward, I punch the back of his head. He turns to me screaming, and I land a hit straight on the bridge of his nose. There's a *snap*, sharp as a pencil breaking, under my knuckles. Jimmy falls to his knees in the grass. He's still wailing, hands covering his face, when the car rocks up over the lavender, bees flying in every direction.

Nirali gets out of the car and helps me transfer Jess to the back seat, all of us ignoring Jimmy's wails. Nirali gets behind the wheel so I can slide into the back and cradle Jess, help her drink the water. Jess is shuddering, and her eyes won't hold still. Nirali is turned, watching behind us as she backs out, when two bloody hands clap down on the windshield. The whites of Jimmy's eyes are visible the whole way around as he screams:

"You're going down for this, Slayer! Of the Spur! THIS IS OF THE SPUR!"

Nirali stomps on the gas, accelerating in reverse as hard as she can, and Jimmy leaves two red arcs of bloody handprints to steer through as we fly up the street, heading back toward Moore.

"Pull over," I tell Nirali. "Over there—stop the car."

"We have to get her to the lab!" Nirali shakes her head. "She needs to be treated, you almost fainted, you both need—"

"*Spur* means secret business for the King," I snap, breaking my oath as Captain of the Guard. "King Max told Jimmy to bring us here."

Nirali makes a hard right and screeches into a driveway choked with tall grass. She rolls down all the windows before shutting off the engine, turning in the seat, and staring down at Jess.

"Jessica, what happened to you? Who put you in the house, do you remember?"

Jess, curled up in my lap in the fetal position, gives me a look. "Who is that?"

"She's from Jefferson, she's on our side." I think? I am not sure what the sides are, right now, because I have no idea what's happening. "Jess, did you go to that house to meet Leo?"

"A couple days ago, yeah. He wanted to let me know he was with that new girl. I told him whatever, cool." She shrugs, face stiff. "Then I was heading back to the school and got caught up talking to Chris from the guards. He was having a kick back at an empty house with some people I knew, so I hung out and ended up, uh, sleeping through Expansion."

"Jess."

She shoots a guilty look at me. "Yeah, I figured I'd get in trouble, so I've been staying at the house. Then last night we were having a little barbecue, when Jimmy turns up. He pulled me aside, said Leo wanted to talk and he could drive me to our spot. I'm like, aren't you supposed to be in the dungeon right now? And he's all, do you want to see him or what." She swallows hard. ". . . And I did."

"Jess . . ." I sigh.

"So Jimmy takes me out to the house. But when I walk in, it's empty. And I remember, I was turning around to ask what's going on, when—" She lifts her hand toward her head. "BAM. Jimmy just—I guess he thought that was all it would take. One big hit. I started running. I made it out to the cul-de-sac, but he was faster . . ." She closes her eyes for a moment. "The next thing I remember is Jimmy yelling 'She's alive,' when I was in the grass."

"She was supposed to be dead," Nirali says, unemotional. "And I was supposed to find her, in Leo's house. Who would send Jimmy to do that?"

"If Jimmy *was* in the dungeon, the only person who could get him out is King Max, but Max loves Jess, he would never—"

"Jessica?" Nirali cuts me off, addressing Jess, her voice very kind. "Do you remember a guy named Kyle?"

And Jess, who told us about almost getting killed with no self-pity, bursts into tears.

She clutches me so hard, the whole time, as she talks about the party with Jefferson's president, so many weeks before. A memory of Kyle pulling her down to the bed. She'd told him she had a boyfriend, but she didn't feel like standing up again. She'd had a Drive pill from Leo. When Kyle kissed her, he fished it out of her mouth with his tongue.

The more she talks, the colder Nirali's eyes become.

"He wouldn't wake up. I ran and got King Max." Jessica's hands are over her face now. "We tried CPR, we put him on his side, I tried to give him his inhaler, Max tried to give him the stuff that makes you throw up. We tried *everything*, but he was gone. He was already gone."

"Leo never—" Nirali's voice is hard. "Leo didn't find you and Kyle? He didn't punch the bed, or—"

"Leo? He's never been in the principal's office," Jess says flatly. "Not that night or any other night that I'm aware of."

"And the inhaler?" Nirali asks.

"I hid it in the costume room when we got back. From where we put him."

"Where did you put him?" Nirali's voice is gentle, but her eyes are flat and black, the broken windows of an abandoned house.

"We dragged the body out to one of the Escalades, me and him." Jessica's face crumples. "King Max said we'd drive it out somewhere we weren't expanding any time soon. I drove a car behind him, helped him open the panels, 'cause there was no guard out yet. We found a little house just past the far fence."

This is why she's been drinking so much.

"Jess, I'm sorry," I manage.

"You didn't do anything. It was me and King Max, and I made an oath not to tell anyone. He backed the Escalade into the garage, and I drove him back. Peach Street, it was called Peach Street." Jessica sighs. "Kyle's body is in a blue house on Peach Street."

"It was an accident," I tell Nirali.

"Until they covered it up," Nirali says. "Why hide Kyle's body, Jessica?"

"She was almost killed," I remind Nirali. "She doesn't need you to interrogate her."

"She was almost murdered, by the King, to cover up his other murder."

"No, no way. Kyle was an accident, and Max would never hurt Jess! He might have sent Jimmy to find her, that's the Spur thing, but Jimmy went rogue. Max didn't know Jimmy would . . ."

But no one knew what Jimmy would do. He'd pulled a knife on Kay. And Max sent him after Jess, when I was unconscious and couldn't protect her?

I look down at the fragile, familiar curve of her ear, and my heart makes a fist around the only two things I know to be true: Max is my best friend. Jess is my sister.

If he could hurt her, I don't know him at all.

"Why don't we ask him?" Nirali says, looking right in my eyes. "At the Trial."

SUR-VEIL:
TO CLOSELY WATCH OR MONITOR

NIRALI

Death, the Chariot, and the Emperor. *You will see him again soon, and live happily ever after.* The upside-down Queen of Swords. The tarot reader had tried to tell me what happened. Kyle's dead body in the back of the missing Escalade, driven away from the school by King Max. Who was he afraid would overhear?

As I pull up to the parking lot, as close as I can get to Moore's gym, the thought echoes through me: *I'm not supposed to be here.* But this is exactly where I'm supposed to be. I'm supposed to announce I'm marrying King Max today. "Supposed to" means exactly nothing.

Drive was supposed to be just for the Auto Shop mechanics. They did not take Lucid; that was supposed to be for the opposing faction at Moore. But with Jessica, they crossed over, and then perhaps Kyle's inhaler and his drinking interacted with these drugs as well. Kyle's death was a senseless, tragic accident. But the cover-up was deliberate. And that I cannot forgive.

There's a screened-off corner of the gym for patients whose wounds require them to undress. Brick and I carry Jessica to a cot in that corner. I tell the nurses to not bring anyone else behind the screen, that no one must know she's being treated here. They're surprised but don't dare question me.

Brick falls into a small chair beside Jessica's bed.

"Oh no, you don't," I tell him. "You're coming with me. I need someone to back me up on what's just happened."

"I can't see." Brick is staring into midair. Beads of sweat stand out across his forehead; his eyes are dilated. "It keeps going black."

He hasn't eaten yet; I haven't taken his vitals. I'm ordering the nurses to find him some juice and cookies when he reaches out and catches my sleeve. Then Brick pulls me toward him so hard my nose almost bumps his terrible face, his voice a whisper.

"You *cannot* confront the King about this in front of other people," Brick warns me. "Promise me you'll pull him aside, don't corner him where people can see."

"I promise." I have no intention of confronting the King at all. This is a job for Merlin.

I stride through the lobby's hordes of people in formalwear who erupt in excited whispers as I pass. My mind is coldly telescoping my options into a new plan.

When I tell Merlin about Jessica, she will see to it King Max has a real Trial. She is a just person, and she's the one with all the good ideas—*she* should be in charge. I can convince her to go for his throne, let her know Jefferson will support her claim. Together, we could unite the two schools, no King required.

This could be a golden age for Jefferson and Moore, each learning from the other, sharing our complementary strengths. And what I do in the next few minutes could very well bring it into being.

By the time I reach the Cavern, I am radiant with possibilities.

"Merlin?" I call. There's only two remaining patients, both sleeping peacefully. I stride to the back of the lab, to the office where Merlin keeps her bin of Lucid. She's not there. I'm turning to go when there's that strange crackle again. A tinny voice leaks from her desk drawer.

I pull the office door closed behind me and take hold of the handle. The drawer rolls open smoothly and silently, the crackling freed to bounce around the room.

Inside are rows of baby monitors, all different types and qualities. Each fastidiously marked with masking tape and labeled in perfect cursive. I pick up the crackling one, labeled *Throne Room*, and turn the volume up to hear a staticky iteration of Max's voice:

"—drums of course to bring everyone in, we'll start them at noon—"

I read the other labels:

1776, Dressing Room, Gold House, Costume Room, Guest Room, Principal's Office.

I pick up the baby monitor for *Guest Room* and see my bed in the corner, the bathtub mercifully out of frame. My hand is so cold, my blood feels like slush in my veins.

This is why the boy with black hair had to read my tarot, instead of just telling me. Merlin has been spying on rooms all over the school. Merlin knew Kay had the inhaler because she'd bugged the 1776 house. She destroyed the inhaler because she knew Kyle was dead. King Max talked about getting medication for Kyle, but he and Jessica didn't even know what ipecac was called. I have no doubt he asked Merlin for help.

I have no doubt she knew Kyle was dead all along.

She would know the Spur guard phrases, of course. For all I know, she ordered the hit. Merlin might let me be one of her chess pieces to push around. But under no circumstances will she let me check her King.

The Trial is supposed to start at noon. That can't be long now. How do I stop the Trial and get Kay out of here?

Tyler isn't going to help me. Brick could collapse again at any moment. But Leo!

He could be reasoned out of a fight and into making a proper case in front of the school. That is my only play now.

A needle of pain flashes through my temple as I put the monitors back carefully, then race toward the office door. Opening it, I walk straight into Merlin.

"There you are!" she says, then pauses, watching me. "Where've you been? I've been looking for you."

I raise a smile like a shield: big, showing all my teeth. "Oh, you know! Running back and forth to the gym. There's a patient I thought might need transferring, but it was a false alarm." I try hard to look like I've suddenly remembered something. "Though I think I may have left some inhalants down there—"

"We have more in the library." She is watching me so intently. "How are you?"

"A little nervous. Big day, right!"

"Right." She nods, then comes closer. "Nirali, I hope you know that I will do everything I can to make sure you never have to choose between being happy and being Queen."

What the hell kind of double talk is that? Is she saying she'll secretly cheat with me?

"If you mean last night," I say primly. "That won't happen again, I promise."

This does not get the reaction I was expecting: she smiles. "Wait. You're happy, about last night?" Her eyes shine, like at one point she doubted it, and the dull ache sings through me again, my fathead heart starting to race.

Who are you, Merlin? What game are you playing? Does the King know you're always listening in? Are you listening in on him, too? Are we all just pieces on your board, and to what end? You wouldn't just order a hit on some party girl to protect your King.

Would you?

"I'm just so confused." I bite my lip. "Are you going to tell the King?" .

"Never," she says quickly; she means it. "The King can never know."

"Won't he find out, though? Have you ever had to keep something this . . . damning from him?"

She moves closer. Her hand drifts forward until it brushes the side of my leg, an invisible ember at the end of her fingertip that burns to my bone.

"I could," she answers quietly. "If you wanted me to."

"Wizard Merlin, hey!" someone calls. She turns, all control, no panic, and nods calmly to the massive figure now filling the door: a guard in a Viking helmet and a hockey jersey with the sleeves cut off, along with nunchucks tucked into his belt.

He nods excitedly. "Your Majesty! I'm Chris, your personal guard. King Max just assigned me."

"Hi! A guard, wow, okay, that's . . . new." My throat tightens, my eyes sliding from his smiling face to Merlin's neutral one and back again. How the hell do I get to Leo now, without either of them knowing?

I smile at them, too hard. "I wonder if Artemis could come help me get ready?"

+ + +

Once inside my room, Chris outside my door, I stand before my bed, a blue ball gown laid out on it, crisscrossed with ribbons and lace and embroidery. I surreptitiously scan the shadowy ceiling for the baby monitor camera. It takes me just a moment to find the little red dot, wedged behind a fire sprinkler, and my eyes bounce away with a thrill of shock.

Is she watching me right now? If I put the dress on out of range of the camera, will she guess that I've found the monitor?

I hang my lab coat on the clothing rack, then turn back to the bed. A pins-and-needles awareness washes over me as I try not to look at the hovering red dot of the camera again. There's no way to tell if she's watching me or not, but as I pull my shirt over my head, I can't stop imagining her staring. Not that it matters now, but I don't think she was faking her attraction. She has every other advantage here at Moore, but that one is mine.

I step out of my jeans and stand, shivering, in my underwear. I feel almost feverish, waves of heat washing through me, goose bumps rising along my arms.

I look up, and my eyes lock on the red light.

A loud knock. I instantly throw the huge puffy blue dress over my head. "Coming!"

In another moment, Chris announces Artemis, who hurries in with a giant satchel of makeup slung over one round shoulder and dark circles under her eyes, her arms full of the white wedding dress.

"You *do* need help." She raises her very-drawn-in eyebrows. "That's on backward. The corset ties up the front."

"Is it the right dress at least?"

"Yes. Blue for the Trial. Always introduce a Queen in blue." She hangs the wedding dress on my rack of ball gowns. "Blue is the supernatural-feminine signifier. From Disney princesses to fairy godmothers to Mother Mary, from the ocean to the sky, blue signifies the unknown of the horizon and woman as man's channel to all supernatural yada yada." She drops her theatrical affect and says wearily: "We'll quick change into the white after the pool, in the closet with the old ice machine, between the proposal and the ceremony. I had to guess your measurements, but I have a shit-ton of safety pins so—"

"Well, hey, look," I cut in. "I have a very specific style for my hair I was hoping you could do? Can I show you?"

"Uh, sure." She seems thrown by my sudden enthusiasm.

Artemis sets the bag on my bed as I grab the notepad and a pen. I scrawl something quickly, then hand the pad to her with the message:

Merlin can hear what we say > baby monitor camera in the room > don't look for it

Artemis's eyes practically bug out of her head. She starts to scan the ceiling; I take her wrist firmly and hold her gaze: *Careful.* She nods almost imperceptibly, then warbles, "Maybe you could add a little more detail while I brush your hair out?"

"Exactly what I was thinking!" I say, still smiling with all my teeth. "How about I'll sit on the edge of the bed, and you sit behind me. And I'll try and clarify what I need you to do." That way I can keep the notepad on my lap, and she can read it over my shoulder while blocking it from the camera.

Artemis, fumbling with her brush and bottle of detangler, gets in position behind me. I start writing, the letters slanted and spidery because my hand is shaking so hard:

We found Jessica. KM ordered Jimmy 2 kill her. She's w Brick in gym rn.

Artemis drops her hairbrush with a clatter. I retrieve it from the floor, then sum up the morning's events as succinctly as I can while she creates an elaborate braid crown. Once she's caught up, I write:

J can testify if L will accuse KM @ trial. What can I do 2 help?

"How is Brick doing since yesterday?" Artemis asks.

"He's much better!" I say, then scrawl:

B won't fight. No one fights. We can settle this w words.

Furious as I am, I don't want to see anyone disemboweled in a joust.

When KM and I stand up 2 announce mrrge, I'll set up L 2 accuse KM. I'll call J 2 testify. Can you help me tell L?

"Well, I better hurry." Artemis's hands jitter nervously as she pins the last section of my hair in place. "I have to do last looks on the combatants after I'm through with you. Give my final costume *notes* to Tyler and El Martillo."

Got it. She'll see Leo, but they won't be able to talk privately; it's safer to pass a note. I turn the page and write out:

Leo, it's Nirali.

After Kyle overdosed at the office party, King Max hid his body and has been covering up his death. He ordered a hit on Jessica and had her hidden in the 1776 house to frame you, which is where I found her this morning.

Jess is going to be all right. She's being treated in the gym and

remembers enough to testify against King Max. Please send some of
your people to secure her immediately.

Confront Max with this crime today, and you'll have my—and
Jefferson's—full support.

I fold the note up, tight and small, and pass it to Artemis. When
I glance back at her, I'm surprised to see her hand is over her mouth,
nostrils pink and flaring.

"I'm so sorry about your boyfriend," she whispers in my ear as
she finishes up my hair. Hot tears spill from me then, so many she has
to redo my eyeliner.

Once she's finished, I pull Kyle's worn, filthy varsity jacket off the
rack. I hang it over my shoulders, our Senators mascot falling over
my heart, right where it's supposed to be.

+   +   +

There's a steady drumming that gets louder as we walk toward
the Moore athletic hall. Through the open windows I hear guards
bellowing across the front lawn:

"TRIAL! ALL TO THE TRIAL!"

All the Moore kids are crowding into the pool doors. But when
they see me approaching in my elaborate blue gown, Artemis holding
my train, they start swarming me instead, smiling and waving. Chris
and the other guards have to corral them toward the wall to let me
through. I keep my smile on until I'm out of view.

By the shallow end of the pool, where the wheel of lane lines
is usually kept, eight drummers beat massive timpani drums in
perfect rhythm, their faces grim. The empty pool's tile has been
scrubbed porcelain white, the hot noon sun that pours in through the
tall windows making it almost too brilliant to look at. Thousands of
fantastically dressed Moore students breathlessly fill the bleachers,
electrified by the tension between the promise and the containment
of violence.

The guards lead us toward an enclosed office set slightly above the rows of bleachers, its soundproof plexiglass panes removed so the drumming continues to hammer away at my head. Couches have been dragged in for the King's guests, along with a couple trash bags of popcorn and a warm keg, and two easy chairs pulled right up front for the best view.

King Max is leaning on the back of one of these, acting relaxed but giddy underneath. He's made an effort: under his swimmer's coat, he wears a vintage maroon velvet tuxedo and a pink frilled shirt, and his habitual paint-spattered Converse.

He stands up straighter when he sees me and gives me his huge white smile. I want to shove his teeth down his throat.

"You look incredible." He steps toward me, and I step back involuntarily. I will vomit if he touches me.

"Your Majesty!" Artemis bobs, about to hurry off, but he stops her.

"Don't go. I had them save a space for you on the couch."

"Cool, I'll be right back. I just have to do last looks for Leo and Tyler."

"Nah, don't bother. No one's going to be looking at them. Not while Nirali's around." King Max flashes his boyish grin at me again. "I'm about to go down to the high dive and kick things off." He puts out his good elbow. "If you want to come with me, my lady?"

Artemis's eyes flash over to the visitor bleachers on the other side of the pool where Kay Kim sits, two guards flanking her, four solid rows of Los Martillos glowering behind her. She's in a coarse gray shift. With her shaved head and huge, staring eyes, she makes me think of Joan of Arc. Not on the battlefield, but when they burned her at the stake.

Artemis shifts her weight to her back foot, making some excuse as she goes for the door. But King Max reaches past me and grabs her hand, laughing.

"Relax already! You just pulled two all-nighters. Now you get to put your feet up and chill, and that's an *order*. Someone get her a beer!"

Then he looks down at her hand, and my heart contracts so hard my vision pulses.

"Oooh, what's this, a note? For Leo?" He says it teasingly, but his grin is slightly too tight. "A *final goodbye*?" Artemis's neck goes red up to her jaw, cut short by the matte line of her foundation. "You know, whenever people told me Heather has a thing for Leo, I said *that* dude? No way. But maybe I was wrong?"

He snatches the note easily. Artemis, desperate, grabs the King's wrist and yanks it back. The room goes: "WHOOOA!"

"Easy there."

"Look how red her neck is!"

One of the Motorheads rips the note away from her and holds it over her head. Artemis leaps and claws for it. They laugh at how her full figure bounces, and she cries:

"*Give it back!*"

I've been frozen in terror this whole time, but now Artemis looks to me for help and King Max catches the look. His face changes. The Motorhead guy, confused by the sudden tension, looks from her to the King to me, still laughing. "You want it, Your Majesty?"

"What is it?" King Max smiles at me, confused. "You know what it is?"

I scramble for some lie, mouth opening and closing.

"Here, Dan!" King Max cups the air with his hands, and the Motorhead guy steps back and flicks the note like a paper football. King Max catches it as another Motorhead grabs Artemis's skirt to keep her from rushing him, pulling her in by her hips as she tries to tear herself away.

"*Stop it!*" Artemis shrieks. "Give it back!"

"It's a drawing of my wedding dress!" I cry in panic. "It's a surprise, don't look!"

But he's unfolded it enough to see the writing.

It's like a nightmare, watching him read my plea to Leo. Waves of cold panic go through me as his face changes, grows harder and more focused. He shakes his head a little when one of the Motorheads, laughing uncertainly, asks:

"Well? What is it? What'd she say?"

When King Max looks up at me again, it's with new eyes.

"You would've liked me," he says. "But the fact is, you don't have to."

He crumples the note as he orders the guard behind me:

"Sit them down. Don't let them get up again. They're both traitors. We'll deal with them after."

Ca-tas-tro-phe:
A DISASTER

NIRALI

I step toward King Max, but Chris pulls me back easily. King Max hands the balled-up note to Merlin, who's just come in, before stepping past her out of the enclosed box. A cheer rings through the tiled room as Merlin looks to me in consternation. She unfolds the note and reads.

The guard herds me into the easy chair, hands heavy on my shoulders. I watch Merlin's face, but she's inscrutable. At last, she approaches me, note fluttering in her hand.

"You were going to give this to *Leo*?" She's so angry she can barely get the words out. "*Are you trying to start a war?*"

This was not what I expected.

I thought she'd make some denial, or cover frantically. Even an evil cackle and a monologue about how easily she'd checkmated me would make more sense than this.

Instead, she's acting like *I'm* the bad guy. When they *let Kyle die*, they *tried to kill* Jessica, and *they lied to my face about everything!*

"You don't deny it, then?"

"The time to ask me for explanations," she says through clenched teeth, "was before you wrote this! Why didn't you come to me?" Her voice breaks. "You could have come to me. But instead, you go to these traitors and try to *destroy us?* Who the hell are you?!"

I can't fathom her point of view, can't even pretend to. I let out an involuntary sound, between a sob and a laugh, and Merlin says to the guard over my head: "You heard the King. She's a traitor. Don't let her speak again."

In another moment, a box cutter blade grazes my neck. I stiffen, instantly nauseated, and watch King Max climb the stairs up to the diving board. He strides out right to its end, suspended on the thin blue plank above the drained pool, as the drumming reaches a crescendo and then strikes three last slow beats.

A breath of silence, then wild applause, and King Max holds his arms out as though to embrace the crowd.

"Thank you, everyone," he calls, "for being here to see justice be done! The rules of Moore's first Trial by Combat are simple. Fighters may not leave the pool. If they try, they forfeit their lives." He indicates guys in boxy prom tuxedoes, red ties, and cummerbunds, standing every ten meters around the pool. Each holds a pitchfork.

"If either of these fighters *can't handle it* and wants to *give up*, they can always yell out 'craven.' And then the King decides if they may go." He smiles his big boyish smile. "Or, uh, not."

The braying laughter after this sickens me.

"So please give a *big Moore welcome* to our first fighter, my royal champion—Tyler, with the Motorheads!" he yells, and Tyler steps forward, hoisting a sledgehammer skyward. He has a motorcycle helmet with red plumes and soda-can chain mail spray-painted gold. There's a modified hubcap for a breast plate and a short hunting knife and hammer on either side of his belt.

"Our second fighter should be here, too. Maybe someone's seen him?" King Max looks to the benches of Los Martillos around Kay. They're all wearing black jumpsuits, with black lines painted under their eyes like football players, and they glare back at him with total hatred. "Maybe he's hiding out in the bathroom? Leo? Helloooo?" King Max yells, the board bouncing a little under him at the force of his cry. "Is he coming or what?"

"I'm here," a voice calls from the other end of the pool room.

Gasps and cries ignite across the long bleachers as everyone turns to see Leo, all in black. Black work boots, black baseball leggings, and a black sweatshirt under what looks like a full suit of black chain mail. But this is not made from soda tabs; this is something crafted in the Auto Shop, something real. He has a huge black shield made from the beaten hood of a '60s Cadillac on his left arm, his gold helmet gleaming on his proud head, and a black titanium ax in his right hand.

Leo looks to Kay. He raises his ax and bows his helmet in salute to her. He might as well be a boy band, the screaming cheers that follow are so lascivious. Kay, blushing, bows her head in return.

"Ready, Leo?" King Max snaps.

"Yes. But first, I have to say something as Kay's champion," Leo begins. The whole length of the echoing pool room falls silent, and I dare to hope. "Kay was accused of causing the attack in the gym. But only because she came too close to a terrible truth. So I am here to expose that truth. That you, King Max of Moore, killed the president of Jefferson, Kyle Meyer."

"Yo, what the hell did he just say?" Chris blurts out, his box cutter still grazing my throat. A sputtering uproar breaks out along the bleachers and just as rapidly falls silent as Leo keeps talking.

"And when I win here today," Leo addresses everyone in the bleachers across from him, "it will prove you, 'King Max,' are not fit to be King at all. You are nothing but a *murderer*."

Shocked silence. Then the room fills with the ocean crash of everyone talking at once: heated objections, confusion, people screaming "TREASON!" at Leo, and Los Martillos breaking into a thunderous, coordinated cheer: *"MAR-TEE-YO, MAR-TEE-YO!"*

King Max looks unimpressed. He just starts taking off his swimmer's coat, and then his tailored velvet jacket. He looks down to Tyler and says something. Tyler looks surprised but unsheathes the hunting knife from his belt.

"Well?" Leo yells, his face red in between the panels of his golden helmet. "Do you deny it?"

"Leo," King Max says contemptuously, and the whoops fall silent as the audience holds its breath. "I'm glad you finally got around to saying to my face what you've been saying to half the school. Tyler, you go ahead and sit this one out—"

Everyone starts screaming as King Max climbs down the stairs of the diving board and then walks the length of the pool, all the way to the shallow end, directly across from where Leo stands.

"I'm going to kill this piece of shit myself," King Max announces, in just a button-up shirt and velvet tuxedo pants and Converse. He has his crown on and Tyler's hunting knife, and that's it. No shield. No chain mail. And only one arm. I can feel the affection Moore has for its King, their pride at his recklessness stealing through the bleachers as he lowers himself in. Even Los Martillos look impressed.

"Come on in." King Max stares up at Leo from down in the pool. "Water's fine, dickhead."

Leo lowers himself into the shallow end and gets in a centered stance, ax held expertly. He's so much better equipped than King Max, not just with all his gear and weapons, but with his ready calm. King Max is twitching with adrenaline, but Leo is carved in stone.

They circle each other slowly. It will take just one good swing from Leo to King Max's right arm to end this, because the left one is useless. It's curled into his side in its thin sleeve, his right hand brandishing the hunter's knife. When Leo moves toward him, King Max retreats, and there are whoops of disapproval. Leo comes for him again, with an ax swing that King Max dodges. The bleachers ring with shaky, nervous laughter at the close call.

Then King Max charges Leo fast, nearly gouging his right shoulder, but Leo steps back at the last moment. King Max tumbles forward like a kid slipping on a wet lawn, his knife fumbling out of his hand and rattling across the tile.

Gasps ring out as King Max reaches with his right arm for the weapon, just barely swiping it back with his fingertips, the injured arm pulled into him. He's laughing a little too hard, and now it's obvious to everyone that he's injured. Still, he grins breathlessly up at Leo.

"Whooo! Now we're talking! Come on! *Come get me!*"

He's going to be slaughtered. I have to stop this, but how?

I try to stand, but before I so much as lean forward, the guard pins me back to the chair, box cutter digging deeper. The roar of the crowd is amplified by the empty pool as though it were a porcelain speaker, the cheers and screams echoing back so thunderously, they'd drown any scream I could make.

Leo advances on King Max again. His shield must weigh a ton, along with his mail, because he's already sweating in the bright noon sunlight. King Max skitters away in a strange crabwalk, refusing to turn his back on Leo as he half dances, half springs to his feet. Then he nearly pratfalls down the steep incline that starts halfway across the pool and sinks rapidly into the twelve-foot-deep end. Leo needs to slow down on this incline; the polished tile is slick. But King Max is tantalizingly close and jeering at him: *You can't touch me!* And then King Max yells something, and while I know it's impossible with so much noise from the crowd, I swear I hear "Jessica, too."

Leo charges forward, and that's all it takes. The weight of the shield going down that incline is too much momentum. Leo falls heavily, his huge shield rattling down the white tile slope like a sled and dragging him after it, revealing his arm strapped to its black steel mass.

Los Martillos spring from their bleachers just above him, screaming: "Get up, Jefe! *Levántate!*"

But King Max is faster. His Converse sneakers squeak against the tile, and now one of them is on Leo's shoulder, and the crowd gasps as he lifts the other knee high and stomps hard on the shield, bending Leo's arm backward against the angle of the pool's incline. I can practically hear the bone break. Leo screams in pure agony just before King Max swoops down and stabs him hard in the side.

"NO!" I wail. The entire audience lets out a cry of protest as King Max hunches over the golden helmet and stabs again, and again. *"NO, STOP! PLEASE!"*

Leo pitches to his side and struggles free, but way too much blood starts fanning into the grid between the white tiles. A broad smear of scarlet trails Leo as he crawls on all fours toward the deep end, pulling himself forward with one arm, the distended limb and Cadillac hood dragging behind him like a broken wing. Leo strains and slips until he gets to the twelve-foot-high tile wall below the starting blocks, and curls up against it, groaning in pain.

King Max, chest heaving, scurries after him, and Leo holds up his hand: *Please.*

"Cra-a-" Blood drools from Leo's mouth. *"Craven. Craven!"*

"No," the King says.

I can't look. I don't hear any cheering in the silence that follows—only Leo's pitiful screams as my fingers dig into the armrests. They shatter against the tile and refract back into the dreadful silence of the room, so it's like he's dying all around me, his anguished moans hitting from every side, on and on, until I'm moaning along with him, sobbing with him, right up until his last breath sputters out. Leo is gone. And then the only sounds are Max's high frenzied breaths, the slaps of his hand against Leo's side as he plunges the knife in a few last times to make sure, and the wild sobbing of Kay Kim.

I look up to see every face around me is stupefied with horror. King Max stands over what used to be Leo, his dress shirt and velvet pants drenched in blood. He wheels around, horrible eyes darting over the room, teeth bared.

"See?! *See?!*" he screams. "This proves it! This proves I'm not a murderer!"

There isn't a sound from the crowd as he walks back up the incline to the shallow end, red footsteps following him. He climbs up the chrome ladder, blood gloving his hand, and walks around to where Kay stands.

He says something to her then, up close, right against her ear, and

Kay recoils, shocked. A long, heavy beat follows before she shakes her head. He smiles angrily and calls out to Tyler:

"Kay is your prisoner now. Your first job at Moore is to put her to death for treason. However you see fit."

"*Please.*" I get to my feet. This time, my guard doesn't stop me. I think he's in shock, like Merlin, who sits stock-still in her chair, both hands clamped over her mouth. "Please?" I call out through the silent room. This is her only chance. All I have are words, but words have power. "I beg you, O great King Max, please. Please, great King Max, please—"

Sympathetic faces turn to me hopefully as I walk out of the box and down the concrete steps, down through the silent bleachers, to the tile around the pool, all the while begging "O great King Max, please, please, I beg you" like a mantra, until I am ten feet from him. And it's no act, as I sink down to my knees then, the big shiny blue dress pooling around me. I believe I am at his mercy, I believe he will decide Kay's fate. And I believe he is capable of stopping this, still. I hold his eyes for a moment, then bow my head and crawl to him on my hands and knees.

"Please, great King Max, I beg you, please show mercy to my friend Kay. I will do anything you ask, great and merciful King. I'll give you my kingdom, my crown, anything you want, it's yours, okay? Just please, great and wise King Max, merciful King, *please don't hurt my friend.*"

He walks over to me, so close I can smell Leo's blood, still warm, radiating off him.

"Look at her!" he calls to the crowd. "Beautiful! So beautiful. I *am* merciful, Queen Nirali. But I am just, too. Jefferson set the dragons free that killed so many here at Moore. So Kay must die." His voice rings through the still room: "Jefferson is ours. Their Queen is mine to use as I please." And then, to a guard, as he walks past me, "Lock her in the North Tower."

THE KNIGHT

KAY

"You want to be Queen? Beg me to stay. Beg me, right now."

I was sobbing so hard I didn't realize Max was walking toward me until he was trembling right beside me. His stare was searing, eyes too wide and blank, haloed by pinpoints of red. Leo's blood freckled his clear face, his lips; flecks of Leo's blood were dissolving in his mouth. I'd shuddered back, horrified, before it really hit me what he'd said, what it meant. The depravity it took to make that offer, moments after Leo had died protecting me, made me feel dirty. I felt the kind of hot, itchy guilt I hadn't known since I was a young child.

What had I done to make him think I would possibly accept?

It wasn't a real offer, it couldn't have been. He just wanted to make me beg for mercy, so he could turn down Leo's "girlfriend." One last humiliation to the broken boy in the pool just below. The huddled, pitiful shape of Leo, arm distended, blank blue eyes, I can't bear it, I'm going to throw up—

"Stop fighting!" Tyler yells, jerking me forward. "You lost!"

He clicks his key fob, and the sedan in front of us beeps in answer, its trunk lid popping above its silhouette.

He's going to put me in there.

"Tyler!" I scream, grinding back on my heels, pulling away from the car with all my strength. "I never hurt you! Why do you want to kill me? How is this fair? What have I done to deserve to die?!"

"What have you done to deserve to live?" Tyler spits back. "Pushing a pen for Student Council, taking minutes no one reads!" He grips the back of my neck like he might just finish me in this parking lot and save himself the drive. "My friends died because they were brave and strong. You lived because you were scared and weak. That wasn't fair, but you went along with it. You wanted to go to Costco so bad? You should've gone yourself. You should've had to go through that, not them."

He picks me up like I'm nothing, throws back the trunk lid, and tries to push me in. He's so much bigger, still in his armor, and hopped up on unspent adrenaline. But I keep twisting and clawing, like a cat refusing to take a bath, until he hits me straight across the mouth.

Stunned, I become easy to collapse. He shoves me backward into the trunk and the lid comes down, SLAM.

I lie in the dark, airless space, upholstery biting into my hands, pain radiating all along the side of my head and neck. It's too much pain to even think at first, but then the engine turns over and the car starts to move. Tyler is eager to kill me, and I have no idea how long it will take to get to the scene of my future murder. So I have to start rescuing myself right now.

I reach down my dress, fumble in Amy's borrowed sports bra, and pull out her multitool that I transferred from my coverall before the Trial. I writhe in the black, tight space, wrestle myself toward the trunk latch. The hinge of my jaw feels almost offset from the blow and is swelling fast. I grope for an emergency release lever. Finding none, I focus in on the trim panel, the thin plastic lining that covers the latch of the trunk, forcing the screwdriver into the crevice between the panel and steel. Its edge scrapes at my fingers as I pry it back.

The car is speeding, with only tight swerves left and right, accelerating all the time. We must be on the highway.

And then I realize where he's taking me.

The Costco. Where his Scavenging friends died.

With a shaky scream, I tear the thin panel away from the trunk lid, then grapple in the dark through the wires, feeling around for the trunk release cable.

The car downshifts and swerves hard as we follow the curve of an exit, rolling me away. I can picture the Costco parking lot rising up to meet us as I fight back into position. Teeth grinding, wail rising in my throat, I fumble until my hand finds a cable on the other side of the latch. I pull it hard, and the trunk lid releases; I catch it before the wind forces it upward, whipping through the small crack of daylight.

The car is going too fast to throw myself out. I clutch the trunk lid to keep it from flying up in Tyler's rearview mirror with one hand, and cycle through the options on the multitool with the other, praying for a knife blade but settling on the largest Phillips head. The car gallops over a set of speed bumps and careens around the abandoned cars of the Costco parking lot.

If I hop out and run, he'll see me and chase me with the car. I must wait until he's out from behind the wheel and hope his soda-can armor slows him down.

And then? Then I don't know. I may only gain minutes to live before I run into a Grown. But while there is a possibility of life, I will chase it. That is all I need to know.

The car shudders to a stop, and I fist the screwdriver as the driver's-side door slams. Tyler clanks around the car, soda-tab chain mail rattling, and when he reaches for the trunk lid, I shove it upward and knock him in his stupid face as hard as I can.

I hop out, ready to sprint, but Tyler catches the tail of my dress and I burst out in a feral cry; he's really going to make me do this.

I turn and thrust the screwdriver at his face. The metal tip catches his flesh, then splits through with a horrible rubbery sensation like tearing a pencil eraser, the sweat on his forehead coating the side of my hand. Then I turn and run without looking back through the sea of gleaming cars.

The Costco is both exactly and nothing like I remember.

The same broad white store, but its tile columns are streaked with dried blood. The same red steel picnic tables, but they lie upended on their sides. Like two giants were playing knucklebones, then got up and left the jacks scattered. Shattered glass and soccer mom vans crushed flat all declare: This is Growns' territory now.

I don't know what I'm more afraid of, the guy chasing me or what I could run into, when brakes screech to a halt beside me. A hot car grill grazes my midsection as a truck slams to a stop.

Through the windshield, our eyes lock.

I have never been so happy to see someone in my entire life.

"BRICK!"

"KAY!"

He leaps out of the truck and runs over to me, and I throw my arms around him helplessly.

"You're awake," I weep. "You're awake! Are you okay?"

I lean back to smile at him. He's pale as he takes me in, eyes leaping from the multitool clutched in my hand to the bruise gathering at my jaw, and then to a third vehicle screaming down the highway on-ramp above, its radio loud enough to make its doors buzz. The cheerleaders' Jeep? Is help on the way?

Brick locks on to something over my shoulder. The unscarred half of his face becomes more terrifying than the scarred half has ever been, and he pushes me behind him.

Metal rattles across the asphalt as Tyler approaches us warily, dragging six feet of heavy chain behind him. A thick bead of red from the gouge in the middle of his forehead winds down the side of his nose and lines his furious sneer.

Tyler wordlessly starts swinging the chain in a circle, a big hook at its end like they use to drag trucks with.

The Jeep has turned off the highway into the parking lot. Help is on the way if we can just hold him off. I'm so focused on the approaching Jeep it takes me a moment to notice Brick trying to furtively hand off the truck keys to me.

But the instant I move to take them, Tyler sends the chain flying at Brick. The keys go soaring as Brick throws his arm up to block it. The heavy metal chain wraps around his thick forearm, but he barely winces, catching the hook with the other hand before it strikes his face and then yanking Tyler forward onto the asphalt. Tyler's short, though, and athletic enough to maintain his balance and drop to a controlled kneel. He leans back hard then, pulling against Brick with all his might.

The chain squeaks taut between them as they strain to pull each other off balance. The truck keys glitter on the ground between them. I'm about to duck forward and grab them when the cheerleaders' Jeep lands beside us with a shriek of axles and Leila and Stokes leap out.

"Stop in the name of the King!"

Stokes has one of the royal crossbows in her hands. I've never seen one of them so close; it's terrifying, the wooden stock like a rifle's, the severe arc of the metal bow promising deadly force.

Brick releases the chain abruptly, and Tyler falls forward. Brick is on him, his arm around his neck. I let out a breath of relief when Stokes yells: "ENOUGH!"

There is a mechanical whisper, then a bolt hits the pavement at Brick's feet with such force it flies up and scratches a red line across his arm. It would have struck his unmarked cheek if he didn't step back in time.

"What the hell are you doing?" I yell at Stokes.

"Come on, Brick," Leila says, not looking at me. "We're under orders to get you back to Moore."

"What?" I cry. "You're going to take orders from Max, after what he did?"

Stokes, muscles standing out in her neck, pulls back the next bolt with a mechanical creak, then raises it level with my face in answer.

My eyes blur like she's slapped me.

"Kay." Leila says my name, but she's staring at Brick, eyes swollen from crying. "Leo lost. And the King's command is that his Captain of the Guard does not interfere with the results of the Trial."

Stokes's crossbow is still trained on me. "Get in the Jeep, Brick."

"Run, Kay!" Brick cries.

But I can't move, can't leave him like this. Where could I even go where I'd be safe? If I could get the keys and get in the truck, maybe I can—

Tyler follows my gaze to the keys, grabs them, and stabs them straight into Brick's injured leg. The howl that comes out of Brick almost brings me to my knees.

And then the three of them—Leila, Stokes, and Tyler—go completely still at the sight of something right behind me.

The next moments happen in what feels like slow motion, as I turn around and my adrenaline-soaked brain races to absorb it all:

A tall figure, covered in silvery cloth. A black welder's mask pulled down by a gloved hand. The soft hiss of the cylinder on his back. The metal nozzle gripped in his other, heavily gloved hand. A muffled command:

"Put the weapon down!"

Stokes tightens her grip on the crossbow, eyes cutting from me to him. She shifts her weight. Her jaw sharpens. She keeps it level.

With a click, the hissing sound becomes louder, then there's a rush of sound like a fire hose. A burst of blue flame arcs up and above us, with a snap of black smoke. Blue fire, bluer than the spring sky, and Leila's jaw drops.

"*The Blue Knight.*"

Stokes's face is bathed in sweat as the Blue Knight brings the nozzle level with her face. He is standing just beside me now, towering over me. I'm too afraid to run away.

"Put it down," the Blue Knight says again, voice deep and calm.

"Like hell." Stokes grimaces, tears mixing with her sweat now.

His hand flits to his tank, and the hissing sound starts again. Stokes swears, and lets the bow go slack.

"On the ground," he says coolly. "Kick it my way."

The crossbow rattles across the asphalt.

"Everybody back up," the Blue Knight yells.

Then a stream of blue fire swallows one of the King's royal crossbows, and Stokes drops to her knees on the hot black asphalt, screaming like she's the one on fire. When the flamethrower finally chokes off, she reaches for the warped T-bar, then recoils with a shriek.

The Blue Knight lifts the welder's mask and turns to me.

His narrow brown face is stern, covered with days of black stubble, but softens when he smiles. "Hey, new girl."

My knees go weak. "Starr?!"

The guy from under the car, the one who the jack collapsed on. It's him. *He's* the Blue Knight.

"Can you tell me what's going on here?" His large dark eyes flit down to Tyler, scowl all bloody, and then linger on Brick. "Which of these dudes is giving you a hard time?"

"My friend Brick here"—I walk over, set my shaking hand on Brick's shoulder—"has been trying to keep the other guy from killing me."

Brick's hand goes over mine, and hot tears sting the back of my eyes.

The Blue Knight takes this in stride, though his upper lip curls a little. "And these two?" He gestures at Leila, who is still staring at him open-mouthed, and Stokes, sobbing on her knees. "What's their deal?"

"YOU HAVE NO IDEA WHAT YOU'VE DONE!" Stokes howls up at him. "THAT WAS THE KING'S!"

"*King?*" Starr laughs.

Then the sound of trees falling on the other side of the parking lot silences all of us. The shadows of fleeing birds sweep the ground below.

"Inside," the Blue Knight says. "Everybody. Right now."

And we all start running for the bloodied entrance of Costco.

Enough of Everything

BRICK

This is the weirdest day since Before, and that's saying something. Like, there have been some weird days, there have been some *twists and turns*, all right.

But nothing has been quite as surreal as helping the mythical Blue Knight bring down the massive metal garage door that shields the entrance to the Costco, and then realizing, once it's locked to the floor, that the lights are on and music is in the air because Costco *still has electricity somehow.*

I back up, staring at the fluorescent lights overhead, wanting to stare them down until my eyes stream tears. On the store radio, Pharrell is telling us all to clap along because happiness is the truth when Tyler punches me in the back of my neck.

I grab his ear and get my arm around his throat before the Blue Knight pulls us apart:

"*BEHAVE YOURSELVES!*" He throws Tyler off me.

I put my hands up. Tyler isn't as cool—he tries to push through and get another hit in—but my new best friend shoves him to the ground, gets a knee on his chest, and pulls out a zip tie.

"That's it!" He cuffs Tyler's wrists in front of him, then pulls him to his feet. "Keep playing, I'll put you out there! All of you!" He glares at Leila and Stokes. "You hear me?"

At least four car alarms are going off now as the dragons frolic on the other side of the metal Costco door. It's dented from the inside, which is reassuring: If it kept rampaging dragons in, it can keep them out.

"*Do you hear me?*" the Blue Knight repeats.

Immediately, everybody nods and mumbles yes.

"All right, then." He shoves Tyler over to Stokes to babysit. "This way." And he turns toward a wasteland of brand-new stuff.

I look over at Kay, and she's staring at me. Her heart-shaped face goes the color of a Valentine. I can't get over her in that dress. She looks like a fairy-tale princess who fronts a punk band. She walks over to me.

"How's your leg? There's red coming through the bandage."

Oh, she's just worried about me keeling over again. Tyler poked a hell of a hole with the keys, but I don't think the wound is reopened. I hope not, at least.

"I think I know where I can get another one," I joke, nodding toward the store so my hair falls between her and my face. Kay stares, starry-eyed, out into the fully lit warehouse.

"Look at it . . ." she breathes.

At some point Costco's towering shelves, taller than most houses in our town, toppled into each other like dominoes. I'm guessing dragons must nest—must circle up before they lie down to sleep, like Frank does—because the floor of the Costco is a frozen ocean of stuff: whirlpools of new jeans, a tsunami of bulk cracker boxes and soaps and bags of gummy bears crashing into vortexes of hardcover books and laundry detergent bottles. Loose noodles and jellybeans and snack crackers carpet the floor, ground fine as flour. But almost everything seems still good, still usable, and there's so *much*.

Enough of everything, for everyone, for years to come.

We follow the Blue Knight through the mess, Kay so close her arm keeps brushing mine. Whenever we touch, it's like hitting my funny bone, but through my whole body. A jolt that goes up my arm, down to my fingertips, and echoes in my stomach. But Kay looks straight ahead, like she doesn't notice. So I focus on not slipping in conditioner as we follow the Blue Knight through a pearly canyon of Pantene bottles.

He takes us to a brown microsuede sectional couch and La-Z-Boy living room suite, positioned in front of a wall of dark flatscreens.

"Are there any active TV stations?" I ask. Active stations mean active adults.

"No, not that I could find." He shakes his head. "But there was a loop of high-res images going that I turned off. Bee on a flower, that kind of thing."

"How do they have electricity still?" Kay asks.

"I figure they had some deal with water and power. Or the world's best generator. The meat's rotten, but it's cold. And the frozen stuff is still good. There's cans and nuts and every kind of chip. Speaking of which . . ." He pulls a fifty-count pack of Lay's snack bags from under the coffee table and points out a flat of blue Gatorades.

"You're really the Blue Knight," Leila says, not a question.

"The who now?"

"That's what we call you back at Moore," I say. "You're a big mystery because of the blue fire."

"No mystery there. I burn alcohol and alcohol burns blue."

"I'm Brick." I hold out my hand, and he takes it after a moment.

"Starr." His eyes bounce off my scar, but then he looks me straight in the eyes. "Can I ask what happened?" He points to his own cheek.

"Dragon clipped me as it was dying."

"Because he killed it," Kay pipes up, and my face heats.

"Yeah, well. Thanks for getting things under control back there."

"I'm just sick of everyone being so cruel to each other." He looks around the group. "Like it isn't hard enough these days."

"You don't understand the situation," Tyler says from the couch where Stokes has plopped him. She and Leila are on either side of him now, but I'm not counting on them to keep him from acting like a fool. I keep him in my eyeline, perching on the arm of the recliner Kay is curled up in, ready to go if they come at her again.

"So explain it to me. She said y'all were about to kill her out there, and I don't hear you denying it." Starr sets the flamethrower tank down with a clunk and rolls his shoulder. "So please. What situation possibly justifies killing a fellow human being?"

"You seen the blood out there?" Tyler says. "That's from my friends. Half my friends are dead because she got the bright idea to come open up this Costco."

"And then those dragons came through our gym." Stokes pops open a bag of Chili Cheese Fritos. "Killed twenty of *our* friends. And then another guy got killed today, defending her grim reaper ass—"

"Leo," Leila says softly, hand floating up to her eyes. "I know I joke a lot. But I think I really was in love with him."

"You're blaming Kay for King Max killing Leo?" I ask Leila.

"She let him fight!" Stokes answers for Leila. "And if he'd won, and King Max was lying dead back there instead? *She'd* be Queen right now. And she wouldn't be complaining about it, either. *But she lost.*" Stokes leans forward, mad-dogging Kay. "And that's the only reason you're crying, bitch. So wah wah wah all you want, I don't care."

"You saw your boyfriend get killed today?" Starr asks Kay.

Kay doesn't answer. Her hands just cover her face, and her shoulders start shaking. The urge to comfort her is overwhelming, but I don't have the right. I'm the henchman for the guy who stomped and butchered Leo. I still can't believe what I saw, what I heard.

The roars from the pool kept echoing down the hall to the gym. They went from cheers to something else, something awful. Jess was being looked after by several nurses, so finally I went to watch. I entered the pool room just as Max stomped Leo's arm.

One thing I will say. Max was sobbing while he stabbed Leo. I knew the sound even from the back of the pool room, when the crowd went silent in shock. That low noise deep in his throat hit me hard. I've only heard him cry like that once before: the night his parents told him they were getting divorced.

I know Max didn't want to kill Leo. But he did it. Oh, he did it all right.

And I *defended him*. Kay tried to warn me. She saw King Max for what he was at once. And I lectured her! *Told her she couldn't move in with me?*

She must hate me now.

I fist my hands to keep from touching her.

"He was stabbed to death," I say. "By the King of Moore during a Trial by Combat."

"Trial by Combat?" Starr looks like he's hoping he heard wrong. "Like in the Dark Ages?"

Leila puts up her hands. "It's not something we do all the time or anything. This was an exceptional circumstance."

"But it *happened*." Starr leans away from us, eyes wide. "Like . . . y'all watched two kids fight to the death today, to settle a dispute? And no one called out that that doesn't work? Like, might does not actually make right, this has been established again and again in history—"

"Especially in this case." I stare at Leila. I know her, I know she has a good heart. And she can get through to Stokes if I can just get through to her. "Because Kyle is dead, and Kay was right. King Max covered it up."

Kay looks up at me then, eyes gleaming with tears.

"I only found out this morning," I explain. "When we found Jess."

I tell them about the house. What Jess said in the car. By the time I finish, they're all staring. Watching me fight not to cry.

Kay's hand presses against my arm, and I stand up, try to suck it up. Punch the top of the recliner until I can keep it in.

"But then the King didn't lie at all! He didn't *kill* Kyle," Stokes is saying. "Kyle died of an overdose. By accident."

"Kyle overdosing isn't the point. King Max ordered Jimmy to kill Jess to cover it up, Tiffany," Leila snaps. "Do you not see the problem with that?"

"Well. I mean. If Jess got clocked in the head that bad, maybe she's remembering it wrong—"

"*Tiffany.*" Leila glares at her. "Stop."

"I don't believe it! Sorry, but I don't!" Stokes yells. "Why would the King go to all that trouble—put a hit out on someone!—to hide some rando from Jefferson who overdosed? Why not just explain what happened? Like, it's *sad*, but accidents happen! And no one at Moore gives a shit about Kyle! I'm sorry, but we don't. Why would our King get in the pool and *risk his life* fighting Leo, instead of just explaining there was an accident?"

Leila waves a hand in Stokes's face to get her to stop ranting. "Because the Trial wasn't about Kyle, not at first. I was at the dinner. The Trial was about whether or not Kay caused the attack on the gym."

"And she did!" Tyler says. "She forced us to come out to this Costco. We opened the doors, the Growns came out, and then they crossed the highway, they crashed straight through the fence—"

"But they didn't crash through," I say quietly, my guts in knots again. "My fence guys stopped me on my way out. There were no breaks in the wall. They said the panel wasn't closed right, *that's* how the dragons got in . . ." I look around the living room set. "You can open a panel with two people, but you need three to lock it right. It wasn't *locked right* . . ."

Shit, shit, shit.

"What's the matter?" Kay's voice sounds far away, but her eyes bring me back.

"King Max and Jess took Kyle's body through the west fence on their own, before the guards were out. When they came back, they couldn't close it right—there's no way to close it right with just two people. That's how the dragons got through. No one goes out that way to raid, we always expand east, so . . ." Say it. Say the words. "So the attack on the gym was King Max's fault. But he was going to let Tyler and Leo fight instead of admitting it."

All of them look stunned. Especially Tyler.

Leila leans forward, kneading her temples like her head aches. "So King Max straight up murdered Leo. He *tried* to kill Jess. He was going to let Tyler kill Kay. And he sent us after Brick, his best friend, with a *crossbow*." She looks around at us. "So what do we do? Can we get Jess to, like, testify—"

"To who?" Kay says. "You don't have a court, you have a pool."

Stokes shakes her head, face grim. "We still don't *know*."

But she does know. We all do. We're all picturing the frenzy in King Max's eyes when he yelled he wasn't a murderer.

"Okay. First off." Leila turns to Kay. "I owe you an apology. I am so, so sorry." After a beat, Leila looks at me. "Brick, I won't force you to come back to Moore. Hell, I don't think I can go back now."

"Of course we're going back. Where else do we go?" Stokes says.

"Honestly?" Starr gets up and walks over to the broad white side of a freezer case, where a rough but impressively scaled map of town is sketched out in black Sharpie. He picks up a dry-erase marker. "There's not a ton of options. They're damn close to eating each other at Briggs"—he crosses out a yellow square downtown—"and I'm not going to even go into the twisted shit at Sharpe Academy." He crosses out a blue square up in the woods north of Jefferson.

Briggs was where the "bad kids" got sent to if they were expelled from Moore. If you had a parole officer, you went to Briggs. I never talked with anyone from Sharpe Academy, a private boarding school, but I'd see them clustered up on the train platform in their stupid blazers with the gold crests in spring and fall.

"What school did you go to?" Leila asks Starr.

"I was homeschooled. My dad was a professor. He had some pretty deep feelings about education." Starr clears his throat. "And you can *survive* alone. But it's no way to live. I was *hoping* to join up with Moore." He rubs at the stubble on his jaw. "Seemed like y'all were doing it right. Or at least better than the rest. But now . . ." He puts a big black X over Moore as well.

"We should all just go back to Jefferson," Kay says.

"*Jefferson?*" Tyler laughs. "Do you *remember* Jefferson?" He looks from me, to Stokes, to Leila. "You have no idea, no fucking clue, how good you have it. Why do you think I was willing to kill a guy with a sledgehammer to join a room at Moore?"

"Because you're a homicidal maniac," Kay says, matter-of-fact, and my laugh surprises me. "Jefferson's not all set up, like Moore is." Kay turns to me. "But it could be. We could build fences. You could show them—"

"No one's letting Skeletor into Jefferson," Tyler cuts her off. "They see that freak coming, they'll bolt the doors."

He has a point. But the cheerleaders are shoving him now.

"Don't talk about Brick like that," Leila snaps.

"You're ugly with no excuse, and we still let *you* in!" Stokes adds.

And then Kay says, like it's basic math, "Brick is the most valuable person in town."

I cut a glance over to her. She isn't blushing. No tells apparent.

"He can kill dragons," she goes on hotly. "He can build anything. Everybody who knows him, loves him. If anyone at Jefferson has any objections to Brick, I will deal with them myself."

Loves him.

"And so will Nirali." Kay lifts her chin. "Once I break her out of Moore."

"Uh, that's not happening," I cut in.

"Who's Nirali again?" Starr asks, leaning against the freezer case.

"The doctor at Jefferson."

"But now she belongs to King Max," Stokes adds.

"Belongs? Did I hear that right?" Starr blinks. "She belongs to the guy who *stabbed somebody to death*?"

"No, she doesn't, and I'm not leaving her with him." Kay looks at Leila, her voice steely. "So thanks for the apology, but if you really want to make it up to me, you will help me get her out."

"Leila is not helping. No one is helping because there is no way to get Nirali out." I shake my head. "As soon as the fence guards see you, you're done."

"They won't see us, because Starr knows a way in," Kay says. "The Blue Knight has been crossing the fences this whole time, right?"

Starr shrugs. "There's a tunnel."

"Doesn't matter!" I say, too loud. "Even if you get past the fences, even if you *somehow* get in the building, King Max said to put Nirali in the North Tower."

Leila sucks her teeth, and Stokes laughs through a mouth of Fritos: "Yeah, that's not happening."

"What's the North Tower?" Kay asks Leila.

"The machine room of the elevator shaft. Brick knows more about it than I do since he basically built it."

"Oh really?" Starr's eyebrows go up. He holds out the marker. "Could you draw it?"

Moments later I'm up by the freezer case, drawing a clumsy cartoon blueprint of the elevator with a squeaky erasable marker.

I draw the column of the elevator shaft, a square for the engine room above it, and a circle for the pulley that the engine helps control.

"This is the North Tower," I say, then draw three lines across the shaft, one for each floor, and two lines going up and down the shaft: the cable for the elevator car, the cable for the counterweight.

"The second-floor entrance is closed off. There's a guard at the first." I add a stick figure carrying a little arrow spear. "Let's say somehow you get in the school, knock out the guard, and get into the elevator." I draw the elevator car at the first floor. "Now you don't have someone managing the counterweight. Because that's what the guard's for. He's what we use for an overspeed governor—"

"Governor?" Kay frowns.

"It's not a title. It's the part of the elevator that makes sure the counterweight doesn't drop too fast when the car is light." I draw a line from the guard's arm to the counterweight hanging above the elevator. "Because this weight is *heavy*, okay. It's designed to counter the car itself, Merlin, her chair, and a guest. And our horsepower up top can fluctuate. So, you need a guard on that counterweight. Otherwise, the car could go flying up and *bang*." I clap my hands as hard as I can, staring right in Kay's eyes. "Pancake time."

"I could help with the counterweight," Leila offers.

"Can you bench two-fifty?" I fold my arms.

"Can *you*?" Kay asks hopefully, and I shoot her a dark look.

"I'm not going to help get you killed, Kay." King Max condemned her to death back at the pool. What does she think would happen if he caught her now? He's been after her since she walked in the throne room. I've never seen anyone get so under his skin.

"Look, Brick's right. No one should be getting in this elevator," Starr says, and my shoulders release. He stares at my drawing appreciatively. "This is some cool engineering, though, man. Where's the counterweight housed when the elevator is all the way up?"

I tap the very bottom of the elevator shaft I've drawn, below the last line. "Basement."

"And when it's all the way down?"

"Held by a braking system in the machine room, in the North Tower."

"And what, a guard holds the car up at the first floor?"

"No, they let it rest in the basement until Merlin needs to go up again."

"So . . ." He picks up another dry-erase marker and draws a red stick figure on the counterweight itself. "If someone got on the counterweight, and then Merlin was called down, couldn't they ride the counterweight all the way up to where Nirali is?"

I glare at him. He smiles apologetically but goes on.

"She wouldn't have to knock out a guard or anything. She'd just have to sneak into the basement and get a ride straight to Nirali without anyone seeing her. You're what—" Starr points toward Kay with his marker. "Ninety pounds? Guard won't even notice the extra weight."

"Yes!" Kay cries, face glowing.

"*No*." It comes out of me too loud, but I can't help it, can't stop myself. "Absolutely not."

"Why not?" Leila says. "All we have to do is get Merlin to come down to the throne room." She jerks a thumb at Stokes. "We could demand an emergency meeting with her and the King, because, um . . . we found the Blue Knight! Which we really did, so that's perfect."

"We can coordinate with walkie-talkies," Starr says. "There's all kinds of 'em here." He gestures to a pyramid of silver plastic and LED screens just left of the television displays. "And all kinds of batteries. They've got ropes, ladders, a gardening section in the back . . . This place has just about anything you can think of."

"We can do this," Kay says deliriously. "Leila and I will get the gear together. Everybody else can help Starr load up the cars with food for Jefferson—"

"We got the Costco eighteen-wheelers," Starr says. "Refrigerated."

"Even better!"

And now I'm on my feet, hovering over her. "Kay, *no*."

"Brick, yes."

"How many times are you trying to die today?" I wave at the others. "And if it's not you, it'll be one of them. Listen to me. I am the Captain of the Guard and the *guy who built the elevator*. Someone is getting caught and dragged in front of the King tonight. Any of you care to beg for your lives from King Max right now?" I look from face to face, feeling their dread at the thought. Good. They should be scared; they should be terrified. "Jefferson's all about *voting*, right?" I turn back to Kay, who's glaring at me now. Fine, hate me. I don't need you to like me, I just need you to be alive. "So, let's vote. Who here is willing to risk their life on the one in a million shot we can pull this off?"

Stokes crosses her arms. Leila looks at the floor, arms at her sides. Tyler's hands are still tied, but he makes a point of dropping them even lower.

Kay is the only one with her arm in the air.

"Nirali is a doctor, right?" Starr asks the group. "And we're absolutely sure she doesn't want to be at Moore, right?"

Kay looks pointedly at Leila. "She's being held against her will by a homicidal maniac who *murdered Leo*. A handsome, brave young man who did nothing wrong, and who some of us *allegedly* cared about."

Leila glares at her, but raises her hand. "Damn it all to hell, fine. I'm in. For Leo."

"And I'm in." Starr raises his hand. "I've always wanted to save a princess from a tower. Doctor's even better. Anything else we can say for Nirali? Like, she do anything nice for anybody here?"

Kay looks at me then, and my stomach drops.

"Well," I admit, "she did save my life."

Kay takes my hand and lifts my arm up.

"Looks like the ayes have it," Starr says.

+ + +

"The tunnel's left over from colonial times," Starr explains via walkie-talkie. He's in the driver's seat of the Costco truck crawling ahead of us, loaded down with as much food as we could stock before dark fell. Now we're driving through that same dark in the open.

I've driven around before dawn outside the fences at Expansion, but never at night. It's claustrophobic because our vision is narrowed to the Jeep's headlights. But Starr's crackling voice is calm, like he does this all the time. "It was dug during the Battle of Brockton."

"What battle? You guys heard of a battle?" Leila whispers over her shoulder. Kay, next to me, shakes her head. She's dressed like a cat burglar after raiding the piles of Costco clothes: black hoodie, black leggings, black beanie.

"It was the militia captain's house," Starr goes on. "The tunnel originally went from his root cellar to the mouth of the Brockton River, but of course that was diverted in 1912."

"Of course." Stokes's eyes roll in the rearview mirror.

"So now it opens out on a stream. My dad took me by the house. I met the little old lady who lived there back when I was doing my local history unit. She was really nice. But she, uh, had a lot of cats."

Crackling. "Anyone allergic?"

"Oh, I love cats!" Leila says. "I want one."

Starr laughs, and not in a good way, before his walkie-talkie cuts out.

The massive Costco semi turns off onto a narrow road and shimmies to a stop. Leila pulls alongside him, and the last thing we see before the Jeep headlights go out is a dark red house, half-buried in fallen leaves and ivy.

Inside, the air is so thick with cat piss you can taste it. Our new Costco flashlight beams slide around the cramped living room, flattening everything they touch into crime scene photographs: a bowl of fruit buried in white mold, a worn pink slipper filled with spiderwebs, a mountain of heavy furniture pulled clear from the walls and piled in the middle of the living room.

Old people furniture for sure: dark heavy wood cupboards and chairs and tables, all crashed together. One decomposed hand reaches from the tangled mass.

"What happened there?" Leila is horrified.

"That was the old lady," Starr says. "I guess some furniture fell on her."

All the furniture fell on her, somehow. Like it decided to come to life and jump her all at once. I've never seen anything like it. Kay looks as puzzled as I feel. Leila circles the heap suspiciously, her flashlight casting jagged shadows across the flower print walls and catching iridescent eyes. There are cats hiding in every crevice of the heaped furniture pyramid, and they're all making that demonic growl cats make right before they pounce.

I zip-tie Tyler to a fallen bookcase; he's gagging too hard from the piss smell to protest.

"The trap door is under here." Starr kneels on the floor and throws back a braided rug. There's a latch in the floor with a sliding bolt that slides back silently, like it's been recently oiled. The trap door comes up with a thin creak, its wood planks maybe six inches thick.

A rickety ladder starts just below the floor and drops into a hole deep and narrow as a well.

I start down first with Leila, Stokes, and Kay following after. When I land, the ground underfoot feels like packed dirt. I can't see; it's pitch black and so cold. I back away to let the girls come down and the damp stone walls close in around me so tight I have to hunch my shoulders to fit. We wait for Starr, but his headlamp isn't turned toward the floor.

"Starr?" I call up the ladder.

The trap door slams shut overhead, plunging us into total darkness.

✝otal ✝raitor

BRICK

"*Starr!*" Leila is back at the top of the ladder, banging on the bottom of the trap door. She can scream all she wants. There's no way anyone will hear anything.

"It won't open!" Her voice breaks.

Who is this guy again? Where the hell does this tunnel lead? Is it even a tunnel, or just a pit to keep us until he's ready—to what? Kill us? Carve us up like deer and sell our meat to the cannibals at Briggs?

Maybe. My best friend killed someone today, killed him so close he got the other guy's blood in his eyes. Who knows what anyone will do?

"*Open up!*" Leila fights to push the door open. Spots slide across my vision, amoebas made of light. If the ants are coming back, there's no way to tell; it's darker with my eyes open than closed.

Then Kay's hand is on my arm; her cool fingers brush against my cheek as she turns on my headlamp. The LED washes her whole face in angelic light.

"You okay?" she asks.

I nod, and my headlamp rakes the walls. There's bright green moss, and spiders booking it back into the shadows. And then the entrance to the tunnel ahead. Not a pit. A tunnel, like Starr said.

The trap door flies open and Starr climbs down the ladder, hissing between his teeth, "Damn cats!"

Leila hurries down to make room.

"Any of them get down here?" he asks. There are angry red scratches across his hands. "I was stashing my pack under the couch, and three of them jumped me at once!"

Leila laughs a little too loud. "We were wondering what the holdup was!"

"So sick of those cats, man—" He looks up, his headlamp beam landing straight on my face. "Hey, bro, if you're waiting on me, you're backing up."

I stumble into the tunnel, Kay squeezing my hand again before her fingers slip away and we fall into single file.

We're about twenty feet in before the going gets rough. Roots rise out of the increasingly muddy earth, snagging our shoes. The wood struts that appear every few feet overhead—the things keeping the ground from collapsing on us—are clearly rotten. The ants ring the edge of my vision; I'm already exhausted and we're not even there yet. Though the tunnel runs pretty straight, there's no end in sight. The future is just a gray haze past the beam of my headlamp.

"How old is this tunnel?" I call back to Starr.

"Battle of Brockton was 1779, so almost two hundred and fifty years."

So Brockton was once a battlefield where guys my age bled out in forests. The same forests that are now, like, the ShopRite parking lot. And now the ShopRite probably has a dragon sleeping inside it.

Normal is supposed to be forever, but it's not. If you are among the luckiest people in history, you might get ten years of normal. And you probably think it's boring.

Starr calls, cheerfully: "Almost there!"

The air starts moving around us; the ground rises. The blackness at the end of the tunnel thins to a circle of navy blue, and then dangling ivy vines catch the light of my headlamp, just before its beam leaps into the open. I jog forward into the wind, gulping down the fresh air. We come out from what looks like a large sewer drain, under a small pedestrian bridge, beside a stream running through a wooded ravine. I recognize the bridge; we're maybe a block from the 1776 house.

And inside the fences.

It's a short walk to the edge of the Auto Shop parking lot, but it's made longer by the fact that we have to switch our headlamps off and walk by starlight. Once we're in sight of the school, we crouch in the long grass at the edge of the Auto Shop parking lot.

My guards will have their hands full tonight: a line of Los Martillos, all in black and carrying torches, are marching from the garage entrance along the side of the school, across the parking lot and out to the football field. There, in the middle of the field, they've built what looks like a massive wooden tower. They're singing a slow, creepy song, and every face seems searching for an excuse to throw hands.

My guards are dealing with this with no plan and no idea where I am. Shame burns from the back of my neck to the tips of my ears. I've never let down my team before and, damn, I'm letting them all the way down now.

Once the last Martillo torch has flickered around the corner, we all turn on our Costco walkie-talkies. Kay squeezes my hand again, with the same ringing effect in my bones.

"See you soon," she says, just to me. Then she flits through the open door of the now-empty Auto Shop. From there it's one floor down to the basement elevator entrance, where she will enter the shaft and get into position on the counterweight.

"Ready?" Leila asks Starr. He turns so she and Stokes can loosely tie his wrists. Leila nods to me just before they haul him toward the nearest guards.

"Hey!" Leila calls to Sam and Chris, stationed in front of the music wing exterior doors. "We need to see the King and Merlin. It's Spur business."

I told her to say "of the Spur," but Sam, my second in command, is too frazzled to catch it. "You find Brick?" Sam asks hopefully. Then, seeing Starr's face, "Who's this?"

"That's what I need to talk to them about. You can announce to His Majesty and Merlin that we have the Blue Knight here to see them."

Chris turns excitedly to go tell the King, while Sam opens the door for them and follows them in. It hurts to see my men fall for it so easily. But they trust other Moore kids. After this, they won't. That same trust we've been building since kindergarten in another hour will be gone.

I wait a few beats, then hurry into the music hall through the unguarded doors.

The plan is for me to get up to my room and open the skylight so Kay and Nirali can climb down to meet me. Then we'll sneak out through the music hall and back to the tunnel, while Starr is distracting Merlin and King Max. Once we're through, we'll signal Starr. He will pretend to escape from Leila and Stokes, and they'll chase him all the way back through the tunnel to meet us.

I scan the hall for Frank, expecting him to come running, but I don't hear claws on tile. His bowl, by the Cage doors, is empty. The doors are unchained for some reason.

Maybe he's up in my room?

I move quickly through the unchained doors, stopping briefly in the Cage to take one thing from the shelf, and continue up the narrow stairs to my room.

The walkie-talkie crackles on my hip.

"Brick?" Kay's voice.

"I'm here."

"I went into the elevator, but the weights—the counterweight you described, the stacked metal plates like at a gym—they should be on the ground, right?"

"Yes."

"They're not there," she says, panicked. "But the elevator car is, so Merlin must already be downstairs."

Shit, shit, shit.

"Brick, what if I just climb up the car cable?"

"Don't."

"I could still get there, right?"

"Climb an oiled cable four stories?"

"I'm a climber, remember?"

I can hear her smile. It makes me frantic. "What if they come back up? You could be thrown off, or crushed—"

"Well then, let me know if they come back up," she says. "Over and out."

A brainless laugh echoes through the door to my room. *Jimmy.* And then whimpering. *Frank.* I sprint up the last few stairs and throw open the door.

All my stuff has been pulled down from the walls, my CD player tossed on its side with its batteries pulled out, my scattered Coldest Lakes CDs shining all around the floor. Jimmy's shit is heaped on my bed, and a half-empty Bacardi bottle sits on my overturned desk. It smells like the other half is on the floor, sopped up by my strewn-out clothes. But I don't see Frank. There's another whimper, and I notice a figure against the wall, leashed to the torch holder by a rope around her neck.

Jess.

Jimmy stumbles at the edge of my peripheral vision, nose all swollen, fully drunk. "I'm Captain of the Guard now! This is my room! I'm Captain! Just ask King Max! I'm guarding her!"

I grab the side of his head and run it into the concrete wall.

+   +   +

"I'm not going," Max had said that morning, as I waited outside his bedroom door. I'd gotten up at three to pack my cooler so we could get on the road at four, and it was now four thirty. "Why don't you just take Brick?"

"Hey, Sport. You don't cancel a hunting trip the morning of, after

I get you the license and your own crossbow," Coach said cheerfully, snapping on Max's bedside lamp. "It's time for you to handle a weapon that doesn't hook up to your Wii."

"It's not a Wii." Max pulled the pillow over his head. "Just go and let me sleep."

"You can sleep in the car." I went over to his bed and yanked off his comforter, dodging the punch I knew he would throw. "Let's go!"

"I don't want to go kill deer!" Max pushed me away, too hard. "You want to go kill something so bad, just go do it, asshole!"

". . . I don't," I said, and Coach looked at me, puzzled. But it was true. I just wanted to hang out with Max and Coach and drink coffee in the woods. Killing stuff was the cost of that. But I didn't *want* to kill anything.

I still don't.

I pull back just before Jimmy's head hits the cement wall, my arm flinching so Jimmy spins instead onto the rum-soaked floor, still shrieking, "I'm Captain! The King said!"

There's only one person with the authority to pull someone out of a hospital bed. And he turned her over to *Jimmy*?!

Jessica's head falls to the side when I take her shoulder.

"Jess?" Her eyes don't move. "Jess, please."

I'm going to kill Max. *I am going to kill him.*

Screams echo up from the music hall. Stokes's voice, heated. Leila trying to interrupt. And then King Max's booming yell: "TREASON!"

Shit, shit, shit.

I scramble for the walkie-talkie, press the call button. "Kay? Kay—"

The thick strap of Frank's leash wraps around my throat and twists. The walkie-talkie flies from my hand, hitting the floor so hard the casing cracks off, batteries vanishing into the black corners of the room.

"*You're gonna die like the dog you are,*" Jimmy hisses in my ear, knee in the middle of my back, blocking access to the box cutter in my back pocket.

I claw for the walkie-talkie and Jimmy chokes me so hard my ears ring. I have to get the batteries, I have to warn Kay, but ants are rushing faster and faster into my vision as a ball of light swoops down behind me.

WHOOSH.

The flames shoot so high, burn so bright, they cast the shadows of Jimmy's individual hairs on the wall. They shrivel up as the smell of bubbling skin fills the room and high-pitched animal shrieks break out over my head. Jimmy lets me go to pull at his rum-soaked clothes, blue-and-orange flame swallowing him. I roll out from under him and see Jess holding the torch, her neck still leashed to the metal flag holder, watching Jimmy burn.

"Go, Brick," she says, then drops the torch.

No.

I pull the box cutter from my back pocket, slide the blade out, and cut the rope leashing her in one downstroke. I wrap an arm around her before throwing us backward through the door as flames explode across the room.

"What were you trying to do back there? Kill yourself?" I slap at the fire traveling up her flowy dress, and she collapses against me.

"I can't do it anymore," she weeps. "Leo's dead? He's really dead?"

". . . I'm sorry." I hold her, and she sobs hard. I hoist her up in my arms. I have to get her out of the smoke, so thick now I get down the stairs on pure muscle memory, then throw open the Cage doors to find a knot of theater kids. They all freeze at the sight of me. The throne room is empty, the guards gone. In the crowd of terrified faces staring at me, a shock of hair like the top of an asparagus spear catches my eye.

"DAMON!"

His face goes slack at the sight of Jess. He reaches for her, and she curls into him with a sob of relief.

"Can you get her to the gym? And stay with her?" Off his nod, I sprint down the hall. I need to get to Kay.

I take the cement stairs up, two at a time, down the hall by the library, pushing past stunned faces.

"Brick! Brick's back!"

"Hey, you're bleeding, man!"

"Yo, that's my sword!"

I snatch a flea market ninja sword from Nate of the Lone Stars, who keeps his blades stupid sharp.

I don't know how much time I have before I black out again. And the elevator is running, I can hear it, the car is rising, I might already be too late.

I race toward E Hall, toward the elevator, wrenching the wood trellis off the opening and throwing myself into the pitch-black elevator shaft.

I land hard, sprawling across the elevator car roof. I hear Merlin: "What was that?" Good, she has a guest; between their weight and mine, the cables grind to a halt. I stare up at the cable, but there's no sign of Kay. Was she thrown when it started moving? Did she fall? I'm starting to choke on panic when Kay's voice floats down from above:

"Get up, Nirali, come on, we need to go, we need to go right now, please, Nirali . . ."

She made it to the machine room!

The cables whine and the car strains higher, the scene in the North Tower coming into view: the high room with its slanting skylight, Kay's hook rope dangling from it, and Nirali lying in a blue pool of her own glittering gown, her face half-hidden in a filthy Jefferson varsity jacket. Her cheek is on her hand, and her eyes are staring; she's not responding. Kay kneels over her almost in tears.

I reach for the edge of the floor and hoist myself up, the elevator speeding once my weight moves off. I race for the engine in the corner and hit the manual stop, the elevator grinding to a standstill as the brake engages. King Max's and Merlin's cries ricochet up the shaft like frightened birds.

"Brick!" Kay reaches for me. "Something's wrong. It's like she can't hear me."

For a second, I think Nirali really might be dead, her face has such a strange purplish cast. But then she blinks.

"Go up through the window," I tell Kay. "I'll hand her up." I gather Nirali off the floor. "Okay, doc, I need you to help me," I say, spots swimming across my vision again.

Nirali moves like a sleepwalker, but she lets me lead her to the rope as Kay calls down encouragement from the roof. Behind me, the engine lurches back to life, and the brake releases. I'm supporting Nirali now, so I can't cross the engine room to stop them coming up.

"*Brick!*" King Max yells. "What the hell do you think you're doing?"

"Nirali!" Merlin cries. Nirali's eyes seem to clear at her voice. Max lunges for us, but Merlin puts her arm out.

"Hold on!" she says. "Everyone. Please! Can we just talk?"

Nirali, slumped against me, breathes harder.

"Where are you going?" Merlin asks Nirali. "To Jefferson? What happens when you get there?"

"You *starve*," King Max says. "I'm not sending Jefferson shit if you're not here."

Merlin gives him a warning look, then wheels forward, her voice softer: "Today has been hell. Things have happened on all sides we should regret. But that doesn't mean we can't work this out."

"You were lying to me," Nirali says to her quietly. "About everything."

"To *prevent a war*." Merlin shakes her head. "There were people who needed to know things at Jefferson, and people who didn't! You covered up about Kyle not calling in, how is that any different?"

"*Because I could have handled it!*" Nirali bursts out, then gets herself under control and goes on: "I'm another ruler, not one of your subjects. I could have *handled it*. But you kept his secrets from me. And you kept our secrets from him."

Merlin's expression darkens.

"'Our secrets'?" Max's voice, still hoarse from the pool, breaks now.

"She'll say anything at this point," Merlin says, but she doesn't look at him.

"We kissed last night," Nirali tells Max, but her eyes stay on Merlin. "She kissed me, and I kissed her back. I only agreed to marry *you* so I could be around *her*. Because I am a *fool*." Her voice hardens in the last word, and only then do her eyes travel to Max. "If you don't believe me, ask Marissa."

Max looks to Merlin, but she is staring at Nirali like they're the only people in the room.

"Check." Nirali smiles coldly. And then she starts climbing.

King Max strides toward the rope and I pull out the katana, bringing it between us.

"Stay back," I tell him.

"The hell, man?"

"Stay. Back."

Nirali's hand wraps around the sill and King Max rushes for the rope. I grab him by the back of his neck.

"GO!" I scream to Nirali, hurling King Max away. But she stands for one more moment, eyes locked with Merlin's. And then King Max's fist connects with my jaw.

+ + +

The night after I committed to University of Florida's baseball program, Coach took me and my mom out for dinner at this super nice place. It was a big deal for me. But Max showed up so high all of us could tell. At the end of the night, waiting for his mom to come pick him up outside the restaurant, he knew I was mad but wouldn't acknowledge why. And as her car pulled up, he insisted on shaking hands.

When we did, he jerked my arm, hard. Too hard.

"Ooh, watch yourself! Gotta protect that arm!" he laughed. "You lose that batting arm, *what do you have?*"

King Max knows how hard I can pitch and how far I can hit, so he should understand how hard I can punch. And if he didn't, he does now.

The katana clatters to the floor as we fall on each other, grappling like we're back on Max's living room floor after school, like any moment he'll stop and yell, *"Time, time, seriously time!"* and I'll laugh and apologize. But then he makes that low noise in his throat, the noise he made hunched over Leo, and I remember he's not my best friend anymore.

I don't know who this is.

I push away from him and pick up the katana, feeling too light as I stand, like my heart can't keep up with me.

King Max pulls a broadsword from his belt, some Renaissance faire collector's big splurge, and swings it to meet my katana. I half expect my blade to snap in half, but it holds. Maybe because King Max is only using the force of one arm, the left hand draped over the handle of the broadsword with the fingers loose. He clocks where I'm looking and jerks his sword away, pacing across from me, left arm curled into his side the way it was in the pool.

He's trying to fight me one-handed. He should throw down his sword, but instead he runs at me, swinging. I block him, catching his blade with mine so the two edges sing and then grind together.

"What, Leo wasn't enough for you?" I say. "You're going to kill me, too?"

King Max blinks, and my blade rolls over his good hand before he can react. The cut is deep, the blood dark. We both freeze, horrified, like when I accidentally gave him a black eye in eighth grade, play fighting. I cried so hard he ended up comforting me, defending me to his mom when she came in. But his eyes aren't like they were then. They look like the eyes of the dead deer in the back of his dad's truck. Like flies could settle on them and he still wouldn't blink.

I throw my katana down, grab Max by the collar, and hoist him against the wall, trying to get him back. "What are you doing, Max?!"

"I'm keeping us on the throne!" he shouts back. "You think I'm happy about today? I wanted a wedding! I wanted a *party*, not this shit! You think this isn't the worst thing that's ever happened to me?"

"I think it's the worst thing that's ever happened to *Leo*."

"And I bet he would've let me walk out of that pool, right? After everything he did to get me into it?"

No. No, he wouldn't.

His eyes scan my face. "You know he shot you in the gym, right? That asshole shot you with the crossbow I'd just given him. To take you out, so he could come for me. He tried to kill you, so I killed him. *You're welcome*."

Is he serious? There are only three crossbows, and one is in my room. So either Leo shot me . . . or Max did. I watch his face carefully. "Did you tell Jimmy to guard Jess?"

Max blinks. "What?"

"Jimmy had Jess tied up in my room. He said it was on your order."

"You're going to trust anything that comes out of that kid?"

"He's your new Captain of the Guard, isn't he?"

"Because you're sick, dumbass!" Max shouts. "You need to be in bed, not chasing people past the fences! Why'd you think I sent the cheerleaders after you?"

To kill me, probably. He found out Jess was still alive and I had spoken with her, and he knew our friendship was over.

"I fucked up, okay?" Max says, his voice all high. "I got all up in my head about Nirali and I fucked up! But I *need help*, Brick. I'm so fucked . . ." He peels back a bandage at the top of his left arm, exposing fresh black stitches. I cringe back, and he grabs the rope with his good hand and stares up toward where she's gone with furious desperation. Then he looks back at me, and I know he's about to ask me to go after her, and I start shaking my head in disbelief.

"*Someone* has to help me, or I'm done, okay? And it's all fucked—"

"Help *me*, Max! Help me understand what the hell is going on! Kyle died, and you hid his body?"

"What was I supposed to do? Leo was looking for any excuse! A body in my room? He would have twisted that, tried to radio Jefferson about it, who knows! Holding on to Kyle's car like that—you *know* he wanted a war. He doesn't care who he hurts, as long as he gets control—"

"So you drove out Kyle's body and left the west fence wide open."

His expression changes. He didn't realize how much I knew.

"And you told Jimmy to shut Jess up about it, so *you* could stay in control." I am barely holding back tears. "And you let Tyler blame Kay—told him to kill her!—for what you'd done! It's all *already* fucked! Because of what you did!"

I want him to contradict me. To have an explanation that makes it all okay. But he doesn't. And my friend is bending down for his sword, slowly, with his bloodied hand. So I grab my katana and level it at his throat.

"It's hard to be King." He shrugs, his face stony. "That's why you wouldn't take the job. Because being King means *crushing your enemies*, Brick. You don't like to get dirty? Fine. But someone has to."

That's his answer. *That's his answer!*

I swing the katana. King Max's broadsword barely makes it up in time. He moves left as I strike again. He blocks. I punch him right in his stupid stitches and his sword clatters to the ground. The tip of my katana is at his throat, and it does not shake.

"We're brothers," King Max gasps. "Half brothers."

"*What?*"

"Your mom. My dad. My parents' whole divorce! Why do you think I stopped going hunting?" His eyes are dead but steady. "We're brothers, okay? You stay, I can prove it."

Hot salt blinds my eyes, burns the back of my throat, like the moment a wave knocks you down. He's the biggest asshole in the world if he's lying about this, and if it's true and he's been keeping it from me, he's even worse. I can't look at him, but I can't turn my back, either. Swearing, I throw the katana to the ground with a crash and jump for the rope, climbing as fast as I can.

"ALL GUARDS TO THE ROOF!" Merlin yells into her walkie-talkie. Max tries to get on the rope and follow me, but I kick him backward with my good leg and climb into the night. Leg bleeding, teeth grinding, I keep climbing up until the only thing above me is stars.

Coach's smiling face across the table at dinner, squeezing my shoulder on game day: *"I'm so proud of you."*

I scream so loud it feels like my guts will come up, like I'm flattening the trees going down in the distance, but it's just dragons. Focus, put it away. Get the rope up, get it over your shoulder, you're not done yet.

It's game day. Come on, focus, son.

"Brick!" Across the gravel expanse of Moore's roof, a graceful figure waves to me, a column of smoke blurring the black sky behind her.

"Your whole room is on fire," Kay gasps. "We can't go through!"

"There's another way." I take Kay's hand and lead her and Nirali to the skylight over Artemis's room, what used to be the choir director's office. It's identical in layout to the band leader's office, which is mine. Kay breaks through the glass with one well-aimed kick. I help knock the shards out and then hold the rope fast as she climbs down. I help Nirali find her footing; she's out of it again. We land in a room stuffed with heaps of fabric and piles of sheet music and Artemis zip-tied to a chair.

Her eyes widen, and she starts screaming through her gag. I cut her wrists free, and she pulls a sopping bandanna from her mouth, her makeup cried away.

"Brick, what's going on? Nirali! Am I glad to see you, honey! Girl, are you okay?"

Nirali leans against the wall, staring.

"We're taking her back to Jefferson," Kay says.

"Really? How? You know what, I don't care. I'm coming, too. How do we get out of Moore?"

"We go back the way we came—" Kay's interrupted by her walkie-talkie going off. Leila's tinny voice rings through the small room:

"Kay! Stay away from the tunnel! Do not go back to the tunnel! Kay! Do you hear me?"

Kay hits her walkie-talkie button with a crunch. "Leila?"

"Stokes turned on us," Leila sobs through patches of static. "Starr and I got out—had to burn it down—Tyler ran back just as—it all collapsed! It's completely collapsed—"

Shit, shit, shit.

Kay plugs one ear, face steely. "So how do we get out?"

Static is the only answer. What can Leila tell her? There is no other way out.

"What about the lake?" Artemis hisses. "Couldn't we swim out that way? There's no fence on the other side."

Kay looks at me, and after a beat I nod. It's dangerous, but so is everything we do, from this point out.

"Leila," Kay says, trying to keep her voice from shaking, "if we swim across Mill Pond, can you pick us up?"

+ + +

Torch in hand, Artemis leads us down a back stair to a narrow hall behind the stage, the flames shrinking in the airless concrete passage. I follow with Kay just behind me, Nirali dangling from the end of her arm like a drowsy kid getting dragged to bed. Artemis stops at an old fire exit at the very back of the stage, cracks the door, and peers through. After a beat, she pulls back with a hiss.

"There's like a million guards out there!" she says, wide-eyed, and moves aside to let me look.

I peer through the dark. It's not just my crew; it's also Motorheads and a couple other large rooms ringing the perimeter of the building, their flashlights angled toward the roof.

"Gotta come down eventually!" I hear someone call. Others are nervously talking about Jimmy, burned alive in my room.

"Brick is *wilding*, man—"

"I can't believe it. Brick, turning against King Max?"

There's so many of them. They've all got flashlights; they're all keyed up, watching that roof like they've got Charles Manson up there or something. There's no convincing anyone to give me a pass, not with a dead body in my room.

So what's the play now? Wait until morning? They'll root us out long before then.

Shit, shit, shi—

"LET ME GO! LET ME GO!"

Jess sprints out of the music hall toward the parking lot. The guards try to clothesline her, but she's too fast. She breaks through, and their flashlights turn away from the school and train on her figure as she runs for the chanting circle of Los Martillos, out on the football field.

The guards all along our side of the building sprint after her, and suddenly the sidewalk just outside the music hall is clear.

"Let's go."

I grab Kay's hand, and we book it across the parking lot, veering off toward the woods at the edge of the football field. Jessica has been met by Los Martillos, who are helping her over the fence. The chain link strains and sings as the chasing guards throw themselves against it and are shoved backward by angry mechanics.

"Send her back over!" the guards yell. "The King wants her under watch!"

"She's with us now!" a Martillo yells back. "Leo loved her, and she loved him! She's with Los Martillos! Your King has no power over her now!"

Jess disappears into a protective knot of mourners. They keep yelling at the guards on her behalf:

"She stays! She stays! We don't want your killer King!"

There is the wet sound of fist meeting mouth, and a fight erupts as the Martillo girls protectively usher Jess toward the tower farther down the field.

A familiar bark rings out behind me.

I whistle his dinner call, and Frank is at my side. He was watching for my truck in the parking lot like after Expansions; he must have been waiting all day, poor guy.

But this has pushed my luck too far.

"YO!" a guard yells. "IT'S *BRICK*!"

I push Kay ahead of me, and Nirali follows after her, stumbling over billowing skirts she can't contain with both hands. Artemis is tilting forward she's going so fast, and once she's by me, I'm bringing up the rear.

"HE'S GOT THE QUEEN!"

A firework shatters the left side of the sky, and sparks stretch overhead. The mysterious tower of wood Los Martillos have been throwing their torches into starts sending out pinwheels and rockets and Roman candles in every direction. A stray curve of white sparks sets off a glint of gold at the top of the tower: the Duke's helmet, still on Leo's head.

The tower is Leo's funeral pyre, and Moore's peace is burning with him.

Los Martillos surge over the chain-link fence at the guards as though this explosion has loosed them. This means only two guards are free to break off and chase us, and the glittering pond is already breaking through the trees ahead.

Artemis dives in and starts swimming as Kay tries to coax Nirali in. Nirali balks, and Kay darts behind some rocks. She returns holding a huge pool float, shaped like a wedge of watermelon.

"Get on, Nirali!" she calls, voice shaking with exhaustion. I grab the other handle and we splash into the water, stumbling and sliding through the muck until we're deep enough to float. The guards yell for us to stop, then air rifles crack overhead. We paddle, breathless, at an angle from shore, toward the lily pads. They'll help hide our silhouette from the shooters.

I kick as hard as I can, expecting every minute for a shot to ding the float, for the two of us to have to wrestle a drowning Nirali back to shore, for my vision to go black. But we keep going, the two of us, pulling side by side.

"Brick?" Kay says between gasps. "You okay?"

Yeah, except for my own guards shooting at me. And the war

breaking out behind us, and the fact that I'm leaving Moore and Jessica to King Max and his dead eyes.

"I'm a traitor," I tell her. "A total traitor."

"No. No, Brick, you're saving us," she says. "You're saving me, you're saving Nirali. You're doing the right thing, I promise."

"I thought King Max was right, and he's messed up in the head." Silence, for a moment. Then I ask, "What did he say to you, after he killed Leo?"

"I couldn't really tell," she sputters. "He wasn't very coherent, you know?"

He'd acted like an animal in that pool. I never would have thought he was capable of anything like that. My best friend. *My brother.*

Could he have been my brother this whole time, and I didn't know it? I see Coach smiling at us over his travel mug of coffee, out in the woods: *This is the life, me and the boys!*

"It's like I don't even know him. I don't even know who I am."

Coach's son? Coach's *unacknowledged son*?

The dark water pulls me down; the dank taste of it slaps at the back of my throat, fills my ears with my own muffled heartbeat. The ants swarm the stars like they're grains of sugar. But Kay says something, so I kick hard enough to get my ears above water.

"What?"

"I said I know who you are." Her voice is steady. "You're a Coldest Lakes fan. You're Frank's favorite human. You killed the first dragon. And . . . you're a total nine."

My ears go hot all the way to the tips.

She flashes me a smile, bright even in the dark. "Maybe even a nine point five."

"Cranberry," I say, not sure how to react, but she doesn't laugh. She isn't kidding.

"I know who you are," Kay says. "You ever forget, I'll remind you. Okay?"

". . . Okay." And I'm cutting through the lily pads like it's nothing. The stars shining like she wiped them clean.

She can't really think I'm a nine. But she keeps acting like I am. That night on the cot. She tried to kiss me. And I choked so hard. I haven't done anything with anyone since the first time I almost died, since I got like this. I didn't want to inflict myself on someone else, let alone someone I was guarding. But Kay keeps trying. Her hand holding mine, in the truck. She left the dance to meet me, she said she wanted to ask me something. The answer is yes. Whatever she wants from me, my answer will always be yes.

When we get to shore, I'll make a move to kiss her. If she shrinks away, I'll never try again. But I have to try, at least once.

The rising floor of the pond meets my foot a second later, like reality is calling my bluff. We've reached the shore; I'm up to bat. I'm psyching myself up as we climb out of the water, help Nirali off the float. She stumbles over to where Artemis is squeezing water out of her hair, closer to where Leila's Jeep is parked. They're far away enough it feels like just me and Kay in the dark. I turn to her, hyping myself up as hard as I can. Her black clothes are all wet and hug her like shadows, her face shining the color of starlight as she calls over the water:

"Frank! Come on, Frank!"

Frank's dark head rises twenty feet from shore. And stays there. Bobbing like a buoy, whining. This is weird. Frank hates water. I have to throw him in for his monthly bath.

"Here, Frank!" I call.

That's when the birches beside the lake crash into the pond, folding under the biggest dragon I've ever seen.

Making Out

BRICK

I pull Kay toward Leila's Jeep Wrangler, Leila accelerating as we climb in, and lean out the back, yelling for Frank. He books it toward us. I grab his collar and haul him up over the side of the car, both of us sprawling backward onto Kay and Artemis, who's come in the other side of the back seat. Dripping wet, Frank scrambles to regain his footing on their laps as Leila wheels the Jeep around, tires screaming.

"Did someone get Nirali?" I yell over Frank shaking himself dry.

"She's up front! We got this!" Leila swerves around a low stone wall at the edge of the pond's gravel lot when the dragon whips its head straight in front of us, sending a lightning bolt of shattering glass across the windshield.

Its upper and lower teeth catch the headlights and its jaws open, the inside of its slick red throat filling the entire windshield as Leila reverses, twisting in her seat and steering backward sixty miles an hour down the pitch-black main street.

"*Starr? Starr?*" Kay yells into her walkie-talkie. "Just go to Jefferson! We're in trouble!"

"Where y'all at right now? I can help."

"Coming up Mill Road!" Leila screams, then makes a 180, lighting up the claws of the chasing dragon as she wheels around. "Mill Road and West Rocks!"

"I'll be there. It's going to get hot," he says. "Roll your windows up."

"WE DON'T HAVE WINDOWS!" Leila yells, but trees are falling so close their crashing drowns her out. Her face goes perfectly still as she stands on the accelerator, flying down the winding, wooded road as the dragon swipes at the back of the Jeep.

The spare tire flies apart in shreds.

"*GO LEILA!*" Artemis screams. "*GO GO GO!*"

"I'M *GOING*, HEATHER, DAMN!"

I scan the floor of the cheerleaders' Jeep and see an ax from Expansion and Tyler's chain. I grab the ax and stand, feeling Kay grip my belt as I steady myself against the roll bar and turn back toward the dragon, winding up the ax like I'm on home plate. Game day mindset. When the dragon lunges for us again, I drive the ax into its snout, the ax head lodging into bone, the handle tearing from my hands. The dragon is stunned enough to pause and shake its massive head, and we gain half a block before it stops trying to shake the ax out and starts chasing us again.

Faster now. Like it wants revenge.

"WEST ROCKS! GET DOWN!"

Four hands yank me below the side of the car as the Jeep gets bathed in a stream of blue fire.

Overhead, the dragon's whole face is illuminated by flame, jaws fully open to reveal a mouth the size of a coffin. Blue fire glistens off its wet tongue and tall, hooked teeth. The eyes along one side of its head burst and melt in the steady stream of fire Starr trains on it. As we speed forward, I sit up and watch Starr, hanging out the passenger window of the Costco truck, the visor and line of his arm traced in neon blue. But then his light sputters.

"He's running out of fuel!" Leila moans as Artemis and Kay slap out the flames licking up Nirali's dress. Nirali doesn't seem to care; she sits still in her burning skirt, her grody old jacket blackened with smoke, and lets them figure it out.

The half-blinded dragon sets a claw into the side of the Costco truck.

"*STARR! YOU GOT TO GO!*" Leila yells into her walkie-talkie. He's disappeared into the cab. The engine is making sounds like he's putting it back in gear, but now the dragon is climbing onto the roof of the refrigerated container. I'm cringing, certain its claw will swipe through the cab next when something I've never seen before happens: *The claw gets stuck.*

Dragons can tear through cars, but cars are relatively short and built to crumple. The side of the refrigerated semi is longer, thicker, and compacts enough to trap the dragon's claw as the truck pulls away.

Maybe we can all make it out of this alive, after all.

I grab Leila's shoulder. "Will you help me?"

She's vibrating with fear, eyes bloodshot from smoke and grief, but her gaze is still sharp and clear. She's Moore's best driver. If anyone can do this, it's her.

"Can you keep up with him?" I ask her.

She nods, getting it at once, and puts the car in a higher gear.

"I'll be leaning right so stay on his left," I cry down to her, grabbing the roll bar again. "But we're going to need space to react."

"Got it." She hits the gas. I pull the wet rope from around my shoulder, Kay's rope, grateful I didn't throw it off in the pond, and thread its hook through the last links of Tyler's chain as fast as I can.

"Here we go!" Leila yells as we race toward the towering 18-wheeler. It's careening wildly down the curving two-lane street ahead as Starr attempts to shake the monster half dragging, half prone on top of him.

I hang out the right side of the Jeep as Leila gets closer, swinging the rope where it joins the end of the chain, letting its weight pick up momentum, scared any minute a low-hanging branch will catch it or sweep my head off. I spin the hook faster and faster, winding up my arm like I'm about to pitch. And then I throw it forward.

The hook bounces off the dragon and flies back, almost nailing me in my good cheek and nearly slipping under the wheels; I retrieve it just in time. But now he knows where I am. The dragon twists its massive head to face me. Just the smell this close makes me choke, takes me back to that first day when I stood over that dragon and fired up the chain saw. It blinked awake, and with its last sigh nearly took my head off.

This dragon's mouth yawns open, and the smell of certain death pours out.

"What you got, you got. Only difference is, today you're afraid," Coach told me the day the scout from the University of Florida showed up. "But you got it, whether you're scared or not. When you get to game day, you tell fear to shut its ugly face. I want you to go out there and show them what you got, son."

I throw the hook again, directly into the dragon's mouth. It catches on one of the massive curving teeth up front. The chain goes taut.

"GO ROUND!" I call to Leila, giving the rope all the slack I can, keeping it high as the Jeep slows enough to fall behind the truck, then swerves around to its other side, dust and fumes turning the beams of its headlights milky white.

It works: the chain wraps across the dragon's head and pins it to the top of the truck, my hold on the rope and the Jeep's speed keeping the chain tight. The eyes on the exposed side of its head are melted, so it's effectively blind now, the claw facing me buried in the truck, its back legs and tail dragging in the street.

"I got you now, you poor bastard," I say through my teeth. But that's not true; the rope will only stay taut as long as both vehicles are at speed. Either one slows, the dragon's back in control.

"We're almost there!" Leila screams.

The shape of Jefferson looms on the hill ahead, cut out against a pale pink sky. The gears whine. The truck will slow as we climb up the long driveway to the Jefferson parking lot.

I have to end this now. I wrap the rope around the roll bar and hand the end of it to Artemis.

"Keep this tight!" I yell. "Don't let it go, no matter what happens!"

"BRICK!" Kay screams. "NO!"

I dig into my pocket and pull out her locket, press it into her hand. Her eyes widen with surprise.

"*I'll see you soon!*" I promise.

With a last look down at the ground streaming between the Jeep and the truck, I grab the rope and hoist my feet up. With a throb of pure pain, I cross my ankles over the rope and climb hand over hand along its rough length toward the top of the semi.

The road climbs, the truck slows, and the rope goes slack. One and then both of my heels slip as the girls scream bloody murder. But Artemis yanks it taut again, and I swing for the edge of the semi like it's monkey bars. The top edge of the truck digs into my hand, and I pull myself up beside the dragon's grotesque shoulder. His arm is flinching wildly as he tries to free his claw. Hatred rolls off him like steam, desperate to kill me.

Same.

I shamble toward his back, crouching low against the wind as the truck whines uphill. The smell of death is overpowering as I straddle the dragon's neck, bits of unincorporated corpse in his hide clearer up close: fingernails and eyelashes and earlobes mixed together, like a pile of corpses run through a thresher. Trying not to puke, I grab the ax handle jutting from his snout, yank it loose, and fix myself on the ridge at the top of the dragon's spine. His tendons jostle me as he tries to thrash me off. I rise up, gripping the handle like a baseball bat, and bury the blade in the monster's neck.

Black blood blinds me. The girls' screams meld with the screech of the brakes and my own primal yell as the tires hydroplane through the long grass of the lawn in front of Jefferson. The blood tastes filthy and stings my eyes like hell. The ants swarm, the dragon below me in a cloud of black. I just keep striking. I can't stop until he stops moving; leave him one last blink, one last flinch, and he'll take the rest of me with him.

So I squeeze my eyes closed against the black blood, and swing. I swing and see Max's blood coming out of his hand, dark and deep. I swing and see Leo's arm distended, the other hand up, begging. I swing and see my own flayed face the first time I woke up, red meat and black stitches. Pain rings through my shoulders and blood drenches my face and still I keep swinging.

The dragon and the truck below me shudder and go still, almost at the same time. I stop, panting, and the dead dragon materializes below me as the ants retreat, clearing a blurry circle in the center of my vision. Gasping, I pull myself to my feet on top of the truck, trying to mop his filthy blood off my face.

The sound of wood breaking. More dragons?!

No, it's from the school—the plywood behind the shattered-glass front doors is being pulled away, and then the doors wobble open. An emaciated girl staggers out.

"It's okay, Denise!" Kay says, jumping out of the Jeep. "Tell them they can come out! The Growns won't go near their own dead!"

The girl's eyes are too big for her face. She winces in the soft dawn sunlight. But she keeps going, hobbling toward us, staring at the fallen dragon.

"It's dead?" she says, in wonder. Then: "They can die! THEY CAN DIE!" And she falls to her knees, head bowed, and starts sobbing. More scrawny figures come out after her, cringing in the sunlight.

"What is this?" A guy pushes through the crowd. He is flanked by figures in all black: black jeans, black hoodies, black gloves, and black motorcycle helmets that hide their faces. The guy, in round scratched-up glasses, looks too old to still be here. He can only be eighteen, but he seems more like forty when he squints up at me, shading his face with his hand against the bright pink sky. "What are you doing, bringing one of them up here like that? Who are you?"

"Can't you tell, Simon?" Nirali says, her voice strong and clear.

I turn to see Nirali has climbed on top of the truck. She's framed by the glowing dawn, her singed blue gown billowing around her, long black hair loose in gleaming waves around her shoulders.

She picks her way toward me, over the dead dragon, but slips in the iridescent black blood. I catch her before she goes flying off the top of the truck, and that's when she grabs me by the collar with both hands and kisses me.

THE REAL MVP

BRICK

My face is covered with dragon blood, but Nirali doesn't seem to notice as she forces her tongue inside my mouth. I'm so shocked I don't know how to respond. Her hands are sliding up my arms and around my shoulders as she goes at me like it's the last dance at prom.

The crowd below us starts howling. No, cheering. They're *cheering*. And then someone yells:

"Is that *Kyle*?"

I break off the kiss, but Nirali stays clamped to me, one hand flat against my chest, smiling so hard I can practically hear her teeth grinding. I turn my head, the edge of the truck bobbing drunkenly in my vision, and see Kay looking very far away, down beside Frank in the grass.

"Let me do the talking," Nirali says in my ear, and then the world goes black.

+ + +

The smell hits me before I open my eyes. Something in the air, bitter and musky and so strong it has an aftertaste. The darkness takes on forms and becomes a room. There's Artemis, all in white, sitting on the cot I'm lying in. And Starr, perched on the edge of a teacher's desk facing me, and Leila, leaning against the cement brick wall behind him.

There's a doorway to another room lit just slightly brighter than the one we're in. I sit up, about to ask where Kay is, but Artemis's hand covers my mouth. Nirali's voice carries in from the next room, though she's trying to whisper. Shouting back at her is a male voice I don't know.

"—you also somehow managed to *bring back Kyle.* Really? Really."

"Yes. *Really.*"

"Well, great. I can't wait for you to show him off to the whole school at the Tribunal tomorrow. If Kyle *is* under all that gunk, I'll be the first to welcome him."

"Simon. Surely you realize he's going to be heavily bandaged once I get done stitching him up—"

"Right!" Furious laughter. "Of course! How convenient."

"There's nothing convenient about surgery, Simon. What, you're going to deny Kyle *medical care*?"

"Like I said, *if* that's Kyle, I'll be the first to welcome him back. But I'm not holding my breath." It sounds like he's heading for the door, but she calls:

"What about Kay? Will she be at the Tribunal as well?"

"Why would Kay Kim need to be at the Tribunal?" Simon says coldly.

"Tyler said you ordered him to drag her out."

"Tyler said that? And where is Tyler?"

The silence hangs a few beats. Then Nirali says, "Kyle will be at the Tribunal if Kay is there, as well. Now I need to do some sutures. So either get some gloves on and help or get out."

"Good night, Nirali."

The door slams.

Starr looks at me, shakes his head, then looks away as Nirali hurries in, shutting and locking the door behind her. She's out of the huge blue dress and now in a Jefferson sweatsuit, but she's kept the disgusting varsity jacket. She flicks on a camping lantern beside Starr, throwing a wheel of light against the concrete wall. Cockroaches as big as fun-sized Snickers dash into the shadows. That's what the smell is. Cockroach musk. I almost dry heave.

"How long has he been up?" Nirali asks Artemis, ignoring me.

"Just a minute or two."

Nirali pulls a penlight from her pocket, and then runs it back and forth across my line of sight. I reflexively snatch it away from her, wincing.

"*Where is Kay.*"

Nirali grabs it back. "Kay is fine—"

"That's what you said last time!" I try to get up again, but Artemis helps her restrain me. I'm so weak it's not a contest.

"Would you calm down?" Nirali says. "You keep pushing it, you're going to be out for three days straight like you were at Moore. And then who'll help us?"

I stop fighting and fall back on the sour-smelling pillow.

"Kay is fine. She's in another part of the school, but she's fine. This is Jefferson—*we* have *laws*." She sneers. "And too many people saw her for Simon to try any of his tricks. Simon just doesn't want us to . . . collaborate on a story, I guess."

"And our story is that *I'm Kyle*?!"

"Would you shut up and listen to me," Nirali snaps. "King Max warned Simon we were on our way. They've been radioing back and forth the whole time I've been gone, and now Simon is going to try and make some proposition from Moore at the Tribunal. Unless we can bluff him into backing down."

"I'm sorry," Starr says. "But what exactly is this Tribunal?"

"It's a public Student Council meeting. The school sits in while the council debates something." Nirali stands. "But whatever King

Max thinks he has to offer, the school will want Kyle instead. And Simon knows that."

"Yeah, well," Leila says uneasily, "that Simon dude didn't sound like he was buying Brick as Kyle, like, at all."

"That will change when he sees *the school* buying it." Nirali looks around, eyes just a little too wide. "Which they will. You saw how well they responded to the kiss."

She has a lot of nerve bringing that up.

"Nirali," I say through clenched teeth, "there is no way anyone is going to think I am Kyle."

"I don't know, Brick . . ." Artemis tilts her head. "You're his height, same hair color, same build. We can do a lot with just the walk, you know? How you stand. And your face will be bandaged."

Leila squints at me. "I mean . . . if he's bandaged? Like . . . maybe."

"That's why I told Simon he was getting stitches," Nirali says quickly. "And that will also explain why he can't talk."

"So now I can't talk?"

"Not while you're pretending to be Kyle. We're talking a *couple of hours*," Nirali says, sinking down beside my cot so we're face-to-face. "Please. This is a chess match between me and Simon, all right? And I can beat him. But *not without a king*. So please. Please, Brick. Just for a couple of hours, make him think the king is still on the board. Not just for me. For Leila, and Artemis, and Starr. And Kay. *Please.*"

I can't help thinking of Nirali crawling in front of King Max, pleading with him. She shouldn't have to beg anyone like that again. No one should.

And I don't need convincing to help Kay.

"What do you need me to do?"

+ + +

Artemis helps me get dressed the next morning. She makes me wear Kyle's old jacket; it's all singed and rank, but it fits right. She winds gauze around my entire head *Invisible Man*-style, and Nirali helps secure it in place. Nirali has commandeered protein powder (Kyle's favorite, apparently), which I have to eat from an old coffee can before I'm allowed to stand up. I need help getting to my feet, still cashed out from blood loss. Artemis even gives me tips on how to stagger.

"Shoulders back, take up as much space as you can. Keep your chin tilted up, and stare down Simon, okay?" Artemis directs me. "Like a gorilla at the zoo! Like you're going to rip his arms off and beat him with them the second the Tribunal is over."

"But no one can see my face," I point out.

"They can still feel your intention," she insists.

"Too much, Heather," Leila says, and it's time to go.

Though it's day, the halls are darker than Moore at night. And empty, except for the roaches crawling over one another's backs to get away from the lantern light. There's no other sign of life till we get to the first story. Then shivering bass and the thunderstorm rumble of a crowd grow at the end of a long hallway.

"What's that?" Starr says.

"Everyone in Jefferson is in the gym," Nirali says, "waiting for us."

"But like, is that music I'm hearing right now?"

"They turned on the generator for the Tribunal. Shh, Simon's people are up ahead."

Her lantern light warps across several motorcycle helmets in the middle of their athletics hall. Nineties' drum machine sounds and thumping bass rattle the closed doors of the gym as they pat us down for weapons, and then it's showtime.

The jock jam might as well be playing in a morgue for all the energy the crowd musters when the doors crack open. Every cold, dazzling fluorescent light in the gym is on, keeping the roaches out of sight but laying the Jefferson student body bare.

And they are a damn sad sight. So thin their skulls seem ready to break through their faces, clothes all muddy gray like they've been boiled together. They sit in cliques of five or so, elbows out, glaring when any outsider comes too close. No waves, no smiles. The ones sitting alone have multiple plastic bags, crammed with personal items, tied to their arms like human spider egg sacs.

No wonder Tyler ran through fire to get back to Moore.

At the sight of Nirali, there's clapping. They whisper when she reaches down and takes my hand. We should've been hand in hand when we walked in, but I was so thrown by the sight of Kay I forgot.

Kay is next to Simon in one of the folding chairs arranged in a semicircle for Student Council, opened out toward the bleachers. Her thin wrists are zip-tied like they were the first day I met her, and like then it sickens me. She's staring down at the floor, lips pressed tight, bouncing one leg on the ball of her foot like she's next up to bat. Half her face is still bruised from when Tyler hit her. I move toward her, but Nirali quickly steers me to the last two empty chairs, at the opposite end of the semicircle.

I will Kay to look at me, but she just stares through the gym floor, a carpet of filth over honey-colored varnish. Is she mad at me for playing along with this Kyle routine? Or is she trying to help, trying to keep from giving us away?

Maybe she's afraid I'll trigger her tells, since I'm a walking lie.

The whispers build along the bleachers as Simon walks to the mic in the center of the semicircle, the jock jams cutting out with a sting of feedback.

"This on? All right. Hello, everybody"—he adjusts his round glasses—"and welcome to the Jefferson Student Council meeting. Today our representatives and student body must discuss a proposition from our friends at Moore, who've been so generous with their food."

Scattered applause.

"But first, I have to share some sad news. As you all know, I've been in contact with Moore High's leader, King Max. And just this morning he told me that Moore scavengers found Kyle's empty car on the highway."

All sound breaks off at once, like the silence after a hard slap.

"Which leads me to believe that Kyle, who risked his life for all of us . . . actually died on his way back home."

I'm not prepared for the reaction this gets. Some people break out in wailing sobs, others in hysterical shrieks of denial. A firestorm of protest and grief ignites through the bleachers, some people standing to point at us and others yelling for me to take off my bandages. Simon takes a step back. Seven unknown council members lean forward to stare at me.

"What?!" a scrawny girl in the chair next to me shrieks. She smells like sour milk. "Simon, are you serious? What does that even mean?"

A guy in the way back, the top bleacher, leaps up and yells, "YOU CAN'T SAY THAT! RULE BREAKER! *RULE BREAKER!*"

"DESTROYERS!" comes a rallying cry, like someone has scored a point for an opposing team. A lanky guy next to Kay sits up at the word, then hits the siren button on his megaphone. He narrows his eyes into the audience and speaks through the megaphone:

"Order! Order right now!"

"Freaking *fathead*," Nirali says under her breath.

She's glaring at Simon but clenching my hand so tight my fingertips are going purple. What the hell is her play now? She better have something up her sleeve other than me sitting around in these bandages.

"Thank you, Representative Yashpal," Simon says to the lanky megaphone guy, leaning into the mic again. "Everybody, please. It truly hurts me to tell you this. We were all holding on for Kyle, I know that. And Nirali knows that, which is why she's claiming he's back. But once I knew there was no chance that was true, I had to ask myself . . . *who the hell is this guy?*" He swings around and points at me. The floor squeaks under his feet, then there is no sound whatsoever for a long beat before he goes on. "This *very* masked man, in Kyle's jacket? Who the hell is this?"

In the chair next to me, the scrawny girl has turned to stare.

"Then King Max told me about a fugitive who disappeared from

Moore the same night Nirali did. A guy named *Randall Brick*, who is wanted at Moore for *burning another student alive.*"

The crowd in the bleachers heaves forward, staring harder at me. The lights seem to get brighter, fill my vision with their glare. I feel pinned in place.

"Well? Aren't you going to deny it?" the scrawny girl asks.

"Kyle can't talk!" Nirali answers for me. "His mouth was injured yesterday."

"Seemed like it was working when you kissed him," Simon says into the mic, and there's an *"Ooooh"* from the crowd. "You've had a busy week, I hear," he goes on. "You got engaged to the King, for starters—"

"That's not true."

"Nice ring," the sour-smelling girl chimes in, nodding at the fat diamond flashing on Nirali's knuckle. How did I miss that thing? It should have blinded me when she was masking me up this morning, but it didn't register. I'd been too nervous.

"Yeah, nice ring!" Simon yells into the mic. "Show it off, Nirali! We all want to see!"

Nirali lifts her chin. I awkwardly put my arm around her shoulders when Simon gets in her face, grabbing for her hand.

"What a rock! How *do* you get a ring like that? What did you have to do?"

I set my hand on his chest and press him back, calmly but forcefully, and the crowd lets loose a delighted whoop. There's a ripple of movement from the guards, so I look to each of them, hands up, making it clear I'm not the one causing problems. Simon backs away, before turning and sneering into the mic:

"If you're wondering why our doctor came back looking like she's been working the streets instead of the hospital"—shocked laughter from the bleachers—"it turns out Nirali spent the last few days going to parties and feasts and calling herself *the Queen of Jefferson.*"

Hisses of disapproval from the bleachers now.

"Her Royal Highness didn't *just* get engaged to the King. She

THE MERCILESS KING OF MOORE HIGH

also got involved with a rebel gang leader at Moore, Leo from Los Martillos—" He pronounces it wrong, and someone in the crowd who speaks Spanish corrects him. He waves his hand. "Whatever. It means the Hammers. Apparently, she goaded 'Leo' from 'the Hammers' into challenging the King of Moore, who had welcomed her with open arms—"

"These are all lies!" Nirali protests, but Simon steamrolls her.

"So when King Max put her and these other traitors under arrest—" He gestures to Artemis, Leila, and Starr, sitting on the edge of the first bleacher, the guys in black with motorcycle helmets standing all around them. "She promised Randall Brick, the Captain of the Guard, that if he betrayed Moore and helped them escape, she'd make him *King of Jefferson*. And here we are. The would-be Queen and King of Jefferson, lying to your faces, while Kyle *lies dead!*"

I try to stand up. I'm too weak; I slam back down in my chair. Across the semicircle, Kay is still staring at the floor, leg bouncing harder than ever. Nirali is trying to yell over the outraged crowd, furiously denying all of this, but the ring has cost her.

"I get a rebuttal, don't I?" Nirali cries.

"Oh, I'm not done!" Simon goes on, mugging for the crowd. "Your love life isn't the point of this Tribunal, Nirali. The point is, King Max has an offer for Jefferson." He looks each member of Student Council in the face, then turns to the bleachers for the big pitch. "If we send Nirali and 'Kyle' back to Moore, they will keep sending us food. All through summer, all through winter." Simon looks to the guards around Starr and Leila and Artemis. "No more scavenging. Ever. And all we have to do is agree to turn over a *murderer*, Randall Brick. And the so-called Queen of Jefferson. And their accomplices. For a fair trial."

Shit, shit, shit.

Nirali stands, chair screeching back. "I believe I get to make a rebuttal. About the ring and everything else Simon just—"

"I don't care about the ring or what you did at Moore." The representative beside me shoots to her feet, shaking like a struck bell.

345

Simon runs over to her with the mic, happy to keep it away from Nirali. "All we care about is surviving. If this *is* Kyle, did he find help? Is there anything outside Brockton? Are we just on our own?"

Simon strides away, mic in hand. "Good point, Natasha. Even if we were in some alternate universe where this *was* Kyle . . ." He turns and stares hard at Nirali. "So what? The truck of food out there will be gone in days, and then what? There's no food for *miles*. When we tried to cross town to get some, more than half of the Scavenging Team *died*. We either starve to death, or we take King Max's deal. That's our choice." He turns to the audience. "That's what we're here to vote on. Do we starve, or not?"

Nirali walks into the spotlight and snatches the microphone from him, her ring flashing. "NICE ROCK!" someone yells as she straightens her shoulders and begins:

"Just to quickly address some of the outrageous things Simon—"

"ANSWER THE QUESTION!" someone yells from the bleachers. "WHO'S EATING?"

She opens her mouth. She closes it. She's at a loss. She's like a kid called on by the teacher when they weren't paying attention.

"It's time to vote," Simon says.

"*It's time to tell them,*" Kay says, rising to her feet.

The attention of the entire gym refocuses—away from me, away from Nirali—and fastens onto Kay, as she crosses the semicircle toward Nirali, her face pale and severe, her dark eyes huge and steady.

As a shocked Nirali turns to her, the mic swings close enough to amplify Kay's next words:

"Nirali, we need to tell them about the secret mission."

Whispers rise through the bleachers. Nirali hesitates for one beat, then gives her the mic.

"Shut up!" Simon bursts out laughing. "*Secret mission!* Do you hear yourself?"

"Nirali sent me to find Kyle at Moore. That's why I walked out." Kay stares him down. "*Why else* would I have done that?"

He steps back as she steps forward, clutching the mic in both her bound hands.

"Simon doesn't really have a handle on what's going on," Kay says, her stare driving straight through him. "Like, he told a lot of you I was dead, right? But here I am."

Now she's done it. The air crackles with the unmistakable tension right before a lunchroom fight.

"That's why he believes whatever Max tells him." Kay keeps advancing. "Because they've never actually met. But I've met Max." She turns to the bleachers then. "The first time I did, he made me bow to him. Everyone bows to him, at Moore. They kneel when he walks in and when he stands to leave. He likes that. A lot. That's why he's trying to bring us to our knees, too."

Then she turns to me, letting the mic fall far enough that it seems she's not speaking into it at all, but close enough it still catches her words:

"Kyle, I am so sorry your homecoming started like this."

Our eyes meet, and my heart jumps up like it's her dog.

The scrawny representative, Natasha, leans forward and examines Kay. But Cranberry, for once, is not blushing. There's no embarrassment in those black eyes, just determination. And while the apology was addressed to Kyle, I think she really did mean it for me.

Kay jerks her head back to the audience and goes on:

"He can't speak to defend himself. Because he got his face torn open, killing that massive dead Grown in front of the school."

Big applause from the bleachers at this.

"A lot of you didn't even know that was possible. I didn't, until he trained me. I, too, have helped kill a Grown. Because he knows how to kill them. You saw him do it!" She points at me but doesn't look back again. "He could teach *everyone in this gym*."

Roaring applause, whistling. A couple people yell, "HELL YEAH!"

Simon doesn't like this, obviously. He's starting to object, making a move to take the mic back, but the crowd hisses at him until Yashpal makes him sit down.

"I think we all want to hear what Secretary Kay has to say," Yashpal says, and the crowd applauds.

"We sent Kyle out to get us help," Kay goes on, striding across the gym floor, "and that's what he did. Not because he found some adults who will make everything okay. But because he learned how to deal with the world the way it is now. Kyle has come back to set us free from this school, from our hunger, from the dark. He will show us how to kill Growns, hunt meat, and live in the light again."

The bleachers are in the palm of her hand.

"That's why Max held Kyle prisoner."

What.

"To learn his secrets." She takes a deep breath and looks at me like it helps. Still no red. I'm impressed. "You see, he was badly hurt killing a Grown and completely under Max's control. When Nirali found out, she sent me as a spy to go find out what I could. Then, courageously, she came herself to free him. But Max decided he wanted Nirali, too. Jefferson's doctor and Jefferson's only hope were both captives at Moore. But because of the bravery of Leo of Los Martillos and his rebels—"

She points to Artemis, Starr, and Leila. They look around nervously. Artemis does a fingertip wave.

"—we were able to free Kyle so he could come home. Just like you always knew he would!"

A strangled sob from the bleachers makes me tear my eyes away from Kay's radiant face, and back to the crowd.

They're all crying, but it's happy tears. Some have their hands knit together as though in prayer, some are on their feet like they want to break out dancing; all are hanging on her every word. We don't have TV anymore, but Kay is giving them drama better than the shows from Before.

"Kyle never stopped believing in us." Kay is crying too now, crying with them. "He fought so hard to come home. Now we are asking you to keep believing in him just this little bit longer, to believe in each other. Max wants us to lose faith in ourselves. To hand over our chance at being free and independent, in exchange for scraps. As if the food won't stop coming *the moment* he decides he has no use for the rest of us!"

Angry boos and hisses erupt like spot fires through the crowd.

"Well, I say *no thanks, asshole*." Kay's voice rings through the gym. "I say we keep our school. And our doctor. And our president. I say we welcome Kyle home and take Brockton back for Jefferson!"

The crowd stands, a spontaneous wave that spreads until everyone is on their feet, clapping over their heads. A cheer starts up in the back, either "FREE THEM!" or "FREEDOM!" and Simon shrinks down into his chair.

Yashpal takes the mic from Kay, thanking her and resting a long hand on her shoulder. "Secretary Kay, it is a . . . surprise to see you back," he says. "Simon found a note that seemed to indicate you walked out. Which I found hard to believe, as many others did."

Applause from the audience, but Yashpal waves for silence. Then he turns on Simon with tired eyes.

"How do you guarantee that Max will keep sending us vans of food?" Yashpal asks.

Simon squirms. "Well, there are several options. I'd be happy to make a more detailed presentation at a later—"

"Sum it up for us." Yashpal indicates the watching school.

"We could have him sign a contract."

There's scattered laughs from the bleachers. Yashpal turns to me then.

"Kyle." He says the name with gravity. "We all saw what you did to that Grown. Can you teach us to do that, too?"

I nod. Wild cheers erupt: stomping, clapping, whistling. *A lot* of Jefferson kids want out of this school, and frankly I don't blame them.

"Well, then," Yashpal says. "That's a clearer choice, I think. And Simon?"

Simon's going red.

"I had pneumonia this winter. I almost died. I am only standing here now because Nirali nursed me late into the night, caring for me like I was family. I consider her family now." He shakes his head. "To make up a story that Nirali would get engaged to a guy she just met, when Kyle was out there . . ." He turns to the bleachers. "Any guy in this whole school who Nirali has ever made a play for since getting together with Kyle, please. Raise your hand."

The audience stares back. A dry cough, and silence.

"Yeah. That's what I thought," Yashpal says coldly. "I'm absolutely disgusted you would try to shame our doctor that way."

"But the ring?" the girl beside me cries out again. "Why'd she hide it, then?"

Nirali reaches for the mic, clasping Yashpal's arm as he hands it over, composure restored.

"Well, we haven't told anyone yet. We wanted it to be a surprise." She smiles shyly at the crowd, then raises her hand to show the rock off properly.

Shit, shit, shit.

"This ring is from Kyle. He asked me to marry him. And I said yes."

She just hit the ball out of the park.

The crowd loses it. People stomping and cheering like they're trying to bring down the bleachers. I'm trying not to puke protein powder through my gauze. Nirali turns her big smile on me and helps pull me to my feet.

I catch Kay's face, confused, eyes trying to find mine. How do I tell her, in front of all of them, this wasn't my idea? But then Nirali is kissing me again, more carefully this time, over my bandages. And then she gets right in my ear and hisses:

"Put the jacket on me!"

What choice do I have?

I take it off and slip it around her narrow shoulders, and the moment I do, the floor shudders, as thousands of students thunder down from the bleachers, storming us like dragons, screaming with joy. Dozens of hands reach for me. The crowd swallows us, then we're suddenly lifted above it. They pull us onto their shoulders, these cheering skeletons, and carry us around like we won. One of us sure did. Nirali didn't just outplay Simon; she beat us all. She figured out how to turn her king into a pawn.

THE AWAY TEAM

BRICK

The cafeteria cooked probably half the food we loaded into the Costco truck. Simon had planned an "Alliance Celebration Feast," but they're making it an Independence Day picnic now. The Jefferson kids are charming once they're fed. They make a ring in the center of the cafeteria and break into the electric slide to music they all sing together, at the top of their lungs.

Nirali stays arm in arm with me, happy to do all the talking, which is good because Kyle's millions of best friends keep leaning in to whisper inside jokes I have no reference for. Every moment I play along, the trap closes tighter. I should get up on a table right now, rip off these stupid bandages, and call her out.

But then what happens to Kay?

Kay is across the cafeteria, keeping Frank's leash short so he doesn't rush me. He stares and whimpers. Kay doesn't look over at me once. She's busy introducing Leila and Artemis and Starr to her friends. One in particular, a girl with a braid crown, is hanging off her, tears spilling over every time their eyes meet. A best friend? A relative? There's no way to ask.

All of Jefferson seems starstruck by the new kids. Artemis has drooling Jefferson guys circling her like she's Marilyn Monroe; Starr has had three different girls bring him plates of food. Leila has her own share of admirers, but I notice her hand keeps drifting up to her nose as she speaks with them, like she's desperate to smell something clean.

Despite every kid in school coming up to welcome her home, Kay seems down. She smiles hard at her friends, but when they look away she droops. Maybe she's just burned out from carrying the game back there in the gym. I don't know how she did it.

"Honestly, he mustered his strength for the Tribunal, but he really should rest now." Nirali has decided it's my bedtime. "Kay? Where's Kay?" She looks around until someone relays her request through the cafeteria, and at last Kay comes over to us. Though she still doesn't look at me.

"Kay, could you help me take Kyle up to the hospital?" Nirali says. "Starr, maybe you could help? And Leila and Artemis, I can show you where you'll be tonight?"

Starr gets my right arm, Nirali my left. Kay is behind us, managing Frank. Of course, fifty thousand people have to wish me good night first. Nirali keeps promising she'll be back down to give them the details of my romantic proposal. Guess I'll find out what they were tomorrow.

Once we're at the third floor, I kneel down and wrap my arms around Frank, who's shivering with excitement. I look up at Kay, words sticking in my throat.

"Thanks," I tell her.

"Of course," she whispers.

"Come on." Nirali pulls at the collar of my shirt as she walks toward the door. "Everybody inside. Let's go."

Okay. Enough.

"What the hell was that?" I yell the second the door is closed. "You told me hours! Now I'm trapped in this goddamn roach motel, pretending to be your boyfriend? No. Hell no!"

"I made you president of Jefferson." Nirali is all shocked.

"More like president of jack shit!"

"Still an upgrade," she says coldly, "from King Max's head thug."

The room goes very still. I shake my head, disgusted.

"Lady, if you think I'm going to stick around here to be your personal sock puppet, you're out of your mind. I'm done. Soon as I can walk, I'm taking Frank and that Costco truck and—"

"Why don't you both just take a breath." Starr steps in between me and Nirali. "I see why you did what you did, Nirali. But Brick has a point. He never agreed to this." Leila nods emphatically. Artemis gives me a sympathetic cringe. Kay doesn't look up from the ground. "But most important, it's what Kay promised this school that got us across the finish line back there. Jefferson wants to learn how to kill the monsters. So how can Brick teach Jefferson if he can't talk?"

"I'll translate for him or whatever," Nirali says.

"You're not talking for me. Not when you're coming up with all this stuff out of nowhere. A *wedding*?!" I adjust the gauze, clammy against my hot face. "I don't even *know you*—"

"It is *purely* a political alliance." She sneers at me. "Don't flatter yourself."

"It's a fraud!"

"It's a story." Artemis steps forward. "A story that's keeping us safe. Don't get it twisted, Slayer. The crowd didn't sweep you onto their shoulders just because you're good with an ax. Nirali is absolutely right. They bought you as Kyle because they need a win. This school is desperate for a happy ending. And I know how to give it to them"—she does finger guns at me and Nirali—"if you put me in charge of starting a theater department?"

I start laughing furiously. "No one is going to believe I'm Kyle long term!"

"Fuck belief." Nirali's voice is ice cold. "If enough people *agree* something is true, *important* people, everybody else will keep their goddamn mouths shut. Lucid was nothing but sugar, but everyone at Moore claimed it made them fearless and *no one talked about when it didn't*."

And that's when Kay steps forward.

"None of us wanted this," she says quietly. "But I don't know any other way for us all to stay safe and stay together. I'm sorry, okay? I'm so sorry, Brick. But please don't leave."

I have to lean back on the desk for support.

"If you stay, I'll make sure you can talk. You could write down what you want to say, and I'll read it out loud if you want. And if there's anything Kyle would know that I should add, I can do that . . . but otherwise I won't change a thing," she says. "I promise."

"You'd have to be with me, like, all the time," I point out.

"I'd like that," Kay says. "I'd like that a lot."

Does she have to say it like that?

". . . All right," I say. "All right, then."

Nirali rolls her eyes and lets out a dramatic sigh of relief.

"But as president"—I glare at Nirali—"I'm telling you, we need to put everything we have into getting the first fence up. We've got maybe a week and a half before that dragon disintegrates."

"Maybe," Starr says, "a moat would be faster?"

It's such a brilliant thought it knocks the rest of the anger out of me. And he's asking *me*, like it's *my call*. Because it is. I don't have to clear it with Merlin or King Max. I can just do what needs to be done.

"That could be great." I nod. "But we'd never dig it out in time."

"Weren't they adding an underground parking lot to the Kohl's right Before?" Leila says. "I bet they'd have a backhoe."

Starr lights up. "That's what, two blocks away?" he says.

"Who's in charge of the Auto Shop?" I ask Nirali.

"We're a magnet school. We don't have an Auto Shop."

"*Are you kidding me?!*"

"There's a gas station with a garage on the corner." Leila speaks louder now. "Maybe we move some remains there and incorporate it."

I turn to her. "Leila, will you take charge of that?"

"What?" She laughs, surprised. "The *Auto Shop*?"

"Yes. You're the best driver in Brockton. Who else?"

"Of course." She smiles. "Are you kidding me? And heck, if we could get a couple of Starr's flamethrowers made before Expansion—"

"Now, *that's* a thought." I'm getting excited now. I've got a talented crew around me and a school with electrical capacity still intact. And the city's Department of Water and Power is just a few blocks away. "Hell, maybe this could really work."

"The only way this works," Nirali says in her teacher voice, "is if we make sure 'Brick' never leaves this room. Do you understand?"

Damn.

She looks from face to face. "I need you all to swear. That if any of us ever tells, the others will kill them."

"I'm sorry, what?" Leila gasps.

"That's the only way this works," Nirali says, dead serious.

"Honey." Artemis's voice is gentle but concerned. "What if we all just give you our word that—"

"Words are cheap," Nirali snaps. "I need more than words from you. From all of you."

I could still go. I could demand the truck from Nirali in return for leaving quietly. Maybe Starr would even go with me. But all my Coldest Lakes CDs burned back with Jimmy. There's only one other person who remembers how they sound.

So I hold out my hand to Nirali, and she clasps it as we stare at each other.

"If I ever tell, Nirali, you can take me out," I vow. It's not exactly what she wants me to say. But it's enough. And I'm done with being an attack dog.

Nirali nods, then looks at the others, eyes hard. And one by one each person in the room steps closer and lays their hand on top of ours, staying so close we can hear each other breathe. It's like they're all channeling something into me as they swear on their lives to keep my secret, something powerful and frightening. Merlin would call it magic.

"All right," Nirali says, breaking our circle first. "I should go back down. *Kyle*, you should stay here in the hospital for the night. The rest of you are free to sleep or go back down to the party. Thank you all. And welcome home."

Starr claps me on the shoulder.

"Moats," he says. "I'm going to start drawing tonight."

Leila hugs me goodbye before going out into the hall with Artemis. Only Frank is at my side.

And Kay, in the corner, hidden in shadow.

"You going to go back down to the party?" I ask her.

She shakes her head and edges toward the lantern. It stars her black eyes with tiny lights.

"I wanted to ask you something," she says. Then: "Could you take your mask off?" Her voice goes up a little too high. "I like to see your face."

"You're the only one." I fumble with the gauze, and she hurries to help. I lean in toward her as she unwinds the bandage. When the mask comes off, we're so close our foreheads almost brush. She steps back, her face going pink.

"So you *can* still blush," I point out, and the pink deepens. "How did you keep from going all cranberry at the Tribunal?"

"I tried to just say things I knew were true. But with the names switched around. Because I believe in you, Brick. I believe you could really save us."

"Brick?" I say lightly. "Never heard of him."

She laughs, but not really. Shifts her weight like she's about to turn and leave.

"Kay—" I start, and she turns more toward me again, but hangs her head like she can't meet my eyes. "Thank you for—for saying that. I am going to do everything I can not to let you or Jefferson down as king—"

"President," she says quickly, then her chin dimples like she's trying not to cry. "I know it must seem like I put you in a situation where you have to be king for everyone else, when that's the last thing you wanted. It's not fair, that you have to cover your face and not talk and not be yourself. I feel terrible, okay? This wasn't what I wanted, ever. But all I was thinking, that whole time on stage, was *I cannot lose Brick*."

Holy shit.

"And now you're with *Nirali*," Kay's voice cuts off with a high, hopeless break at the end of the name. Her hand flits up to her eyes, and she blurts, "So I lost you anyway!"

"Kay—"

"I get it! I get it!" She shakes her head, eyes squeezed shut tight. "I know how loyal you are. I'm not trying to get you to say anything against your fiancée—"

"*Kay.*" I hover right over her, willing her to look at me, smiling.

"But I promise, *I* won't let *you* down, as—as your secretary. I don't care what it takes, I don't care *what* I have to do or say." She shakes her head. "The truth gets you stabbed in a pool, and lies set Jefferson free. If that's how it works, I'll lie every day. I'll be the most evil person in Brockton, if it means I can keep you with—"

I pull her into me so abruptly she almost stumbles. Like when I grabbed her by the zip tie that first day. But her eyes aren't scared now, they're pleading. They fix on my mouth, asking for the thing I want most.

Adrenaline is tearing through me, all of me hyperaware. It's like I see her more than I ever have before. She's different up close, so unbelievably lovely: her long eyelashes, the freckle just above her eyebrow, the bright flush of her cheeks, the shining heart of her mouth. And then her beautiful hand is on my scarred cheek and she's meeting me halfway. My arms wrap around her waist, her arms around my neck. I bend her back in the kiss, and she melts.

I will never see a movie again, but it feels like I'm in one now. Like there's background music surging, like we really could live happily ever after. And when we part, she's completely smiling, like she's learned my secret. That my heart is her dog, that she makes it come running. That it's been hers, for a long time.

"Kay," I say at last, when I get my breath back. "What were you going to ask me before the gym? After Expansion?"

THE MERCILESS KING OF MOORE HIGH

"I was going to ask . . ." Her eyes sparkle. ". . . Can I stay in your room tonight?"

And I turn out the camping lantern so fast she laughs.

EPILOGUE

EL MARTILLO'S FUNERAL

JESS

It's hard to tell if Leo has started burning, there's so much haze from the fireworks. But it's not like we have anywhere else to go. None of us is allowed inside the school again, the guards said. The Motorheads get the Auto Shop now; all Los Martillos, including me, are exiled from Moore.

See, Leo? I finally joined your room, after all. You got your way, in the end.

I refused all the times he asked for the same reason I never told him I loved him. I don't want to belong to anyone. I want to do what I want, when I want, without being told I'm a disappointment. The only people who've understood that and loved me anyway are Brick and Mom, and Mom didn't really have a choice and Brick is loyal as a dog. But even he saw I was a mess, by the end.

But since he's run away from Moore, now is the time to do it. Once Leo is up in smoke, I'll sneak up the fire stairs to the roof and walk off into the dawn. The only reason I'd been holding off since the Kyle thing was I figured Brick would get stuck cleaning me up.

The fire crackles and spits, sends waves of heat and smoke over me and the girls standing around it. They've adopted me already, these mechanical-minded girls, but they'd come to hate me if I stayed longer. Their boyfriends would flirt with me, and they'd start giving each other looks when I came around, make it clear I should sit somewhere else. The only people who talk to me anymore are guys who want to sleep with me. And Kelly and Damon.

"The guards won't even let Kelly bring us our stuff." Damon is fretting, shivering hard beside me. "Like we're supposed to just live out on this field and no one can help us or even talk to us, full stop. I told them you need medical care, and they were all, 'too bad'—"

"Don't worry about it," I say.

"Don't worry about it?!" Damon pulls his hand through his curly hair. "Honey, where the hell are we going to live?"

Once I kill myself, King Max will let them back in, but I don't tell Damon this. King Max is afraid I'm telling Los Martillos all about Kyle and whipping up some kind of movement against him. Like I care about any of that shit. I told Kelly, but Kelly can keep his mouth shut. And if I hadn't told *someone*, I would've walked off the roof already.

I wish I had, I'm so tired of being stuck in my head, stuck in my memories, stuck in this world where everything only gets worse. I just want to be up there with Leo now. Oblivious.

Leo's helmet glints through the haze as the flames lap higher. They put it on him, after they pulled off his armor and washed the blood away, along with the coverall he got knighted in. At least, I think it's his helmet glinting. But then the gold glint floats up further still. Maybe more fireworks got set off in the pyre? But I didn't hear anything.

The silent spark keeps rising. A black shadow grows below it. And I could swear the shadow is staring down at me.

Is he *still alive*?

My heart leaps like it hasn't in a long time. What if Leo's revived? What if he just lost a lot of blood but now he's okay?

"Leo?" I call up to him, voice breaking. "Leo?"

Damon puts his arm around me, not understanding, so I point, my throat closing, because now the shadow is *climbing down*.

A thing that is and is not Leo spiders down on all fours, head-first, fast. The skin of his hands hisses as he gets closer, but he doesn't flinch. His clothes catch fire, gold flames licking up his coverall and turning up the edges of his collar; he doesn't notice.

Leo lands in the grass but stays on all fours, scattering burning flames like wildflowers where the grass is dry enough to catch. As he scampers around the pyre, the other mourners back away, looking to one another in disbelief.

"Leo?" Seth moves toward him, hands outstretched. "Hey, man, what—"

Leo looks up. The burning collar lights up his whole face: his beautiful blue eyes have gone completely black, from eyelid to eyelid. There are shrieks now, people running. Seth steps back, but it's too late. Leo rises to his feet and leaps at his friend. In the ring of fire around his neck, I see Leo's teeth sink into Seth's cheek. I watch his hands flex as they force Seth's head back at an angle no neck can go.

"Come on," Damon yells, pulling me away. "He's turned or something, come on!"

"Let me go!" I scream, fighting him off. "*Let me go!*" This is how I want to die. In Leo's arms, one last time. "LEO!"

Leo stops, like a dog catching some scent in the air. Seth falls from his arms, and I've seen enough dead boys to know that's what Seth is now. Leo, though, is something else. He turns and sprints on all fours through the grass, toward the west fence.

Damon is so shocked, I throw him off and sprint after Leo, still calling his name. But he won't turn back.

When this Leo-shaped thing gets to the fence, he starts battering it with his head. The very first strike leaves a burst of blood and one of his front teeth embedded in the wall. I scream uncontrollably, and the guards on watch open the panel fast, just wanting him away from them. They're in such a rush to let him out, they don't try to stop me following.

The moonlight through the trees covers the ground in blue leopard spots. I run as hard as I can but am hardly able to keep up with him. Leo is sprinting now, back up on two legs, dashing himself straight into the low-hanging branches and sharp hedges. Like he wants his clothes off and the only way is by shredding them. One arm dangles limply as he runs, swiping himself hard against tree trunks and thorny briars. Once the clothes are all torn off and the bloodless stab wounds in his side exposed, I know without question the thing running ahead of me has been dead for hours.

My head aches unbearably, the pain meds from the gym long worn off. I ate some cookies and juice, but they aren't enough. I'm going to collapse out here before I can get to him.

But then Leo stops.

He goes still at the edge of a clearing and drops down on all fours again. Then he strains, hard, every muscle distorting and distending in his back, like he's trying to pull a tree root out of the forest floor. His spine, purple in the moonlight, breaks free of his skin. The sound is like a watermelon falling to the ground and splitting.

Then I see the dragon in the clearing, just beyond him. It ducks its head down through the tree branches and sniffs.

Leo shambles into the clearing on all fours, the top half of his rib cage flayed out above him, bones standing white against the night like grotesque wings, his spinal column twitching back and forth at an angle from the top of his hips like a scorpion's tail. He leaps for the dragon, clambering up its side like a kid climbing up a jungle gym: joyful. As he does, his body dances apart from itself, muscles falling loose from bones and nerves unknitting from tendons. The dragon's horrible skin clings at Leo's limbs like clothes right out of the dryer, wrapping around his parts before they rain loose onto the ground. Leo's dark muscles nestle into the dragon like leeches; his bones stab themselves into foul dragon flesh that swallows them greedily. The golden helmet is the only thing the dragon cannot digest. It falls heavily onto the ground and rolls to my feet.

The dragon arches its back and shudders. Two new rolling black eyes appear in its broad, flat head and blink down at me.

This is it, then.

"Okay!" I yell at the dragon, stepping out of the trees and into its way. "My turn! Here I am!"

It stares through me like I'm not even there.

"Hello?!" I yell. "I'm right here! So kill me, huh? Kill me! Kill me right now!"

It stands totally still.

Come on, I don't want another dragon to kill me. It has to be this one, the one with Leo in it. Come on! What does it take?

I never thought I could hit an animal. But I don't know if that's what this is anyway. I draw back my fist and punch its big leg as hard as I can. It's like punching a telephone pole. I swear and shake my fist, sure I've broken a finger.

The dragon steps back.

"I'm *sorry.*" I burst into tears, knuckles already swelling. I collapse against its horrible skin. With my eyes closed, it feels warm and gritty. Like asphalt at sunset. "I'm sorry, okay? But could you please just kill me? Please? Right now?"

The embrace is one-sided. The dragon continues to back away, until I fall forward onto my knees. It turns away from me, and I watch it leave, feeling rejected in the strangest way. I want to run after it, but I'm too exhausted, my head ringing deeper with pain. Roof it is, then. If the fence guards even let me back in.

"Jess?" Damon's voice, shaking hard.

I turn to see him. The fence guards and several of Los Martillos are behind him. They are all wide-eyed, staring at me.

"Jess, do you understand what you just did?" Damon is crying.

I look down at my swollen hand.

I hit a dragon. And I lived.

One of Los Martillos darts forward, takes up Leo's helmet. He kneels, trembling, and holds it out to me.

Not sure what else to do, I take the heavy gold helmet. It slides over my bruised head easily.